Praise for the Work of Lev Raphael

Secret Anniversaries (

"Lev Raphael's moving collection of stori
ness and variety of his concerns: faith, f
means to be a Jew, what it means to be a
tender heart."
—Elizabeth Benedict, Author of *The Practice of Deceit, Almost,* and *The Joy of Writing Sex*

"Lev Raphael's stories are as thrilling as his thrillers, but for an entirely different set of reasons: the psychological perspicacity, good humor and deep empathy with which he approaches all the secret anniversaries of the heart—his lovely title—that make up his characters' wonderfully flawed humanity."
—Jonathan Wilson, Author of *An Ambulance Is on the Way: Stories of Men in Trouble* and *A Palestine Affair*

"Lev Raphael takes us into uncharted literary territory where Jewish identity, traumatic history and homosexuality collide and sometimes resolve in surprising ways. His stories, set in college dorms and family living rooms, enlarge and enliven the scope of American fiction."
—Helen Epstein, Author of *Children of the Holocaust*

The German Money

"What a gift for a writer to be able to sustain unflagging, sweaty-palm suspense in a novel. This is what Lev Raphael pulls off in *The German Money*, a mystery whose shocking denouement is so organic to the whole thing that it feels as if a boiling volcano has finally let loose. *The German Money* combines his multiple talents with his understanding of Holocaust survivors and their families to produce one of the most powerful suspense novels in years, a kind of Kafka meets Philip Roth meets le Carré."
—*Washington Post Book World*

"If you're starving for a powerful novel, buy Lev Raphael's latest book, *The German Money*, a potent, contemporary story about the complicated lives of three Jewish siblings, descendants of a mother who survived the death factories of the Holocaust, and had a closely guarded a terrible secret."
—*Fort Worth Star-Sentinel*

"Lev Raphael delivers the goods in a thriller with a wicked twist. It is a fast, engaging read, with glints of insight, and a deeper, twisting message about the ambiguities of history and human nature."
—*Jerusalem Post*

Dancing on Tisha B'Av

"The power of Raphael's stories comes from his passion for telling the truth, however painful."
—*Hadassah*

"His characters are voices of reason, observers rather than judges…The prose is poetic in its simplicity, the sex scenes sweat with passion."
—*The Los Angeles Times*

"Raphael writes with loving compassion, taking bold steps forward in the revelation of cultural secrets, the preservation of memory, and the fight to be visible."
—*Lambda Rising Book Report*

"Each story is a spellbinding delight."
—*Booklist*

Winter Eyes

"*Winter Eyes* works so well precisely because it is scaled to intimate human dimensions. Raphael's book resembles a piano sonata, a piece he knows so well that his fingers breathed the music."
—*The Los Angeles Times*

"Raphael writes about the legacy of the Holocaust in a way few writers do. About remembering and not remembering, and about what people do to survive the darkness of their past."
—*Sacramento Bee*

"Raphael is a writer of vision like Ralph Ellison and James Baldwin."
—*Jewish Bulletin* (San Francisco)

"One of the most affecting, absorbing, and quietly powerful American coming-of-age novels."
—*Booklist*

Secret Anniversaries of the Heart

Also By Lev Raphael

Fiction:

Dancing on Tisha B'Av
Winter Eyes
The German Money

Nick Hoffman Mysteries:

Let's Get Criminal
The Edith Wharton Murders
The Death of a Constant Lover
Little Miss Evil
Burning Down the House
Tropic of Murder

Nonfiction:

Edith Wharton's Prisoners of Shame
Journeys & Arrivals

Co-Authored:

Dynamics of Power
Stick Up For Yourself!
Teacher's Guide to Stick Up For Yourself!
Coming Out of Shame

Secret Anniversaries

of the

Heart

New & Selected Stories

Lev Raphael

Leapfrog Press
Wellfleet, Massachusetts

Published in 2006 in the United States by
The Leapfrog Press
P.O. Box 1495
95 Commercial Street
Wellfleet, MA 02667-1495, USA
www.leapfrogpress.com

Printed in the United States

Distributed in the United States by
Consortium Book Sales and Distribution
St. Paul, Minnesota 55114

First Edition

"Free Man in Paris" appeared in *Crimewave 3*, "Dreamland" appeared as "History (With Dreams)" in *American Jewish Fiction: A Century of Stories*; "Your Papers, Please" appeared in *Criminal Kaballah*; "Gimme Shelter" appeared as "Shelter" in *Genre*; "Nocturne" appeared as "Listening to the Silence" in the *Baltimore Jewish Times*; "Welcome to Beth Homo" appeared as "Beth Homo" in *More Like Minds*; "The Pathfinder" appeared in *Frontiers*; "The Story of a Plant" appeared in *Reconstructionist*; "Roy's Jewish Problem" appeared in *Commentary*; "The Children" appeared as "Split Decisions" in *Inside*; "You're Breaking My Heart!" appeared in *Forward*. The remaining stories appeared in *Dancing on Tisha B'Av*.

Library of Congress Cataloging-in-Publication Data

Raphael, Lev.
  Secret anniversaries of the heart : new & selected stories / Lev Raphael.--1st ed.
    p. cm.
  ISBN-13: 978-0-9728984-7-8 (pbk. : alk. paper)
  ISBN-10: 0-9728984-7-6 (pbk. : alk. paper)
  1. Children of Holocaust survivors--Fiction. 2. Jewish gays--Fiction. 3. American fiction--Jewish authors. I. Title.
PS3568.A5988S43 2006
813'.54--dc22

2005027524

10 9 8 7 6 5 4 3 2 1

for B.
then, now & always

The holiest of all holidays are those
Kept by ourselves in silence and apart;
The secret anniversaries of the heart.
—Longfellow

Contents

The Tanteh

Those rare times the Tanteh talked about the War, we all shifted nervously at the table, unable to change the subject or know how to respond, captured like a circle of unwilling believers in the occult, whose medium has sunk into a trance. What she said would be like a violent telegram: "Once I stood in mud and rain. Two days. Naked." Or: "The day we were liberated, the Elbe was flowing with bodies." When she stopped, we went on eating, passing dishes, cutting, spooning, the surge of mealtime sweeping us away from her wasteland.

Ours was a large formal dining room in a dark rent-controlled Upper West Side apartment, with sliding doors stale from seventy-five years of paint, glass-doored china cupboards set into the wall, plaster stars and arabesques bubbling the high ceiling. The Tanteh made that room more natural and fitting than any of us could, because she was a woman of bearing. Straight-backed and hard like an old upright piano, she was gray-haired, gray-eyed, and handsome as much for being seventy and firm as anything else. We called my mother's Great Aunt Rose "the Tanteh," as if she, the only close European relative of ours who had survived not only the Nazis, but Russians and Ukrainians, would always live and speak in capitals. She had come to stay with us five years after her husband, a rich dentist, had died; I was twelve then and my sister, Melanie, had moved to California to join an architectural design firm. The Tanteh filled Melanie's large empty room with books in six or seven languages, the strange gold-stamped spines leering at me from ceiling-high shelves, like eager gypsies. Many books were by writers behind the Iron Curtain, cries of outrage, cries for help, she said, or cunning little parables that mocked and buzzed.

I envied her, but it was more than just the books; it was everything I dimly understood her to represent: Europe, sophistication, travel, a larger, more glamorous world. For other Jews, I suppose their old-country relatives summon up a personalized *Fiddler*, a glowing cartoon, but the Tanteh was so resolutely un-Jewish—and her parents before her—that I couldn't imagine her haggling in a market, whistling a mournful Yiddish tune, attending a Zionist meeting, doing anything ordinary and Jewish that mass death had made seem otherworldly. Rather, I saw her as one of those lustrous women in Thirties movies, forcefully in love, her stabbing words like brisk steps taken in a walk to mend her health, stalking her sleek young man (Francis Lederer, perhaps), with a large leather bag clutched under one arm and a cigarette waiting to be lit. The Tanteh smoked with spiteful grace, one arm close in and parallel to her waist, palm up, supporting the elbow of the arm that leaned out slightly from her body, as smoke twined up from her Sobranie Gold.

I thought I loved her.

Dad, an accountant, found her affected. No one in his family spoke with an English accent or read more than a weekly magazine. He glanced at her books suspiciously and never commented when she talked about school. After moving in with us, the Tanteh had decided to take classes in French literature and criticism at Columbia, and the comments on her papers amazed me. I had never leapt from all those cute little French tales of kids getting into trouble and making puns to the world of Great Books, so the Tanteh's familiarity with writers I found impossible even in English (when I tried) awed me. She seemed to glide through that alien world like a dangerous debutante cutting across a dance floor with all the decision of great and untried beauty.

When the Tanteh mentioned a paper or one of her classes, Mother looked away, perhaps paying the Tanteh back for her criticism of the Jewish things we did, like lighting candles on Friday night, keeping kosher (at home), observing a number of holidays.

Once, soon after she moved in, the Tanteh had peered at Mother as she covered her eyes and blessed the candles in their tall brass stands.

"What are you looking at?" she asked the Tanteh, finished.

The Tanteh shrugged with all the distance of an anthropologist unwilling to influence the primitive life he was studying.

Mother slid the lace covering from her head and said with great dignity, "I light candles because I am a Jew, so was my mother, and yours."

The Tanteh nodded, wickedly slim in gray silk and pearls.

"I believe in God," Mother said, heading for the kitchen.

"They prayed," the Tanteh called after her. "And still they died."

16

I knew who "they" meant—all the lost Jews who spoke to us in pictures, films, and books, so terribly nameless in their millions.

"But some believed," Mother retorted, bearing the steaming blue tureen to the table. The Tanteh shrugged. "Whatever you say."

Dad came in from the bathroom, smoothing back his hair, scrubbed face as shiny as the challah waiting for his knife.

The Tanteh avoided our Passover seders and candle-lighting at Chanukah, happily sweeping off to a concert, party, or film that would spare her the affront. The rustle of her cape and her lush scent—White Shoulders, I believe—would mockingly crowd the air and we would all want her there with us: Dad because he said she was our responsibility, Mother because she was family, and me because somehow, with the cosmic vanity of adolescence, I hoped the Tanteh would "convert." I hoped our vague but steady faith would warm her, heal the past I knew so little.

But she appeared content in her world of books, chatting about editions, critics, translations, conferences (I'd hear her on the phone sometimes—flashes of English bursting from sentences in other languages). We rarely met her friends; she entertained them in restaurants, as one did in Europe, and she often seemed less to be living with us than visiting until a more suitable arrangement presented itself. Did she miss her large home on Long Island, or the furniture she'd donated to Jewish charities? I didn't know; the Tanteh was as private about the recent past as about the War.

When she had trouble with a paper, she'd call me to her curtained room and. hold out a page wrenched from her old typewriter.

"Is it good?" she'd ask, which meant, Was it English? It was, usually, but always with a trace of another language, like the remains of a figure incompletely painted out on a canvas. She knew Russian, German, French, Hungarian, and Czech, so who could say what was stirring in her mind as she resolutely typed?

If I told her it was good, she'd lean back, slim, stern, and explain the paper in a lecture that could last half an hour. Her talk was bright and blinding, and if I did comment, she nodded regally.

My parents were glad I talked to her. She was so foreign and disapproving; at dinner, the table could often seem impoverished by her air of acquaintance with finer meals, more elegant company—though not for me, of course. It was precisely her detachment I adored. She was the perfect figure of romance for a teenager-someone I saw a great deal but knew mostly through my imagination. My visions could not be blurred by facts: her occasional ugly limp, due to arthritis, her rumbling stomach, her spotty wrinkled hands, from which she'd long since removed all jewelry to make them less noticeable, her gray hairs in the bathroom sink. When she contradicted Mother or Dad about, say, politics, they deferred to her history while I enjoyed the pageantry of grimaces and frowns. Because she was the Tanteh, we were more ourselves, too. The Americans, possibly. Or the Ungrateful. It's hard to say. The Tanteh was so much a presence in our large shabby apartment with its leprous windows and gouged parquet floors that maybe we were simply an audience, or even less: a background.

It was the Tanteh, and her talking to me in a pungent voice smothered by years of smoking, who brought me out of the blindness of youth. She was the first person I observed wholeheartedly, and with greed.

"You're so American," she sometimes said, and the word always came from her with surprise, as if she wondered how such a creature could be related to her. That thrilling reproach filled my mind with fireworks of speculation, great bursting cascades. She was not American, and the difference was no mere attribute of geography or time; it was more, mysterious.

The older I got, the more I found myself watching her, studying her: the hand extended to the hollow of her neck, fingers gentle there, the matchbooks she often twirled and tormented when bored. In senior year of high school, when an English teacher asked us to do a character sketch of the most unusual person we knew, I chose the Tanteh.

My teachers had always said that my writing had "flair," but now I realized I had something more: a treasure. The Tanteh was mine, someone to write about, rich with possibility. I was important; I imagined writing a book someday that would gleam down from her shelves. I brought together the years of reports, skits, and sketches and put all my writing in a box under my bed. I had a history.

I wrote a little story about her, about having dinner with her, her classes, her books and ankle-length mink coat, everything, her contempt for my parents, but what I concentrated on was when she would blurt out parts of the past. How I felt helpless then, trapped, assaulted by each unbearable word that I could not really understand. Writing, I realized how the Tanteh crushed us with what had happened to her, and how I hated it, hated her, even, just a little. My teacher said the story had energy and pushed me to submit it to our yearbook. His praise was so nagging that I finally took it to the small yearbook office seething with posters, photos, clippings, and files, to a thin, bleary-eyed girl who accepted it from me impatiently, as if I was late.

I was excited and triumphant without knowing if it would be printed, as if those few pages were brighter and more alive than the Tanteh would ever be. The story was my child and seemed perfect.

Three months later, bound in a heavy red and black cover, crammed with class pictures and poetry, the yearbook frightened me. Mine was the only piece of fiction—relevant, I guess, because the class was 90 percent Jewish—and it said too much, revealed too much about me and how I felt. I had mistaken simple observation for creation, the amateur writer's ugliest confusion. There was no distance, no shaping, no disguise. It was too raw.

I was ashamed.

"So where's the yearbook already?" Dad asked me the week it came out. Mother smiled expectantly and I muttered about a printer's delay.

I imagined falling at the Tanteh's slim small feet, her walls of books a judgment of my crime, begging her to understand, to feel for me forgiveness, mercy, love. I saw the Tanteh accepting me for the sake of literature; we would cry, be close. She'd become my muse and guide.

It wasn't like that at all. Before I could figure out how to prepare them all, a friend's mother brought a copy over, beaming, a little jealous: "My Marcy also gave in a story, but she wasn't so lucky as you."

The Tanteh waited for me one Thursday afternoon, in my room, the desk chair turned to the open door, smoke wreathing the curtain rod, her eyes cold. We were alone.

"How could you?"

"It was just an assignment—"

"Why do you want to hurt me?"

"No, I love you." But I didn't know if I believed it.

She rose with a quivering face and I expected her to advance on me with her cigarette and burn my desperate tongue.

"That's love?"

I fled the room, grabbing my jacket from the bench in the foyer. I missed dinner that night, staying out to see a James Bond movie twice, hiding in the shadows and the light of the balconied, gold-ceilinged Depression-era theater. When fatigue brought me home, there was more: the Tanteh had gone to stay with a friend for the night.

"How could you write this?" Dad asked, holding up the yearbook as if it were the photograph of a desecrated synagogue or grave. We sat at the dining room table like survivors of some dreadful break in customary time, the cool mahogany reflecting our hands. "What's wrong with you?"

I shook my head. If he'd accused or threatened me, I could've yelled something about art, I guess, but he was only disappointed, hurt.

Mother, sitting in the Tanteh's place, clasped her hands. "I've never seen her like that."

The Tanteh's cold rage was alien, none of us had seen her "like that," seen beneath the languages, the pearls—except when she suddenly spoke about the War in those terrible few lines.

I wasn't close to my sister, Melanie, who was fifteen years older, but I called her that night, hoping she would take my side. What was my side, though?

I pictured her sitting out in her lush English-style garden complete with gazebo, oak benches, and elegant, expensive shrubs.

She was curt. "Don't do it again, kiddo. And you'd better apologize fast."

"The Tanteh can't sleep," my mother told me. " She keeps dreaming about you, that she's trying to climb out of a pit, hanging on the edge, and you're a Nazi, stomping on her hands." My mother was pale, wide-eyed, as if the dream were true. She shook her head. "Why couldn't you leave her alone?"

A week later, the Tanteh decided not to finish her semester at Columbia, and to visit friends in Brussels. She was quickly packed and gone. The days before her flight were bitter; she stopped eating with us entirely and wouldn't talk about what had happened, about not sleeping anymore, but playing the radio in her room softly through the night, reading, reading.

I feared more disaster like a child, some nighttime curse that would tumble down my walls or smother me in books, her books. But the Tanteh said and did nothing. Hers was the cruelty of silence.

She wrote to my parents from Brussels; then Paris, Marseilles, Madrid, Rome, Venice, Vienna. The postcards, even the stamps, dazzled me. She was triumphantly the woman of Europe, distant and immense, but colored by my shame now. I shot off several wild letters of apology she might have received and even read; I never found out.

The Tanteh died in Prague on the eve of Yom Kippur and was buried there by a distant cousin of her husband.

"It's a saint's death to die then," my mother said, hushed, surprised, repeating a Jewish superstition I'd never heard before.

Did the Tanteh go to get away from me? I believed that at first. I imagined her feeling humiliated by my words, powerless, exposed, forced to plunge into the volcano of her past, which we knew only in its rumbles and flashes of fire or steam. I must have seemed perverse to her, a snake of disapproval and contempt, spying on her soul, or thinking I had.

"Another month," she told us once at dinner. "The Allies would have found nothing. No one. Cholera," she explained. "Dysentery." If her camp had been liberated in May of 1945 and not April, she would not have lived. Spring was more to her than weather or a song.

Did she go to find her past? Why was she in Prague—to see if her home still stood and who lived there?

In synagogue on Yom Kippur with my parents, I cried for the first time, not even knowing that she was dead, beating my heart as I recited the collective prayer of guilt—the *Ashamnu*: "We abuse, we betray, we are cruel. We destroy, we embitter, we falsify. . . ."

I had to atone for writing about her, but she wouldn't let me, and begging God's forgiveness did not seem like enough. My father squeezed my arm through the prayer shawl, whose fringes I knew were supposed to remind me not to follow the desires of my heart. What had I done?

A postcard from Prague came to me two weeks later, well after we had heard the Tanteh was dead. I don't know why or how it was delayed.

"You had no right to steal from me," it said. "My life is not an assignment."

I remembered overhearing her on the phone one time, years before. "Americans are like vampires," she said, then switched to French: "*Dégoutants*." Disgusting. She went on in English: "They feed on everyone's disasters because it makes them feel happy and safe. *Pauvres petits*."

And I heard all the times she had marveled at me: "You're so American."

War Stories

Ira's father had an odd, stubborn way of standing: His hands were inevitably in his pockets and all of him seemed to lean forward, as if he'd placed himself in your path and the next move was up to you. In his father's presence, Ira often felt as if he had to excuse himself; one look of those narrow dark eyes would put him so much on the defensive that even a hello could come out apologetically. Ten minutes alone with his father could exhaust Ira. Luckily, his father rarely spoke to him.

But his mother never stopped. She read several newspapers and weekly magazines and was endlessly fascinated by politics; she talked about her neighbors and friends; she talked about his school and what it was like for her as a girl. And she could talk about the War so calmly, no, not even calmly, because her expression at such times wasn't peaceful, but blank. She seemed then to have no connection with the experiences she related in a stifling monotone. Ira would suddenly see how old she'd become; see not that broad, grinning, sweet face on the other side of a large birthday cake years ago, but a face that belonged to a survivor. The face of a woman who had been forced to stand in the snow for many days, without clothes; the face of a woman who had fled four hundred kilometers on foot through forest, only to be captured by pistol-whipping soldiers. Her hair was starting to fall out, so that the skin showed pink above her forehead through the teased graying mound. Her eyes seemed to have wept flesh they were so pouchy, and her hands were blunter, wider.

Ira hated being outside her in that way and feeling the ruin; each line in the sagging flesh held him, glared at him, hurt him. He had an image of his mother—glowing in a white summer dress that was splashed with big yellow flowers, leaning across the table over that cake and helping him blow out the three candles, then sweeping masses of thick red hair off her forehead, bracelets jangling, laughing and saying, "You're three! You're three!"—that was destroyed whenever she told him a War story.

The distance between them would grow intolerable as she forced word after word on him, until he thought something had to break. But nothing did. He never screamed, never said anything, just nodded, helpless, listening to what he had no real way of understanding. Oh, the words themselves made sense—but slowly strung together, the pictures they created crushed Ira. How was he to deal with the unimaginable? His mother could talk about the War with her friends because they had been through it and were able to discuss dates and camps and trains and punishments and bombings. They had lived with the unbelievable for years, had fought off searing moments when a man—"Over there, on the corner . . . see? The one with the head tilted."—looked like a commandant at Treblinka, or a guard with a chair leg at Matthausen, or even an uncle, a cousin, a beloved friend whose ashes went into no urn.

If Ira's father never talked much, and then only about commonplaces, at least he never mentioned the War. If anyone did, he would announce, "I'm walking out of this room," and did so, leaving a chorus of knowing nods. And then the nodders would discuss Ljuba, who was still seeing an analyst, and Fania, who never used the glittering copper pots that hung in her kitchen, and, in fact, lived in the basement of her immaculate white-on-white house, and all the others who were more visibly battered than the rest. Many sighs, many shrugs, many "What can you do's?" in Yiddish, Russian, Rumanian, Czech. Those times when his father left the room filled Ira with a longing to follow and touch his arm, to make his father understand that he didn't want the gap of comprehension that was between them.

Ira had decided that it was because his mother was unable to share her stories with his father that she told them to him. In a way, he felt touched, but what about his needs? Yes, she loved him. Yes, she'd taken him wherever he wanted to go, baked him cookies or marble cake when he was sad. Yes, she'd helped him with his homework and advised, consoled, and berated him when he most needed all three; but was listening to her War stories the price he had to pay for his mother's love?

When he was younger, all that he'd heard were marvelous descriptions of the first snow in Riga and the special crunching sound snow in America didn't seem to have. Dark carriages laden with heavy worn blankets had gone hurtling down those streets, filling the snow-thickened air with the faint jingling of their horses' bells (a sound he imagined was like that of his mother's bracelets). Gradually, the visions of her home had changed and there were troops on those streets, first Soviet and then Nazi, and bombs falling on the Jewish cemetery during a funeral, and then the ghetto and then the camps. So imperceptibly had the shadow of the War fallen over her stories that it was as if Ira himself had relived her life, slowly becoming aware of being trapped in the horror and unable to stop it or escape.

Once, while putting on her coat, Rushka, one of his mother's friends, sang very softly, as if the words couldn't bear hearing them selves: "*Es brennt, briderlech, es brennt. . . .*" "There's a fire, little brothers, there's a fire. . . ." It was a pre-War line of warning that for Ira didn't come so close. It had nothing of the brutal clarity of his mother's stories.

Ira had no idea what his father did with his part of the War. He had gathered something about his father standing in front of a fascist firing squad as the RAF bombed wherever it was, but Ira knew little else. He had no sense at all of his father's past, and sometimes he wondered if his mother wasn't incorporating his father's experiences into her own stories. Had his father perhaps told her everything and forbidden her to repeat a word?

When Ira was sixteen, his mother had been at the very beginning of a story, in the kitchen, standing at the stove and stirring a pot of soup. She broke off when the front door opened and his father walked, in early. He nodded, put his meter, coin changer, and call sheets on the table. No one said anything. As his father fingered the meter and his mother stared into the pot, it occurred to Ira that there was a gap between his parents, too: the War, which should have bound them in understanding, divided them. After that, Ira had trouble seeing his situation in black and white; there were flashes of color, wild and upsetting. It had been so easy, resenting his mother and fearing his father. The two feelings began to switch back and forth now with a will of their own, and for all their intensity, lacked true definition.

His father talked mostly about the people who got into his cab, and then only to his mother. She would sit at the table, her face tight, hands folded like a petulant schoolgirl's. She didn't like his driving a cab, even though he owned it. Ira was unwilling to probe those feelings of hers, but he had figured out that she thought it was undignified. One night when his father was two hours late for dinner, his mother muttered something about "lower-class."

He envied his father's freedom and couldn't imagine seeing and talking to so many people in one day. His father looked wonderfully scrubbed and tall, leaning over the wheel of his Checker cab, wearing the perpetual white shirt, his dark hair brushed back off a wide forehead, handlebar mustache looking thick and dark against the pale freckled skin. In a wildly confident moment, Ira had once ventured asking his father if he could sit up front for a whole day to see what it was like.

"What're you . . . a baby?" His father spaced the words carefully, as he always did when angry. Those cool dismissive questions of his would stalk Ira, mostly at night, pouncing just as he was falling asleep. Strap marks would at least have faded.

Soon after, Ira started having his dream. He'd been frightened, hearing his mother and her friends talk about this one's husband and that one's sister screaming in the night and seeking some magic from analysts. A plump dark little woman who always made a point of asking how Ira was doing in school, and listening, once told his mother, "Analysts are fine for these Americans—what do they know about real problems?"

The light—that was the beginning of the dream. His eyes would open and Ira would find himself in a large feather bed piled high with white quilts. They seemed to shine; everywhere there was a clean white glow. No rats, no lice, no dirt, no death, no people. It's over, he would think, I'm safe. And just then, the whiteness would rip apart and images would come stabbing through the glow: a graying rabbi on his knees, his beard on fire; an overturned carriage, the blankets bloodied; a grinning, monocled doctor with a scalpel. On and on they came as the blankets turned into a putrid fog that smothered him.

He never told his mother about the dream because somehow it didn't seem to be his. He'd wake up afterward, not frightened, not caught up, not; even out of breath, but instantly aware that he was in bed, at home—and disappointed. He was almost ashamed of the dream because he felt it was a distillation of his mother's stories, and things he'd seen on TV or read about, though he couldn't pinpoint the details. Ira hated not being able to respond from the depths of himself. For all it mattered, he could have been dreaming of a car accident. Why was this dream so obvious and what was it trying to tell him? Was it simply that the horror he felt was too oppressive to let him settle into peace at night?

His father was usually home around six and they watched the news over dinner, a tradition that began in fourth grade when Ira had to do public-events reports. The reports stopped the next year, but dinner went on being served at six, maybe because then they could talk about the news and not have to talk to each other. The older he got, the more Ira welcomed the TV's distraction; the tension, at table was so strong. Eating at a friend's house was a treat; at home, Ira worried whether his father thought he ate too fast, too slowly, too noisily. His father hardly said anything personal to him, and that made Ira feel his standards were impossibly high. He came to suspect his mother's easy approbation; it was as if she was still speaking the young mother's dialect of indiscriminate praise for her infant: everything he did was "Wonderful!"

On an evening a week before his seventeenth birthday, Ira lay stretched on the couch in the living room, reading the *Times*. His mother was in the kitchen with a crossword puzzle. He didn't see how she had the patience to work on them; he gave up after being stumped a few times, but she plunged on, intent, muttering, steadily darkening each white square. When the doorbell rang, Ira assumed it was a neighbor. He sat up and heard his mother ask a sharp question out in the foyer. His father entered, headed for the wall unit, opened the liquor cabinet, and took out a bottle of vodka someone had given them last New Year's, and a shot glass. Ira had never seen him drink except on holidays.

His father turned, shook his head and crossed to the couch. His cheeks were beet red, as if someone had slapped him. Back straight, his father set the bottle and glass down on the large square table on top of the Chagall book, opened the bottle, very slowly poured a shot, and downed it as if he wanted to feel pain. He had another shot in the same exalted, self-absorbed way.

Ira's mother stood at the door, hands thrust into her apron pockets. His father signaled and Ira poured another drink for him. He had never done that before.

"I was at Kennedy Airport," his father began softly. "And a woman, my age, nice-looking, got in. She gave an address and something . . . something in her voice made me look: at her good. '*Foon vanent koomt a Yeed?*' I asked her. '*Foon Litteh.*' Lithuania—"

"Stop it!" Ira's mother leaned forward, rigid, her face pale. "Stop! You'll make yourself sick!"

"And then the woman stared, saw my picture and name tag hanging on the dash. 'Wolf Landau?' she said to me. 'But I'm your Betsia!'"

"She was Betsia, my mother's a cousin. They told me she died at Treblinka, everyone said. She's been here, in America, for years. She thought I was dead—she never could find me after the War over there. She gave up."

"But where is she now?"

"Not far—Kew Gardens. She's coming soon with her husband, and two sons."

Ira reached for the vodka and then looked at his father, who nodded, gestured for him to drink. He had a family. It was no longer true that all his parents' relatives had died in the War. They were no longer so alone.

His father sat stiff and silent, hands on his knees, and stared out into the room, trembling. Ira could almost feel it. He reached out and touched his father's arm. His father started to sob. Ira's mother rushed forward and Ira leaped up, grabbing her arms to hold her back. She pulled away, bracelets jangling.

"Let him cry," Ira said. "Let him."

A New Light

With the traffic noise outside the office window as loud and familiar as New York's, I sat wondering how I'd gotten into sparring about Yiddish, in Chicago yet, and at a Jewish newspaper! The senior writer whose office I'd been sharing for a month had found me during lunch reading a many-paged letter from my parents. Even though he was supposed to be training me, Leon Grossbart generally sneered at whatever was on my desk. I had been hired to write features, like a recent story I'd done about older women getting bas mitzvah'd. He covered the Middle East and considered my work negligible, but this time he stopped and peered down.

"Yiddish?"

Thin, pretty-faced, precise and critical, Leon had the air of suffering the constant violation of his standards. He was the kind of man whose sharply-creased suit pants made you think his legs were creased, too. My parents would have simply called him a *Yekkeh*—uncomplimentary slang for German Jew.

"It's not even a language," Leon said that October afternoon. "Hebrew is. And Russian, German. But Yiddish—it's just a mess." He shrugged.

"Have you ever studied Yiddish?" My wood swivel chair felt more uncomfortable than usual. "Or read Peretz? Sholem Aleichem?"

"Scribblers, not writers. You buy a basket at a street fair, but it's not sculpture, it's not art."

All I could say was, "You don't know what you're talking about." But I knew that he was just parroting generations of arguments that Yiddish was a "jargon," an ugly bastard child of the Diaspora. It was a point of view that had strangely survived the Holocaust and even all the romantic outbursts of enthusiasm for Yiddish across the country that you often heard about: a

27

club, newsletter, a college minor. I'd even written a feature about Yiddish being "reborn" in the Chicago area.

Just then Martha, Leon's girlfriend, appeared at the door for him—a large, lavishly freckled, tawny-haired woman with the grace and vigor of an athlete—and he was gone with a satisfied nod.

The crowded high-ceilinged office seemed to cheer Leon's exit, the file cabinets hulking around me like "I told you so" cousins. I was new to Chicago and to writing full time, so having a letter from home was a special treat. Until then, I'd done free-lancing for Jewish newspapers and magazines, and this was my first real job. The money was terrific, more than I would have made starting out as the journalism professor my parents had hoped I'd become ("We sent you to Columbia to write stories?"). But I kept explaining there was plenty of time for me to teach if I wanted to—I was only twenty-six. My parents, who'd emigrated from Poland in the mid-1930s, were proud of me in their blundering way: I was doing something good for the Jews, making a living, and if I didn't always date Jewish girls, well surely that would change over time, given the world I worked in. I can't claim a relationship with my parents that's especially enviable, but their letters and phone calls had always pleased me because Yiddish was what I'd spoken as a child, and still spoke to them at home. I had learned French in high school, but it was a transplant that never really took. Despite my teachers' propaganda and a blaze of posters, films, and travel anecdotes, I found French not beautiful but simply foreign. Perhaps because French meant exams and drilling, while Yiddish was my mother reading rhyming children's books to me, or my worn copy of Peretz's collected stories, or my father sarcastically murmuring about people we passed on the street.

I had gone to a Workman's Circle Sunday school for years, regularly leafed through *The Forward*, and was more startled by an English word in my parents' Yiddish than the reverse. They spoke English well enough when they had to—and with little accent, but it always sounded hard, unyielding, a language of necessity. I felt closest to them speaking or reading Yiddish.

Leon's arrogance offended me so much, I was still angry that evening when I went back to the bright office to review some notes I'd forgotten to take home. The *Jewish Journal*'s offices were in a converted loft and much brighter and cleaner than I'd expected—not at all gritty or decayed. It was beautifully carpeted and a bit too methodically mauve and gray (like a motel where the paintings match the drapes). Even rushing to make our weekly deadline, panic and frustration seemed muffled there. Employing over twenty people, and despite all the files and computers, the *Journal* was more like the home of a subdued Jewish charity than "The Front Page."

I was doing a short series on women who were having bas mitzvahs. They fell into two groups, young "converts" (from all kinds of things) who wanted the ceremony to mark a new stage in their Jewish lives, and women in their late forties and fifties, many with their children gone to college, who had always felt left out and inferior at services and had decided to end their sense of exclusion. I envied their seriousness. I had done a bar mitzvah to please my parents, to get enough money in gifts for a stereo and to start saving for college. I had memorized all the Hebrew—and sung it quite nicely—with no interest in understanding what it meant. Afterward, like all my friends, I stopped going to services, having run my mock spiritual marathon. The women I'd been interviewing were infinitely more thoughtful than I was or could have been at thirteen.

The first one, Mrs. Rudner, a tiny woman adrift on an enormous white and gold couch, had been reserved, almost suspicious, until I took a chance on her accent and switched to Yiddish. We chatted for two valuable hours, once she could stop marveling at how well I spoke. Now, though, reviewing my notes, I was struggling. I'd written some in very sloppy Yiddish which kept colliding on the page (going right to left) with phrases and sentences in English. I thought of Henry Higgins singing "And the Hebrews learn it backwards, which is absolutely frightening."

Leon's bare shiny desk grinned in the fluorescent light. I settled in to decipher what I'd written, gradually losing myself in the work, eased by the big old building piled around me in the cool evening. I heard the distant slide and groan of the janitor's cart, jangling keys, and slamming doors. At ten o'clock, there were footsteps out in the receptionist's area.

Martha burst in, red-cheeked, squinting, a ring of keys in her left hand.

"Leon's not here," I said.

She stared at me, hands vague at her sides. And she surprised me by saying "Good." I watched her cross to his desk, sit on it, her strong back to me, wild hair a tumult of light. She was very striking in jeans and gray turtleneck, jeans jacket.

"I thought he'd be here," she brought out after a moment, as if wondering why she'd said "Good" before. When she turned her beautiful full face to me, the white light slashed at her wide cheeks and made her look a little like Marlene Dietrich. I studied the grayish eyes, long eyebrows, nose and mouth. I had seen her only a few times, and never like this.

"Do you have a mezuzah?" she asked.

"What?"

"At home, on your doorpost? You are Jewish, right?"

I told her that no, I didn't have a mezuzah.

"Leon didn't want me to have one because he doesn't." Martha stood, pulled a chair over, and sat loosely in it like a dancer after a grueling class, gracefully exhausted. "Leon said it would happen, someone would rip it off. I hate when he's right."

"Someone stole it?"

29

Martha shrugged. "It's gone. Just two little holes where the nails were. He said it would happen."

I didn't add that's why I had never had one for any apartment I lived in outside New York. I'd imagined it destroyed and a swastika smearing my door in jagged black paint.

"He doesn't want me to be Jewish," she went on, hands clasped thoughtfully, eyes pained. "He doesn't like that I'm a secretary at Hadassah. It's too Jewish for him."

Then why was he working here? I wondered. But I just shuffled together my notes and suggested a drink, without imagining she would say no. I was that sure of myself.

We strolled out to the closest bar, a little place plastered with Toulouse-Lautrec posters. Sitting with Martha was exhilarating because she was so beautiful, with a face I found not perfect but fine, shaded and unexpected. For the first time, I felt I could be deeply at home in Chicago.

"When I saw it," she said, "I wanted to scream. Run up and down the hallway, on my floor, pound on doors, find who did it."

"You felt powerless."

"I felt Jewish. I felt someone violated me as a Jew."

"Was it just kids, maybe?"

"No, I hammered it in too well." She grimaced. "It makes me sick thinking of someone touching it, throwing it out somewhere."

Martha's father, she told me, was not Jewish and her mother was "only by birth," but in college Martha had dated a guy who later went to the Jewish Theological Seminary.

"It started being important to me," she explained. Leaning back, gorgeous with anecdote, hands commandingly still on the table, she went on: "Once in this introductory psychology class, the professor said something like, Freud's view of man as basically evil was from Jewish tradition. Well, what did I know about Freud or anything, but it sounded funny, so I asked Ron, who I was dating. Next class, I told the professor that Jewish tradition emphasized man's free will, the choice between good and evil. He just stared."

"What happened?"

"He asked if this was a new development in Jewish thought. I said no, just the mainstream of Judaism for over two thousand years. One girl in class told me later she wanted to applaud." Martha smiled. "I started reading a lot, books Ron gave me, history, fiction; I felt pretty dumb. I wanted to know where my mom came from."

We left without having mentioned Leon. I walked her to the blue Volvo parked in the lot near our building. I took Martha's hand to wish her good night and drove north to Evanston to think about another man's woman.

My parents would've called that *grub*—Yiddish for coarse, dirty.

I sat up late in my rigorously modern apartment with its glaring white walls, motel-like sliding windows, a place of pure and boring lines unlike my parents' West Side New York apartment with its archways, moldings, and deep windows. I was as intrigued by Martha as by her story, and I wondered why Leon was hostile to her being Jewish. Drinking a beer, I wondered how else she was discovering herself to be a Jew. I wondered how I could help.

That was Monday. Thursday, Leon went off to a four-day Zionist conference in St. Louis, and the next day, which I had off, Martha called me at home.

"Alan, would you come shopping with me?"

I said yes and dressed, without having asked why, what for.

All that week, Leon had been annoyingly polite, as if he felt he'd bested me in our discussion of Yiddish, so when Martha arrived at my apartment building, I stepped into her car with a keen sense of annoyance. She wore red that day, looking cool and deliberate. As we drove to Skokie, I felt we were escaping in the provocative sunshine that urged action, movement, life.

"I want to go to Tamaroff's, the Jewish bookstore. I've never been there."

I assumed Leon wouldn't go with her.

On the short drive over, we had the half-furtive preliminary conversation I'd had before, sharing our romantic pasts, or highlights from them, anyway, in a mature casual fashion: emotional historians. I told her about the Rumanian girl in college I'd almost married; she told me about her affair with an English professor. The details—my poor comprehension of Balkan history and her labored villanelles—weren't of real consequence.

As we drove through the flat modern suburb replete with shuls, Jewish community centers, kosher food stores, bakeries, and delis, I felt almost lazy, suspended in the present.

Tamaroff's was a small store in a shabby mall, crammed with glass shelves full of menorahs, kiddush cups, spice boxes, candlesticks, kosher wines filling one corner and books spreading in every direction on shelf after shelf: popular Jewish novels, books on the Holocaust and Jewish holidays, scripture, and then higher up, great gleaming-backed Hebrew volumes that seemed too beautiful to touch. There were bumper stickers, song albums, holiday cards, kids' T-shirts, cases of tallis bags, and rows of glass-fronted drawers jammed with yarmulkes, phylacteries, and things I couldn't make out. It was a flood for me; I gawked along with Martha, who reached and pointed and stared and held as if she had been released from some prison. Even I, who'd grown up in Manhattan, had never felt such richness before—perhaps because I was with Martha. I wanted everything, and I wanted to share it with her.

I bought a heavy black and gold scroll-type mezuzah whose weight said something wonderful to me. The gold letters spelling *Shaddai*, Almighty, were hypnotic. I saw Martha choose a plainer mezuzah, two low brass candlesticks, and a wooden board with Shabbat carved into it. The bearded man at the counter asked if she was getting married. She laughed.

In the car, she opened her bag and handed me a blue velvet yarmulke.

"I was thinking we could go to Russian Tea Time, that restaurant near the Art Institute, but I'd rather have *Shabbos* dinner tonight with you," she said.

"It's beautiful." I had not worn one in years, since a cousin's wedding. I tried it on as if expecting to be seared with a vision. "You're gorgeous, Al."

I took it off.

But driving back, I enjoyed her approval. I had my father's looks—we were tall, wide-shouldered men with broad, strong features, curly dark hair, intense dark eyes—and growing up I had resented being his copy. I struggled to blur the resemblance, first with a mustache and then a desperate little beard, but for a few years now I'd felt more relaxed; after all, no one in our family was exactly a "raving beauty," as my mother would say Martha's, compliment delighted me.

As if her gift had freed us, we talked about Leon.

"He hates being Jewish." she said. "He had it shoved at him all his life."

"By his parents?"

"Oh yeah. I was lucky, I guess, but Leon's parents made him go to Hebrew school and have a bar mitzvah."

"That's not so terrible."

"His father beat him if he didn't study. All his friends had to be Jewish, he couldn't bring anyone else home. It was kind of crazy, so he hates it and he hates Jews, most of them. You like being Jewish, don't you?"

I told her how important Yiddish was to me, though talking to Mrs. Rudner I'd wished I was more fluent. I told her that in college I had drifted away from going to services not because they were meaningless, but because I found too much meaning: obligation, history, challenge, belief. I struggled against a way of life even though I sometimes fantasized about living in Israel or going to a yeshivah to immerse myself in Jewishness.

Martha was quiet for a time, eyes ahead, but her fine hand rested more easily on the wheel, I thought, and her shoulders were lowered, relaxed by my words, perhaps. In that car, the vague de longing to find some authentic way to be Jewish came back to me with the intensity of regret.

"Have you ever read Lawrence Kushner?" she asked.

"I've heard of him."

"He's mystical, he says somewhere about holiness, 'Entrances are everywhere and all the time. You don't have to become something other than yourself, because you're already there.' "

My parents would definitely have called Leon a *mawdneh mensh*—a strange unpleasant fellow—I thought the following Monday afternoon in our office. He smiled stiffly when I said hello.

"Did you like Skokie?" he asked, settling at his desk.

I turned, hoping I didn't look guilty. "I didn't really see it."

"Well, Tamaroffs, then."

I nodded.

He glanced aside. "Martha's always magnetic on the run."

"On the run?"

He leaned back in his chair, smug-eyed. "I'm sure you think her interest in Judaism is exciting. It is. All her interests are exciting. For a few months. What a devoted jogger she was! Read the magazines, learned the language, changed her diet. And that red sweatband, wow. Yoga? Three kinds. Bio-feedback. Adopt an Asian child. Save the baby seals. Disco. Tanning. She tries everything—it's like having your own *People* magazine, she tells you what the trends are. She probably thinks you'll make a Jew out of her. I bet you had a lovely *Shabbos.* . . . I saw the candlesticks." Leon sat rigid, cynical, unblinking. "You probably imagined having a child with her."

I flushed, trapped by his guess.

Leon nodded triumphantly while my shamed silence rose around us like a flood. "What'll you do, Alan, when Martha decides to go to Mass? She's half Irish, you know."

"But her mother's Jewish—"

"So she's all Jew? Martha isn't all anything. She couldn't be. I know."

I wanted to pull a bookcase down on him or strike and strike at that knowing, vicious face—but my rage made me feel doubly helpless, like a small boy cornered by his father.

"Why do you stay with her?" I managed.

This seemed to amuse him. "I can see right through her, no surprises. That helps."

Leon went off for a meeting with the managing editor, and I jammed stuff into a folder and left early, calling "I don't feel good" to the frowning receptionist as I fled. I was sure that Leon's malice was practiced, that he'd outfaced other men before about Martha.

At home, lying in the tub, lost in steam, I fought Leon's slurs. Perhaps Martha had other enthusiasms, but Chubbiest had been too real, too beautiful. When she lit the candles, simply, unpretentiously, I sensed in her a *Yiddisheh neshomeh*, a Jewish spirit. When I salted the challah, that rite connecting us to the incense in the Temple, I felt that we were two pilgrims emerging from different deserts. Was it wrong to picture introducing her to my parents, teaching her Yiddish, reading to her from Peretz, to enjoy being Jewish with her, to feel romantic that evening?

I worked at home until Martha called to say she was coming over, and then I felt nervous, suspicious. Maybe Leon was right about her. . . . But then I thought of the women I'd been interviewing, all so dedicated and serious, and how proud their families and rabbis were. I wondered how many women were struggling like Martha to be Jewish in some way that made sense to them.

I expected Martha to be harassed or crying when she showed up, but we rarely get to play out the scenes we imagine. She was warm, relaxed. We sat on the couch with some wine and watched the sky darken, the city light up. She spoke calmly; we held hands.

"Leon was so nasty when he found the candlesticks. He asked if he should buy me a head kerchief and lumpy shoes and throw out my makeup. He started humming things from *Fiddler on the Roof*! But it didn't touch me, he was just spinning his wheels."

"Where did you meet him?"

She grimaced. "Two years ago in a bar."

Then I told her what Leon had said.

"But it's true, Alan. I have done lots of things and got bored. This isn't the same, though; that's why Leon's fighting it. You're different." She laughed. "When we went out last week, I thought, God, he is so normal." After a silence, she asked, apparently thinking of Leon, "Did your folks beat you?"

"No."

"My father did, sometimes, when I was little, but I used to scream so loud, he couldn't stand it. Do Jews beat their kids?"

"You're not supposed to. You can only hit a child if he's refusing to do a mitzvah."

"I know what that is: a good deed."

"Right. But that leaves out kids who're too small to understand a what the mitzvah means, and you can't hit a kid old enough to hit you back, you'd be causing him to sin."

"Is there more?"

I grinned. "You can only hit a kid with something that breaks easy.

"Which leaves out hands."

"Right. Basically, you can only use a reed."

"A what?"

"A dried reed."

"How do you know all that?"

"A friend in high school asked his rabbi, after his mother slapped him around for something."

"She must have been mad when he told her."

"She was ashamed."

"You know so much," Martha said, shaking her head. "No, you do." There was a flattering hunger in her eyes that filled me with enthusiasm. Years ago, I had been a Jew, had prayed, with my family, with friends, or alone, but never with anyone like Martha, never anyone for whom being

Jewish was so much a problem, so promising and so alien. Cause a new light to shine upon Zion, I thought, *Or hadash al tsion to-ir*. Shabbat melodies began to stir in me.

"Would you take me to services someday? Would you teach me?" She was as open as a child sharing a secret.

I wanted to tell her about my series, maybe introduce her to some of the women. She could have a bas mitzvah, too, and I could help her study.

"What about Leon?" I asked.

"Forget him."

"We share an office. He's supposed to be training me."

She shrugged. "Train him back."

"Seriously, what about Leon?"

Now Martha rose. "He doesn't own me," she murmured.

She went off to the bathroom and I surrendered to memory: seeing my father cry one Yom Kippur as he beat his heart; practicing the Torah blessings with my mother; the Passover seders; the Chanukah *gelt*; fasting on Tisha B'Av. The simplicity of Martha's hunger for the unknown, the guessed at, had opened me to my old longings for a commitment that filled as well as bound. I wanted to reenter that world of possibility, with her, and when she came back to hug me and I smelled the jasmine of her perfume, I realized that we were already there.

The Cossacks

Like the first and second violinists of some glorious defunct orchestra, Sam Levine's parents, refugees from pre-War Poland, had a dim estimation of almost every expression of American Jewish life. Example: They winced every time they heard someone pronounce *rebbe*, the Yiddish for rabbi, as rebby and not rebbeh, the way you were supposed to, the way they did, because they spoke a pure and refined Vilno Yiddish. But that treasure they had saved from German thoroughness seemed like the chestful of Czarist rubles Sam's father said his father had brought from Moscow to Vilno in 1917, convinced that the Czar would restore order. A colorful relic, interesting, perhaps, but valuable only as history. And Vilno itself, that Jerusalem of Poland in which their families had flourished for three hundred years, the name did not provoke awe or even respect here in America. It was like Atlantis, mythical, sunken, lost.

Because of their criticism of anything Jewish and American, Sam decided not to tell his parents right away that he wasn't going to move back to his dorm at Case Western Reserve, but off campus, to the Hillel co-op. He just moved, and wrote them a week later, and by then he knew he would have to say as little as possible about what the co-op was really like. He could describe the two-story Tudor house ringed with maples and elms, the beautifully furnished room he had, the small wood-paneled shul with its ark set into the wall, the large modern kosher kitchen downstairs, the cozy lecture rooms and lounge. All that would be okay, would get a neutral response, as almost anything else about his school life in Ohio.

Sam had come to feel less like their son, or even a relative, than a cause they supported with regular and generous checks in exchange for newsletter reports and—possibly—a sense of purposeful commitment to something outside their daily life. For he, too, was American, and so, unreal to them in a way, or at least insignificant.

But he could never tell them about Rabbi McGee, the Hillel director, who looked like a chubby Richard Dreyfuss. A rabbi whose father was Irish? Only in America, Sam could hear them sneer, typical.

And what would they think of the co-op members, like Fred, the six foot two blond, blue-eyed Viking whose swimming, weights, tennis, and lacrosse gave him the bulk and curves of a magnificent Fifties Chevrolet? Fred was supposedly majoring in advertising, but almost always talked about vitamins, diet, cramps, marathons, equipment. Sam's parents would have called Fred goyish and vulgar, *prost*, in Yiddish.

That first day, Fred came into Sam's room sweating, toweling his red and heaving chest, and offered him the use of his weights next door, "any time." Did Sam work out? Swim? Sam admitted that he was from L.A., where staying in touch with the latest film, book, song, clothes, club, and expression was his kind of workout. But he mentioned running, which his girlfriend Mandy and he had taken up in high school as soon as brunch spots had begun filling up with sweatbands and mesh tops on Sundays. The look—after all—was so hot.

Fred grinned. "I can run." Fred made a 7:00 A.M. appointment with him for the next morning; there was a good track nearby at a middle school. Before Fred went out to take a shower, he said, "You met Tony yet? Don't mind Tony. He gets confused sometimes."

Tony Hernandez, from Dayton, had the room opposite Sam's, but the first time he saw Tony was in the shul (the sign read CHAPEL) downstairs, with a yarmulke and prayer shawl on, kneeling down near the Ark. He knew that Jews only knelt on Yom Kippur, and many not even then, so Sam was shocked. But over a Coke in Tony's room that night, Tony told him that his Jewish mother and Italian father had tried to give him and his sister a choice about religion. It worked, and it didn't work.

"Okay," Tony said. "So my sister's a nun. It's not so bad. I mean, she's got a steady job, and how many people can say their brother-in-law is Jesus, 'cause she is a Bride of Christ, you know."

Sam asked what her name was.

"Maria. She teaches at Fordham University, in New York." Tony tried to say it again as "Noo Yawk."

They talked about cities for awhile and then Sam met Lori, the other co-op member. Leaning in the doorway, she was tall, tanned, blue-eyed and blond, with the dazed shy grace of Botticelli's Venus. Which is why Sam didn't expect her to say, "I'm so bored." He thought then of those "haughty daughters of Zion" in *Isaiah*, and imagined Lori hung about with jewels, shawls, corselets, and bells.

"Don't let Father Tony convert you or anything," she said, and then faded back into the hall. A door opened, closed. "Wow. "

Tony nodded. "Fred and me asked the rabbi to get another girl to cut down the competition, but you were the only one that applied." Tony shrugged.

Sam couldn't understand. The co-op rooms were cheaper than the dorms, the facilities better, more private, the building was on a quiet old street ten minutes from campus, the bars, bookstores, movie theaters.

The next morning we all met in the lounge to work out cleaning schedules. Lori picked at her blue nail polish. Fred was silent, wiped out after his two hundred morning push-ups and the seven miles he had run with Sam at the track, and Tony kept drifting off the subject, which seemed to leave Sam in charge.

"Marsha was our president," Tony explained.

"Why did she move out?"

"Pregnant," Lori said.

"Fat." Fred glared at her. "She got fat."

"Because she was pregnant."

"Marsha did not like men," Tony said, and they were all silent, as if a detective had revealed the key piece of evidence to a roomful of suspects.

"Wouldn't be the first time," Lori said.

"Fat," Fred insisted.

Sam never did find out for sure why Marsha, a sophomore, had moved; each of them had a wildly different opinion, just as they were ill-sorted in their religious leanings. Lori called Fred "Joe Shabbat" because he thrived on the intricacies of *kashrut*, which he only observed at Hillel because it had a kosher kitchen. So when Lori claimed to be a Reconstructionist, Fred snarled, "You can't even spell that."

"I feel it."

They both agreed, however, that Tony would either join Jews for Jesus or become a Jerusalem black-hatter, throwing stones at cars driving on the Sabbath and spitting at women tourists in short skirts.

"Hey, I don't spit! Do I spit?"

Sam supposed he fit in with the motley bunch. His grim bar mitzvah, the Hebrew school, and the Yiddish classes his parents made him attend (while they sneered at his teachers) were all like transplants he had rejected—nothing took. He guessed it all gave his parents more proof that American Jewish life was an oxymoron.

"This campus is an interesting place," Rabbi McGee said on Sam's second evening. "There's more jewelry than Jewishness. It's a challenge."

The rabbi had found him in the lounge reading the *Plain Dealer* (which seemed like a college paper compared to the L.A. *Times*), and had stopped, to be warm and confiding, Sam guessed. McGee explained that Case was not the most prized post for Hillel directors, despite Cleveland's rich cultural life and strong Jewish community. The students had very low Jewish identification, apparently, and the only other applicant who'd competed for the post had been a former Black Panther converted by a "mitzvah mobile" in New York's diamond district.

Why was Sam there? It was the fall after Israel's invasion of Lebanon, and their campus had been full of leftist and Arab students ringing buildings with DEATH TO ISRAEL picket signs and cries of hatred. The campus paper printed endless tirades against Israel, punctuated by an occasional letter protesting that words like genocide, Nazi, fascist had very clear meanings that were being distorted by flinging them at the Israelis. Sam just got fed up with fellow students saying "Boy, those Jews—" when they talked about Israel. He was angry, but felt he knew only what he read in the L.A. Times his folks had given him a subscription to (as an incentive to stay for summer classes, he bet). There in Ohio he felt exposed as a camouflage Jew. In L.A., crowded with Jewish names, jokes, faces, and concerns, he had fit in because he was never really challenged.

He couldn't tell this to his parents because it would have been taken as criticism of them, which was unacceptable, since they had their own parents' pre-War European ideas of how he should "address" them. His mother and father were often saying, "Don't talk to me like a servant." It opened up a whole different world he could hardly imagine.

Sam tried sharing how he felt about being Jewish with the coop members. Lori was not interested, Fred was clearly restless to be working out, and Tony told him more about Maria, the nun.

"She says God talks to her, through music. *John Denver's Greatest Hits.*"

Tony then tried explaining the Sorrowful Mysteries to him, with the adolescent enthusiasm of a kid taking driver's ed.

At his interview to get into the co-op, Sam had told Rabbi McGee that he felt pretty ignorant—Judaicly speaking, that is. He knew from an introductory psychology course that "I am pretty ignorant" from a nineteen-year-old would've seemed like obtuse bragging. He just wanted to get in, thinking it would be difficult. And he wanted to learn something about being Jewish.

He supposed McGee thought his "search" would change the co-op; the Jewishness there was one of tacit bland concern for Israel, worry about anti-Semitism, a Jewishness of atmosphere, jokes, self-parody. Any bargain, for instance, any advantage, offer, or change for the better was greeted with "Such a deal." Tony said it firmly, Lori dropped it like a dull postcard, Fred made it sound like a mantra. And all three tried for a "Jewish" accent, which would have annoyed Sam's parents, who proudly spoke half a dozen languages between them, with no distorting accent in any.

The four of them shopped and cooked dinner in pairs, and ;given their class schedules, Sam wound up with Fred, who wasn't of much practical help in the kitchen. He could make origami birds out of napkins, and at his cardiologist father's parties in Shaker Heights, Fred had once seen a caterer's assistant run a fork down and around a cucumber to leave the slices ridged, flower-shaped. He insisted they always have a salad, so he could serve his specialty.

It was their first night coking, two weeks before Rosh Hashanah (which was late that year) that Sam found the cross carved on the inside of the building's bask door. He'd gone out to get the last bag of groceries from Fred's Audi and had to kick the door closed because it was sticking: that's when he saw it. The foot-long cross was not very deeply cut into he center of the door, but he had a sudden terrified flash of some movie with a plain swept by horsemen, cossacks, maybe, their brandished swords slicing the air as they charged. When he told Fred, and Fred was done running a finger along each arm of the cross as if tracing a map route, he said, "It wouldn't be Tony."

Which of course made him think that it was Tony. At dinner, though, when Tony heard, he had the sick look of child who has seen his first accident; it didn't seem like guilt.

"The building's open," Lori complained. "It's a public building, except at night."

She was right. McGee taught some classes there; people were always corking by for information, counseling, schedules, with questions abort Jewish observance or history.

Fred objected. "Public doesn't mean nuts with knives."

"Yes it does." Lori popped a red grape into her mouth as if practicing to be Alexis on *Dynasty*, gave it a crunch. "Yes it does."

"Someone should do something!" Tony spoke through a mouthful of salad.

Lori shrugged. "So what else is new, anti-Semitism, in Ohio."

"Go dye your hair."

"Well is it?" Lori asked Sam, as if he was an expert. "Is it new?"

"No. Of course not. But—"

"See?" Lori raised her eyebrows at Tony as if the weight of her disdain could bring him to his knees.

"Someone should do something," he insisted.

They talked then about cemetery and synagogue desecrations they'd read about in Cleveland's Jewish newspaper, like a circle of campers telling ghost stories at a fire they can trust.

Rabbi McGee informed the Anti-Defamation league and seemed pleased to have taken an official step; he also called in a carpenter to repair the damage. For a few days afterward, Sam imagined that anyone he passed on campus or at a bus stop could be the intruder. He wondered if that wasn't partly why his parents had never traveled to Europe, not just because their families and homes there were lost, plowed under, but the murderers, the witnesses, could be next to them at a cafe, or snapping photos at a famous monument, holding their chins up in the breeze of a river crossing to mask their shame. The scene of the crimes would not be empty and fixed for retrospection.

Nina, Rabbi McGee's secretary, told Sam that this wasn't the first incident at all. Cars in the lot behind the building had sometimes been vandalized; last year a brick had gone through an upstairs window over Christmas break when no one was around, and there were phone calls, cursing usually. In her late sixties, model-slim, with a face scored by smiles and attentiveness, and trim in bright linen suits, Nina did not seem fazed by much of anything.

"The best calls are the real ones, though, like from the Christians, the born-againners?" She stroked the white phone machine on her desk. "Last Passover, someone called to find out the schedule for the Paschal Lamb sacrifice, and could non-Jews attend? I'm serious! I wanted to say, Darling, since the Temple times we only do a symbolic ritual, you know, pour a glass of wine on a sweater." She grinned. "Virgin wool, of course."

For some nights after the incident, they all stayed up late, Sam noticed, doors open on the hall, radios and stereos low, drifting in and out of each other's rooms, comparing assignments, talking about movies. They were all so different, Sam kept thinking; you could see it on their walls. He had posters of freeways and the Hollywood sign. Tony's walls were full of family pictures, but especially vacation shots of his sister in Rome, Paris, Chartres, anywhere there was a church or cathedral.

"She sends me Christmas cards, too," Tony said, sitting back on his bed. "She wants to save my soul."

"What do your folks think?"

"About my soul? Oh, Maria. . . . Well, my Dad's proud, sort of, and I guess he's happy she didn't marry some jerk. She dated jerks in high school. My Mom had trouble; it's not like she's real Jewish or anything, but a nun, even if you're not real Jewish, a nun's pretty different."

"But your sister's Jewish, since your mom is."

Tony shrugged. "She got over it."

In Fred's room, which smelled of sweat, mostly, and was crowded with barbells and a weight bench, posters of Bruce Jenner, Arnold Schwarzeneg-ger, Mark Spitz, and Greg Louganis plastered the walls. One night, Fred asked Sam if he'd ever had a vitamin work-up.

Lori leaned in at the door, clutching the frame as if she were a kid on monkey bars, and jeered, "Pizza, Twinkies, nachos, beer. . . ."

Fred gravely shook his head.

She laughed. "Have you ever noticed how nobody smiles in a health-food store? Know why? They're all afraid of dying—that's why they eat that crap."

"She's right," Tony called from his room.

Fred snarled, "Fuck you, Your Holiness."

Lori drifted to her room and Sam followed. Like the cool inside of a shell, it was all subtle gradations of rose and ivory. There was only one picture, a matted and framed print of that sad Manet bar girl.

"Why'd you move in here?" Sam asked.

Lori eased into her fat pink and white striped armchair. "Because Marsha was my friend."

It occurred to Sam then that for all four of them, being with Jews was not just the clearest way of being Jewish, but a substitute for it. And his parents? Well, they were survivors, refugees, like villagers who flee a volcano, they had escaped the flames, the rocks, the death-dealing lava and gas, but they had not left the disaster behind them. They may have made lives of dignity in the United States, his father as a chemist, his mother as a translator, but they were still citizens of the lost and magical Jewish kingdom spread across Europe, shaped by its passing. Sam had no such inheritance and had always resisted creating his own.

The co-op building unfortunately lay along a stretch of streets between some bars and a handful of fraternity houses, which was most obvious Thursday and Friday nights and weekends. It was like being at an opera before a big crowd scene—roaring offstage that swells into curses and boasts, then eventually recedes. Sometimes guys pissed or threw up on the lawn; mostly, they just left beer cans.

Other people's drunkenness can be disgusting, especially magnified by crowds and a reproving nighttime silence, but Sam's room was at the back, so he didn't hear as much as Tony and Lori did.

The night the police came, though, they were all in Tony's room, making popcorn and listening to the new Stones album.

"Here we go," Lori sighed at 11:00 P.M.

They heard the usual strident shouting and then a chorus of "Oy-oy, oy-oy," which faded quickly. Dogs were barking.

"Jewish sailors," Tony quipped, turning up the stereo, but none of them smiled. Fred was flushed and Sam felt trapped, suddenly, wanting to move, disappear, but feeling something awful would happen if he left the room.

Lori hissed, "I hate it."

Tony cleared his throat. "Being Jewish?"

"No. Being here, inside. I want a gun. I want to stand there with a machine gun and go, 'Say it again, asshole. Come on!' "

They stared at her.

Tony whistled. "Lori the Barbarian."

"Well, don't tell me I'm the only man in this place!"

Fred nodded. "I hate it, too."

The record had stopped playing. Tony reached for more popcorn. "They're just dumb farm kids. Hicks."

They heard more shouting then, something about killing Jews, which turned into a loud and solitary "Go back to Auschwitz!"

Fred was out the door and tearing down the stairs before anyone could move. The front door slammed open; Sam heard shouts, and then a harsh cry. When he got downstairs, with Lori and Tony tumbling behind him, Fred's right hand was bloody, and there was no one in sight. "I got one in the jaw pretty good. I dragged him." Lights were coming on all up and down the street. Sam and Tony stood out on the lawn looking at Fred as if he were a massive war memorial; Lori went in to phone the rabbi. Someone had called the police, because before McGee got there, a car pulled up, the flashing light staining them all with bursts of crimson. Rabbi McGee arrived when the gray-haired cop was done taking Fred's statement. Fred's hand was cut and swollen, but he could move all his fingers without much pain.

Rabbi McGee sat him down in the kitchen with an ice pack. "So what happened? Why did you do it?"

"My mother was in a concentration camp." Fred glanced down at his reddened hand, then up at all of them, a wide-open look of defiance and pain.

None of them had known. Sam and the others drifted off to bed, leaving Fred and the rabbi talking in the bright and empty kitchen.

No one filed a complaint against Fred, though he said he was sure he'd broken some of the guy's teeth. Sam began to feel ashamed that his first impulse hadn't been to follow Fred onto the street. After reading a feature-less blurb about the incident in their campus paper, Sam sent in a letter deploring the catcalls and all the other incidents Nina had told him about. He ended saying that his parents had lost all their European relatives in ghettos and concentration camps, that Auschwitz could be a joke only to a very sick mind.

It appeared within two days, and the Jewish friends Sam had, was coming to have, congratulated him. He was proud to feel part of a group, its representative even, but all that praise for a one-page letter was excessive, undeserved. It was as if his cool prose had redeemed the violence of the evening for them, but Sam still felt unsettled.

A week later, his parents called.

"We got a letter," his mother said. "Yesterday. Block print. The postmark is Cleveland. It says: 'Too bad they didn't gas you, too.' There's a swastika, and both too's are spelled wrong: t-o. I don't—"

His father cut in. "What the hell's going on there?"

Sam explained about the drunks, about Fred, Fred's mother, his letter.

"*Shoydelech*," his mother said in Yiddish: terrible. But Sam didn't know what seemed worse to her. "How did they get our address?"

He explained that anyone could find his name and home address in the student phone directory.

"You shouldn't write letters," his father said.

It was the voice that had always cautioned him against signing petitions, any petitions, against demonstrations, no matter what the cause, against joining groups of any kind, no matter how innocuous, against being too free about what he said on the phone, because "you never know."

"I'm sorry."

His father snapped, "Don't be sorry. Just don't be stupid."

"He means don't do it again."

"No," Sam shot. "How can I promise that? I'm glad Fred punched that guy. Next time, I will."

"You're crazy." His father hung up and his mother tried to apologize for him, but it wasn't easy, since she clearly believed he was wrong and had to say so.

They were afraid, Sam thought, when she was done. They'd always been afraid, and he was finally learning what that could feel like.

As soon as he hung up, he went to tell everyone what'd happened, find out what he should do next.

Tony was the only one there, down in the shul, without a prayer shawl this time, but on his knees again near the Ark.

"Get up!"

Tony turned, ready to smile at a joke.

"Don't do that here. Jews don't kneel."

"But Yom Kippur's coming—"

"This is just Wednesday, that's all it is. Get up."

Caravans

My father never won at cards—not for long, anyway. While my mother would pile and twitch her nickels and dimes with fingers that almost grinned, and Sam and Pauline, their neighbors and best friends, lost or won with exclamations and applause, Dad would grow more and more sullen, his round, blue-eyed face somehow flattened, lifeless, as if more than change was draining from, his heavy dark hands. Gradually, the phrase he muttered as if challenging each poker round to prove him wrong would come.

"I'm cursed," he'd say, watching Pauline flutter a full house and gobble up a kitty. She was as unlike my mother as any woman her age I knew: honestly blond, full-bodied, embarrassingly rosy-looking next to her husband Sam, a thin and simple man all shrugs and "How d'ya like that's?" They were all four in the garment industry, which had been doing "bad" for as many years as I'd been listening. That's where they all had met, after the War—not in some Displaced Persons camp, not in a sealed train or on a forced march, but in New York City. It disappointed me that they couldn't trace their friendship back across the ocean; it made the past even darker. Sam and Pauline had never said a word to my parents about what they'd lived through; my mother swore to that. I could understand wanting to keep silent, but not actually succeeding.

Mom spoke sparingly about fleeing Warsaw in 1939 to Tashkent, deep in the Soviet Union, where her parents and sister starved to death, but she did answer my questions, and with remarkable poise, I thought.

Dad only referred to the past, that past, when the cards, or his lack of skills betrayed him. "I'm cursed," he'd bring out. "I shouldn't have lived."

I would be reading on my bed those Thursday nights, with the door open, and even though the hallway from the front of our Inwood apartment to the bedrooms and bath was quite long, you could hear most of what people said in the dining room, which was where they played. When my father's flat awful words caught my ear, stamping out the crack and slide of cards, the tinny click of silver coins on the blue plastic tablecloth, I'd put my book down, transfixed. It was ugly and intimate, but the game went on.

Mom told him to stop. Pauline good-naturedly recounted previous hands that had amazed or amused her; Sam would talk about work. Nothing helped: Once Dad had spoken the word cursed, he couldn't, stop the descent. His life was also "empty," "nothing," "dead" and because he mostly spoke in Yiddish ("*leydig*," "*gornisht*," "*toyt*"), the judgment seemed more solemn and severe. In English, he would've sounded melodramatic.

Once Pauline tried a different approach: "You have a wonderful wife. And such a fine son."

"Hah!" he said. "He dresses like a girl! A *feygeleh*." That was Yiddish for faggot: little birdie.

"No. . . ," Pauline hissed, always ready to defend me. "He just wants to look like his friends. All the boys look like that. It's . . . colorful."

"*Piristaneh*," Mom said, Russian for "Stop it." Russian was the language in which she argued and pleaded, as if she was a diplomat required to mark the formality of his interactions.

I cringed at *feygeleh*, as I always did when Dad made fun of my long hair and bandannas, my bell-bottoms, fringed belts, tapestry vests, my sandals and beads. It was not what I wanted anyone to think of me. But for my father, the anger in that word was only a moment's diversion from being cursed that one night.

Hand after losing hand came the same miserable talk of his "dark fate," his "cursed luck." It was so terrible I wanted to laugh, to burst in on them and discover the joke. But he meant it. And even after the break—in which the table was overwhelmed with honey cake, strudel, cheesecake, tea, coffee, slivovitz, and even later when the cards were put away near eleven o'clock and platters of fruit glistened in the light of our cut-glass chandelier—Dad would look battered, as if each card were a day he longed to forget.

I'd help clean up while Pauline remarked on how handsome I was becoming and Sam made his one joke, meant to get me over my by-now-legendary shyness with girls, I guess: "Got any girlfriends?"

"Three," I'd say. "That's one extra for you."

Pauline would shake her head, say "He's so fresh," and I'd be off the hook again.

When they left for their apartment a floor below, Dad would go to bed, sometimes after taking a bath so hot and long, orchids could've sprung up from the tiles. So Mom said. She was the one who could joke best. Once, in junior high, when the girl I'd finally asked to go steady with me told me she was going with my best friend (who'd encouraged me to ask!), I sat through dinner without a word until Mom wondered what was wrong.

"I wish I was dead," I muttered.

"Then you don't want dessert?"

We cracked up, while Dad just frowned.

Mom and I would often sit those Thursday nights in the kitchen with WQXR playing softly from the little black plastic radio perched on the fridge like a bird on a hippo. My mother, a slim pale woman with deep-set narrow hazel eyes had a dreamy kind of elegance, as if when she lit her after-dinner cigarette or slipped a purse under her arm before going out, she was in a gentler, more refined world. There was something ineffably touching and distant about her: she was as beautiful as a summer garden seen from a speeding train. Her soft voice, for me, lit up pictures of dark paneled rooms, tiled kitchen stoves, thick velvet curtains, tea from a samovar: scenes from a Turgenev novel. I admired her; my friends thought she was "neat," liked her accent, the vaguely foreign coil of dark red hair, the lightness of her attentions. Unlike most mothers, she never fussed; food was offered easily, questions were casual. She had never once said my hair was too long, even when it was almost down to my shoulders (I would eventually cut it short when I went out for the track team); she didn't complain about my tie-dyed shirts and jeans, or make fun of any of the music I played: The Doors, Jefferson Airplane, The Who. And she didn't even complain about Dad, except indirectly.

"They're tired of it," she sighed one Thursday, handing me a dish to dry. "It's not very interesting to listen to him."

"Why does he always lose?"

"Not always. But he plays wild, he can't bluff."

I wondered that night why, after more than twenty years, Sam and Pauline hadn't given up, but the question came to me in bed and I forgot it while I slept. I suppose they were used to him, used to the long after-dinner walks, the summers together in the Catskills or on the beach at Rockaway, the factory, the political discussions, the union banquets, all of it, every link that brought them back and back to the dining room table—the arena in which, once a month, my father fought and struggled, only to fall like a gladiator trapped in a net that readies him for the sword thrust. How could they listen to him, though, when sometimes I wanted to storm in there and slap him so hard I shook just imagining it? I was ashamed of feeling that, but the fantasy of stopping him was so powerful I couldn't control it. Perhaps what enraged me was that I had so little sense of who my father had been as a boy in Warsaw, his dreams, his schooling, his crazy cousins (I figured everyone had a few of those), that to have the door to all that wrenched open and slammed with each bitter "cursed" was too much.

One time, Dad had given me some facts to fill the void. We may have been Jewish, but except for the Yiddish books and newspaper and the mezuzah on our doorpost that was painted over, left by a previous tenant, you couldn't tell. Besides sending out some New Year's cards, we celebrated no holidays by anything more than a special meal, and I hadn't even been circumcised like all my Jewish friends. When I was eleven, I asked my Dad to tell me why, really. Over the years, he'd said things about "health reasons," but that didn't make any, sense, or not anymore.

"Because that's how they knew, that's how they could tell!" he spat. "My Polish was the best, and my German—! I had blue eyes, blue like the sky, but you couldn't hide that.

"This is America," I ventured, and he nodded, contemptuous, knowing, his tragedy crushing my unthinking optimism.

Likewise, when later that year I mentioned wanting a bar mitzvah because my friends who went to Hebrew school were studying for theirs, though I had no real idea what was involved or what it meant, he mocked me.

"You want presents? Bonds?"

I blushed.

"You don't need all that *chazerai*, it's *bubbeh mysehs*, nonsense, junk. There's no God, no Torah; it's only lies. All I learned in *cheyder*, those hours chanting and sweating to be close to God, what did they get me? Tell me that."

"I don't know."

He scowled and turned away from me.

I couldn't really argue, because I wanted a bar mitzvah as I'd wanted a G. I. Joe doll in fourth grade, to join the Boy Scouts in fifth, to collect Man from U.N.C.L.E. books in sixth grade—so that I'd be as much like other kids as possible.

Sometimes I envied my friends their loud or sarcastic or even violent fathers, because. basically mine worked, ate, slept in front of the television, read his newspaper, and played cards once a month. We could have been boarders renting rooms in the same house; he was that much a stranger. What he thought of me came like news bulletins through my mother: "Your father's very proud of you," she might say, discussing my grades or any other achievement. To me he said nothing. At fifteen, I could bristle so easily at any comment Mom made about what I was doing or thinking of—perhaps because I was desperate both for approval and to see myself as a rebel—but Dad's relayed comments had as much impact on me as a list of state capitals.

I couldn't reach him. When I asked Mom why he wouldn't talk about the War, she would smile gently, as if I had blundered so horribly, kindness was the only possible response.

It was in my junior year of high school that Pauline mentioned one afternoon she knew a very special girl. This was a change from her joking.

"That's nice," I said. She and my mother had just come in from shopping and all the kitchen cupboards were open, waiting to be filled.

"For you it's nice. She's a beautiful girl."

I assumed Pauline meant "inside." I shrugged.

"Call her, she lives not far, in Washington Heights. I know the father." To my mother, she added in Yiddish, "Her mother's dead." Pauline went on: "She goes to Bronx Science and she's very musical."

I groaned.

"Her name's Bonnie. Bonnie Rosenthal."

"I know her. She went to P. S. 98." I vaguely remembered a pretty, dark-haired girl good at math.

"See?" Pauline beamed as if pleased to correct a cosmic error.

Mom didn't comment when Pauline left; she never said anything about my dating so little, never pried.

Now, I wasn't shy with girls because I was embarrassed about my looks or anything. I had no zits, and even though I wasn't tall, being on the volleyball team had given me a good body, but when I went out—bowling, to movies, for, pizza—it was with other guys or in a mixed group in which I felt relaxed, mostly because we'd known each other since first grade. My few dates had been inconclusive, maybe because I'd seen the girls so often in class, in the stands at track meets, on the bus, that dating seemed artificial. I kept thinking that I knew them too well to find them attractive.

I felt under a lot of pressure from Pauline and my mom, and I was kind of intrigued by meeting someone "new," so I called Bonnie. After a few slow minutes, we laughed about Pauline a little; Bonnie thought she was "sweet." Bonnie's voice was rich, but it was what she said next that hooked me: "My Dad and Pauline went to school together."

"In Cracow?"

"Sure."

"Your Dad was in a camp?"

Bonnie listed several names that for me were like great searing brands on my map of Europe. I wanted to meet her right then. I told her about my parents and we arranged to have pizza the next afternoon after classes.

I went to bed in a strange state. All my Jewish friends were second- or third-generation Americans, and even though many had lost family in the War, it was distant relatives who were only names or photographs. The barrenness of my connections—we had a cousin in Michigan and a great-uncle in San Francisco—had always seemed a private humiliation. I never discussed what I knew of my parents' War years except with other kids' parents, who asked out of a kind of horrified politeness, if they did ask.

Talking to Bonnie was like Robinson Crusoe discovering footprints on his island: I was not alone.

Bonnie was half Italian and looked it—dark eyes, skin, and hair, figure as full as her creamy voice—and I was surprised I could talk to such a beautiful girl so freely. She looked gorgeous in purple elephant bells and a purple and white collarless knit shirt—and we laughed because we had the same fringed suede belt.

"You're like me," she said, "a clean hippie."

In the noisy, crowded pizza place (she shook lots of red pepper onto her slices) about halfway between our two apartment buildings, I discovered as I described it to her the pain and frustration my father's distance caused me. Bonnie listened the way I imagined a doctor would, her fine face open, receptive. And then she talked about her father's books, a whole room of them, in four languages, all on the concentration camps.

"He never left, she marveled. "He's there every day. You know when you talk to him."

"Someone's staring at us," I said, pointing.

Bonnie looked up at the door and frowned. "That's my brother! He probably wanted to get a look at you." She shook her head. "He's been following me around all my life." Then she grinned. "Well, all his life." Sighing, she waved him over.

Daniel came to sit with us. Fifteen, he was as slim as his sister was buxom, but just as dark and even more striking, with that poignant look you somehow see only in photographs of young immigrants (Greeks, Italians, Jews) around the turn of the century: curly black hair squashed down by a huge cap, eyes incredibly open. His hair was almost as long as mine had been before I cut it.

Bonnie offered him some pizza, but he just sat there, hands in the pockets of his tie-dyed jeans, eyeing me. I felt awkward and exposed.

"Don't you have homework?" Bonnie asked him.

"That's why I came. I need help with physics tonight."

"Okay, I'll help you. Later."

And then he nodded at us both, and left. I wasn't sure what to say.

"He's very serious," Bonnie threw off.

I was puzzled by how much cooler Daniel was than Bonnie, and it bothered me that I was even thinking about him.

On the way out, Bonnie threw the poverty of my Jewish upbringing into high relief after something I said sparked a cascade of questions.

"You've never been to temple? You don't keep kosher at home? No youth group? No Passover? No menorah for Chanukah!"

Her astonishment almost frightened me. I realized more clearly than ever that I was a Jew in name alone, vicariously, through friends at whose holiday celebrations (the few I'd attended) I'd felt stupid and ashamed. I knew so little and was afraid to ask questions that would expose me; I think people assumed I knew more than I did because I understood my parents' Yiddish. I felt Jewish in the vaguest sort of way: My neighborhood was, my teachers and friends were, mostly—so it was a backdrop, one-dimensional, something I tried to know better only when a friend made a reference that meant nothing to me. I did that rarely, because I still cringed for having confused Tisha B'Av, which memorializes the Roman destruction of the Temple in Jerusalem, and Tu bi-Shevat, the Israeli Arbor Day.

We walked down Broadway together, to Bonnie's house, and she asked some more questions before falling into silence.

"I'm sorry," I finally said.

She laughed, taking my hand. She pulled me to the curb and we sat on the huge fender of a white Chrysler New Yorker, a car big enough for a dozen of us, parked right outside a candy store. Traffic was getting heavy, but it felt relaxing just to sit out there.

"I wasn't criticizing," she said. "It's just— Well, I'm not saying we're super religious or anything, but we go to services and other stuff and Mom always lit the candles on Friday night. I've done it since she died." I remembered Pauline's sad aside to my mother about Bonnie, "*Di mamma iz geshtorbn.*"

"She never actually converted, but boy, I swear she knew lots and she liked passing it on to me."

I walked her back to her building, and we met Daniel again, bringing his bike out for a ride in Riverside Park. He didn't seem to like me at all.

Pauline was thrilled when I told her that Bonnie had invited me to *Shabbos* dinner the next Friday.

"She's a beauty, hah? A real *krasavitzah*, right? And musical."

I don't know where Pauline got that from. Bonnie just liked watching Leonard Bernstein on television, but that didn't matter to me. Daniel was the family's musician; he played piano, and Pauline hadn't mentioned him to me, though in Yiddish she murmured to my mother that Daniel was "strange." I wondered what that meant.

After the amazing openness of our first talk, we didn't draw back on the phone, perhaps because we felt safe, knowing something about each other that was intensely personal but transcended both of us. Of course I knew there were other children of survivors, but I'd never met one, and even though I was aware of books on the Holocaust, I'd never seen so many as in Mr. Rosenthal's little study a week later. His books made me want to learn more, to fit the fragments of my parents' lives into something larger.

Meeting Mr. Rosenthal, I felt an isolation far more chilling than my father's, perhaps because it was covered by such graciousness. A professor of Russian at Hunter College, he was a tall, white-haired, frayed-looking man whose gentle voice and handshake were like something awkward and strange out of an old newsreel: the way people *used* to act. "I don't lend books," Bonnie's father told me, but he said he would give me a list of some I could find in paperback—books that would tell me about my parents' world and how it died.

The Rosenthals' apartment on tree-lined upper Ft. Washington Avenue in a six-story building a lot like ours with an equally pretentious name—The Woodmere—was very large and dark, I thought, and almost too clean. The crystal gleamed like a warning, and I felt unnerved by the white curtains and table linen, the white velvet cloth covering the challah, and by the skullcap Mr. Rosenthal lent me.

Bonnie wore a dark blue skirt and white blouse and when she brought in the tall brass candlesticks and set them on the sideboard, she seemed much older. Her father wore a dark suit and Daniel had his hair pulled back into a ponytail. He looked older, too.

Bonnie covered her head with a piece of lace, sang the blessing after lighting the candles, repeating it slowly in English for me, I guess: "Blessed art Thou, Lord our God, King of the Universe, who hast sanctified us with thy commandments and commanded us to light the Sabbath lights."

"Why are there two candles?" I asked.

"Because in the Bible it says 'to observe the Sabbath and keep it holy' and also it says 'to remember. . . .'" Mr. Rosenthal motioned me to sit.

"I like lighting candles because it's ancient," Bonnie said."It goes back thousands of years."

I couldn't imagine anyone lighting oil lamps or whatever in the desert, but watching the small wavering shadows that night, I realized Dad's mother had probably lit candles, too (Mom's parents had been socialists). I felt closer to him, suddenly, surprisingly.

"Does it have to be a woman?" I asked.

Mr. Rosenthal shrugged. "Traditionally—"

Bonnie was smiling, as if she had followed my thoughts. "Men can light them."

Daniel nodded. "I do it, sometimes."

I had long hoped to find my father by knowing more about him, discovering facts, but maybe the truth of the man I didn't know would be clearer if I searched for him through our shared Jewish past, the tradition he had completely abandoned and refused to pass on to me. I felt dizzy then, and more ignorant than ever.

Bonnie said, "I'll teach you the blessing, if you want."

"And you can come to temple with us tomorrow," Daniel chimed in. "Right?"

Mr. Rosenthal said, "Enough. Don't push him, Danny." It sounded like a familiar admonition in that family, because they all smiled, but I thought I might enjoy sitting with them at services, imagining Daniel explaining something in the prayer book to me.

Mr. Rosenthal raised the silver kiddush cup, brimming with wine, and we went on with dinner.

We talked without stop; that is, Bonnie and Daniel did, about their trips to Israel, their youth groups. Daniel seemed almost to be competing with his sister to be more interesting, but since I was an only child, I found that fascinating to watch. And I was glad that he wasn't cold to me anymore. Almost like a little kid pulling at your shirt, he kept grinning at me, trying to top his sister's stories. His eyes were wide and bright.

I felt drunk with *yiddishkeit*, Jewishness, as if I were in a Jewish Disneyland; they all knew so much about history, tradition, customs, religion, books, and legends. I felt the way I imagined Hindus were supposed to feel when they bathed in the Ganges—purified and whole.

They were so relaxed, so beautiful and kind to me.

"*Gotenyu!*" Mr. Rosenthal said when Bonnie brought me a third cup of coffee. "It's so late there won't be any buses."

"I can walk home. It's not far."

Bonnie frowned. "It isn't so safe anymore."

"I can call my folks for a ride."

Mr. Rosenthal shook his head. "You will stay with us."

"Sure," Daniel said. "I've got a double bed, or you could use my sleeping bag. Whichever."

After I called my parents, we talked some more in the quiet living room dominated by the Krakauer baby grand that Daniel's mother had taught him to play. Daniel promised he would play something for me in the morning. The thought of sleep had made me tired, and a little anxious. Bonnie bustled around getting me towels, linens, and a pillow, and in a chorus of good nights I found myself alone with Daniel in his bedroom beyond the kitchen, converted from the original maid's room and pantry.

His walls were painted a glossy dark blue and lined with Velvet Underground and Mott the Hoople posters, as loud in that silent apartment as a car radio heard in a discordant flash on some still summer night.

"So," Daniel said, "bed or sleeping bag? The bed's really more comfortable."

I nodded as he stripped off his clothes, dropping them on his desk. He padded out to the little maid's bathroom.

He came back and slipped into bed. I turned away as I undressed, because I thought he was watching me, with the same disturbing look he'd had at the pizza place.

"You're not circumcised," he said. "Because your parents are survivors?"

I nodded.

Then he said good night and rolled closer to the wall, clicking off the bed lamp. When I was finished washing up, I hit the wall switch, turning off the overhead fixture with four bulbs just like the one in my room, and moved slowly to the bed across the darkened floor.

I got in, adjusted my pillow, and made sure there was as much space between us as possible. I lay there listening to him breathe, wondering how long it would take me to fall asleep. I was still high from the dinner, and it also felt kind of strange not to be alone at night. Before I could even close my eyes, Daniel said softly, "Let's jerk off."

He took my left hand—how did he know I wouldn't pull it away?—and wrapped it around his thin long penis, which felt very cool to me even as it stiffened, surged in my fingers. My whole body suddenly seemed to be pounding like sledgehammers in a quarry. His right hand felt for me, pulled at my foreskin, slowly sliding it open and closed.

"Wow," he said. "It's so different."

We worked at each other like pistons of a strange and timeless machine. Occasionally, I brought back my hand to spit on it when he said, "It's dry." He smelled of Jade East and Johnson's baby powder, fresh and a little silly, but as our thighs pressed together and he began stroking my chest, I gave way completely.

This was what I had never allowed myself, even in fantasy, the touch, the closeness of another man. In a flash, I thought of all the different times friends, guys on the track team, had suggested messing around, or been on the verge of it, and how I'd always changed the subject, or just pretended I didn't hear them. I had always known what to fear, and avoided it. That's why Dad's taunt of *feygeleh* had been so devastating. I hadn't known how to yell back without proving I was. Mortified, afraid, I'd said nothing.

Now all that was gone, and I felt like I'd thrown myself from a skyscraper window. The plunge was exhilarating, mad, inexorable.

I fell into his arms as he pulled me on top of him, and we slid against and across each other. He said that no one could hear us, but I'd already forgotten Bonnie and Mr. Rosenthal at the other end of the apartment.

Daniel groaned, kissing at my neck, my cheeks, my chin. I could feel the sharp spasms in his hairless belly and legs. I clung to him like a storm battering a tiny coastal town, tearing up shutters and fences, downing trees and flooding homes, and quickly collapsed in an orgasm like thunder that shook and seared me.

When I could pull away, Daniel breathed in deeply a few times. He stroked my lips, played with my hair, pushing it off my forehead and back. "I'd like to watch you run," he said.

I felt sweaty and stunned, as if I actually had been in a race.

"When I first saw you," Daniel whispered, "I thought, He's the one. I can do everything with him."

"What?"

"This isn't like messing around with some other kid. Because I love you. It's different if you love somebody."

"But you don't know me!"

Daniel chuckled. "I think I know a lot."

I stumbled from the bed out to the little bathroom and washed myself at the sink, making the water almost painfully hot.

I remembered the Stonewall riots I had read about in the Times that year, read in a fog of incomprehension and excitement, and how my parents had said, "It's sick, like the Nazis." I was sure they meant the police, and their harassment, the beatings, the oppression. But then my father said, "Men with men. It's like the Nazis, disgusting." And I had left the room so they wouldn't see my reddened face. "They did that, you know," he said. "*Parshiveh baheymehs.* Filthy beasts."

I thought of all the times my father had called me *feygeleh*, not really meaning it. What would he say now that it was true? How would I ever be able to reach him? What I had just done with Daniel, what I wanted to keep doing, again, always, would make him despise me. And worse, despise himself even more, and his "cursed" luck. While all his friends would have doctors and lawyers and show off wedding pictures and all the rest, I would force him outside that circle of simple continuity.

I was sitting on the edge of the tub, head down, when Daniel knocked and slipped in. He crouched at my side.

"It's not so bad," he said, lightly. "Hey. . . ."

And when he held my head up to kiss me, I felt like a straggling desert caravan, savaged by bandits, swept up in a sandstorm, that had suddenly emerged near an oasis—still devastated, but humbled by relief.

Fresh Air

Sometimes, watching Mom at dinner, I pictured the wheelchair at the hospital, in which she'd sat shrunken by fear, and I felt afraid myself.

Dad yelled at her, of course, as soon as we knew there was no concussion, no internal bleeding, no visible medical change or problem. "How could you drive through a red light? Twenty years driving and a red light you forget?"

Mom shook her head, all the energy of Dad's words dissipated by her awful doubting voice. "Maybe I'm going crazy," she murmured, like a defeated little girl.

The accident had not aged her but torn away the years of work and stability. Mom taught Hebrew and Jewish history in our Queens congregation's Sunday school, and she always looked so firm and settled, buttoning the last button of her suit jacket on the way to classes—as if the neat little woman she was, curly dark hair cut close at the sides, freckled face patient, serious, had never known another life, had never walked down any street uglier or more dangerous than Queens Boulevard. She was at those and other times like a wonderful bright porcelain doll, shiny, untouched. But the accident, which happened near home, had come like an invisible, cruel hand to mangle that doll.

"What's the matter with you?" Dad blustered. "You're not crazy!"

If I'd expected the accident to change him, I was wrong. Dad was one of those short stocky men, broad shoulders and neck tensed forward, who seem to push themselves through life as if it were an unruly crowd. His words and looks could fall like hammer blows, pounding at your smiles or opposition. He was not a kind man—or better, he didn't know how to be kind, it was not one of his languages. And though he hung over Mom at the hospital as oppressively as stifling dusty drapes, and tried to care for her at home, the anger lurked in his ominous heavy hands and mouth, his hard eyes.

"You're not crazy!"

"I am. I must be."

"What's wrong with you?"

Her helpless pained shrug disgusted him and he shook his head at me as if to say, "See? See what I put up with?"

I didn't see, I never had. Dad's criticism of Mom was persistent, historical, like the character of a people or the climate of a land. Whatever she did or said in her quiet efficient way irked him and they always seemed to be wrangling somewhere in our dark, cool apartment that faced the back of another, almost identical six-story building of postwar red brick. Mom would sometimes explode and practically bark at him, her thin voice high and stretched, but mostly she ignored his pounding questions or seemed to filter the words from the contempt and anger.

They had met in Paris after the liberation of the concentration camps. From the pictures in their black photo album with its crumbling sheets of sepia-colored, protective paper, they seemed as ill-matched then as later: standing on broad avenues, under lampposts, near monuments, they could have been two strangers brought together by a photographer's whim.

But then I had not survived bombings, beatings, typhus, near starvation, and the death of all my family and friends, so what did I know?

"I didn't want marriage," Mom once said quietly after I'd come home with the news that my seventh-grade math teacher was engaged. "It didn't mean anything," she went on, smiling as if surprised by her recollection. We sat in the cozy eat-in kitchen that was like a warm quilt drawn around you at night.

"But your father wanted a new start, and children."

Whenever she called him "your father" to me, Dad sounded like an idea, not a person.

"Then why—?"

She shrugged. "We had to. To make up for what was lost, all the dead."

"One kid isn't enough!"

She nodded, and I felt then more intensely what I think I always did with my mother, that I was not her son, not even a child, but an adult whom she spoke to across a distance no one could ever cross or comprehend—especially not me.

I wasn't angry being told that I'd been wanted not for myself but for reasons that transcended individuals. I could feel myself shrug inside, saddened by the truth, but not really shocked.

It was later that same year—I was twelve—that I raged at something she said. We'd been debating abortion in social studies class because of the

Supreme Court decision legalizing abortion, and I asked Mom what she thought.

"Of course it isn't wrong. I had one." And she said it so calmly, the way you'd mention something that had merely brushed the edges of your life.

"When?"

"Before you. When we were still in Paris. We couldn't afford a child."

"You didn't want one."

She accepted the correction. For days I wouldn't talk to her. I was so mad, I failed two exams that week, the numbers and words I had to work with boiling on the page.

It could've been me.

But I brought myself out of it, remembering how Mom had said they chose to have a child, for reasons of history.

So I was a child of necessity, of duty to the past, named not just for one lost relative but a whole family of cousins in Lublin: the Franks. Frank. My incongruously American first name was their memorial. Perhaps that explained my mother's distance, my father's rage—how could you be intimate or loving with a block of stone?

People like to look back and say "I saw it coming" after times have twisted in upon themselves, but I saw only what I saw and didn't look ahead.

One Wednesday afternoon of my freshman year in college, I walked down our tree-graced clean street to find my mother upstairs, in the bathroom, on her knees, scrubbing the tile floor with a heavy old brush. Beside her, a pail of soapy water sweetened and steamed the air.

"Mold," she said, pushing her hair back with her free arm.

From the kitchen, I heard her scrub for almost half an hour, and the broken hissing was like a curse on that floor.

When I went in later, the grouting did not look much different, but I wasn't sure, and felt foolish for not having really noticed.

"It was the smell," Mom said over dinner. "It wasn't strong, but—"

Dad glared at her. "What?"

"Mold. There was some—"

"What are you babbling?"

Mom changed the subject and Dad was soon reading aloud from the *Daily News*. Accidents and crimes, he savored them, blaming strangers for not being more careful. "They should know better." Maybe he lived in that violent little black and white world because America had not freed him from his past, had been only a change of scene. Sometimes I wondered how it wasn't him in the paper, thundering his delivery truck into a wall, a house, lying splintered and triumphant in the wreckage he had made. I could see it happening.

But people said he was a "sweetheart." Mom told me that without irony.

Who could've said it? Other drivers? A union boss? Cops?

The mold was not the end.

Mom seemed to be doing loads of wash whenever she wasn't cooking or preparing for her Sunday classes. At first I thought she had changed her routine, but she still did laundry on Tuesday and Wednesday afternoons, wheeling the loaded shopping cart in which blaring boxes of detergent and bleach bobbed and settled like buoys in their sea of wash.

I offered to help, but she only smiled and said I did enough around the house. Her extra washing wasn't really excessive, just curious, I thought.

Then she threw out all our towels and bought new ones. "You did what?" Dad was storming at her.

In the kitchen before dinner, he had said, "*Feh*. It stinks in here."

Dinner was overpowered by ammonia and other vicious cleaning odors.

Mom shrugged. "After a day in the truck, of course."

"Expert," he shot.

I said nothing. I didn't want to be his target more than I already was that year. I kept changing my major depending on how well I was doing in a course, and had already gone through history, sociology, French, and linguistics. My silence in response to his needling only provoked him more.

"So? What are you today? Haven't made up your mind?"

My Regents scholarship and work study paid almost all my school expenses, and I reminded him of that.

"*Svolitch!*"

That was bastard, in Russian, I think. I flushed and went on eating, red with shame, unable to look up from my plate or even see anything.

"And who said we needed all new towels?" he went on.

"They wouldn't get clean."

"I never saw."

The silence seemed to echo and mock the assertion. He never saw. Not when Mom bought a new lamp, cut her hair a little differently, lost weight, framed a museum print, bought flowers.

He never saw.

I didn't understand why he was so upset. Who cared about towels; they just had to be dry and reachable. So what if Mom had bought new ones? Dad accused her of wasting the money he earned with his blood, his *blootigeh gelt* in Yiddish. She didn't say that she earned money, too.

That night, if they argued any more, I didn't hear. I retreated to my stereo headphones, playing the Stones' *Exile on Main Street*, loud.

Our bathroom, windowless, was at the center of the apartment, off a small hallway. I was so used to it that the opaque windows in friends' bathrooms had startled or amused me. So I was surprised when Mom started complaining.

"We need fresh air," she said, and so, three weeks after her accident, in the morning, the windows in every room except mine were ripped open even though it was November and curtains flapped and flared at themselves.

"It's too cold!"

"We need fresh air."

"In Queens? There isn't any fresh air in Queens."

My alarm clock became the sudden temperature shift in my room as Mom's fresh air surged under the door to banish the night's heat. The windows were down when Dad got home and I never said anything. I was still at the age where—for most kids, I guess—parents are hardly individuals, but a grab bag of traits and quirks and expressions, most of them annoying. Mom's sudden concern about the air didn't disturb me, just added itself to the private condemning list adolescence writes with such exactitude. She was strange? Well, parents were strange. Besides, she'd had an accident that shook her up.

Our words for other people's pain are sometimes criminally vague; this was such a time.

The windows were followed by an ugly whirring blue plastic air filter, hunched atop the toilet tank, that turned on noisily with the light. It nagged at me each time I even passed the bathroom. Mom just said that the overhead fan wasn't enough.

"What are you throwing away money for?" Dad challenged, the night of the purchase.

Mom slapped her hands together, hard, like an angry magician forcing something to disappear. "It stinks in there!"

"What?"

"You don't care, you don't notice anything!" Mom fled the dining room table, wrenched a coat from the hall closet, and rushed out of the apartment, the slam of the heavy metal-cased black door her last word.

Her exit proved Dad right; that's what I read in the self-consciously satisfied way he finished his dinner and washed the dishes. Each one he stacked seemed to me a smug "I don't need you" to Mom. But she would probably come back from her walk or flight to a neighbor's—wherever she'd gone—and not pay attention.

Because I never confided about my parents to anyone, partly, I think to protect their past and their pain, that night's incident registered inside of me but wasn't connected to anything else. I didn't imagine myself discussing, analyzing, recreating, mocking: I simply went to my room and tried to study.

What would my room have told you about me? All the paperbacks were alphabetized by author and subject (and the subjects were alphabetized, too), so were the albums. The rug was always spotless and the pictures paralleled one another on the sky-blue walls: chrome-framed prints of Impressionist landscapes, shimmering fields and trees. Blue predominated in that room that I thought was cool and ordered, but now I wonder. It was an attempt at control, a bastion, a room that ultimately failed because it summoned its opposite—chaos—unintentionally.

What upset me most after Mom's accident was the new perfume she bought. Small and almost dainty-looking, Mom had always used unobtrusive scents, but suddenly she had all the brashness of a gleaming cosmetics counter in a department store. The laundry, the gaping windows, the air filter seemed somehow a part of the heavy perfume that almost made me dizzy.

I was worried.

Mom seemed unable to concentrate on her teaching, was taking lots of baths, where before she'd preferred showers; she stayed up after Dad was asleep, sitting in the darkness, with her perfume as strong as the blossoms of the Sansevieria plant that bloomed once a year, drenching the living room at night with their sweetness. The picture of her alone in the dark pushed me from my comfort and reserve. One December night, before Chanukah, I rose from my bed, slipped on my robe, and went out to her.

"Mom?"

"What?" Her voice was hoarse and unfamiliar.

"Are you okay?" My eyes began to find her in the dark.

"Why shouldn't I be?"

"That sounds like Dad."

I think she chuckled.

"Mom? Can I sit with you?" I felt like a shy little kid at the playground, desperate to make a new friend. She patted the couch and I moved carefully across the shadowy strange room where everything was blurred in the night.

"You never talked about the accident," I began, surprising myself.

"No."

"Why not?"

In the silence, she breathed in, and I could see her white, white hands clasped in a fist. She sat head down, legs tightly together in her gray wool robe.

"I'm not crazy, and it wasn't an accident. I saw the light. I went through on purpose. I wanted to kill the man crossing the street."

Somehow I asked who.

"A camp guard. The one who killed my brother Yoshkeh. He's here, somewhere in Queens. A Nazi. He stepped on his neck, choked him down in the mud. . . ."

I had never heard how her brother died. "You saw him?"

"He was here, in Queens, crossing a street, in a nice suit. I went through the light to kill him. I shouted 'Murderer!' He knew. He ran away, and I hit the light pole.

61

"Nobody saw?"

"You know . . . only a kid was a witness. She was too young."

I shuddered. "Are you sure?"

"Such a face you don't forget."

There in the room that seemed darker than any I'd ever known, the terrible sick past threatened to swallow me up. I felt I could go crazy; I wanted to, wanted to surrender finally to the madness, to purify myself, to drown out all the voices and the noise, but Mom kept talking, and that saved me.

"You don't know what it was like, Frank. The filth, the piles and piles, worse than death. The smell. Books can't tell you, film is nothing." She started to cry, hesitantly. "It came back. The smell. And now it's on me," she stumbled.

"No."

"It's on me. I can't get it off—" And those hopeless words broke through the night. I reached out to hold her, and for the first time in my life, Mom cried in my arms, heavily, with the desperation of an abandoned child.

I was terrified.

When she stopped, at last, I brought her tissues from the kitchen.

She asked, "You think I should see a doctor? A psychologist?"

"Yes. If you want to."

"Will you help me find one?"

I squeezed her hand. "Sure."

"Don't say anything to Dad. Not yet. He won't talk about the War, won't listen to me, and he thinks doctors are crazy. Maybe they have to be. There's so much," she said softly. "So much to tell."

"I'll help you," I said, not knowing how or when, only wanting to so much.

"You know," she said, as if surprised. "You're a good son."

It was my turn to cry.

Betrayed by David Bowie

I wasn't on the run or even searching for anything when I met Jeff—I was tired. Tired of living in the rowdy dorm where I had started to drink and smoke pot more than study, and hoarded my haphazard encounters with guys I met at the track or in the sauna at the gym, like a widow saving pointless bits of string.

I resisted the temptation to date women as a cover; I didn't care what people in the dorm might think of my being gay. And with a single room, there was no roommate to lie to. But I needed a change, even though it was my senior year, so when I heard about a vacancy, I applied to move into the Jewish students' co-op at the Hillel Foundation building, a large brick house five minutes from campus.

Downstairs at Hillel was the rabbi's office, the chapel, the public rooms for talks, meetings, films, upstairs the six co-op rooms. I got the high-ceilinged room opposite Jeff's, with two windows facing north, full of grandmotherly furniture: mahogany wardrobe, bed, and, mirrored night table. People were always donating old furniture to Hillel, so the house was full and comfortable, but very eclectic, almost bizarre. Jeff's room had boxy modernismo white furniture that looked like a child's plastic toys all blown up, but it fit him, set him off. Jeff Fabiano, dark-skinned, with piercing eyes, had been lifting weights since eighth grade to make up for being only five foot six, and he was as darkly rich and gleaming as one of those stores that sells luxurious leather briefcases, wallets, bags. He seemed incredibly, inhumanly gorgeous to me—and at eighteen, only a sophomore, so young.

"You like Bowie?" was the first thing he said that nasty February afternoon I moved my carload of stuff from the dorm. I hadn't met him when I interviewed for the spot.

I shrugged. I was actually into Poulenc back then, so Bowie was as uninteresting to me as The Allman Brothers.

Jeff waved me into his room, made me sit opposite the professional-looking stereo system, and played Bowie all afternoon, talking about the songs and himself as if there were no distinction.

While he spoke, I was mesmerized by Jeff's heavy, weaving hands that sculpted the air between us as if turning ice into fountains, arches, swans. He looked like Franco Nero, I decided, with the same masculine, seductive face.

I wondered if his last name was Sephardic, which would account for his looks.

"Just Italian. Half—This one is terrific—listen to the break!" He turned it up.

I was surprised to find myself captured by the dry whimsy of early Bowie ("Andy Warhol looks a scream, hang him on your wall"), and the dark visions ("Smack, baby, smack, show me you're real"), the talk of "Homo Superior," the complete fantasy of Ziggy Stardust, the wild changes from album to album, but always that eerie, distant, sexual voice. Bowie's latest, *Diamond Dogs*, knocked me out cold, jagged music on the edge, Punk before people slam danced and dyed their mohawks. Jeff even had some bootlegs and we listened to "John, I'm Only Dancing," which ends with Bowie shrieking to be fucked, years before it was commercially released.

So I sat opposite beautiful cross-legged Jeff in his white Stony Brook sweatshirt and tight gym shorts while he told me what he thought every song meant, where he was when he first heard it, how Bowie did them in concert, and what he wore onstage. And when Jeff played "Rock'n'Roll Suicide" from the Ziggy Stardust album, with its chorus of "Gimme your hand, 'cause you're wonderful," he told me he was gay, and that he'd never said it before.

Jackpot! I thought. Then I smiled: "Once is enough."

Jeff got up to close the door and then pulled off his shirt and shorts. "It's two," he said. "I have to do my push-ups."

I must have looked incredulous at the sudden shift, because he flushed a little.

"I do four sets a day, of a hundred, always at the same time, if I can."

And so I watched him in his black bikini briefs drop to the floor and shoot back up one hundred times, shoulders bulging, sweat dropping from his hair onto the red and black rug.

When he leapt to his feet, wet, grinning, he said, "How 'bout a towel?" His dark nipples were gleaming and tight, buoys riding on a sea of muscle. I got a white bath towel from his closet door, brought it over, and he turned, stretching his shiny hard back to me as if it were as hot and life-giving as the sun. I wiped his back and arms dry, excited by the feel and the heavy, almost vegetable smell of him—like fresh grass cuttings.

"That feels good," he said, turning, and I dried his thick neck and chest, on which the hair foamed in little curls like paint flung on a canvas, down to his groin. I knelt with the towel to dry his heavy thighs and he reached down to pull the towel away, tossing it on the bed. While Bowie was singing "Boys, boys, it's a sweet thing," Jeff brought my head to his bulge, shoving my mouth against the damp cloth. I slid the briefs down and he thrust into my mouth, already hard, sawing back and forth, hands painfully tight in my hair. Before I had gotten used to his jagged, fierce rhythm, he breathed in deeply and came.

"Gotta shower," he said, getting his red and white robe. He left.

"Do you want me to jerk you off?" Jeff asked when he was back from the bathroom.

"It's okay." I'd already done it myself, too hot and frustrated to wait.

At first, I thought all his showers were connected to the weight lifting somehow, but soon I realized it was sex itself that he found disturbing, unclean. If we got off by rubbing on each other, for instance, he grabbed a towel as soon as either one of us came, dabbing, cleaning, like a criminal frantic to erase fingerprints at a murder scene.

"It won't burn," I said once, trying to get him to laugh.

No response. The one time he went down on me (after I had to beg him), eyes closed, face scrunched as if expecting to be struck, he freaked out when I came and didn't give him time to pull away. He spit and gagged as if poisoned, glaring at me, outraged. As for fucking, he wouldn't try it, either way, seemed almost hysterically against the idea of it. "That's what they do in prisons, it's nasty, it's sick." I didn't argue.

After that first time with Jeff, Bowie often entered my dreams, thin and magnetic, singing a song he'd written just for me, or that only I could understand. He represented what I hoped for from Jeff, maybe, but also the time, those years after Woodstock and before *Saturday Night Fever* turned disco respectable, boring, and white, when being different, being extreme was still a great idea. Bowie became a symbol for me, a talisman.

The other co-op members hated Bowie.

"He's so phony." Tammy, the stunning redhead, was a second generation vegetarian and made all her own clothes.

"But that's the whole point!" I countered, and Jeff agreed.

Dennis, the runner who looked like Keith Carradine in Robert Altman's *Nashville*, just sneered, which he could do in French, Italian, and Spanish. Nat and Marie, who looked like brother and sister whippets and dressed like preppies, ignored the controversy. They were in love and barely seemed to recognize our existence, let alone anything we said.

We all got along fine if Bowie wasn't mentioned; we cooked and ate together, kept to our kitchen and bathroom cleaning schedules. We were also more than perfunctory Jews, unlike most kids our age. We attended lots of the Hillel functions downstairs and even went to services Friday nights and had *Shabbos* dinner afterward. Through his father, Jeff was a Cohen, descended, so the belief goes, from the Temple Priests in ancient Jerusalem. I was a Levi, descended from the Temple functionaries, and on Yom Kippur, Levis still washed Cohens' hands (though there was surprisingly no special blessing for it)—something I joked about to Jeff. He told me to shut up. I was surprised at how seriously he took services, and even more, the first Saturday morning that I saw him *shokeling*, the swaying back and forth that intensely religious Jews do, which I had always found a bit alien and repulsive. But in Jeff it was very sexy, imbued with all the power of his beautiful body. I suppose it also made him more unknowable, almost romantic: the man I'd sucked off was at that moment no longer an individual, but an expression of faith and tradition. Watching him made me hot.

Despite Jeff insisting we never sleep overnight in the same bed, and his never letting me touch him at all when other people were around (and not much when we were alone), we were clearly a couple at the co-op, and Rabbi Lieberman didn't seem to mind. He was a veteran of the civil rights movement and had marched in the South, his wife was active in NOW, and both had fiercely protested the Vietnam War, so how could he have condemned us and meant it? We were so good, too, never mistakenly bringing anything nonkosher into the kitchen or mixing meat and dairy dishes, pots, or cutlery; we set up chairs and cleaned up after the Hillel events we attended.

Whether Bowie was bi or gay, what made him greatest for me was that he said he liked men, and did it openly, in the press. It permeated his songs. He was exotic, he was brilliant, he was strong, and Jeff and I wanted to be as cool as his sax on the *Pin-Ups* cover, as lewd as the boys who "suck you while you're sleeping," as funky and dreamy as "Fascination." We never just listened to one of his albums; we entered each song, and traded lines as if we had written them: "Turn and face the strain," "Watch that man, oh honey, watch that man." We were the Bewly Brothers, the Diamond Dogs, the Spiders from Mars, and Jeff told me that he liked those images better than the bar mitzvah picture that his parents treasured and refrained every year, and the other one, the one of him under a wedding canopy that would someday fill their photo album with continuity, the future.

When the *Young Americans* album came out that spring of 1975, I talked about getting gold bracelets just like the one Bowie wore on the smoky, romantic cover. Jeff said, "No way." For one thing, it was just too obvious. But worse—for me, anyway—was that I discovered Jeff was not a person to buy little treats for; he'd unwrap the book, the pottery, the paperweight suspiciously, as if it were a subpoena forcing his appearance in court. Jeff didn't seem to know how to be grateful, and after the first few tries, I stopped. It was just too annoying watching him peer at the present I had imagined he would fondle and delight in.

Instead of getting bracelets, we went in to New York to see Bowie at Radio City Music Hall, and then spend the night at my sister's in Forest Hills. The stately, sweeping lobby that for me had always led inside to Disney delights and holiday pageants was that night full of guys and girls costumed in all of Bowie's previous incarnations (Jeff had refused to dress up or even put on eye glitter). I rushed to the stage during a wild version of "Suffragette City," imagining Jeff up there, shirtless, sweaty, shoulders gleaming in the stage lights as he pounded away at bongos. I was hoarse when we left the ecstatically romantic, Latin-beat show, and strangely purified, as if I'd run some kind of marathon. Jeff seemed happy, too, but more quietly, like someone too old to risk intense emotion.

My sister Laura, a biochemist, a folky who still dressed like Mary Travers did in the Sixties and even looked a bit like her, didn't know what questions to ask about the concert, and Jeff was not good at making conversation, so our night there was strained. We slept in her guest room, but chastely, like brothers, even though Laura was clearly—perhaps too clearly for Jeff—not disturbed by our relationship. "He's very quiet," she said when we had some time alone. I took that to mean she didn't like him much, found his too perfect body and face off-putting. "He seems scared."

"Of what? You? Me?"

In the morning, Laura had coffee ready for us out in her tiny garden, where the rows of daffodils along the fading brick wall were already quivering in the sunshine, the green and white bishop's weed starting to mass at their feet. Jeff just read *The New York Times* while Laura and I talked about school, and our folks, who were vacationing in Hawaii.

When we left; she squeezed my hand and whispered, "Next time it'll be better." I hoped so. I hadn't even gotten together with any friends from college because Jeff had seemed reluctant, embarrassed when I brought up the idea, just as he avoided parties where everyone was gay.

Besides Hillel functions, Jeff and I went out a lot with Tammy and Dennis. Jeff was uncomfortable about going into the city or even anywhere nearby for a gay bar or disco, but sometimes, if he was drunk enough, he would dance with me at mixed parties where no one minded. He was a very hot dancer, locked in the beat, and I loved watching the sweat start to gleam on his broad dark forehead, his shirt start sticking to that chest of mathematically precise twin arcs, loved when he pressed against me, eyes closed, forgetting himself and everyone around him.

Jeff was always talking about his parents' summer place near Providence, so one weekend at the end of May, we decided to go up there. The night before we drove north, we left a terrific party at about 3 A.M., weaving out to Jeff's Triumph. "Keeping dark is hateful," Bowie sings in "Time," and when Jeff leaned down to point his car key, there on the dark, residential, respectable Long Island street I grabbed him, pulled, him around for a kiss. A car slowed down, someone shouted "Faggots!" Dogs started barking in a widening circle from where we stood.

"What's the matter?" I roared after the guy. "You afraid someone wants your ass? You're too ugly to shit on!"

Now lights were coming on up and down the street and I heard some windows opening. Jeff was drunker than I thought, so I pulled the keys from his fist, pushed him inside the car, and drove back to the co-op. He was silent all the way back, and I was still muttering threats when I got him to bed in my room.

"I feel so gross," Jeff said before he passed out. I couldn't sleep. Dennis had a girl over, and through the wall I could hear his bed steadily creaking. After a while, he gasped like a succession of camera flashes and she let out a staircase moan—rising, building, higher.

On the ride to Rhode Island, I could no longer see Jeff as just the guy I wanted to hold. He was something grander, more elemental: freedom from all the ugly shouting in the world. His beautiful body, his glossy dark skin, his gesturing seemed more compelling than ever. But I felt uncomfortable, on the spot, as if he was silently criticizing everything about me. Luckily, Jeff drove, because I was unable to notice road signs or rest stops. The car could've been stationary, with the New England spring unrolling in front of us like the film in an arcade game that tests your driving skill. I had already learned to keep my hands to myself when we were driving. If I even tapped his shoulder or thigh, he'd hiss, "Stop, people can see!" "Right," I would jeer, "they're hanging from the trees." But I did stop.

Jeff talked a little about his father and the Fabiano restaurants in Boston, Providence, and New Haven, about having waited tables the previous summer, and that he wasn't looking forward to joining his father in business, but it sounded like he was trying to keep himself from thinking too much.

"You're upset," I said. "Last night?"

"What if those guys in that car know me, were in one of my classes or something?"

"What if? Now they know you better."

"Don't joke about it, they could tell people."

"So then they'd now you, too. You might make the news: Queer Kisser Sighted in Town!"

Jeff shook his head. I wished that we'd made love the night before, that I hadn't just let him slip off into whatever nightmare and tension had claimed him, only to see him in the morning wake up unhappily surprised that he was in my room.

"Come on, Jeff, you're not even sure who that guy was!"

The house was very large and bland, a lone white and green waif front-ing the Atlantic, which always seems bluer to me, more intoxicating off New England than anywhere else. Inside, the house seemed ready-made, ordered: One Summer Home, Medium Deluxe, dense with wicker, cheer-ful chintz, afghans, needlepoint pillows, and moldy paperbacks, their pag-es yellowed by sunshine, their covers worn by carelessness and sand. We hadn't stopped to eat, so we hurriedly cooked some steaks we'd brought, wolfed them down in the cold kitchen, and rushed to bed in Jeff's unin-teresting room, where we could watch the cloudy sunset and wait for the heat to warm up the house. In bed, we had lots of Lambrusco, and I got Jeff really drunk by the time it was dark. When I greased our cocks with K-Y, I also shoved some into my ass. His eyes were closed. Just as we were about to come, I pushed him onto his back, crouched over him with one hand around his cock, and skewered myself on it. He went crazy, hump-ing into me, screaming "Fuck-fuck-fuck!" With his hands grabbing at my ass, I thought, There's nothing else, and shot all over his face just as he came, but in a minute he tore out of me, rushing for the shower. He left the bathroom light on when he came out at last, unsteadily, drying his face and crotch as lugubriously as a riot victim, hoping there won't be more violence, more pain. He said nothing, just crawled into bed and fell asleep.

Later I woke him up. "I love you."

He rolled over and fell back asleep.

In the morning he seemed very upset, making blueberry pancakes as if he were a museum figure behind a wall of glass, demonstrating something I could understand only by reading the plaque.

I said, "You're letting one word get to you."

"You mean faggot? Or love?"

When we weren't out on the rocky beach, roasting, we had sex recklessly, as if to prove or destroy something. And now Jeff was fucking me with gusto, bending me over a table, a chair, ramming into me, drumming at my shoulders and back when he came. I loved it.

I told him about my very first time, with my friend Bryan at a Zionist youth camp. Slim, blond, dark-eyed, a counselor-in-training, Bryan was al-ways slapping my back, squeezing my shoulders and arms when we worked out together at the little gym, and when he spotted me on a machine, he stood close enough to kiss me, urging me to do "Just one more rep," in a husky, commanding voice. In the showers, he soaped his long thin cock un-til it was almost ready to spring up against his belly. I was uncertain how to begin, and finally he broke up one of our frequent private wrestling matches to say, "I know what you want."

"And he did," I recounted. We snuck out to a field that night, it was all clear in the sky, you could see the Milky Way. He had a picnic blanket, and some Vaseline, and it was terrific, looking up into his eyes, into the constellations.

Jeff had actually had sex with more men than I, but always furtively, and that weekend he told me he wished he was a Catholic so he could confess and be forgiven, saved.

"I forgive you."

Jeff frowned. "Not funny."

"But I wasn't joking."

Jeff was amazed that my sister, even my parents, knew so much about me, and weren't shocked or disgusted.

"Hey—don't be hateful, like Bowie says."

He shrugged.

Even though it was never really warm enough that weekend, inside, Jeff didn't bother with clothes, and I studied him: the rich, curling Botticelli hair, the small high-arched feet, the enormous haunches and dark handful of cock and balls, the heavy shoulders tapering down to an impossible waist, like one of those vase paintings of Minoan athletes. But like those paintings, he was stylized, one-dimensional, a type: beautiful young man. He had kept his body impersonal, and the distance between us, I suddenly felt, was as chilling to me as the ocean which we had been unable to swim in.

Jeff had brought a tape player and we listened to *Hunky-Dory* (my favorite early Bowie album) until it could've been a script we were learning for a play. I reveled in "Oh! You Pretty Things" with its prediction of gay triumph, but Jeff kept wanting to hear "Quicksand," with its grim chorus of "Don't believe in yourself, don't deceive with belief. . . ."

It wasn't until the ride back to Long Island that we talked about the summer. Like the other advertising majors, he had been interviewing a lot for an internship, but he hadn't wanted to discuss his plans, even though we had shared interview strategies. I loved how he looked in a suit, all hidden and contained, as if his tie were the cord on a magnificent sheeted sculpture, and with one yank, everything would be revealed.

I told him I wanted to go to Europe. "My Dad never got to college, and he said if I kept an A average for at least two years, and stayed away from heavy drugs, I could spend a summer there when I graduated. The money's already in my account, but I've never wanted to go alone. I guess I've been waiting for you."

Jeff was not excited, but as silent as someone who's just been told, "We have to talk."

I began setting names out like a caterer creating an elegant and tempting buffet: Athens, Florence, Avignon, Madrid, on and on until he said, "Sounds great."

"But better with two, huh? There's enough money for both of us."

Was he too proud to accept this offer? No, that wasn't it at all. He just couldn't imagine himself traveling through Europe with me; everyone would know; it would be too obvious; it would be hell for him. Where I saw adventure, he saw shame.

I had been trying to release the playfulness I assumed was inside of him, by showing him how to let himself enjoy men, enjoy wanting them, by joking in the car about guys we saw jogging or walking by, sometimes threatening to stop and offer them rides or just plain howl things like "Prime Rib!" or "Lieutenant Sulu, turn on the tractor beam!" Because I had never made myself sleep with a woman—as Jeff had, hoping to purge himself of being gay—my desire for men was more unclouded, and I thought that Jeff could be just as free. I wanted to save him. But it didn't work.

My sister may have been willing to accept him, and my parents, too, but I realized at last that Jeff could never invite me home for a Passover seder (he found the idea disgusting), get an apartment together, buy groceries, be a couple that was open, public, relaxed. And I wanted all of that.

We managed to get through the end of the semester with only one blow-up, when Jeff said he still wanted to be my friend. "What kind of bullshit is that?!" He couldn't explain. I could tell that Tammy and Dennis, even Rabbi Lieberman, wanted to find out why Jeff and I weren't talking much, why I was so moody but I resisted their sympathetic glances inviting me to open up.

I helped Jeff pack up his car to go back to the parents who believed he was just a nice Jewish boy. I asked him not to write me or call. What else could I do? My sister at first said "Try," but I didn't want to end up desperate, hungry, strained—and when I explained Jeff's attitudes toward sex, and about being gay, she agreed: "Nobody deserves that—thank God you got out."

I was not feeling very thankful.

I kept my Bowie albums, and as each new one came out, I pictured Jeff somewhere absorbing it into his private universe of admiration and fear. When the amazing *Heroes* appeared in 1978, I imagined myself and Jeff there in West Berlin, shouting at all walls, all oppression, affirming, "Yes we're lovers, and that is that" (I was ecstatic the Gay Pride Day in New York when Blondie sang "Heroes").

I eventually went to Chapel Hill for my Ph.D., feeling like Bowie's Thin White Duke: angular, tense, remote. I always made sure that Stony Brook's alumni office had my current address, and scanned their class reports for Jeff's name.

I finally read about Jeff around the time of Bowie's "comeback," the weak *Let's Dance* album and tour, the *Time* and *Newsweek* covers, and that vile *Rolling Stone* article, "David Bowie Straight." Suddenly everybody, including Bowie, was saying that the androgyny, the bisexuality had only been poses. A new biography claimed that he'd only been to bed with a man once or twice, as a "lark," and that anyway, the sex stuff was just cooked up to get press attention—and not even by Bowie himself.

I couldn't buy the new album. I waited for Bowie to clarify, to say that he wasn't denying his past, that this was all just some kind of intriguing retranslation of himself, like Ziggy or Major Tom. I wrote angry letters in my head, but even in fantasy I couldn't imagine where I'd send them or who would care.

Bowie was more popular than ever before and his music was the least original of his career. He was claiming to be just like everybody else; forget about "Queen Bitch" or wearing a dress or going down on Mick Ronson's guitar at more than one concert, or singing about trade, a "butch little number," cruising, "the church of man love" being"such a holy place to be," all of it, the obvious and the metaphorical. "The Man Who Sold the World" was selling himself and everyone who'd believed in him.

I finally read about Jeff in Santa Fe—that strange ocher and gold town of looming mountains and low, secret-looking buildings, the streets awash in rich tourists—where I had my first academic position. Jeff's name popped up in Stony Brook's alumni rag, but not in the 1978 graduates column, in the deaths: "After a brief illness," it said. "Pneumonia. In San Francisco."

AIDS. It was now more than a threat to defend myself against; no matter how high I built my walls, the enemy had tunneled underneath.

I canceled my office hours and went home to play my Bowie albums the rest of the day, crying at the lighthearted "Fear is in your mind, so forget your mind, and you'll be free," wishing that I could've known, could've helped him. For a long time after Jeff and I broke up, I had kept away from men because I was so angry; he had seemed as ungrateful as Lord Douglas after Oscar Wilde was freed from prison.

Jeff was the very first of my friends and acquaintances to die of AIDS, and, when I read the news, all I could wonder was this: did he die alone, still hiding, or had he discovered how hateful "keeping dark" really was?

Shouts of Joy

"Weeping may lodge with us at evening,
but in the morning there are shouts of joy."
—Psalm 30

Afterward, they would agree that Ken saw the woman first as she stepped from somewhere to fill the empty seat at his left in the noisy Hillel dining room that Friday night. She was beautiful and still, a slim redhead with bright bluish-green eyes, twenty-five, perhaps, dressed in rich dark colors— plum, maroon. There was a fine gold pattern in her hair like the gleaming embroidery on a prayer-shawl bag, he later decided.

At the long table where everyone waited for dinner, loud joking discussions followed the blessing over the wine. The large room's baseboard heating could only tease the Massachusetts November cold but could not displace it. The woman sat, hands in her lap, smiling at the noise, the evening. When Ken told her his name and his major, and asked if she was a graduate student, her "no" made him look at her more closely. She seemed rested and very content, and her heavy cowl-neck sweater, high leather boots, and wool skirt looked a shade fuller and more luxurious than what people in their small college town generally wore.

"I'm Riva," she said. "I'm just here for dinner."

Hal and Amy, sitting directly opposite, introduced themselves.

Riva seemed so kind that Ken had an inexplicable, frightening desire to tell her he was gay, which he hadn't told anyone here, had hardly even told himself. It had to be obvious, though. He never dated women and he could not stop looking at men. Everyone at Hillel, the students who lived in the co-op upstairs, those who like him came to all the Friday-night lectures and services, even Rabbi Keller, seemed to make a point of treating him casually. "We don't mind," their silence, their distance seemed to say, "but keep it to yourself." He sometimes felt like a drunken wedding guest at a reception with everyone screening him off by their politeness, muffling the explosion they feared he might make. And he was too uncertain and afraid to search out other gays, though he knew he could go to the Gay Council office at the Union Building, or to Rally's, the local disco, for Wednesday's Gay Night, or even to the men's room in the basement of the Music Building.

Before, upstairs, at the, service welcoming the Sabbath, he'd felt more lonely than usual. He wanted to share the service, to welcome the Sabbath bride not just with friends and acquaintances, but with a man—someone like Neil, Hillel's excellent cook. He loved watching Neil. A hotel-management major, Neil was short, tight-knit, with a mane of curly brown hair, and a broad, heart-shaped face, thick short mustache, and startlingly dark eyes that gave nothing away. He handled and served food with a formality that was sensuous, almost embarrassing—for Ken, anyway. And his stocky taut body seemed terribly confined by whatever clothes he wore. Tonight he had on a sexy thick deep blue turtleneck, which stretched across his hard and perfect chest.

What would his parents say if they knew that just fifteen minutes after prayer, Ken was sitting there hoping Neil would, turn around and show the crack of his tight faded jeans, which were a kind of nudity under the long white chef's apron?

He looked away, to find Riva smiling at him, as if she had seen and understood everything. Eyes soft and sympathetic, she shrugged lightly, as if assuring him the future would be okay.

"Where are you from?" Ken asked as Neil wheeled the soup cart closer to their end of the table.

"The East."

"You must hate it here," Hal said from the opposite side of the table. "There's nothing to do, and it's so goyish." Tall, freckled, glaring, Hal was Ken's least favorite person at Hillel. He was from "Lawn Guyland," from one of the Five Towns, and was constantly complaining about how Amherst was nothing compared to New York—too quiet, too dull, too WASP. He always wore an enormous gold-plated Star of David, like some beacon sending off a distress signal.

"But the trees," Riva said. "The valley. The river. All so beautiful." Ken tried to place her accent—it sure wasn't Boston. She was right about Amherst; even though the UMass campus wasn't very attractive, crossing it, you kept catching rich glimpses of the green and gold Connecticut River Valley between buildings.

Riva handed her bowl to Neil, who raised his eyebrows as if mocking Hal. The table was soon canopied by steam and the savor of lentil soup. "Besides," Riva continued, "where there are Jews is a Jewish place, no?"

Hal sneered and went at his soup.

His girlfriend Amy, said, "I have friends in Boston."

"Yes." Riva nodded, which seemed strange to Ken, but Amy smiled as if the two women had just exchanged a confidence. Small, dark, shy, Amy had been dating Hal for a month, and next to him, her little light always seemed dimmer, almost extinguished. Ken hated how when he'd see them walking together, Hal held his hand at the back of Amy's neck, as if steering her or holding up a dead and plucked chicken.

The huge aluminum salad bowl lurched closer, passed by eager, unsteady hands. Ken could hear Rabbi Keller at the other end of the table discussing Carter's recent triumph at Camp David.

"What do you do?" Amy asked, sipping her wine.

"I'm a violinist—"

"Then you must be with the chamber ensemble at the Arts Center to-morrow night. I love the violin."

Hal speared a radish. "Why are you here?"

"In a strange place," Riva said, "I wanted to be among Jews Friday night."

It was said with embarrassing simplicity, and Ken felt as if Riva was speaking the truth of his heart, or at least part of it. Amy studied Riva, smiling a bit oddly, and Hal just rolled his eyes. Meanwhile, the twenty others at the table did their imitations, argued politics, panned movies, talked about *Saturday Night Live*—the easiness and warmth that made Ken feel at home. He noticed a few people eyeing Riva.

"This nothing little place is what you want?" Hal began complaining about Rabbi Keller who was new. His Orthodox background, Hal said, ruined their Conservative services. "I mean, if I wanted *Fiddler on the Roof* I'd see the damned movie, all right?"

Ken didn't listen. He liked how Rabbi Keller led services with quiet passion and authority. He liked being able to lose himself in the service it had taken him two years to fully understand and love. As the son of Reform Jews, the prayerbook's Hebrew rows had looked like impossible walls to him, unscalable, but now he was inside them and knew so many strange things: that he liked praying, that he believed in God, that he wanted to live a Jewish life, whatever that meant.

"We need more English," Hal was objecting.

"Hebrew's beautiful," Amy pressed.

"You can't read more than a line!"

"I'm learning." Flushed, Amy added, "It sounds beautiful."

"Why do you come here?" Riva asked Hal sharply, leaning forward. "Why come if you don't like anything?

Hal just stared.

"Why? To feel superior? To laugh at people?"

Hal shook his head as the table quieted down.

"You think you know all about God, don't you? People like you keep God away."

Hal flung the wine in his glass at her, spattering Ken, too. People jumped up, knocking their chairs. over. Amy shouted "Stop it!" and in the sudden confusion, with knives and forks paralyzed or dropped and people standing, chattering, confused, asking what had happened, Riva was gone.

Amy stood up. "You are disgusting," she said, moving away from Hal.

Someone tapped Ken on the shoulder. It was Neil, handing him a washcloth to wipe his face. Neil said, "Help me clean up, later?"

In the kitchen after everyone else had gone home, when the cleaning was almost done, and all the co-op members were out or upstairs, they talked about Hal's mortified apology to Rabbi Keller, the small storm of gossip, with everyone wondering who Riva was, and people giving different descriptions of her voice, her hands, her hair.

"She sure got to Hal, like she knew just what would hit," Neil kept saying. "It's about time."

"I'd like to see her tomorrow, at the recital." Ken closed the dishwasher.

"You won't," Neil said, tying up a garbage bag. "She's not in the poster up in the hallway."

Ken felt relaxed, as if the wine had washed away his shyness, his longing, and he perched on the top of a step stool while Neil fixed them hot chocolate.

Neil handed him a steaming sweet mug.

Ken stirred his hot chocolate. "She didn't say she was in it. Maybe she's an understudy or something. No, that's dumb. Maybe she was sick when they took the picture. Or we just assumed—"

"—Maybe not. I mean, what was that about being from 'the East'? Maybe you'd say that if you talking to people in Michigan or Montana, but—"

"What do you know about her?"

Neil dried his hands. "I'm just guessing." The large kitchen, with its banks of cupboards, two massive aluminum-hooded-stoves, suddenly seemed private and small.

"What do you know about her?"

"Wait." Neil went out to the hall closet and returned with his backpack. He fished inside for a paperback, searched for a page, and then handed the book, over, open. "This is a book my sister sent me last month. I've been thinking about it ever since dinner. Look at the top on the right."

Ken read half-aloud: "Elijah wanders over the face of the earth in many and varied disguises . . . bound by neither time nor space . . . he acts as a celestial messenger. . . . He brings consolation to the afflicted and chides the arrogant and proud."

Ken put the book down. "Oh come on," he said. "Passover's months away, and Elijah's a man."

"So are you," Neil said, moving closer to slip a hand over Ken's where it lay on the book of folk tales. Then he grinned.

Ken suddenly felt as if he was soaring up in a World Trade Center elevator, alone, rocketing so fast that nothing would be left behind, not a trace of who he had been. The hard insistent beat of his pulse seemed to rock him back and forth like Orthodox men in prayer. He couldn't speak.

"We're done," Neil said, a little flushed. "We can go back to my apartment."

Neil lived in a large studio a few icy blocks from the Hillel building and close to the tiny downtown, at the top of a house with a view of the Emily Dickinson home, though you couldn't see it from Neil's place. The furniture, drapes, and wallpaper were splashed with a floral print of orange, gold, and green. "My sister's a decorator," Neil explained. "She wanted me to feel warm all winter." Two tall bookcases were stuffed with paperbacks on Jewish history, worship, and thought, Jewish fiction—a small library almost as rich and varied as the one at Hillel.

"Have you read all this staff? Really?" As Ken stood scanning the shelves, afraid to turn around, Neil came up and started massaging his shoulders, slowly, with the easy authority of someone doing Japanese ideograms—it was exciting, tense, involved. Ken leaned back into the warmth, the pressure.

"Don't stop," he said, "or I'll think of some reason to leave."

"No you won't." Neil broke away and opened the couch bed as if he were a pirate revealing his treasure. And then he stripped. Ken had seen men like this at the campus gym, had sat next to them on locker-room benches, but they were always figures, not people, not anyone looking at him with open, inviting eyes. Neil stood like a wrestler, poised, tight, his tautly muscled body hairless, except at the base of his fat jutting cock. He was as beautiful as all those men Ken had gawked at in the weight room, or biking through town, arms and shoulders bulging with force, or jogging across campus with Spandex drawn tight across their firm asses and calves.

"Why would you want to leave?" Neil smiled. "Society? Your parents? The Torah?"

"All of that, especially the Torah."

Neil sat on the bed, legs wide. "Do you keep kosher? I didn't think so. Then why choose just one restriction to guide your life, to make you feel like dirt?"

"You've had this discussion before."

"So have you, at least with yourself, I bet. Come here."

"I don't know what to do."

"You'll learn, you'll learn."

Neil slipped Ken out of his clothes so gently, he could have been a nurse. He pushed Ken back on the bed and moved on top of him, massaging him slowly with his whole body, kissing his mouth and eyes, his ears, stroking his hair, his sides, languidly rubbing his heavy penis up and down the length of Ken's, and across until Ken exploded from the pressure, the excitement, and the hungry, commanding look in Neil's eyes.

"You didn't turn off the lights," Ken murmured.

"There's time," Neil said, pushing a pillow under Ken's head and moving up to crouch across his chest, his cock throbbing like a slow metronome.

"I'm real close," Neil said, moving to Ken's mouth. And as Neil pushed Ken's mouth open, Ken felt his lips were as sensitive, as tingling as if he were high. He closed his eyes, with everything in his life somehow concentrated in that one moment. When Neil groaned and clutched the back of Ken's head, Ken didn't pull away.

Neil moved off and lay beside him, and Ken only knew that they had slept when he woke up near dawn, with Neil grinning at him on the neighboring pillow, eyebrows twitching like Groucho Marx.

At services that morning, before the Torah was taken from the Ark, Ken whispered, "Do you really think Riva was—?"

Neil shrugged. "It's some story, huh?"

And when the Torah was brought around, Ken was struck for the first time by the gold embroidered lions flanking the tablets of the law on the scroll's white velvet sheath. Their glass eyes were so very bright, like Neil's, like Riva's.

Ken reached his prayer book to touch the white velvet, and brought it back to his lips.

"It's a great story," he said to Neil as the Torah was borne away.

Big Girls Don't Cry

When I first read the myth of Orpheus descending to Hades to rescue Eurydice and losing her when he turned, I didn't picture the figures in Greek robes; I saw them wearing those gray, horrible striped concentration camp uniforms. And I saw myself as Eurydice, forever lost.

That's because I looked so much like my mother and she had kept her uniform. She was wearing it the last day she saw my father in 1945, soon after the Soviets liberated his slave-labor camp in Germany. Somehow, they got separated again, and he disappeared. He and my mother—Polish Jews—had survived everything: it was only freedom that separated them.

"Maya, I turned around," my mother said, always describing the chaos a week after liberation with the same words, "and he was gone."

No matter what I learned about my father's life in Poland before the War or his sufferings in the ghetto and in camps, he was always someone who had disappeared.

"Gone," my mother would echo, as if the little word would have to explode with its own meaning.

No wonder that when she and I visited our friend Eric for holiday or Friday-night dinners a few blocks down Riverside Drive, mother would sit with her knees and heels together, back straight, gloved hands folded in her lap, her thin face resisting Eric's charm. Going anywhere seemed to remind her of her loss.

Eric would regale us with tales of his piano students and their "impossible" parents. At the table, he chatted about the old days in Cracow when he and my father and mother were students together, days that had no surviving record in photographs. Gradually, Mother would smile and laugh, clapping her hands almost girlishly.

It was only Eric who could work this magic on her; nothing I did could soften the woman for whom loss was not a memory but a shadow hanging over everything she did. It was sometimes in her smallest, most casual gesture that I saw this most; closing a cupboard or setting a pan in the drainer, she would suddenly blur for me as my mother or even a woman, and seem a figure burdened by history. I found it hard, then, imagining her at work in the lingerie shop uptown, with its frills, straps, and pastels. Mrs. Reisen, the bouffanted, puffy-cheeked, awkward owner, was also a survivor from Cracow and seemed to find balance in Mother's quiet elegance.

Almost every Sunday, my mother, Eric, and I went to the Metropolitan Museum. Eric and my mother headed decisively up the crowded stairs straight to the exhibit they would investigate and explore for the afternoon, planting themselves in front of canvases or glass cases, reading all labels, staring, staring, as if there were something concrete and measurable to be borne away. The way my mother dressed those days, applying her makeup with the care of a jeweler putting the last touches on a Fabergé egg for the Czar, she could have been readying herself for some hazardous encounter; Eric always wore a dark and somber-looking suit and tie. I never quite had the stamina to besiege and invest any one exhibit, but drifted; unable to be held by a single work of art for long. I loved roaming from hall to hall, consorting with Junos and knights on armored horses, consoles and urns, surrendering to color and form—the lift of a marble chin or the light on a marquetry top jostling for attention in my mind when later we finally headed out and down onto Fifth Avenue. We made an agreement that I had to keep checking back to see where they were, and often I'd find them both with their heads high, in challenge almost, defying a canvas, a Greek krater to resist their inspection, standing together in a silent but somehow tense harmony.

"This was beautiful," Eric usually said afterward. "Very instructive."

Mother generally nodded, deferring to his opinions on anything cultural.

More than going to the museum, however, I loved the familiar walk down to the brownstone Eric lived in, climbing the steep, pitted stairs to the fourth floor, listening to Eric play Rachmaninoff and Liszt—big showy pieces like a carnival ride that grabbed and shook and excited you. At the Steinway given him by an American cousin—guilty, perhaps, for having spent the War in utter safety—he was commanding. With his large weathered hands and gray-streaked black hair en brosse, Eric looked like one of those musicians you see in movies: fiery, dramatic, obsessed.

He was actually very relaxed, and moved and spoke slowly, as if translating not only his words but himself into English. So his foreignness was ingratiating—not like Mother's, whose voice and manner were often as stiff as her lacquered dark hair. Eric made me think of Maurice Chevalier sometimes—polished and charming. I made the mistake of telling him that once and he shocked me by saying Chevalier had been a Nazi collaborator. Such land mines were often exploding at my feet: when I bought something (like a change purse) and discovered it was made in West Germany and Mother forced me to return it; when I repeated garbled bits of history I'd picked up in school and was set right like a puppy being smacked with a magazine. Mostly it was my ignorance they criticized, and, through me, the America they both agreed was too optimistic and eager, too blind. In high school, I found a Frenchman in a James Baldwin novel saying, "You Americans—you do not know any of the terrible things." That voice, the voice of dark wisdom, was my mother's, was Eric's. That was what united them most deeply, I suspected, and what kept them most apart.

But Mother's knowledge was not just tragic. With her firm decisive walk and the way she never seemed subordinated or nonplussed by her stylish clothes, my mother was a monument to a different vision of being a woman. She was not pretty—her nose was too broad at the tip, her eyes dull—and yet she made herself up and held her head with complete belief in her own attractiveness and chic. It was a conviction and a dignity that I couldn't copy. I felt too dumpy, too bland. I bemoaned the pretty dark eyes that were wasted on me. And it seemed only a fairy tale that someone as prosaic as me had been born in Paris, though fitting that we immigrated to America when I was less than a year old. I had given up trying to learn French when my first French teacher said I had absolutely no ear, no grace, no chance: I was a *chameau* (camel, dolt).

"Maya, you don't have to be beautiful," Mother was always saying. "Be careful." But I never had the sense of detail that in her was like a language learned in childhood—the right knotting of a scarf, the balance of jewelry, bag, shoes.

"Emphasize your best feature," she advised. But I had grown up in a different country, bombarded by grosser and more exacting standards for women. I couldn't even play the piano very well, though Eric was patient with me.

"You're quite competent," he said.

"You mean dull. I want to do something well; I want to be special."

He nodded, and I was relieved that he didn't insist, too kindly, that I was special. This delicacy I thought very European.

Watching them at Eric's—his hands flashing at the piano, Mother cool and composed—it was hard to picture them in a war, starved, beaten, betrayed. Yet I could see it looking around Eric's stark white-walled living room, which seemed so much a contradiction of his personal warmth. The bare lines seemed a reminder to himself, a warning not to be too comfortable. With Mother, too, there was a warning—in her posture, her dry kisses.

When I asked them direct questions, Eric spoke about the War in fragments I had to piece together over the years. Mother would barely get started before she would have to go lie down in her darkened bedroom. I tried to imagine myself with them sometimes—a younger sister, perhaps. But it was to understand them, not myself. I know many people wonder what it would have been like to go through the War, because those horrible years seem to dwarf any pain or suffering since. The camps were not a test, not a trial by ordeal, not a Hollywood movie with the heroine looking beautiful even while she's been heavily made up to look shattered, ill. By twelve, I was already writing in my diary everything Eric told me, as if to make it real.

I never asked Eric about my father or mother, because he was only comfortable talking about himself. Perhaps his own fate was still so incredible to him that he, could believe it only through repetition.

Eric's mother had made a brief stir in Cracow as a pianist. But considered brilliant at seventeen, she was less so at twenty, not at all at twenty-five. When the Nazis invaded, Eric's father, a teacher, was rounded up with many other intellectuals and shot. Eric heard after the War that his mother wound up in a Latvian concentration camp, where when it was learned she was a pianist, her hands were cut off and she died.

After the liberation, Eric was on a train bound for Paris with other displaced persons. At some small town in Germany, a screaming crowd stopped the train.

"I could not believe my ears," Eric told me. "They lost the War and still they shouted 'Death to the Jews! Death to the Jews!' We men jumped out to beat them. It felt very good, I have to tell you. Just imagine. The War over, and still they were shouting. When they ran and the train moved on, a man in our car started chanting and then we all did: *Alles geht voruber, Alles geht vorbei, Deutschland ist verloren, Die Juden sind Frei!*

"At the next stop we chalked it on the side of the train, and we traveled through Germany like this. There was no more shouting.

"What does it mean?" I asked.

"Oh, it isn't so powerful in English. 'Everything passes, Germany has lost, the Jews are free.'" Not powerful? I thought. I was fourteen when I first heard that story and felt so moved, I hugged Eric.

He flushed. "What's this?"

There was too much for me to say.

It was in Paris soon after the Liberation that Eric discovered my mother, stunned by her failure to find out anything about her husband. Had the Russians repatriated him to Poland by force, as they had other survivors and refugees? Nobody knew. No one ever heard from him again, or even said they heard he was alive, somewhere. Many times, when I saw a handsome, pained-looking stranger as old and refined as Eric, on a bus or in a museum,

I thought that it could be my father. What if he'd lost his memory and was married to someone else? I spun endless stories in my head on this theme.

Once I asked Eric if he would ever go back to Cracow.

"Never. Europe is dead for me. They bulldozed Jewish cemeteries! My family came to Cracow in the 1600s, and now there is nothing left . . . not even dust!"

Mother nodded at that, adding they had left France because Germany was so close.

She and Eric seemed so much larger than life to me at such moments that I ached with a desire to do something, to say or create something to give their lives the most beautiful expression I could.

When I started seeing more books about the Holocaust being published in the years after the Eichmann trial, I pressed Mother to write her own memoirs. Mother scoffed at my insistence that she owed it to the world to record what had happened to her.

And Eric said, "I give what I have to my students. No more."

How could I argue with either of them? But I was afraid that something much too precious would disappear, just like my father and everyone else sucked into the black hole of wartime death. It wasn't right—silence was not right. I watched the flood of Holocaust books—history, reminiscences, psychological and sociological analyses—watched all the films with a growing fear that my mother and Eric would never be part of this, that their own pasts—and my father's—would be submerged in statistics, in summary sentences.

Then, in 1975, when I was finishing my dissertation in Jewish Studies at Columbia, Eric apparently changed his mind and finally agreed with me. He enrolled in a course at a small Manhattan college: Adult Autobiography, a class that used tapes, photographs, and interviews to help people in their fifties and sixties recreate the past. He was one of several camp survivors in the class, and they, too, had kept silent, out of pain, and more recently a desire not to seem as if they were being fashionable, self-important.

"Don't tell your mother," Eric warned me, and I couldn't figure out why. But almost as a bribe, I think, he showed me his first assignment—a short piece of "creative writing," flawlessly typed, with no title.

> She can try to forget. The crunch of boots outside. Her father being dragged away. Her friends calling from the back of the disappearing train for them to "Run, run!" But they can't. Faces all around, disappearing each day. Her world smaller and smaller and smaller. Try to forget: her mother on one line and she on another and her mother's line disappearing. "Doctor, I have nightmares." "Well its no wonder, considering that you—"

"Doctor, I have nightmares." But worse than the cold sweat that sticks to her all night afterward, worse than all the beatings, is the fear. It comes quickly, while she is doing the dishes or straightening a picture. It holds her, and she stands, paralyzed, hearing the crunch of boots. She cannot turn and she knows it is the end. It leaves her exhausted, knowing that for her, there is no end.

"My writing teacher said the piece was too emotional," Eric said, frowning, "and that no one writes about feelings these days in fiction—they are passé." He shrugged.

"Did Mom tell you all those things?"

Eric was at the piano leafing through a book of Clementi sonatinas.

He didn't look up.

"You're in love with her, aren't you?" I felt unbelievably stupid not to have seen this before, to have always assumed they were tied only by history, by their youth in Cracow, and by me.

At home that night, I knocked on my mother's door after she'd gone to bed. Her light was on. She looked very pale against the dark headboard and bedclothes; a book lay open in her hand. I asked her why she didn't marry Eric.

"We never discuss it."

"Don't you love him?"

"I have no right to be happy."

"Why? Because everyone else is dead? Because of Daddy?"

Eyes down, she said, "Eric is your father."

"What!" I was suddenly like a tiny child lost in a department store that seemed larger than the world itself, too desolate to cry.

"It was wrong, but I was alone, and there was so much death everywhere. . . ."

I made myself breathe in deeply. "Why didn't you tell me? Why did you wait?"

"I was ashamed," she blurted, clasping her hands.

She looked away as I moved to sit by her. I wanted to shake her as much as hold her. I felt I was my mother's equal for the first time, not in wisdom, suffering, or even courage—but in life. It was our life, hers and mine and Eric's. I thought of all the times we three had walked through Riverside Park, hand in hand, me in the middle; of the years of birthdays, Passover seders, New Year's services, trips to the museum, the coffee and cake, the hours of listening to Eric play, the way he stroked my cheek with the back of his hand when he said goodbye.

"You could have had an abor—"

84

"Never," she said. "Never."

And that made me feel very good. Mother told me her husband was really gone not a week after they were liberated into chaos, but the very day, the very hour. Her pain had always been real, I thought, unable to condemn her for hiding the facts.

When she was asleep, I called Eric to say I was coming over.

"You know," he said at his door, regal in his silk robe. "She told you? You look different."

I nodded. "Mom told me."

We sat on the couch like two strangers waiting for a bus who have exhausted commonplaces but want to keep talking because the night feels lonely through the silence. Eric's hi-fi was playing *Sleeping Beauty* very low, and the plaintive broad sweep of the strings in steady ballet rhythm reminded me of the many evenings at City Center, high up, peering through the opera glasses Eric had given me as a birthday present. Eric and I were usually relaxed there, Mother not at all, sitting with rigid back and fixed stare, so intent on not missing anything, I thought, that I wondered what she did see.

"I thought you would discover us sometime, would feel it."

"Why wouldn't she marry you . . . did you ask?"

Eric nodded. "Many times. She said marriage would be pretending we did nothing wrong. Maybe she thinks he is still living somewhere, your father."

I told Eric the fantasy of finding my father in a stranger. "But why," I asked, "why now? Why are you taking that course?"

He smiled. "We will be old soon, all of us. No one else can tell what happened . . . not you, not anyone. It is mine to do. I am the witness." The unspoken words were: And not you.

I felt relieved, suddenly, of my frustrated and helpless sense of mission, which I had never shared with him, but he had obviously understood.

We were very formal that night. Eric dressed to walk me home, and I kissed him good night on the forehead, holding him by the shoulder, as if I was the piano teacher and he was the student who had just made me very proud at a recital.

Mrs. Reisen died that spring, unexpectedly leaving my mother not only the lingerie shop but a surprising amount of money. When I got my Ph.D., and a job at Indiana, Eric and my mother announced they were getting married, as my "graduation present." They moved into a huge and sunny apartment on West End Avenue with a view of the Hudson from half of its rooms.

I wondered why Eric had chosen just that particular time to risk changing all our lives. I never asked, though I kept imagining what might have happened. He must have seen something to embark on a course that could have left me hating him and my mother, defiant, hurtling into exile. He could have been on a bus or in a cab and spotted someone in a crowd or crossing a street who he was sure was Mother's husband and his childhood friend, even after thirty years. I picture Eric staring, staring at the shocking, familiar face, terrified that he will lose my mother, lose me. Or does he wonder for the first time if my mother's husband had amnesia, or more likely, had deliberately disappeared, had fled from my mother at the end of the War because she would always be a witness to everything he had suffered and lost. And Eric, panicky, perhaps, despairing, had decided he had no choice.

I wanted to know what he had seen, but I never would. I was only an American, and did not understand the terrible things. But I knew enough to write this down.

The Life You Have

It was a mistake at dinner for me to tell Bill that John Gardner had tried for fifteen years before getting his fiction published. He yelled, "John Gardner's dead!" and stormed from the kitchen. I had been desperate to say something helpful because three of his short stories had come back that morning with anonymous rejection slips, leaving him stunned.

I heard the closet door and then the front door close.

Bill disappeared down our dark silent road at the very edge of town, past the condominiums stacked like children's blocks, past the horse farm, trudging with angry hands jammed in his coat pockets. I followed for a bit, to apologize, but his small striding figure looked so sad, I trailed back to our Cape Cod to wait.

We were twenty-four when we met, back in Amherst, Massachusetts. Bill was electric, the star in his graduate creative writing program, winner of two of its prizes, waiting only for his moment. You could see it in the triumphant curl of his thick black hair, the cool confiding smile, the riveting dark eyes always on a vision of himself as special, called.

In the English Ph.D. program, we liked to make fun of the writers and poets doing M.F.A.s, deriding their clothes, their egotism, their romantic chaos, as if they had no claim at all to the peaks of literature we had climbed and planted our little flags on. But even there, Bill was admired, and people went to his readings.

"He's a diamond," an English professor told me once at a department party in an *Architectural Digest* sort of house where the hors d'oeuvres were arranged to look like a Mondrian. "A diamond," he repeated, drunk, confident, as if he were a refugee who had smuggled that gem in his coat lining across an impassable border. I felt momentarily jealous not to have thought of the term myself.

But Bill's gleam of expectation could not withstand the hundreds of rejections, even the kinder "Send us more" or "Try us again" type. It was no longer almost funny, no longer a fantasy of "Won't they be sorry they rejected you when—"

There wasn't any "when." Each manila envelope, each typed label, each trip to the post office was like the part of a painful, empty-handed ritual. The man I loved was a prisoner of his dreams.

And I was doing well. My parents had warned me not to go to graduate school in English, because there were no jobs, but I couldn't imagine a more satisfying life than teaching. So, here I was, enjoying my classes, with half a dozen scholarly articles published or forthcoming, and a contract to do a bibliography of James Baldwin's writing. My chairman said that tenure was assured.

I felt almost guilty; Bill's failure had become like a curse in a fairy tale, a sentence we had no hope of escaping.

While Bill was out, I put everything away, turned on the dishwasher, and settled into the enormous ball-footed leather armchair he'd gotten me for our fifth anniversary, to read the draft of a colleague's article on Edith Wharton. In an hour, Bill stood opposite me, red-cheeked, solemn, coat still on.

"I hate it when you're sympathetic," he said. "It feels like pity."

"Should I make fun of you? Be mean?"

Bill peeled away his coat and came to sit on the wide chair arm. "In the movies, you always see the writer typing, crumbling up the paper, agony, pacing, more typing, a sandwich. That's Part One. Part Two is the letter, the phone call, success. We're still stuck in the agony. . . ."

His sadness reminded me of a war memorial we'd seen in Canada somewhere last summer, a robed woman, head down, shoulders tragically slumped, battered sword at her feet, loss, terrible loss in every line of her face, her robes.

I suggested Bill go to bed.

"Am I tired?"

While he showered, I thought about his work, which he hardly showed me anymore. When he did, it was impossible for me to read anything of his without feeling for the hours he'd sat hunched over his desk, rocking as if to catch a troubling melody, face dark, fingers touching his shoulders, hair, his throat. The nights he worked hardest, I wandered through the house, restless, straightening pictures, shuffling magazines, or stalking the unplanted evergreen-bordered half-acre behind our house, breathing in the silence and the night, hoping. Hoping he had discovered the words I would someday read in print.

I couldn't make it happen. I could fill the house with white lilacs in

May for our anniversary, surprise him with newly published novels he'd forgotten he said he wanted to read, hide jokey little cards under his pillow, cook Julia Child dinners and wear my tux, call him from campus or the mall just to say hi, but I couldn't fill the emptiness of all those unpublished years.

Bill was asleep as soon as he got to bed. I put some dishes away, cleaned up in the living room, and then found myself watering plants that weren't dry. I was nervous. I felt drawn to his study, which I never entered when he wasn't home, I slipped down the hall and into the study, turning on the light after I closed the door. It was a small room, painted a glossy forest green, full of file cabinets and books, but not even the peeling library table revealed anything about him. This room without decoration, pictures, and mementos disturbed me for the first time. It was so Spartan, what was he shutting out besides distraction?

I settled onto the dull green carpeting and slowly pulled open the nearest file drawer. His stories were filed alphabetically by year, and each folder spilled out rejection slips, sometimes dozens. I read those along with ten or so stories, and it all began to seem anonymous, the stories no different from the Xeroxed rejection slips.

I had never read so much of his work at one time, and I didn't like it. While I may have enjoyed individual lines, or scenes, or even characters, reading so many stories in a row, I was disappointed. His work was clever, I guess, but empty, and I found myself thinking of our favorite movie, *Dark Victory*, of the scene where Bette Davis discovers her medical file in George Brent's office and asks the nurse what the words "prognosis negative" mean. How had I missed this?

I cleaned up, checked the bedroom to see if he was still asleep, and sat at the kitchen table with a shot of Seagram's, like my father did when he got bad news—the one drink saying he needed not to forget but to be strong. I was struck by how bland Bill's people were, and how none were even demonstrably gay. Why? Being gay wasn't the center of our lives, exactly, but we'd never hidden it from our friends, employers, or family. His parents had pretty much disowned him when they found out he was gay, and had never expressed an interest in meeting me, but was that enough to wipe it from his stories? And none of his characters were really Jewish, either, which made even less sense: I didn't think we were Jewish enough to feel any kind of conflict between faith and sexuality.

Besides, even though Bill didn't get much out of the holidays or attending services, we had been lucky to find a very liberal congregation in town with a woman rabbi and a few gay and lesbian couples. When we did attend or get involved, there was no sense of exclusion or embarrassment.

Bill's mother had been in a concentration camp, and I was most deeply struck by the absence of any reference to the Holocaust in his fiction. We had certainly talked about it. Just that year, we had watched newly discovered British film of the liberation of Bergen-Belsen. In it, British soldiers forced the SS guards to lift and carry corpses, drop, slide, stack them into four or five pits, "as punishment." The film was silent; there was no creak of carts, no engines stirring into life, no shouted commands—just seven days reduced to black and white minutes on film. The civilized-sounding narrator talked of "graves"—which infuriated Bill. "They're garbage dumps!" I couldn't believe the SS felt any differently, felt repentant while dropping bodies like a gigolo flicking away the useless stump of a cigarette.

"My mother was there," Bill reminded me. "But she won't tell me." And I tried to imagine the dazed and starved survivor wandering somewhere out of camera range.

I woke up late that night, could feel Bill wasn't sleeping.

"They should have thrown the guards in," he said in the dark. "Buried them alive."

"Yes," I said. "I know."

But there was absolutely no trace of Bill's anger or pain in his stories. Why had he cut all that out of his writing?

A motorcycle tore by outside, and I wished then for a galumphing puppy I could scratch and rub and talk to. In all the years Bill had suffered rejection, I had never doubted his work.

"It's late," Bill said at the kitchen door, squinting at my drink. His face was creased and red with sleep, his hair flattened. He rubbed his eyes, pulled his robe together, and came to sit by me. "What's wrong?"

"I was reading. In your study."

I expected him to blast me, but he just nodded, leaning back in the captain's chair.

He said, "It's no good."

We had been at this place before, I dousing the flames of his depression with torrents of praise—reminding him of Amherst, his successful fiction readings, the two prizes there—like a court chamberlain comforting his monarch-in-exile. But tonight I couldn't offer anything; there was only silence timidly filled by the humming fridge and vague grunts from the sink pipes. I felt we had come to the end of something and I was afraid. Our first years fragrant with discovery, the trips to Mexico, Canada, the Caribbean, buying and decorating this house, all of that seemed one-dimensional now, remote.

Bill reached for my glass and the bottle, poured himself a shot and downed it.

"You never wanted to see," he said.

"What?"

"To see my work." He looked down. "You wanted me to be, I don't know, famous, wonderful."

"But isn't that what you want?"

"Not now, now I just want to write something honest. Something real." He stroked my hands. "It's not your fault, it's nobody's fault."

I'm not one of those people who's always being confided in, surprised by friends suddenly announcing "There's something you should know," so I wasn't sure what I was supposed to say or do. I pulled open the fridge and found some leftover veal stew and half a cherry pie to heat up. Fussing at the sink and the stove, I was unable to look at him. Bill came up behind me, gave me a lingering, pleading hug, as if we'd just had some kind of fight.

"I don't have the courage to write about anything that hurts—my mom, being gay," he said to my back.

I felt ashamed then of all the times I'd raved about his writing, gone on and on thinking that I was being helpful, when I was just showing I loved him. It was a subtle form of contempt—I had not treated him as an equal, as an adult, but as a glamorous, talented, demanding child.

"I never have," he said, "except once. It was something I wrote about my mom, her past, her secrets, my secrets. She found it . . . well, I left it out where she could. She went nuts. She said I was sick, I was crazy." He held me tighter, still talking to the back of my head.

"What happened to the story?"

"She threw it out." He broke away. "Wait, I want to show you something." He went off to his study and returned with a deeply creased single sheet of pale blue stationery that had been crumpled up and then straightened more than once, I thought.

"She sent this to me at Amherst. Remember that weekend I drove to Boston by myself and you wondered why? It was because of this."

I read the typed, undated note.

"When we were married your father said we had to have children because of all the lives lost in the War. I didn't want to have any. Now I know I was right."

"She sent this to you? What did you say?"

Bill shrugged.

Feeling suddenly brisk and sensible, I stood up and went to the utility drawer. "Isn't it time for a reply?"

He frowned, not following.

I took the letter and a book of matches to the sink. "Come on." I held out the matches. Bill hesitated, came over, took one, lit it slowly as I nodded, and set it to the corner of the letter, dropping it into the sink when it started to flame. Little black specks floated up above us as the letter twisted in on itself, crackling, vanishing into black powder and dust.

Bill put his hands down in the sink and rubbed them in the ashes, turned on the tap, washing his hands clean.

"Would it change things?" he finally asked, pale now, drying his hands.

He had the look of a desperate client, hoping the lawyer will say, "Yes, you've got a case."

"If you wrote the truth?" He nodded.

Little things in the kitchen suddenly seemed very clear to me: the Boston fern hanging over the sink, the brass cabinet knobs, the Sierra Club calendar near the stove. "I don't know."

He smiled. "Well," he said, "it wouldn't mean I got published, but I'd be honest. Isn't that a start?"

I thought then of my favorite lines from James Baldwin's *Another Country*: "'You've got to be truthful about the life you have. Otherwise there's no possibility of achieving the life you want.'" I said that yes, it would be a start.

Free Man in Paris

"It's like a Picasso or a Braque," Bobby murmured, his green eyes wide as they took in Paris from the narrow parapet between Notre Dame's towers, surrounded by weathered gargoyles and sunburnt German tourists.

Irene squinted against the sunshine. "What?"

"Like one of the collages from when their work was so similar. Remember we looked at that book in the Museum of Modern Art gift shop?"

Irene considered. "Oh. You mean the browns and grays mixed together?"

Bobby grinned. "*Exactement!* Maybe this was what they saw." He stretched out his hands like a welcoming host.

"Well, I hope their feet hurt." Irene cursed the perky, seductive travel catalogue description of her new walking shoes which she was sure had not been designed for the twisting, uneven, vertiginous stairs of Notre Dame. Bobby was standing near her, but further back from the edge than she was since he said he didn't like heights. His cool hand clutched hers as if he were afraid some sudden jostling from the crowd could send him down onto the tourist-packed plaza below.

Cameras around them clicked and flashed or noisily rewound, people squeezing by on the sunny spring day, staring, pointing with grim nods as if verifying that their tour books were accurate each time they recognized a building or a view or bridge.

Listening to clotted German conversations around her, Irene wanted to cheerfully say aloud, "Isn't it great that Hitler didn't blow all this up?"

She watched Bobby, who breathed in deeply as if he could possess the view, the sunshine, Paris spreading west and south and north, the low old roofs broken by enormous monuments that seemed so familiar to her from films and photographs that they were a little unreal and almost boring: the Eiffel Tower, the Arc de Triomphe, the Louvre, the historic and chic Place Vendôme where they were staying.

Their long climb up the endless spiraling stairs had left her sweaty, disgruntled. For all that effort there should have been much more than a view. A snack bar at the very least. Something to make up for feeling lonely. Because even though Bobby was holding her hand, he seemed distant.

He was suddenly the little boy he'd described to her only once, poring over a picture book about Paris he'd saved his pitiful allowances for. Stroking those glossy pages, he must have been like a fairytale miser lasciviously caressing his coins to become part of them, to be them, all gold, all gleam and mystery.

After just a few minutes up here, Irene wanted to be done with this newest phase of Bobby's ecstacy. She wanted to sit down, in the shade, indoors, to withdraw from the blinding loveliness of Paris that hit her like a reproach.

But how could she? The trip had been her idea because she was so grateful for finding Bobby after being divorced for ten years and having given up on remarrying. Bobby had liberated her, and taking him to Paris for their honeymoon had seemed as natural a step as buying him clothes at Barney's or getting him the red Mustang.

Now, though, she felt trapped. Not just at Notre Dame, and not just in Paris, but in Bobby's fantasy come true.

Stuck up here, dreading another encounter with those treacherous stairs (even though gravity would be on her side and it wouldn't be so tiring), Irene wanted to climb down from Notre Dame, to be done with all the orderliness below—the city laid out like some toy village—nauseatingly picturesque—the Mansard roofs—the spires—the graceful bridges—the endless neat array of windows.

No wonder the pitted gray-beige gargoyles around her were leering down at this city. It inspired resistance, contempt.

Their first night, standing on the Pont Neuf near the statue of Henry of Navarre, arm-in-arm, watching the building lights reflected in the Seine, Irene had felt shoved away, rejected by everything Bobby loved. She was as miserable as she'd been in high school jealously watching one of the prettiest girls fish for compliments that always came. Paris was too gorgeous and too damned pleased with itself.

But she couldn't say any of this because Bobby was entranced.

"It's so amazing," he'd said on the Pont Neuf while a tickling light rain fell on them like a benison. And the strange new look in his eyes had reminded her of the Joni Mitchell song about being a free man in Paris, feeling unfettered and alive.

They'd eaten dinner that night on the Rue de Varenne at the exclusive, tiny L'Arpège, which Bobby had assured her would offer exotic haute cuisine as quietly splendid as the pear wood walls set with glass Lalique panels. He was right, she'd thought, savoring the cumin-rubbed lamb with its puree of dates and onions, while Bobby delighted in squab crusted with candy-coated almonds.

"Wow. This is like my birthday," Bobby has said as they sat down, and ordering a $300 bottle of Haut-Brion seemed the least they could do to celebrate.

Bobby repeated his amazement softly now, here at the top of Notre Dame, shaking his head, breathing as evenly as if he'd ascended to the top of the cathedral with the heavenly host in a Baroque painter's cloud of angels, rather than climbed all those hideous stairs. He didn't even look to her for confirmation, not at all interested in sharing his joy. Or maybe he simply assumed she felt the same way.

They'd only been married a week and already she felt he was cheating on her. With Paris! Bobby didn't need another woman, it was enough for him to sigh and drift through the city like Cinderella swept up in a lush embracing waltz by the Prince. Bobby was smitten by Paris.

It had started four days before, when his face took on an unfamiliar stunned look at Orly. As soon as Bobby had stumbled into that frantic dingy airport, he began repeating, "*Je suis en France*" under his breath as if it were a spell. By the time they got their luggage and were in a cab, he was already tearful (but he'd stopped chanting).

In misshapen English, the gap-toothed cabby had asked if it was their first time in Paris. His accent was so thick, Irene half-expected accordion music to burst from his car radio like the corny soundtrack of a TV movie making sure its viewers knew where the scene was set.

Bobby had said yes, adding that even though he'd been born in the U.S., France was "*le pays de mon coeur.*"

The country of his heart! How corny could you get?

But the cabby grinned wildly and after Bobby mentioned they were on their honeymoon and the cabby congratulated them in more mangled English, he and Bobby raced off together in French like speed skaters. To her, Bobby's French sounded as fluent as the cabby's. And he looked French when he spoke, twisting his hands, his shoulders, even his face.

She almost felt nauseous, abandoned, as if she were drowning and he were swimming away from her. No, surely her reaction was jet lag, or instant culture shock, or PMS. Maybe it wasn't so dramatic, so dire.

Unless she was seeing the real Bobby and had married some kind of imposter. What if bringing him to the Paris he had always dreamed of and never been able to afford exploring had been a terrible mistake? What if she were to lose him somehow?

By the time they got to the Hotel Vendôme, the grizzled cabby was as jubilant and surprised as a lottery winner by Bobby's command of French. Helping her out, the cabby said in his painful, lumbering English, "Madame, your husband is—" Groping for a word, he burst back into French, "*Époustouflant!*"

"What the hell does that mean?" Irene asked as a trim, dark-eyed bellman took in their bags.

Blushing, Bobby said, "Impressive. Well, more like . . . staggering."

"Did you tip him extra?"

The hotel, not far from the Ritz, was in a quiet, graceful square of buildings dating back to the early 1700s, windows decorated with ornate grills bearing golden suns representing Louis XIV. Inside the Hotel Vendôme, all was quietly, gleamingly elegant in the way that only the French could manage, she thought, eying the curving marble stairway that was as wide and welcoming as a lover's embrace.

At the front desk, Bobby got another glorious reception from an unlikely source. The frigid-looking slim blonde wrapped in a black sweater dress and hung about with gold jewelry like an icon, well, she positively melted after Bobby rattled on about how happy he was to be in Paris and how he'd loved it from afar all his life.

Irene could follow, but not contribute. It was twenty years since she'd taken a French class, and her once-solid reading skills in French seemed as useful now as the découpage she'd learned in junior high. French had always tormented her in high school and college. Whenever she tried to answer a question, she felt like she was a clumsy little girl again, anxiously trying to jump rope with friends and bound to get tangled. Despite following the language reasonably well on the page, her vocabulary and grammar were spotty, but worse, she had always been hopeless at the accent, the intonations, the rhythm—everything that made a language live. She had never been able to bear listening to herself try to speak French.

"It's not true what you hear about them," Bobby was raving upstairs, after they'd ascended in the tiny two-person elevator. "The French are wonderful people," he sighed, sprawling on one of the satin-covered brass beds that had been pushed together to make a double bed.

"Right. You've met two of them. Both of whom complimented your French. Both of whom are taking your money."

"Our money," Bobby corrected.

My money, Irene thought, as she paced around the exquisite large room with its two banks of windows and enormous double shutters; marquetry chests, writing table and highboy; suite of Louis Something chairs and settee covered in gold and apricot embroidery. An elaborately-framed mirror glowed over the black slate fireplace inset with bronze panels of annoyingly unfamiliar classical scenes. Plaster moldings of garlands, urns and wreaths were picked out against the glowing ivory walls and ceiling in gold, apple green, pink.

"This place needs a shepherdess," she said. The room was so lovely, so charming, Irene wanted to deface it.

"I'll be your lost sheep," Bobby said, trying to baaa.

Sex would do.

In bed she often imagined they were making love under water. Whirling, curvetting around each other like dolphins, completely free.

But when Bobby was in the shower and she drifted back up to consciousness, she realized that even losing herself in him, with him, wasn't enough to blot out the siren song of Paris.

They'd met at her gym on the Upper East side in the pool, or actually she was in the pool doing her hour's worth of laps when she saw him approach. It was mid-morning, but there were people in each of the six lanes—mostly retirees—and he crouched down when she reached the end of hers to ask if she minded sharing. Bobby was slim and sleek in his sky blue Speedo, his thick center-parted ash blond hair falling over his sweet face like twin wings. She'd been intimidated by his youth—he couldn't be past 25—and his looks, but she said okay.

He'd introduced himself and said softly, "We can swim traffic pattern."

"What?"

"I'll swim down on the right and back on the left—you'll follow." He was trying to make it sound like fun, or maybe he didn't want her to feel bad about her space being invaded.

Well, she followed him that day for a while, feeling as goofy in his steady wake as a lolloping dog. Then she gave up, sat on the cool tiled edge and watched him swim back and forth, lap after lap, his flip turns a marvel of speed and deftness, unlike other people at the pool who seemed to think that splashing at the end was a sign of triumph and strength.

"I can help you with your stroke," he said afterwards, when they shared a little wrought-iron table in the black-on-black cafe that throbbed with techno music which she supposed was meant to egg you on to ever more intense workouts. It just made her feel old most of the time, as did the hordes of aerobics junkies with their maniacally-thin bodies, but sitting across Bobby that first day the music seemed to form a sort of halo of possibility.

And so she and Bobby started swimming together every day and having a protein shake or fruit smoothie afterwards. Irene was an awkward swimmer—head up out of the water, legs and arms uncertain. Bobby tried to teach her to lengthen her stroke, to reach: "Whoosh!" he would call, encouraging her. "Whoosh!" Even standing at the side of the pool, demonstrating, his lean shoulders pivoting, arms wheeling and driving through the air, shoulders moving like pistons, high-arched feet mimicking kicks, he was natural, confident, relaxed.

But out of the water he was endearingly reticent and shy. So much so that he blushed whenever he laughed, not only covering his mouth but his whole face, unable to turn away as if he were some strange figure in Greek myth, doomed to paralytic embarrassment.

How could she not fall in love with him when he was so gentle, so undemanding, so kind? When he gave up his dreary coffin-like studio apartment and moved in with her a month after they met, and she had a party, all her friends eyed him like haughty dowagers in a 1930s film comedy peering at a sniveling waif through lorgnettes held with cool and distancing contempt. So what if Bobby wasn't Jewish? So what if he was just a waiter with only vague ideas about the law or police work, she said defensively over endless lunches. So what if he was almost twenty years younger than she was? Men dated younger women all the time—and the movies were full of such pairs: Jack Nicolson and Helen Hunt, Paul Newman and Susan Sarandon.

Unlike her friends, however, Irene's hair stylist, her manicurist, her massage therapist and her acupuncturist all cheered her on in a chorus of "You go, girl!" that made her feel like an athlete training to break a world record. Talking to them about Bobby exhilarated her.

When they got married a month after that in a civil ceremony, there was no criticism at all to dim her enthusiasm, because it was clear that her friends had already given her up as hopelessly misguided. How strange, considering that she felt blessed. All Irene wanted to do was spend the rest of her life watching Bobby sleep. Those moments she woke up in the middle of the night were unbearably precious to her. She stared in wonder at him: he was so beautiful, so young—and so devoted to her.

Which was why she'd suggested Paris for their honeymoon, because she knew he would love it. She'd worried that the language problem would upset her. But what she hadn't expected, even though Bobby said he'd double majored in French and Criminal Justice at NYU, was that he spoke French the way he swam—buoyed by an unpunishing medium through which he moved as if by right.

Paris, which she only knew from movies, from fashion and travel magazines, and from Bobby's rhapsodies, was alien to her and the reverse was painfully true. Bobby delighted in her being zaftig, in her gypsyish thick curls of black hair, and in New York she was considered passably attractive and felt it. In Paris she seemed to herself ungainly, even fat, as the flawlessly-dressed women strode by her like dancers in a graceful, mocking pavane.

"Too skinny," Bobby kept saying, when she'd point someone out, almost testing him. He passed every time.

Sightseeing was okay, perhaps because she could look at her oblong green Michelin guide written in English, but despite the succulent food, meals were awful, since she felt cornered and exposed. At the Picasso museum, at the Cluny, Irene could imagine herself back in New York at the Metropolitan or MOMA. Well, why not? You often heard foreigners there. Even at the cavernous and exhausting Louvre, she could keep up this internal fantasy defense. But at meals it was impossible. The food was too good and Bobby too delighted in ordering, debating selections with the waiters, chatting amiably, winning them over every time, and even apologizing in general for how rude Americans were.

"Well they are, Irene, admit it. They act like this is some Disney attraction. Frenchy Land, and everyone's going to speak cute English with a French accent."

"What was that word you said to the waiter, the one that made him laugh? You know—when you were talking about American tourists."

Eyes down, Bobby said, "*Débèctant.* It means pukey, gross."

She should have been outraged, but Bobby was right. The Americans they passed, at the Louvre, on the Champs Elysée, in the Tuileries, all seemed to be complaining, and loudly, about something—and they insisted on speaking English. She felt implicated in their vulgarity, stained, and had hoped to cut herself off from them.

Trying to do so on their first day, Irene had stumblingly ordered herself *thé avec des glaçons* at a sidewalk cafe near the Samaritaine department store while Bobby was off in the men's room. She thought she had asked for iced tea. The waiter dutifully brought her what she had in fact requested: hot tea, with ice cubes, separately delivered in a small earthenware bowl. She blundered further a bit later after Bobby had returned, when the waiter asked in French if he could clear their plates. Irene bravely responded with, "*Oui, nous sommes finis.*"

In smiling and precise English, the tall, black-vested waiter replied, "Madame, if you *are* finished, I cannot help you. But, if you have finished—" He shrugged.

She wanted to throw herself into the Seine. Bobby stifled a laugh, one hand covering his full-lipped mouth. God, each time she watched those lips say "*Oui*" and pronounce it something like "Way" she felt older and uglier and out of place.

And now! He was clearly embarrassed at her having made the most basic mistake: using the wrong helping verb. She glared at him, and he glanced away, but as soon as he had a chance, he was talking a blue streak with the waiter.

For Bobby, speaking French seemed like some kind of drug. He was completely unlike his English-speaking self back in New York. He was garrulous in French and convivial. To her, his French sounded brilliant. It wasn't just his accent, it was the rhythms and intonations, his gestures and the way his face changed. His French seemed smooth, facile, sensuous. It was a performance. Bobby wasn't just speaking French, French was speaking him. He had become something else with a kind of flamboyant authenticity. Helplessly, Irene watched him seduce people with his fawning eagerness, his joy.

It had been giving her one enormous headache.

She rubbed her temples now and sighed, gazing down at Bobby's beloved Paris.

"Hungry?" he asked. "Ready for lunch?"

They had talked about lunch at the Place Dauphine's Taverne Henri IV, a wine bar near the Pont Neuf they'd seen written up in the New York Times.

"Sure," she said, and they made their way through the crowd to the eerie, cool stairs going down that sliced through the dark and time-worn stones. The air felt clammy inside and they didn't talk as they descended alone. Watching her footing carefully, she was relieved that she was spared having to look at any more spectacular, demanding scenes for at least a few minutes.

Then she felt Bobby's hands on either side of the back of her neck as if he were steadying himself, but the stairs suddenly disappeared from under her feet and she was sliding, falling. Dizzy, terrified, she realized with outrage that he must have pushed her, and she could barely breathe. Her back and head slammed against the ancient stones and she began to tumble raggedly away from Bobby, the stones clutching her all over, slicing, biting. Everything swam in front of her eyes. As she started to lose consciousness, one thought came to her with chilly regret: she simply could not remember the French word for "Help!"

Dreamland

"History is as light as individual life, unbearably light,
light as a feather, as dust swirling in the air,
as whatever will no longer exist tomorrow."
—Milan Kundera

One Sunday in the Metropolitan Museum of Art near the top of the wide main staircase, my best friend Sandy gasped at the Canova Perseus: "That's him."

I knew he meant my brother Paul. It was more than the rich cold marble body, it was the cool contempt with which Perseus, on his pedestal, twice, three times our size, held Medusa's head away from himself: that was all of us, thrust at arm's length, hanging.

Paul was four years older than me, tall, gray-eyed, large and strong, far handsomer than me or our parents. The three of us were small and kind of squat. Paul seemed the son of old-fashioned TV parents, the kind he wanted: those chirpy couples drifting in their large houses, worried about their children's parking tickets and bake sales. Paul was ashamed of Mom and Dad, of the way they could suddenly fling Yiddish curses at each other in a department store when they disagreed about a toaster or a rug; ashamed of how they criticized what we wore, fussing, tugging, yanking. They were triumphantly foreign. Dad with his one after-dinner cigarette, slicing an apple for his dessert, Mom with her quick little laugh that sounded learned from a language tape.

Paul was also ashamed of the past they couldn't share. There was so little—reminiscences of their school days, summer vacations, family dinners almost always brought them to the War, to their bitter losses. They wanted to forget.

My father loved nothing more than lying in the hammock in our little over-planted back yard in Forest Hills, with the high wooden fence between him and the world. He lay in the shade, eyes closed, singing to himself in Russian, a gypsy song, one of those on the fat 78s he occasionally removed from their brown paper sleeves and dusted with amused reverence before playing. But somehow Dad's relaxation annoyed Paul, as if he expected Dad to be busy around the house when not at work—sanding, staining, hammering, nails projected from his lips, as if Dad had no right to such indolence, because he was only a jeweler in another man's store.

One Saturday afternoon while I sat out on a lawn chair breathing in the chaotic mix of scents produced by our scrap of garden, Dad had said, "I just wanted, in the mud, something green, something mine. A tree."

In the silence I felt as if all the cars, lawnmowers, bikes, air conditioners for miles around were frozen, expectant.

"Where?" I asked. "Where?"

"Stalingrad."

And what I knew of that murderous siege and battle in which three of my cousins had died, choked me.

But Paul wouldn't listen. It wasn't France, Italy or the Pacific, it was another, uglier less acceptable war to him. And my father hadn't been a hero, just a Jewish slave laborer for the Hungarians.

And Mom, with her unsteady little eyes, quick jumpy walk like a sparrow snatching at a worm, Mom was not acceptable to Paul either. She wasn't slim and silent enough, but could sometimes talk as if she were a slot machine spilling noisy bright coins. She even talked to herself when cooking, or back to the radio announcer or as she read. Mom loved to shop for food, to eye and handle and sort and squeeze. It took her hours, from which she'd emerge red-faced, ecstatic.

I think the neon-lit plenty was a dream for her after the flight from Poland deep into the Soviet Union, the years of near-starvation, the cities in flame.

Mom and Dad's history of madness was so different from the waves of death back home—ghettos, concentration camps—but no easier to understand. They were survivors, and so were all of their friends, as if relating to someone without a similar past were inconceivable to them. They had a minimal social life. They took walks with their friends, played cards sometimes, the passive pursuits of inmates at a rest home, as if these moments together were merely episodes in a convalescence that would never end. Survivors. It had always seemed an ugly jagged term to me—people ripped from a larger richer life, isolated, drowning in their loss.

I could not, as Paul did, loathe Mom and Dad, even when they drove me crazy. Dad would pass me on the phone in the kitchen, and drop, "Hang up—someone might call." Mom would lurk at the door of my room and wonder, "How many shirts do you need on the floor?" or "What did that book do to you, you treat it like garbage?" These quirks usually made me laugh—at least when I'd tell Sandy afterwards.

I couldn't feel Paul's contempt for them, but I could see them as Paul did.

Mom lost in coupons, labels, sales, Dad selling watches and clocks, chains and rings. Dad was too harsh to Paul, suddenly cornering him and shouting, "You treat us like dirt!" when Paul was younger and refused to do his homework or his chores. Paul simply looked off to one side, blank, lifeless, even when Dad would lunge at him, force him down into a corner, grabbing at his shoulders, striking, kicking. Paul could have fought back, could have hurt Dad or at least kept him off, but he did nothing.

Later Dad would drag himself around the house, mournful, heavy-eyed, his silence a naked castigation I hated as much as his rage. Paul said nothing when he was beaten, but I yelped and begged so much Dad would laugh at me and stop: "Coward!" I'd nod eagerly, smiling, anything was fine for me.

"Just say you're sorry," I told Paul when we were both little. "Say sorry, it's just a word." But he wouldn't.

Mom often recalled overhearing me give Paul that advice, the story sounding like some ancient legend whose figures were metaphors of experience, not her living sons. She made so much of Dad's "sick stomach" after the beatings, proudly telling us how bad he felt, how awful, especially with what he'd been through.

In the War, I added to myself.

The lesson of it all? We shouldn't hurt them.

There were many mysteries in our home, not least of which was wondering who Mom and Dad had been before the War. They spoke so little about their families, how could we tell what in them had changed, what been intensified, what crushed? Reading memoirs of the Holocaust and histories, as I did endlessly, didn't offer a clue. But the War was everywhere, and leaked out especially when something unexpected and terrible happened. Mom would usually just go quiet and grim, seeming to disappear into grief so large it robbed her not only of words but of her very self. And Dad raged around the house, throwing things, cursing in Polish or Russian, Sook in *sin, pja krev*—curses that seemed so much tamer in English: sonofabitch, dog's blood—but sounded grisly dropped from a face all red and dark with rage. Disasters, even small ones, triggered the darkness of their past, which seemed as large and unknowable as a howling sea in which we were just a tiny craft struggling to keep on course.

Sandy and I stepped closer to the Perseus now. "Amazing," he said.

I nodded.

Sandy and I circled the statue, a little breathless. Sandy grinned and murmured so that only I could hear, "Even his buns. Nice and tight."

I had to agree. I'd been getting a good look lately. Paul had been working out much more heavily than usual, and had taken to drifting around nude from his room to the bathroom and back (when our parents weren't around), as if after the months of crippling bench presses at the Y and all the rest of it he had recreated himself as Arnold Schwarzenegger. I had seen

105

him at the gym performing each repetition in a set with grunting violent heroism, like Samson bringing down the temple.

Sandy and I moved on, but I couldn't help turning back to glance at the Perseus, which was more beautiful now that I had to leave it behind. We were only fifteen, but I hoped that while staring at it before, we might have been mistaken for those art students with sketch pads who appeared never to see a work itself, but rather the problem it represented or solved. I did not want us to look hungry or exposed.

Once I asked Paul if he thought our parents' experiences in the War had influenced us.

He said no and didn't even bother changing the subject, just stared at me until I left the room.

Paul did not look inside. He looked ahead, wildly, spouting visions to me of wealth, of yachts and summer homes, travel around the world. He was going to be rich, he claimed, and for many years I listened with the credulity of a child whose friend asserts, "I saw a ghost." He was so blind, so sure—how could he be wrong?

For someone so relentlessly macho, I was a little surprised that Paul's vision of freedom and wealth was fired by late-night Thirties reruns. Over and over he watched TV movies on Channel 2 like *Midnight, Holiday, Bringing up Baby*, movies of wit and style, the elegance sharpened by the grey, black and white screen. I'm sure he saw himself smoking a cigarette in a Rolls, or crossing a lavishly statued marble hall, or sipping brandy in a barn-wide library, flirting on a veranda under a private moon. I couldn't enjoy the movies he had memorized. The world of villas and repartee seemed too cold and unreal; the Thirties were ugly years, the glamor Paul clutched at, a lie.

Even the girls he dated seemed plucked from those movies, but not the stars, the minor actresses sitting at nightclub tables or getting into limos, sleek and blonde, alien, remote. His girlfriends looked alike and had some of the vacant intensity of those young dancers surging in pigeon-toed waves around Lincoln Center, those blank silent girls with anchored-back hair and gleaming foreheads.

"They don't seem Jewish," Mom said once in our small wall-papered kitchen nook where she, Sandy and I feasted on fresh marble cake and coffee. I'd watched before with greed as she had poured the two batters together, anxiously licking the corner of her mouth as if she were handling plutonium. Sandy was always over at my house, and Mom liked him so much she hardly spoke to him.

"I mean the Jewish ones," my mother explained.

"Well, they're American," I said.

"American Jews just don't make it," Sandy said seriously, as he had to me many times before. "They don't know things."

"Like what?"

"We have too much—we're too lucky."

"Am I American?"

While my mother's back was turned, Sandy mouthed to me: "You're cute."

Sometimes, when Sandy tickled my chest or the hair coming in on my toes and called me "Hobbit," I felt cute. He, on the other hand, was indisputably much more than cute, always sought after by the girls for his looks and his attentive respectful silence, admired by the boys for his skill at baseball. We'd been schoolmates since kindergarten, and Sandy's popularity had been a constant.

My mother nodded and said to Sandy, "You're right about Americans." She had said this before, that because Americans had been spared centuries of murder and lunatic pride as national boundaries sliced across Europe like a strangler's wire, they did not, could not, know how lucky they were, how free.

Now she burst out, "Okay, your father's a boy in Ohio. Did he have to run away to Michigan because bandits from Pennsylvania burned his village and chopped up his family? There were armies ready to crush his people? What did his family die from? Sickness, drowning, accidents, tornadoes. In Poland—hah!—we had human tornadoes. Russians, Ukrainians, Poles, *zol zey brennen in fire*, they should burn up!"

Sandy and I nodded, a little scared by her intensity.

Later, over at Sandy's apartment a few blocks away in Rego Park, he said, "Your parents are so real. I think about that a lot."

I looked around the living room, a lavishly curtained little box with bowls of grinning fake fruit and lamps all in the form of buxom gold goddesses lost in swirling robes. Crystal pendants gleamed from unexpected corners.

"For us being Jewish is like someone else's buffet—a little this, a little that." Sandy leaned back on the streaky gold tufted velvet sofa and spoke as if to history: "It's not that important."

"What d'you mean?"

He shrugged and I reached to stroke his neck. He stopped my hand, gripped now by what he was thinking and trying to say.

"Why's it bother you?" I asked.

"When I'm with your parents, it's like, they know so much I'll never know."

Well that was true for both of us, but we couldn't talk about it then because Sandy's parents would be back from Alexander's, and we only had an hour in his room. We left the door open, and a Monopoly game set up, so that we wouldn't be surprised when they returned, and they would surely think we were flushed with the excitement of the game.

Walking back home later, I thought about what he'd said. Sandy's family was fitfully Jewish, some years deciding to keep kosher and *kashering* the kitchen, some years ignoring all the holidays, and dropping or changing Jewish magazine subscriptions, changing congregations, flailing for some consistent way to make a Jewish life. Both Sandy's parents taught at Queens college, and so they had a lot to say. Their Jewish discussions were long and exhausting. My father privately dismissed both Sandy's parents as *yentahs*.

But Dad liked Sandy very much, because he was so respectful, because he was an ardent Zionist. Dad and Sandy would talk politics and agree with delight on most issues. It could be very peaceful the four of us sitting out in the back yard on a late spring or summer weekend, eating seedless grapes very slowly, savoring each cool little globe before crunching it open, drinking iced tea, with Mom idling through a newspaper, occasionally reading aloud to us in a comic high-pitched lecturing voice. She'd read fragments of articles without introduction or explanation and those darts of news would whiz from her chair.

Sometimes I'd think: they may have suffered, but they have this, and I'd feel grateful that I was not, had never been a disappointment. I made few waves, had no rowdy friends, did consistently above average at school (Paul was the real brain) and had discovered great talent in French, which entered me like a magic potion the first year of junior high. I'd won our school's French award and my teachers pressed me to consider taking a summer study program in France when I got to high school, or even a year abroad. My parents were very proud and agreed it would be good for me.

Paul was a disappointment. He was inaccessible, sneering, more aloof as he became a remarkably handsome man. Girls were always leaving messages for him and after Mom took them she told Dad it wasn't dignified, though what she said in Yiddish was *nisht shayn*, not nice or decent.

Sandy didn't like my brother, but the most he'd say against him was that the two of them were "very different." Sandy tried not to malign people; he was on guard against *lashan harah*—Hebrew for evil talk. "It's so easy for things to just pop out, and then you're stuck."

"What if it's true?"

"Doesn't matter."

Sandy seemed to watch Paul as if waiting for trouble, and he was right.

The time when Paul and I were friendly, when we enjoyed each other's company, when he tied my little shoes and taught me games seemed prehistoric to me in Junior High. What followed was years of snarling and insults, as we drifted further apart. Paul's flood of girlfriends made him insolent, as did his weightlifting. I would find him constantly posing in front of the bathroom mirror, body oiled and shiny, wearing a tiny swim suit, making his muscles bulge and dance. His strong hairless body was like a holy relic borne in a procession in some huge dark canvas, shining its own light. I'm sure he wanted me to admire his strength, his masculinity, but I couldn't, because it seemed inhuman.

So did Angela, when I first met her. I thought, "Yes, she's the one." Not a girlfriend for Paul so much as a consort.

Angela went to Fordham at Lincoln Center, the Catholic college Paul had chosen, I think, not for its small size or midtown location, but because he'd encounter few Jews there, unlike City College, NYU or Columbia, which had all accepted him.

Paul brought Angela by one afternoon of his sophomore year. She was tall, bleary-eyed, blonde, with the slack-shouldered elegance of someone like Jean Harlow. Despite myself, I saw her trailing one of those silky Thirties gowns with feeble straps, diamonds bragging in her hair. I was alone at home and Angela just sat in our plant-crazy living room as if she wished she were a hovercraft and could float her designer jeans above the couch that suddenly looked a little shabby to me.

They pretended an interest in me for a bit before I left for Sandy's and had dinner there, trying not to feel angry. Paul and Angela were both so disdainful and aloof I wondered at first how they could converse or even touch each other. They seemed like two exquisite parallel lines, drawn on to their glorious and separate futures.

Angela lived in Queens, too, but in Kew Gardens, in a Tudor frenzy surrounded by reverential big trees with a low stone wall cutting along the edge of a half-block plot. I didn't like the house when Sandy and I walked by it a week after Angela's first visit. People who don't know New York are often surprised there can be these lovely-tree-swathed neighborhoods with magazine houses, but I felt embarrassed to see Paul was dating that house and that street.

"It's so corny," I told Sandy. He didn't ask what I meant.

"Angela," Dad said. "Italian?"

"I don't think so. Her last name's White."

"And what else?"

I hesitated. Dad looked up from his basement worktable seething with bits of metal and tiny nonsense stones. Around us were drills, buffers, a small kiln and piles that would eventually give birth to jewelry or junk. He looked up, but not at me.

Mom had more to say. "Why doesn't he bring her to meet us?" she wondered at dinner. "He's ashamed she's a goy? I won't like her because of that? Believe me, I can find something else if I have to!"

But Angela was not a goy, not exactly. Her mother was the daughter of Russian Jews who'd fled after a pogrom. They had slipped their Jewishness like an anonymous corpse over the rails of their ship into the hungry Atlantic and raised Angela's mother American—that is, dreaming ready-made dreams, yearning for what she might never have. She died when Angela was three, before her husband's real estate career brought him the Tudor home, the Caribbean condo, the BMW's. Angela's father was a Unitarian, from Maine.

"What is that?" Mom asked me. "Unitarian."

"They believe in units."

She laughed, "America!" In their international shorthand in which Germans were killers, Poles thugs, the English anti-Semitic snobs, Americans were crazy. And even after thirty years that craziness was to Mom and Dad a perpetual delight—the way parents marvel at their infant's eyelashes, smiles. And a source of sorrow. The infant will grow into something unpredictable.

Paul's stream of girlfriends, his perplexing (and goyish) fascination with his own beautiful body, made some sense to them, fit into their larger understanding of America. But their steady reference to the broadest context sometimes struck me as restricted, draining away the day into history. I remember a wave of grave desecrations in Jewish cemeteries on Long Island and how I fantasized forcing the black spray paint cans down the mouth of whoever thought swastikas were funny. Dad reminded me, calmly, that anti-Semitism sparked in bad times.

"Yes," Mom nodded, oddly secure. "It's the recession."

And I, I felt cheated of my rage. Likewise with Watergate. They had long predicted that Nixon was dishonest and so couldn't raise their voices about the scandal. Sometimes, though, the historical perspective was funny. Like when in fifth grade Paul was rude to his teacher before Parents' Night and she demanded Mom and Dad punish him as she had done. Mom said that—as she understood it—the Constitution barred being punished twice for the same crime. This became a minor family legend, told with ceremony as if it grounded us in the past and explained our present.

I don't think they were threatened by Angela. They seemed to pass her off as the vision of escape many Jews yearn for, the soft-haired Lorelei, seductive on her rock.

And I was glad Paul spent so much more of his time away from home, at parties, movies, whatever.

The first time Angela came over for dinner, Paul told a news story of some honeymoon wife falling naked from a Midtown hotel window to a fatal street. Angela grinned and topped him with someone burning to death sliding down a plastic emergency shoot off an airplane that didn't explode. They were united in contempt for the unfortunate.

That first dinner was alternately very noisy and painfully quiet, and I drank five glasses of wine despite Dad's heavy glances. Sandy tapped my foot under the table now and then, but whether to slow my drinking or just connect, I don't know.

Overdressed and wearing too much perfume, Angela had loudly proclaimed how cozy our dinette was, as if she were a media-conscious monarch posing gracefully in a hovel. She signaled Mom's garnet ring for her attention, admiring it so loudly I felt a billboard had smashed into the dining room, smearing us with letters too large to read.

But Mom beamed. "My husband made it."

Angela nodded, eyes sweeping the dish-heavy table. "How long have you been a jeweler, Mr. Levy?"

"Since before the War."

Angela frowned away the ugliness of that reference and turned to me.

"What does your father do?" Mom asked warmly as if eager to discover hidden qualities in Angela.

"He owns things."

That's when I poured my fifth glass.

All through dinner, Angela took such mingy portions of salad, roast, potatoes and corn you would've thought her determined to make a show of delicacy. When I found myself silently counting the kernels on her plate, I knew I was drunk.

"She didn't like our food," Dad muttered in the kitchen when Paul took her home.

"How could she tell?" Mom shot. "She had, what, three bites?" Then they switched to Yiddish and moved to Russian. Sandy and I listened to the heavy cadences of the language that always sounded dark and sad to me, even in marching songs. From the kitchen, I heard a snarled "*Amerikanski*" a few times.

Sandy and I sat in the living room for a while before he went home.

"She's a lot like Paul," he finally said, with my parents' conversation drifting out to us, tantalizing, unknowable.

Oh yes, I thought, she was like Paul: cold, beautiful, critical. She'd glanced around our home as if every picture were crooked, cheap and vile, all the furniture needed dusting but she would overlook it. Watching Angela, I'd thought of the Greek and Roman sculpture galleries of the Metropolitan—those high rooms of tender light and silence. I never understood the raving about "classical beauty." Those private faces perched above tunics, cloaks, vague draperies seemed too removed from life to be beautiful. Now Sandy, he was beautiful, dark and romantic-looking.

"God, I'm lucky," I said to Sandy, who flushed with pleasure, understanding I meant him.

In bed, later, reading *Paris Match*, the room around me blurred, tenuous, I found myself wishing for things. Wishing I'd learned Russian as a child and taken Yiddish more seriously so that I could know my parents in a deeper way, think with them in languages they had not learned so much as lived. Paul was not alone in hungering for another life.

I longed for escape in my own way—what else was my dream of France, of barges on the Loire? Of wandering through Vaux-le-Vicomte and Chambord? Of exploring the bastide towns in the Dordogne? It was all a delightful patchwork for me: vermouth cassis, de Maupassant, Monet. My France was untouched by Dreyfus, Vichy, transit camps or De Gaulle's anti-Zionism, it was La Belle France, Europe's jewel, civilizing the world, the fantasy land that had infused each ringing high "*Bonjour!*" of my first French teacher. I imagined myself biking home with my baguette, writing letters in a Boul' Mich' cafe, smoking a Gitane on a train snaking down to the Mediterranean. It was a strange sort of return across the Atlantic, a retreat in time, wiping out history and death.

I adored my name pronounced in French; Robert became Row-bear with that wonderful rolled "R." But I shared these fantasies and visions with no one, especially at school where I covered my facility at translations, my mastery of the subjunctive with adolescent *je m'en fichisme*. Sandy disliked the French, so I couldn't imagine him my *copin*: "Everyone says they're nasty. My folks went there and hated it."

Sandy's dream was Israel, but not as a tourist (which he'd done) matching life to film scenes or photographs, not as a pretend kibbutznik for a few months. Sandy wanted to live there, work, travel, study Torah in Jerusalem.

"When I'm ready," he said, which meant after college. "Life is important there, you know why. You have to—it's a choice."

Maybe all dreams are a choice, a way of plunging reality, like a piece of sizzling, forge-worked metal into a barrel of water to cool its form.

Sandy was always bringing back loads of books from the library, reading Buber, Wiesel, collections of Yiddish stories in translation, essays on religion, the Sabbath, anything, everything, as if preparing himself for a long and hazardous voyage. He talked about his Jewish reading, and I listened in admiration, with a little distance.

Like Paul, I had lost my interest in being visibly Jewish after an undistinguished bar mitzvah, so Sandy's appeals for me to join him at synagogue, sometimes, any synagogue, were annoying. I could still follow a service but it led nowhere, the words heaped around me with each turned page until I felt stifled, trapped. Luckily our seders at home were brief and every other holiday, including Rosh Hashanah and Yom Kippur, was less celebrated than talked about, passed around in conversation like a strange carving that gathers speculation with the heat of each hand. If I'd lived outside of New York I might have done more—but who needed to be Jewish in Queens when someone else could do it for you? I wanted to be French, to feel the dusty red medieval walls of Carcassonne as mine. I had no desire to grow old in Queens or Israel.

"You think because you're not like Paul," Sandy snapped one evening, "that anything's all right."

"What did I do?"

"Nothing—that's the point." Sandy wanted me to join a Jewish youth group, march for Soviet Jews, sign petitions, to do something more than dream of going abroad. He claimed I'd never really come back from France, or wouldn't want to. "It's the same thing. You'd forget about me! And Paul's going to marry Angela!"

I knew Paul wanted to, after graduating. He'd been strutting around nude a week before, scratching at his heavy rich chest and bragging about how Angela was his "slave," how she'd do "anything" for him.

"And she loves this." He flicked at his crotch.

"You're gross."

"That's right. Big." He gave it a shake.

After a pause, I said, "You want her money."

He smiled. "I'm not gonna be like Dad and his lousy little yard. Look at him, he's nothing."

"What about the War?"

"Plenty of people made it after the War."

Bastard, I thought in English, then in French: espece de salaud.

"And I sure won't be like you," Paul went on, leaning on his door frame. "You'll never get to France, that's bullshit. You'll stay here jerking off with your little Golda Meir."

I froze.

He laughed. "You think I couldn't figure it out? What a little homo!" He turned and slammed his door.

I fled to the bathroom, ripped off my clothes and stood under the violent shower while I heard Mom come upstairs from the basement to ask about the noise.

They knew Paul and I didn't get along, but Mom kept trying. There was the abstract approach: "It's nice for children to get along." The apocalyptic approach: "He's all you'll have when we're gone." And even the ethnic approach: "It's a shame for the goyim to see brothers not friendly." To which I'd reply, respectively, "Yes it is"—"I hope not"—"They don't have to look."

Right about that time, Paul was bragging about an MG he'd bought from a friend at school with money saved from summer jobs. I, who spent all my earnings on movies and books and hanging out places with Sandy, had jealous visions of Paul in an accident or arrested for drunk driving, with Angela running from the scene or just sobbing her shame and fear in a greasy station house. I couldn't believe how jealous I was!

One May afternoon of my senior year of high school, and Paul's at Fordham, I came home with Sandy and heard Mom weeping in the kitchen. I had never heard her cry like this, with hysterical heavy gasping sobs that seemed wounded, alive. We stood inside the front door as if trying to fight the energy of that grief, but it pulled us through the house to the kitchen, where she sat in a chair pushed against the wall, head back, legs together, arms and hands dead on her thighs like one of those serene Egyptian tomb effigies.

"Your brother," she moaned. "Your brother and his *dripkeh* are junkies!"

I dragged a chair to her, sat close.

"Junkies!"

I didn't understand. Wouldn't I have seen the tracks?

Dad, she said, was upstairs. The doctor had been to give him a sedative. I made tea for her, brought a dishtowel soaked in cold water for her abused eyes and Sandy and I sat at the empty table while Mom told the story.

A professor at Fordham had discovered Paul in a basement bathroom handing an envelope to another student who tried to duck out the door. It was cocaine. Angela and Paul apparently had a little business going (the money for his car, I thought). But no one was arrested, they were just expelled. The school wanted to protect its good Catholic name and the Chancellor made calls to keep the story out of the news. I knew that was possible; the same thing had happened with a suicide at Fordham the year before.

"A junkie!" Mom said again. "And don't defend him!"

I didn't try.

Angela's father, a large handsome man with glamorous white teeth and hair came over that night, but there were no voices raised. Together, they sat hushed and defeated by their own ignorance, drinking vodka in the living room, like the victims of a flash flood marveling at their enormous unexpected loss.

Paul moved out. Angela was shipped to relatives in California. Dad abandoned his workroom, and even in his hammock strung from two big trees that were his vision of security and peace, he looked miserable. Mom took to chain reading mysteries, walling herself in with shiny paperbacks.

"We lived so long like dogs," she said to me and Sandy. "I only wanted for my sons to be happy."

I knew then that I could never tell her who I was.

Your Papers, Please

"Hey—is your name really Dark? I've never met anyone with, like, a soap opera name! Is that cool or what?"

Dark looked up at Peter Cohen, one of the beginning Masters students, thin, green-eyed, flushed with just having harangued their shy hostess to can Mariah Carey and play some big beat and techno CDs he'd brought with him. Peter was so skinny you could draw straight lines down each side from his shoulders past his hips—it was as if nothing in life had touched him yet. But his voice was full of phony New York sophistication.

Up until now, the English Department party had simply fallen around Dark like heaps of confetti he was too tired to brush away. Alone in his corner, he had been content to just get drunk and hazily watch people laugh and dance, watch especially the newer graduate students like Peter—some right out of college—whose youth whipped the air like crackling fresh flags.

"It's short for my last name—Darkow. Russian."

"But you look Jewish. Come on, it's a Jewish name, isn't it? Confess!"

Dark nodded very reluctantly.

"I knew it! You look just like my Uncle Morty—but he's eaten way more corned beef than you ever will. I mean, you must have, what, 10 percent body fat? 8 percent? No way! Dude! But you're big, too. You have that triangle thing, man. Maybe we could work out together some time, I'm really hopeless, no muscles, a super wimp. So, tell me, with this Russian vibe you've got going, do you read lots of Dostoevski?"

"Not really."

"I like Dostoevski. The people are so outa control, not like in Henry James."

"I'm doing my dissertation on *The Ambassadors*."

"Oh, that's right, I remember I heard you'd been working on it for, what, ten years? Seven? Whatever. But James—why bother? Wasn't James senile when he wrote his last coupla books? I mean, nothing ever happens in his books: somebody just moves a piece of furniture and finds a dust ball behind it. Gimme a break. That pathetic crap about 'Live, live all you can!' when he was dead from the waist down. And he was so fucking anti Semitic. Just like Edith Wharton and Henry Adams. How can you read that clown? Seriously, you should do some therapy and deal with your internalized anti-Semitism, man. Maybe that's why you can't finish your dissertation."

Before Dark could begin an angry lecture or just tell Peter to shut up, Peter bullet trained ahead: "I'm doing my masters thesis on David Leavitt. Talk about your fucked-up shame-based Jews! I'm gonna call it 'The Rise and Fall of a Crypto Jew.' I mean, it's so cool that he ends up getting busted for plagiarizing Stephen Spender's memoir, but doesn't even steal one of the best parts, about Spender being half Jewish in England and what it felt like. How perfect is that?"

Despite himself, Dark said, "I didn't know David Leavitt was Jewish." He'd read some of Leavitt's pallid, over-praised stories years ago and had no idea—not that it mattered.

"See what I mean!" Peter whooped. "You can't really tell!"

"But you admire him? You like his writing?"

"Fuck no. Are you kidding? He's old news, he's the '80s, just like Tama Janowitz. But he's a great case study. And he hasn't published a whole lot and none of it's deep, so it'll be pretty easy to write about. I already have a publisher at Indiana University Press who wants me to turn it into a book."

Dark cringed at the unspoken assertion that Peter would never take years to write anything.

Peter grabbed his arm. "But what's the point of another Henry James dissertation anyway? Wasn't your father a Holocaust survivor? Why not write about something connected to that? Like—" He hesitated. "Oh, how about rhetorical Holocaust pornography—you know, the way everybody and everything gets compared to the Nazis and the Gestapo? It would be awesome."

Before Dark could reply, Peter strutted off to dance as a thumping Fatboy Slim song came on. Dark hated techno and electronica and big beat and all of that, but he felt obliged to keep up with contemporary music; reading SPIN was just as much a vain conjuration against aging for him as vitamin E.

Dark studied Peter, who didn't seem to be with anyone. Though his basketball shirt, baggy jeans, high tops were drab, Peter moved with such confidence he was like a lighthouse beacon offering promise in the fog.

And Dark wanted to punch his lights out. He couldn't believe someone just entering the program knew about his father, and worse, knew he was having trouble finishing his dissertation. What the hell had he become, the Ancient Mariner? How humiliating that Peter wasn't just telling him what to write about, but had tossed off a brilliant idea like it was nothing.

Dark spent a few fierce moments trying to remember who in the department he'd told about his father's past. But the anger faded into despair as he listened to the hateful music and watched people dance. Dark never danced anymore because it made him feel too old. His students, Peter, everyone danced so differently now—like they thought they were gangsta rappers on MTV, moving their arms and hands in ways that seemed as alien as kabuki.

But then everything these days seemed like a performance he didn't understand or care about. Dark was on another College of Arts and Letters fellowship this year, having used up his five years of assistantship support and two extra years the chair had wangled for him because he was a good teacher. And because the department needed cheap labor.

Having long since finished his course work, taken his comprehensives, he was mostly alone writing, or trying to write. Even the people he knew here, people he had gone drinking with, the ex-girlfriends, were no more than carousel horses, passing quickly and smoothly in their private bright circle, eyes dead, manes and legs frozen in painted delight. He was too tired to argue theories, share complaints about illiterate students, or slander professors. He was too tired, and people no longer expected him to show up when he was invited: "If you were an Indian," one of the department secretaries had said, "your name would be Dark Cloud, honey." His work seemed impossible; each new book and article on James filled him with dread as if he were watching a horde of lemmings surge to their strange hypnotic death.

What had happened to his love of Henry James, the sense of discovery and escape when he'd read *Washington Square* and *The Portrait of a Lady* in college, and imagined himself alive in a different era, alive and purged of the Jewishness he quietly, fervently loathed?

His advisor in college, Mrs. Olson, had warned against James. She urged him to choose a minor writer no one had handled, as if dissertation topics were grapefruit at an open air stand. That seemed like brilliant advice now in this dreary apartment which even music, food and guests couldn't rescue from mediocrity. The orange '70s-style plaid furniture supplied by the landlord, the sagging bunchy curtains, the Pullman kitchen, the flimsy unpainted doors, the windowless bathroom with its noisy useless fan were duplicated all over town. Worst were the matted but unframed cheap Renoir prints, their colors greasy, the smiles and poses somebody's idea of freedom, ease—as pathetic in their own way as the kindergarten wish of a child to ride delirious fire trucks through traffic frozen by their blare. If not Renoir, it was generally poster-size nature photos so artificially beautiful they could've been painted on velvet, or cheaply dramatic wall hangings: geometrics, rainbows, trees.

Dark drank some more Seagram's, mulling over his morning's news. On a routine physical, his doctor had found what he thought was a heart murmur and had urged Dark to see a cardiologist. He was only 35, but suddenly those digits were like the room number at the end of a hospital corridor where he saw his father seated in a wheel chair a year ago, eyes crushed shut by pain, thin white hand circling over his stomach. When his father's cancer—sudden, voracious—had struck at their family, Dark had felt himself stronger than random crazy cells, felt he could counter anything and not disintegrate.

But this was new. His own body, his lean, diet purified, marathoning body, safe passage through the realms of sickness and death, suddenly seemed jeopardized, as if the government extending his permission to travel had collapsed in revolution and he was unprotected by its mottoes, interests, seals.

"So what's your real first name?" Peter asked, sailing over to sit by him. Behind Peter the party lurched and weaved like a furious baroque canvas of historical mayhem. "Gregory."

"Puh-leeze! What did your parents call you?"

Peter's thin smooth face was as intent as an obnoxious television interviewer's, convinced that truth was only a question away.

"None of your business." Wasn't there any way to made this asshole shut up?

"Whatever. You're definitely Dark."

Yes, he was. Because of his black hair and tanned looking skin his mother had often called him "Gypsy." Some girlfriends had wanted him to be French or Greek, whatever they thought was sexy and exotic, and made up nicknames to match. And Dark had never said he was Jewish, had kept his background mysterious. So when Sophia in high school had first called him "Dark" it was less a joke or wish than a discovery. Since then, seeing "Gregory Darkow" on paper, even when he'd signed it, had been like driving by a desolate war memorial where each carved name is merely space pushed into stone: form without substance.

Peter leered. "People tell me you've dated a lot of women in the department."

"Most," Dark said flatly, wanting, for effect, to add "All." He thought, dated and negated.

"Really? And?"

Dark flashed to himself at twelve, confidently explaining the garbled world of sex to an open mouthed nine year old cousin whose curiosity was mingled with disgust and shame.

"And what? You want details?"

118

Peter looked down and Dark studied the spiky brown hair dyed blond at the tips, the two small gold hoops in each ear, the thin blue and red wreath tattooed around his neck. He felt sudden loathing for this . . . kid. Rising to leave, he wished he were really drunk, or that he'd gone into the bedroom where the cocaine was; then he wouldn't care. "Jewboy," he thought, despising Peter's big nose, his accent, his arrogance. Peter had suggested working out together; Dark could imagine helping Peter lift a barbell over his chest and then letting it go. How many ribs would it crack? He smiled.

"Hey, I'm sorry," Peter offered.

"I guess you are."

At home he thought of calling Susan, but she would be up from Providence tomorrow and she didn't like him waking her girls. He could hear her saying "You couldn't wait? What's the problem?" Susan could not even pity herself. A promising pianist, she had fallen from a tree at fourteen and broken both her hands; her father drank himself into kidney failure and death a few years later; her first lover had abandoned her when she was pregnant, revealing he had a wife in Florida; she had lost the child and spent months in a mental hospital. There was more: two miscarriages, a vicious divorce, all of it like the awful printed cards he remembered deaf mutes thrusting at you in the New York subways, unfairly forcing pity, shame.

But even at forty, Susan did not look battered. She was beautiful, slim and graceful, gray eyed, with dramatic foaming black curly hair like a Restoration wig, extravagant hair, sweet smelling, soft. Years ago, he would've admired her past like some historic plundered marble frieze reproduced in a glossy catalogue, found it exciting, the promise of life. How he'd loved sad novels in college, feeling he must surely be spiritually expanded for reading them. But that was distant suffering, pain that was observed, not experienced. Now, since his father's death, it was all too real, and so seeing Susan every other weekend when her ex-husband had the girls was enough for Dark.

On Saturday mornings they usually talked first, casual diarists of the week, dropping news and information like cards in a leisurely summer time game on some back porch shaded with honeysuckle. But he couldn't this time. When Susan set her weekend bag down in his living room he pulled at her sweater, jeans, wanted to devour her and time. Their sex was ecstatic, quick, surprising him, amusing her. That was a relief, because for too long now, he'd been feeling his body reminiscing with Susan, like a cart horse with blinders on, plodding home, the world reduced to always what's ahead.

From the floor she said, "I guess you were glad to see me, huh?" Later, in bed, she asked, "So what's wrong?" She was smoking with cynical grace, ashtray on her Caesarian scarred belly.

"Me—my heart." He explained what the doctor had told him. He didn't mention his dissertation. He never did.

Susan pressed for facts. "But you're not even sure it's bad? You won't know right away?" Susan shook her head. "Dark, don't be a baby. Plenty of people live with a little heart murmur, swim and climb mountains and live for ever."

"But I *feel* bad." It sounded illogically petulant, unequal to what was inside. He wanted to shout, "I'll die before I ever accomplish anything," to punish her somehow, but the words made him dizzy. He had never told her about his father, never told her he was Jewish, had kept as much of his past a secret as possible.

As if hearing his inner moans, Susan said, "God, I am so sick of this. Everyone I know is crazy because they're getting old. Women who can't have kids; this writer, he's thirty-seven, never been published; musicians who couldn't make it in Boston, hell they can hardly make it in Rhode Island; real estate guys want to earn double their age but don't and never will. That's all I hear. Someone told me last week at a party: 'I feel like killing myself.' I said, 'You want a medal? You think it's brave saying that? Try doing it.' I live in a goddamned cancer ward and everyone's terminal."

He winced, thinking of his father's death, his father's ugly deathbed wish: "Make something of yourself! Do something for God's sake!" It was a bitter assessment of how little he'd achieved so far, especially when measured against the life his father had lost in the camps, never recovered, never discussed. That absence had sucked the life out of his home, driven his mother to alcoholism, himself to— Well, to what? Endless delays?

All his life, Dark had listened to his father complain. Why had he come to America? Why hadn't he left the DP camp for Australia, England, wherever his friends had gone? All of them had become rich. Why hadn't he? Wasn't it enough he lost everyone and everything in the camps? Was he cursed here, too? Dark's father was so profoundly ashamed that when old friends visited the United States, he was sullen, unwilling to talk about his history of business failures. "*A groyser gornisht*, a big nothing, that's all I am," he would mutter out of their earshot.

And Dark had somehow been supposed to redeem it all, the War and its aftermath, but that was never going to happen at the rate he was progressing.

"A professor you want to be?" his father had sneered, shaking his head. "*A nechitiger tog*—it'll never happen!" As if Dark were doomed to repeat his father's failure.

Showering, Dark felt diminished by a lifetime of scorn, like a tiny tile set into some vast and horrible Bosch like mosaic, insignificant by itself.

The water drain seemed slow, and he reached down for a small slick ring of hair that for some time now had been growing there every time he showered, like a pearl responding to the irritation of time. His hair line was creeping up, but hair was appearing in strange places, on and in his ears, across his knuckles, like weeds and wild flowers claiming an empty house and yard.

"You're upset," Susan said at lunch in their favorite restaurant. "But that's good. It's better than being miserable. Maybe it'll get you off your butt. You'll end up like some dried up old man in a Henry James story if you don't do something."

"Is this, what, an intervention?" Did everyone have to hector him?

"Of course not. I'm just tired of people being afraid to get old. It's not death they're afraid of, it's life. My students write about it—freshmen!" She grimaced, and there at the small crowded table in a halo of wine sipping couples, he wondered why he'd bothered talking to her last year at the Yale conference, or why he'd wanted more than one weekend together.

"You're not listening," she said.

Chianti. Pasta primavera. Peanut butter pie. Espresso.

They could not decide on a movie, endlessly quoting reviews, friends' comments, suspicions. He did not want to go for a drive. She did not want to shop or make love again. Neither wanted to scrounge up someone to visit.

"It's not a good weekend," he managed.

"No." Susan was no longer critical, dismissive, seeming suddenly like a little girl stifled by her expectation of a treat. He did not want her soft or sympathetic, not today.

"I'll go home," she said. "Call me."

Dark slept until 4:00 A.M., woke sweaty, uncertain, pulled himself into the kitchen to brew coffee. He read until dawn, magazines, the Times book review, and then slept again, went off for a bike ride at noon, tearing past the subdivisions and little farms there at the edge of town, lost in his body, in the pumping of his legs. Then he watched *Abbott and Costello Meet Frankenstein* and *Tora, Tora, Tora*.

In the evening he dragged himself to a local bar hung with a nightmare of Mexican baskets. While he ordered his third Seagram's, he saw Peter walk in, recognize him with a huge smile. Peter headed over, his walk part dancer's glide, part saunter. Tonight Peter was costumed very differently, wearing Gap chinos, Topsiders, and a red and blue striped shirt. Dark thought of Gudrun in *Women in Love* liking those two strong colors together, but she was so complex, and Peter had nothing but his youth.

Peter said, "I'm sorry I was such a creep Friday night. I like to talk, but when I'm happy, and drunk, I can be rude."

"Happy?"

"Yeah—my interview."

Peter ordered Dubonnet on the rocks.

"My Philip Roth interview, coming out in *New York* magazine," Peter went on. And through a sinking deadness, Dark heard Peter talk about the Zuckerman books and his editor father's friendship with Roth. "That's how I got into the program here. Roth wrote a letter of recommendation for me, an awesome letter. Not that I deserved it. I mean, my grades weren't really hot, but the letter—"

They drank a lot, Peter raving about New York, his luck, and Roth, while Dark more and more understood the madman in the Poe story bricking up his wife's corpse in the cellar. Peter was pushy, Peter had connections, Peter would end up on top—without deserving it.

"You're pretty lucky," Dark said.

"I am. I am lucky. It's all luck so far. I really haven't worked hard at all. I never have. Things always just turn out right for me."

Dark seethed. Peter was young, brash, connected. He had no illusions about his work being "a contribution." It was clearly just a hoop to jump through. He'd find a job without a problem, ending up at some hip media-savvy English department awash in cultural studies where everything was race, class and gender, or texts had no meaning outside their textuality.

Dark thought of all the papers he'd done at conferences, none published, the articles he had sketched and planned, and bought file cards for but never finished, and his degree. In college, it had seemed like an elusive gleaming story book treasure, but now, within reach, not much more than the campus stickers you bought so that you could park in certain more convenient lots. Yet he still couldn't finish. And if he did? Who would want to hire someone whose specialty was Henry James?

"Is there really a waterfall near here?" Peter was asking. "People tell me it's great."

"It is. Want to see it?"

"Who's driving?"

"I will."

Dark's Saturn was back across the street and they drove twenty minutes along the desolate interstate.

"You know, since we're getting to be friends, Dark, you should know that—"

"You're gay."

"How. . . ?"

"Dubonnet on the rocks."

Peter laughed nervously, and Dark felt as if Susan's contempt had been animating him.

"It doesn't bother you? You're not like a Republican or anything?"

"I don't care," he said, finishing the sentence silently: "about that."

Dark felt the night air had plucked away his haze by the time they stopped at the edge of the state park. As they headed down the unmarked path, he was murderously clear and determined to act. The full moon's silver on and through the maples edged everything with a grim brilliance. He walked without speaking, neared the low heedless roar. At a space in the wall of trees Dark said "This is it." He plunged down the slope; the waterfall gleamed above them, cruel, private, eating up their silence. Dark was glad to see that the stream was deeper than he remembered, and as Peter moved closer to the water, Dark thought, Now, shove him in now and hold him under.

He grabbed Peter's meager shoulders, but Peter whirled around with a surprised, wild, eager grin on his face and fell to his knees, grabbing at Dark's crotch with eager hands.

When Dark kneed him in the chin, Peter grunted and fell back, his head and shoulders down in the water and it was very easy then. Dark crouched down and straddled his scrawny waist heavily to hold that clever, empty head under the ice cold water as Peter kicked and struggled. Eyes closed, Dark squeezed as if he were getting the proverbial blood from a stone, and it wasn't very hard. He was so much stronger than Peter, and had more to lose now.

Shaking the water from his suddenly cramped hands, drying them on his jeans, he wondered how many people had seen them leave the bar together. Could he hide the body?

He was surprised that these thoughts came to him so calmly. He thought of Henry James's cryptic line, "So here it is at last, the distinguished thing." If he could pull this off, he could do anything.

Like steal Peter's topic, change his dissertation committee and finally get his doctorate.

It was time to get to work.

Gimme Shelter

Michael was still on the phone with his father when Paul came out of the steaming bathroom, toweling his dark hair. For a moment, taking Paul in, Michael stopped listening. Even after all this time, he still loved rediscovering Paul's body and face. A Sephardic Jew, Paul was often taken for Hispanic. Paul's mesmerizing deep-set brown eyes had lids so dark they seemed dusted with eye shadow, and they always stirred Michael with the image of Paul's cock which was the same brownish-grey color—like powdered cocoa mix.

Paul had gone running early this Saturday morning, and then stopped at a gym down the street from their hotel, consumed as usual by keeping fit out of town. Paul—even at forty—was so muscular and trim that today he seemed almost a mockery of Michael's small, round, pale, frightened father across the country, trapped by inoperable cancer like a little boy lost in a haunted house, never knowing when he would turn a corner and be frozen in terror.

Michael felt an unspoken adjuration in Paul's running and work-outs. Paul obviously wanted Michael to join him, not just to stay in shape or even keep him company, but to flee the heaviness of his despair. Rather than cajole, Paul seemed to think that looking as good as an underwear model in an International Male catalogue—and breathing heartily—would convince Michael to come along. But who cared about exercise? Michael's father's case was hopeless. There was no cure.

"Michael—are you listening?"

"Yes, Dad."

Michael's father went on to ask, "Say a prayer for me today. Say a *Mi She'beyrech*."

Until that moment, Michael and his father had been talking lightly, his father trying to be jocular about the side effects of the chemotherapy. Michael was willing to adopt the same tone, because it seemed to comfort his father the morning after he'd been so dizzy and nauseous he could barely sit up. And because Michael was unable to fly out to New York as often as his 75-year-old father wanted. So sturdy optimism seemed the easiest way out. But sometimes on the phone with his father, Michael heard his own hearty comments the way they might sound to a stranger: inane, naive—like the loud remarks of a foreigner shouting poorly-learned lines from a phrase book in a desperate attempt to be understood, or at least not silent and invisible. Things would shift when he talked to his sister Marge, who had taken their father to live with her now that she was divorced and her boys were in college. Then he would sound even worse, like a character in a soap opera mouthing beautiful platitudes: "Dad has to have something to look forward to" or "Dad has to believe he can get better"—as if illness were merely the result of boredom, spite or doubt.

"Of course I'll say a prayer for you, Dad."

Putting down the receiver, he felt chilled thinking about the Hebrew prayer for the sick, the *Mi She'beyrech*, even though the small hotel room was bright with San Francisco sunshine. It was an ordinary little room, made exceptional only by its view of the city's hills climbing to the light.

Despite all the years of services he'd gone to with his family or with Paul, and the more recent ones with other gay and lesbian Jews, he had never really had anyone of his own to pray for, anyone whose recovery from illness seemed so hopeless that he could surrender himself completely to the image of begging some vast and impersonal power to show mercy, just once, just for him. His mother had died in her sleep years ago (before he met Paul and started attending shul regularly), dying with no hint or prelude of illness. And most of the people he knew who had died of AIDS were Paul's friends: other journalists, writers, editors.

Paul asked him, "Which service do you want to go to?"

The national conference of gay and lesbian Jews they were attending offered some choices this *Shabbos* morning: Reform, Conservative, and a Women's service.

"The Women's, for sure. I'm tired of the same old thing." Together, they had watched how separate men and women were at the conference, sadly, unconsciously recreating the barriers between men and women in the straight Jewish community. Michael had mentioned this to a few people whose silence and lack of response was as frustrating as the way in which Jewish magazines had consistently not reviewed Paul's book, a Jewish version of Neil Miller's *In Search of Gay America*.

"You got it." Paul padded over to the bureau to pull out black bikini briefs. Michael sighed. He loved watching Paul walk nude: the slim dark cock bobbling below his balls, and his ass—tight, high, round as if perpetually offering itself up to you for veneration, for attack. Michael stood and walked with the erect, perfect carriage of a toreador—an image made even more complete by his slim hips and wide shoulders.

"Don't you ever slouch?" Michael asked, feeling particularly shlumpy today.

"I could take lessons," Paul said, smiling. Michael sighed again as Paul slid the black briefs on. It was like the riveting moment in the London hotel room near the end of *Maurice* when the young gamekeeper pulls on his long underwear and the waistband shoots his long cock up against his belly before it's tucked away.

"But let's not go downstairs just yet," Michael said.

Paul smiled. "You want to put the dick in *shabbosdik?*"

Michael laughed for the first time in days. He felt buoyed up by that laughter and moved across the room. He made Paul bend over and put his hands on the dresser for balance. "Yes I said yes I will Yes," Paul whispered, quoting Joyce's Molly Bloom.

But Michael wasn't laughing anymore. He'd seen his own face in the mirror: pale and devastated by talking to his father.

He closed his eyes, pushing into that perfect ass as if he were making love in a James Baldwin novel and riding an ecstatic slow train.

They were almost late getting downstairs, but given that the conference ran on a combination of Jewish Time and Gay Time, there was still not much of a crowd milling around to chat and pour coffee. They walked into the featureless mauve and grey meeting room where the women's service would be held; a table was pushed well back and semi-circles of chairs radiated out from it. A small thin woman with curly red hair glanced up at him, eyes momentarily uneasy. He was used to these sudden changes in expression or body position when he startled a woman, but it pained and humiliated him to be considered a threat when he wasn't. The afternoon before, on a jaunt surveying the hotel's terrace pool, Michael had come across three women conferees sitting and sunning, who kept talking as soon as he was in sight, but warily, he thought. It was like the time a woman in one of the classes he taught at Ohio State had asked everyone how many women were afraid at night on their vast campus, and every woman's hand went up, while the three men in class stared, and then looked down at their notes.

"Good *Shabbos*," he said now, and gestured with the bag holding his prayer shawl as if he were rattling keys in a parking structure to reassure a lone woman not far off that too he was headed for his car, truly. The woman nodded, and then smiled a little.

Still, Michael stood at the door until Paul pushed past him.

"You're Paul Tores!" the woman said, grinning, and came over to shake Paul's hand. "I've read your book twice. The first time, I couldn't believe I

126

was reading something about us, about lesbian and gay Jews!"

Michael moved to one of the outer circles, content to let Paul "be important" as the two of them called it. After years of struggling to get published, to get known, everything had changed. Paul's prize-winning book of interviews with lesbian and gay Jews had made him visible and sought after; at the conference, he was one of the keynote speakers. Last night at dinner, Michael had watched people fawn over Paul, wanting to sit near him, hear him speak, even touch him as if he were some sacred tree in a pagan grove. Sometimes the hands lingered, tentatively squeezed and assessed. It was annoying, but Michael didn't say much about it. Paul had been writing articles and book reviews without acknowledgment for too many years, had been too hungry and deprived of not only praise, but a sense that his work had any possibility of moving people.

What was worst for Michael was when they'd ask what *he* did (when they did ask), and barely listened to his reply. He had been thinking of giving up on "I'm an English professor at Ohio State" for more colorful and attention-getting remarks like "I'm a famous nuclear physicist—haven't you seen me on TV?" Perhaps that would make them see him as more than Paul's "partner." Even last year at a university-sponsored Gay Studies conference in Florida, the same thing had happened, and Paul wasn't even on the program.

Michael was so mad that he had blurted out to one of Paul's academic admirers there, "Why don't you slip upstairs and stop pretending you just like him for his book?" The three of them were all drunk, it was late, they were almost alone in the hotel bar, they ended up in bed together and it was a disaster. The bearded hairy little Ivy League stud who claimed to be a Neo-Deconstructionist (whatever that was!), turned out to have a ludicrously huge dick which he wielded with all the subtlety of Jackie Gleason in *The Honeymooners*. He took up too much room, and when he wasn't posing for admiration, he basically ignored Michael except for some inconsequential pats. Paul clearly looked embarrassed and bored. They all came, safely, stingily—and the nasty romp was over.

"I think your fans should stay dressed from now on," Michael said wearily as soon as the little professor was gone.

"Amen," was Paul's reply.

The room was filling up quickly now, with many women wearing skull caps and prayer shawls; they greeted each other, chatted. The conference couldn't be more than ten percent women, but there were no other men here besides himself and Paul. For that reason, perhaps, there was less of an edge than among the groups of men at the conference, less sneering and preening, and when people touched, it was softer and not so sexual.

"This I have to share with Paul," Michael thought, "And he can put it in some article." Over the years, he had watched anecdotes he shared with Paul, observations and even jokes wind up in Paul's writing: transmuted, profoundly changed by the way Paul claimed and shaped them. It was disconcerting at first, but being in Paul's work had come to seem like an honor.

Paul sat by him, whispering, "Where're the guys?"

"Maybe they think it's Women only."

Paul pulled out his conference program, which listed the service as "Drawing on Women's writing and led by women."

Michael shrugged. "Women's writing—you'd think that would have brought at least one Judith Krantz queen."

Paul was slipping on the enormous rainbow-striped Israeli prayer shawl that came down to his ankles and made him look like a prophet. The first time they had attended services together, Michael had been amazed to see Paul disappear like an actor getting into character when he put on the prayer shawl, opened his prayer book as if it were the doorway into another world. "He believes all this," Michael had thought, surprised, not even sure what "all this" really meant, just moved by the intoxicating sense of distance and concentration. In a way, he was reminded of watching Paul writing to meet a deadline—he would wander around the house, or just sit in one place, eyes slightly unfocused. Or it was like driving down a heat-baked highway and watching the light shimmer and disappear—magnetic, intense, a little strange.

"My Dad— He asked us to say a prayer for him, a *Mi She'beyrech*."

Paul nodded. "I wish he were here. To see this, to see us."

"Are you kidding? He'd go to the Conservative service—he'd think a women's service was weird—just like he thinks lesbians are weird—`So tell me what are these lesbiankas doing without a man?'"

Services began, led by three women Michael did not remember having seen the night before.

"It's going to be a little distracting," one of the women said, gesturing to the wall behind her—actually it was just a movable partition, carpeted, but apparently not sound proof. Everyone laughed a little. The conservative service was rumbling into life with the opening prayers—and Michael smiled, imagining a mighty herd of Hebrew letters surging like buffalo across a river.

Paul murmured, "They're kind of loud."

"Tell me about it." But Michael also felt part of the other service somehow—it was the familiar masculine chanting that he had found so moving when he shared it with Paul—and so erotic. To be overcome by the strength of that male intensity and conviction, to be so lost in prayer that he was not himself at all but far more than himself, expanded, completed, filled—it was sometimes amazingly sexual for him, and exhausting.

He followed along in the mimeographed service that was culled from various sources, suddenly feeling how strange it was to be a minority within a minority within yet a third one. He tried not to sing too loudly—which Paul always accused him of, especially now when the male voices on the other side of the partition were pounding each Hebrew line into submission. There was as much contemporary poetry as Hebrew in the Women's service, and it all felt immediate and real. Saying "She" instead of "He" made him read more slowly, and think about the prayers.

Because this particular service was unfamiliar, Michael felt carried along on a wave of women's voices, and more struck by each and every word: "I might imagine God as a teacher or friend," they all read together, "but those images, like king, master, father or mother, are too small for me now."

He entered these words, found a summer stillness, as if he were home on a blistering hot day sitting in the back yard, in the shade, the smell of seared limp grass like a wall between himself and any movement.

He read and reread those lines, and then, "God is far beyond what we can comprehend."

Right before the Torah portion was read, one of the leaders said, "Please say aloud the name of anyone you're praying for when we come to that place in the *Mi She'beyrech*."

And around them, like strange sad incense rose a small cloud of names, "Peter Fisher," "Hannah Green," "Marty Perlmutter," on and on—as if this was a dark version of the census in *B'Midbar*, the Book of Numbers. Michael couldn't breathe, couldn't say his father's name until Paul said it for him, and even then Michael merely repeated the syllables.

Too late, he thought, unable to hear what followed. Too late. When he was in New York six months ago, his father—just hit with the news of his hopeless cancer—had said for the first time in his life, "I love you."

Michael had felt stunned all the way home. His father had finally begun to talk about Michael's life with Paul, after they'd been together for seven years, asking how Paul was doing, whether his book was "selling good." Paul suddenly existed for him, and Michael felt his resentment slipping away.

But his father had only a few months to live. Michael had been clinging to every piece of good news so fiercely that when Paul merely nodded or listened, Michael felt criticized and exposed. Paul's silence was all the realism Michael needed. It made his humor, his hope clatter like a lonely sea shell in a child's plastic pail. The sun was going down, the beach growing cold and uninviting.

Paul tapped him to stand up. "Kaddish," he whispered. The prayer for the dead that didn't mention death at all, but praised God's power and majesty.

And Michael realized that he had completely tuned out during the Torah service. Where was he?

"*Yitgadal v'yitkadash. . . .*" They all began Kaddish, except for Michael.

He looked down at the familiar Hebrew words, trying to remember where he had read that the whole point of the Kaddish was for the congregation to respond with "May His great Name be blessed forever and ever" (*Yehei Shmei raba mevorakh l'olam ul'almei almaya*)." Not today, he thought. He could not say a word of it.

On the other side of the wall, lusty out of tune voices bellowed one Hebrew melody after another—all of it like the defiant shouting of someone afraid of the dark—these were no shouts of joy. Or were they? Would he be as loud there, as determined to fill the air with himself?

Suddenly Michael was plucked from his wondering, his annoyance, lifted, saved, shocked. One of the leaders was reading from the service.

" 'I've learned that in the course of life we leave and are left and let go of much that we love. Losing is the price we pay for living. It is also the source of much of our growth and gain. Making our way from birth to death, we also have to make our way through the pain of giving up, and giving up, and giving up some portion of what we cherish.' "

The room was so quiet it was as if they'd all entered a space consecrated to grief. Michael felt almost dizzy and couldn't read from the mimeographed stapled sheets he was trying to hold steady.

Paul slipped an arm around him, holding him firmly. Paul had uttered each word of the Kaddish as if cementing bricks in a wall.

At the end of the service with the booming men next door somehow reduced to the tame wildness of a can-can, people were linking arms for the final sung prayers. Michael wished he would never have to leave the haven of this room, never have to leave Paul's arms, could keep swaying and singing. Paul drew him even closer. Both of them were swallowed by that enormous rainbow-striped prayer shawl.

For a moment, he felt shielded from misery and death.

Nocturne

My sister Rose escaped at eighteen, thanks to a scholarship, off to school at Michigan State University where our mother couldn't tell if her dates were Jewish or not. Mom was always quiet and cool when Rose's high school boyfriends came over, as if she barely noticed those muscled pimply boys. But later:

"Rich Habek?" she would ask. "His name, what is it? Czech?"

"Polish," Rose dropped.

"A whole high school to choose from and you're dating a Pole."

"He's American. His grandparents came here in—"

"He's a Pole. You don't know what they're like. I know." And Mother told us again of the Polish woman who had spat on her as she and hundreds more starved and desperate Jews were led from her ghetto when it was being "liquidated." And the anti-Semitic riots before the War, and how Jewish university students had to stand at the back of lecture halls—a world of humiliation that I could never connect with the pretty postcard Europe I was always seeing in movies, and on TV.

What could we say when Mom laid out her proofs of the world's cruelty to Jews? Dinner, or breakfast, or whatever would drag on in silence. Rose didn't argue, just sat with her eyes down, lips tight, looking then so different from Mom.

Mannish, gray-eyed, broad-shouldered, tall and dark, Mother was too magisterial to yell at, and too distant. She often had the air of a burly sculptor longing for his studio, forced to spend time with people who had no deeper vision than their plans for the weekend.

After their exchanges, Rose would sulk in her room or go off to see a friend in the neighborhood—Washington Heights—that formerly German-Jewish and Irish hilly, park-lined enclave edging towards the north of Manhattan that has long since been absorbed and overshadowed by Harlem. When we lived there it was as quiet and clean as a suburb, with lush old trees canopying some streets, cool-lobbied Depression-era buildings, a neighborhood with roots in the city's past—the plaque marking a battle of Washington's on 153rd street; the uptown cemetery of Trinity Church, the museums built where James Audubon's estate used to be; the wooden houses glimpsed on side streets; the cobblestones spotted where tar had worn away. All that seems erased or blurred by drugs and murder—but growing up we felt both part of New York's excitement and promise, and distant from its dangerous rush, safe on our uptown hills, the highest part of the city. We could never be flooded there, my mother assured me once after we watched a news report of the ravaging Mississippi. I felt relieved.

While Rose was sulking, Mother would play the piano. Enthroned in the living room, it was her one luxury: dark and gleaming, with a rich caressive tone that was as brown as the wood.

She played simply, eyes closed, moving only her hands and arms as she had been taught as a girl. When she sank into Chopin, a Nocturne perhaps, I could imagine her in another world, of school books and a uniform blazer, platters of food on a heavy-legged sideboard, cousins dropping by on holidays, city walks with her smiling parents who called her Masha—a whole world of lovely fragments, pieces of her past that had popped out of her conversation like grains from a sack with a tiny unseen hole.

She said so very little it was all shadows to me, except the War I had learned about from books, which was a pall of dust thrown up by the traffic of time, settling on us all no matter how we might have struggled to be clean. But when she played even the saddest piece, her body rigid, head held back from the keys, I could imagine and love the girl she had been, the life that was stolen from her.

When Rose would come back or come out of her room on one of those painful evenings, nothing was said. Mother never apologized. Eventually, after a strained day or two, she would rumble back to life like the engine of some damaged machine and Rose and I could act normally again, or try to.

But there were too many of those outbursts as Mother watched slim, blonde Rose grow prettier, more popular, rousing Mother's heavy questions and fears. I wondered sometimes if she had promised Dad (who died when I was two) to see we married only Jews, though that was not something I could ask. Mother could not speak of him for long, as if this newer, American loss had forced her even further into silence.

Sometimes I asked what he was like, wanting more than dates and places, photographs, but Mother could only deliver garbled anecdotes that drained away like water into sand. Rose's memories were of a large loving force of a man—a beautiful fairytale. He was a fourth generation American, and his meager Jewishness had fit Mother's, it seemed.

Her parents had been completely secular, like his, and our being Jewish amounting to sneering at the "vulgarity" of Christmas; blundering holiday meals at which Mother rejected any talk of religion; a menorah we didn't always remember to light each Chanukah evening; the awareness of who in the news, criminal or star, was Jewish.

There was not much more, really, but it was apparently too much for Rose, who in Michigan quickly became a "calendar relative," marking birthdays and holidays with a card or a call. Her visits were rare; she always had "too much work." So did Mother, who more and more lived in the high school chemistry classes she taught. Michigan seemed like Japan to me, distant, exotic. When Rose left, I felt powerless and much younger than twelve.

"You'll see," Mother predicted. "She'll marry a goy. A Catholic."

But Rose said very little about her life in Michigan except that it was a beautiful state with miles of beaches, all of which was hard for me to picture. Truthfully, I was not that interested. My determination in junior high to excel in some sport, any sport, brought me to the swim team. I also discovered a bent for writing, and edited the mimeographed school paper, then the yearbook. It was my own world, separate from Rose's, and from Mother's.

When Mother died six years later—so ugly: falling down a staircase at her school and never leaving her coma—somehow I blamed Rose, hated the strange assurance with which she descended on our barren apartment and made ceaseless calls and arrangements. She looked, in her boots and long, belted fur-collared coat, like someone from *Dr. Zhivago.*

Her Master's in Art History had somehow led to opening a boutique with a friend and she glistened with success. She was a stranger, an adult, and I hated her fiancé Moshe whom I had only heard of and spoken to on the phone. Small, bearded, thick-lipped, he looked like a shtetl Jew even in his snazzy dark suit.

My contempt for him, my rage at being abandoned pulled me like a blind wind through the funeral, the mourning visits of teachers, students, neighbors and stray relatives. Moshe, a biochemist, was staying in Brooklyn with his sister and I wondered why Rose didn't stay there, too.

"I wanted to be with you," she kept saying as she fussed around the apartment, perhaps guessing my thoughts.

All of a sudden you have a brother, I jeered, wishing I could say it.

One night, Rose sat at the piano, small fingers stroking the silent keys while I read a magazine, ignoring her. Her grey wool dress irked me; it was too soft, too beautiful.

"You know, Ben, it's natural to feel all kinds of things now. . . ." She went on like that and I sat back in the creaky broad-armed sofa wishing I could break something, throw something, despising her kindness.

"How about applying to State? You could live with us, or near us."

I cursed inside: I was eighteen, I didn't need her.

So it went for days as I discovered how easily I could rage at her in silence while she reached out and out to me.

But when Rose was gone I knew I couldn't live in New York after graduation, when she and Moshe would be back to deal with "the estate." The furniture would have to be sold or stored or given away; the books sorted, saved or brought to the library; my life there ripped thread from thread like a miserable carpet.

Mother had tried so hard to teach me piano, but I had sat uncomprehending, sweaty and flushed while she explained the theory that was twice as onerous as math homework. And I wondered why my hands were so stupid. Alone now, I tried a scale or two, softly, a progression of chords, a line of a piece, the piano resisting me, dull, mechanical.

I supposed we would sell it.

I wouldn't allow any of my friends over, or their solicitous parents, because I wanted to be close to Mother's books and plates and records and combs and scarves and all the rest—to feel it there around me. I went through drawers, cabinets and shelves, looking at everything she had ever touched.

Then one night, a month after the funeral, with the television and the kitchen radio tearing holes in the stillness, I found what I could never have hoped to look for: a message.

From a kitchen drawer crammed with nails, string, buttons, pennies, I dug out a worn-cornered red leather book marked 1955 I had never noticed. Inside, on the yellow-edged pages were appointments, phone numbers, occasional scrawls left by the struggle to start a pen, and almost nothing else but two words on a day late in April. They were in Mother's hand, in Yiddish, which I had once tried to learn. I sounded them out, slowly: *Mein ba-frei-ung*. My liberation.

I sat on the kitchen floor with this book. The *idea* of liberation.

Her slavery. I had seen pictures of those cadaver-faced men and women staring from the graveyard of Europe. She had looked like that in the last camp when the Americans swarmed into the trembling German city. Her tall strong body had been assaulted, melted, reviled by years of hate and mad efficiency.

The horror had never been so real to me. She was gone and through her, a world I could never know. A world that was rightfully mine, but lost, bulldozed, bombed and burned.

I wanted to cry.

I decided to delay college for a year. There was enough money for me to travel if I wanted. I had fantasies of picking my way across Europe, avoiding palaces and cathedrals to find the tombstones of Mother's youth. Sometimes I just wanted to go to California and fall in love with a girl who surfed and admired me.

But first there was Rose's coming marriage.

The Lansing airport was larger and newer than I had expected, and crowded, too, but once I hugged Rose I saw very little on the drive to Moshe's house. Sitting with her in the new Intrigue as red as her slim linen suit, I felt emptied, suddenly, of purpose and feeling, as if I were one of those unclaimed bags back at the airport looping round and round on the conveyer.

Rose chatted about work like someone methodically piecing together a puzzle and searching for "one with a little sky in the corner." I nodded and made noises of response, but inside there was emptiness.

Moshe's house, left him by his parents, on a long quiet street not far from the huge campus, was two stories, brick, looking secluded and important behind a cordon of hedges and trees. Inside, I quickly saw it was a home, rich with plants, pictures, books, mementos, clocks—a living place all greens and browns. Rose led me upstairs to the warm gold guest room, and I put my bags down, sat on the bed, a bit awed now by how settled and mature she was. Rose seemed to look at me with a deep knowledge of herself and her place there.

"You know, I was never really sure, Ben, if I loved you. But I do. I'm glad you came."

"That's great," I managed.

Moshe was still at his lab. We went down to drink coffee in the kitchen hung with glass-doored cabinets. It was Friday afternoon and in the formal diningroom I could see that the table was set for three, for *Shabbos* dinner. In the center, red and white roses hung richly over the white linen and china, the bright silver.

"Mom didn't say much when I told her Moshe was Jewish," Rose began, slicing a piece of chocolate torte for me with graceful deliberation.

"Mom didn't say much," I agreed. "Ever."

Rose smiled. "Like you," she said softly, and then passed the plate, grey eyes steady, inquiring. She smiled again when I did.

"I told her Moshe was observant, and how I was starting to go to services. Sometimes I never thought anyone intelligent could believe in God. But Moshe does." Rose tilted her head and blinked the way people do when they say, "Small world, huh?"

"Do you?"

"I think so. I want to. I like being at temple. I feel safe."

"Happy," I suggested, tasting the rich nut-filled torte, sighing.

"Happy, yes."

Eating, I wondered who Moshe really was. All I knew of him was his age, thirty-seven, his job, his clear gray eyes, his respectful pleasant silence. I wondered how much of Rose's change was due to him.

"Usually we go to *Kabbalat Shabbat*, you know, welcoming the Sabbath, on Friday nights, but Moshe said he wanted us to spend time alone with you tonight. Family."

I felt almost dizzy and closed my eyes. The phone called Rose away, and I felt an explosion of possibilities. I could go to Europe—or even Israel—or stay with Rose and Moshe for a while, maybe longer—or do all of that.

I could be a Jew. Maybe it was time to learn what that meant.

I went to get my mother's datebook for Rose, who didn't know I had found it.

Talking in the bright living room, Rose gave me a little wave as I headed upstairs. I waved back.

My liberation.

Welcome to Beth Homo

Flinging one end of his knee-length wool tallis over his shoulder as if it were a lush sable stole, Larry said to me, "Maybe we should start our very own synagogue, Beth Homosexu-el. Beth Homo, for short." He held his head up like Huck Finn declaring he would go to hell. "And everyone could join the Sisterhood! What do you think?"

Larry had been about to put his blue velvet tallis bag away this Saturday afternoon, but had suddenly unzipped it and whirled out the impressive black and silver striped ivory prayer shawl, entering its folds like a magician about to perform a fabulous escape. When I clapped appreciatively, he said, "Thank you. Now you may kiss my fringe."

Just then, through the open windows, we heard the roar of what must have been another Ohio State touchdown. It was going to be a terrific season, but without me. I hadn't attended a single home game this fall, unlike my freshman year, when I painted my face red and white, and left every game hoarse, exhausted, triumphant. The camaraderie in the student section was electric: on the warm days most guys didn't wear shirts, and the heat of their skin when I'd pummel friends and even strangers after an interception, a great pass, or a terrific second effort was all I could ask for. College football is almost a religion in Ohio, more so than anywhere else in the Midwest, I think, and I worshiped happily, not having to let anyone in the stands know that privately, I also belonged to what David Bowie called The Church of Man Love.

That fall, however, I was spending all my Saturdays at the Hillel co-op which wasn't far from my dorm, to go to Shabbat services at Hillel's Conservative *minyan* with Larry, have lunch and then hang out in his room on the second floor in the former fraternity house where we dished and talked about men. Quietly. So we wouldn't be overheard.

My first time there, Larry had fondly pointed out to me that what was once a lounge and now used as the chapel was on one side of his room, while the men's room was on the other. "That's me all over: between the toilet and the Torah!" His room was hung about with purple paisley Indian coverlets, like someone's idea of a dope den in the '60s. All it needed was Janis Joplin and Hendrix posters, but Larry had nothing on his walls to distract your eye from the filmy purple cloth, and the way it set off his dark eyes and skin, as if he was some Silent Screen vamp lurking in a dusky fur-lined boudoir, and every shadow and fold deepened his mystery.

I had actually come to Hillel to hear a faculty speaker address the rising incidence of anti-Semitism in Europe: the cemeteries being vandalized, synagogues being fire-bombed, Jewish kids being beaten up. I guess I went because the news made me feel helpless. It was my first appearance at any campus Jewish event. It proved to be a disappointment until I met Larry. There were lots of people there, mostly Hillel nerds—the kind of guys who dressed and looked like they were still high school outcasts. Mid-point, I went looking for a bathroom, but the one downstairs was occupied. I rushed up the stairs to the second floor, where there was an Out of Order sign on the public restroom. Desperate, I pushed open the heavy door marked Private, Co-Op Members and Their Guests Only, and gratefully saw a little Men's Room sign.

Inside the blue-tiled bathroom, my urgency blurred and shifted. Standing in one of the shower stalls, drying himself off, was a guy with the shy sad grace of one of those beautiful and commanding dark-eyed imperial figures in a Byzantine mosaic: long face, hands, nose, everything. In fact, Larry's dark good looks (though not his height) came from a Sephardic grandmother, he told me later.

Right then, he said, "I don't grant interviews in the nude, you'll have to come back later."

I laughed, and went to use one of the urinals.

"Are you a guest?" he asked. I told him my name, and washing my hands, explained about the lecture, trying not to eye his body too obviously as he dried off, then wrapped the towel around his waist.

"So, Steve, aren't you going back to the lecture?"

"It was boring," I said. "How about you?"

Larry shrugged. "I don't go to meetings or rallies—it's a waste of time." Then he said, "I'm right next door." I followed him, not knowing what would happen, but hoping he would kiss me. It had never happened before—why not now?

He slipped on jeans, a Polo shirt and loafers. Then he got out Perrier from the tiny refrigerator in his closet, sliced a lime, and we sipped our glasses with the silence of old friends. He sat at his desk and I sat on his bed. Behind me, I heard some kind of hum, and when I reached back to touch the cotton-covered wall, there was a kind of vibration under my hand.

"It's the power of the Torah," Larry said, smiling. "The Ark is right on the other side of the wall."   He smiled. "I'd love to hollow out the wall, and hide in there sometime and when they opened the doors during the service I'd pop out!"

"I would kiss you, if they carried you around."

He frowned. "We can be friends, can't we? Okay, then. Listen—There are six rooms in the co-op, but Carol got mono and had to go home last week to Chicago. You could move in, if you wanted to."

I didn't. I explained that I wanted to stay in the dorm my entire four years at State. Why would I ever want to leave the constant show of male flesh, men padding around their rooms barely dressed, even naked, unconscious of how much a gift just a glimpse of beautifully defined pecs could be for me. The descriptive words themselves excited me: definition, separation, vascularity—so cold and mechanical in the abstract, but signaling such richness in the flesh.

And my roommate, Thomas, had the most casual relationship with clothes—pulling himself out of them as soon as he got back from a class, a meal, a date, wandering around in silky black bikini briefs like John Travolta's in *Saturday Night Fever*. The briefs were a great choice, I thought, because Thomas even looked a bit like Travolta (though he was somewhat more intelligent). His constant nudity—as if we were in Florida and not Michigan—knocked me out, made studying very difficult at times. Dressed for the gym, Thomas was a stunner—wearing spandex biking shorts with mesh panels that revealed a ripe high butt while clinging to his runner's quadriceps.

I loved rhapsodizing about Thomas to Larry until the day he said, "You've got the hots for a straight guy. So typical. So neurotic."

I looked away, stung, but I had to smile when Larry added, "Sorry. My parents are both shrinks—sometimes I can't help myself. I wish they'd been something else—like bakers. . . ."

"Right," I said, "And then you'd talk about buns."

He did, anyway. We both did. We talked.

My parents were proud of my regular attendance at services, especially since my brother Ronnie had married a Roman Catholic. My stock in the family had risen steadily once he started dating her. Though he was a lawyer, had always been a B+ student or better, he was no longer the star, and all I had to do to maintain my position was not cause trouble.

So I was certainly not going to tell them that I was gay. In high school, I had seen openly gay guys—or some who were just suspected of being gay—have their lockers vandalized, get beaten up in the parking lot or the locker room. One very effeminate kid, who never talked to anyone, so enraged the captain of the basketball team that he poured gasoline on the kid's head during lunch and threatened to take out his lighter. This was after *Will and Grace* had become a national hit and news reports were talking of "a new openness" about homosexuality in America. What I saw was open hatred and disgust.

Larry was lucky in a way. "My parents always knew," he said. "I was a queen at three! Clomping around in Mom's pink nightgown, with all the ruffles, and when I was twelve she found me in the attic wearing this old dress of hers—layers of black and white chiffon, kind of like that dress Grace Kelly wears in the opening of *Rear Window*. Isn't that an incredible movie—the first time I saw it, I laughed, I cried, I burst into flames!"

"But what did your mother say to you about the dress?"

"'Lunch is ready, honey—time to change.'"

"Wow, what a story."

Larry wriggled his shoulders. "Just call me Sheherazade."

And I was his captive audience, seduced by the muscled slim dark body, the penetrating mournful eyes, his hands, his lips, the flashes of camp.

Larry told me lots of stories, not to keep disaster away, as the Indian Princess did, but to spin a web. To impress me. It worked.

Like the time he was cruising in Jerusalem on *Shabbos* with a friend in the *gan*, the park, near the building housing the Chief Rabbinate, and a little black-suited, black-hatted man, *tzitzit* and *payess* flying, rushed past them and screeched to a halt like a cartoon character. "Honey, you could almost taste the dust and practically see the skid marks vibrating in the air above his pious little head." The man turned to look them up and down, checked his watch, and then shook his head sadly and raced off to services!

"Would you want to live in Israel?"

"With all those Jews? I'm not sure."

"Is that why I'm not your type? Because I'm Jewish?"

Larry shrugged.

While I didn't move out of the dorm, I started studying over in Larry's room, and staying for dinner. Even though I helped cook and clean up, no one in the co-op seemed to like me or care that I was around. No one was friendly to Larry or me. Two of the women, Jane and Sandy, were graduate students deep in studying for their comprehensive exams, so they mostly talked to each other, or sat in a stunned and prohibitive silence through meals. When Larry and I cracked a joke, both of them seemed to shudder the way someone seriously ill might do, passing happy healthy drunks on New Year's Eve.

Cleo, the third woman, dressed like a drunken biker, I thought. Larry called her Miss Faux, because "Fake!" was her favorite term of derision. The co-op members were all fake Jews, of course, but then she seemed to think that Judaism itself was a fake religion. Once she overheard me asking Larry to attend a pro-Israel rally, which I wouldn't go to alone. Larry declined, because he said that services every *Shabbos* was enough Jewish commitment for him. She laughed and shouted at us. "Praying to what? Some bullshit phony asshole God? You don't believe that shit—you're just faking it!"

"Bullshit" was her other favorite epithet. From Larry's room, I sometimes heard her down the hall shouting on her phone, or maybe just to herself, the word "Fake" alternating with "Bullshit!"—her voice like a slapping unoiled screen door. I couldn't imagine her as a landscape design student—wouldn't she be constantly ripping shrubs up to hurl them at people she disliked?

She certainly despised Larry. Another time at dinner, Larry was dishing some girl's hair on campus, and she hissed, "Faggot! What the fuck do you know about hair!"

"Sweetie," he murmured, "Faggots invented hair."

The other co-op members looked at us as if wishing we were dead. Did we have to keep causing trouble, did we have to be so gay? I assume that meant being gay at all. It irked me that they had—correctly—assumed I was gay as soon as they say me with Larry, but there wasn't anything I could do about it.

They did not talk about AIDS, which despite all the years it had been raging, still seemed like one of those bloody civil wars in a Third World country that most people couldn't find on a map. For Larry and me, it was hardly more immediate: no one we knew had AIDS, we'd never been to New York or San Francisco, we didn't subscribe to any gay publications. Our gay life was mostly in our heads, though Larry said he sometimes picked up guys in one of the library men's rooms.

Except for meals, Larry and I were rarely with the co-op members for any length of time, which seemed fine for everyone, including Rabbi Meyer, the Hillel director who was an ardent Bush supporter and had even started a campus group of Jews for Bush. Meyer was always looking at Larry and me as if we were some burdensome project in home repair he didn't quite have enough money to take on. Meyer frequently complained that none of the people in the co-op really cared about doing anything Jewish, let alone being Jewish. Each program or fund drive he tried to start there never worked. The fact that Larry regularly attended services didn't seem significant to Meyer, who counted Larry and me for the *minyan*, but never called either one of us up for an aliyah.

And Rabbi Meyer resisted any attempt to be drawn into discussing gay rights, or the question of gays and lesbians as Rabbis, or even considering that Judaism's view of homosexuality could change. Larry kept making programming suggestions to cover these issues, but Meyer said, "It's not a problem we need to deal with."

When Larry told me that, I exploded. "We're a problem?"

"That's right. That's why he's for the federal amendment banning gay marriage."

I was embarrassed to tell him that I thought my parents, who weren't wild about Bush, supported the idea of an amendment, because they somehow thought gay marriage was a national threat. I'd asked my father "How? How would it threaten you and Mom?" and he chose to take that as a joke. "Very funny," he said. "What a clown."

But knowing a rabbi was as narrow-minded and fuzzy in his thinking somehow seemed worse.

"Shit," I said.

"What'd you expect? The rabbi's got those Bush Cheney stickers on his Volvo."

"How can you live here?"

"Like the dorms are an improvement? Ever try putting up a Star of David or an El Al poster on your door? See how long it lasts. Or hang out with gay guys at a party or something and let them hear your last name. Watch their expression when they say, "'Are you Jewish?'" Larry's last name was Shlomberg, and he'd been frequently asked why he didn't change it to something "normal." Once someone even told this joke: "What's the difference between a Jew and a pizza? Pizzas don't scream when you put them in the oven."

"Steve, nobody flinched! Some people laughed, and one guy said, 'That's so gross.' I walked out."

We were sitting on his bed, where before he mentioned Rabbi Meyer, he had been telling me about giving a ride to an Israeli soldier who looked like Colin Farrell, and how they went to a nude beach. I reached across now and took his hand, brought it back to rub his long dark fingers through my hair.

But he pulled away.

"We're some pair—" he said.

"How? What do you mean?"

He sat up, his back against the cloth-draped wall, looking so still with the wild purple print dancing behind him. "We're hiding out. I've been thinking about how I never want to go to anything Jewish that you bring up—meetings, whatever. Neither one of us does anything publically gay, like the dances, the LGBT rap group. Nothing. We're hiding out."

And I hadn't told my folks that I even knew Larry or tried bringing him home for a weekend visit. Because they'd know instantly about both of us as soon as he started talking.

Larry went on. "Sometimes I feel like I'm still up in the attic, dressing up, with nobody there, just me, and an old mirror."

"Remember what you said about Beth Homo? Why don't we start it, not a synagogue, but find some more gay Jews, lesbian Jews, don't tell me there's just you and me at a school this big."

"Would two bisexuals equal a full member?"

"I'm serious!"

"I'm not, not often."

"There are all these other student organizations, why can't there be one for us?"

"But what would we do?"

I didn't know.

Larry shook his head. "Steve, I don't think I could be that Jewish, or that gay."

Hearing those words, I realized I could have said them with as much honesty. I thought about how often I'd been glad I had red hair, blue eyes and freckles, could even pass for Irish, and glad my last name wasn't Cohen, Schwartz, Feinberg, but White, an Ellis Island gift; about all the friends whose Jewish jokes I hadn't objected to; all the films and books on the Holocaust I'd avoided; all the images of bearded black-hatted Jews on television I'd been repulsed by; all the discussions about Mideast politics I'd pretended not to care about; all the silence and lying, years of it, years of dimly hoping somehow that I wouldn't exactly have to be Jewish—and yet snatching up books on Jewish history, or novels by Jewish writers, reading them with the furtive embarrassment and confusion of little kids talking about sex.

It was the same with being gay. There was the way I had circled Gay Literature sections in bookstores, hovering, nervous, terrified someone would see me, report me, announce on the loudspeaker: "There's a faggot in Aisle 7." I'd snatched up Andrew Holleran's *Dancer from the Dance* with relief when it showed up in one store's Fiction section, but been afraid to buy it, because the paperback had a bare-chested man on the cover, and I'd even thought of trying to steal it. I bought six other books as camouflage. I read books like Holleran's in secret. Seeing any gay character on television or in a movie made me wince, no matter how he or she was portrayed: I felt humiliated and exposed. It only took one article or a brief news report about AIDS to spoil my entire day. Even if I hadn't read the article, or had turned off the radio, the TV, the assault had touched me and humbled me.

I tried telling all of this to Larry, who didn't move to hug me or even take my hand.

"I feel the same way," he said, eyes down. "Basically."

And we sat there in silence, not looking at each other, like the only two kids at a prom who have no date but are ashamed to even smile at each other, too miserable to dance.

The Pathfinder

"Do not sleep with any of the guests!" my sister Stephanie warns me. She's always been a little haughty with me; it's her being seventeen years older and more like a third parent. She's also a Young Republican, and it's not that long after Nixon's waved goodbye from the helicopter steps, so maybe she thinks chaos is headed her way, too.

What's going on is that my sister's having a huge party, with people from her publishing house (one of New York's oldest), agents, and some famous authors, she hopes. She's angling for a promotion to senior editor, and I suppose she thinks I could queer her chances, so to speak.

Her voice is soft but very firm now, as if she's a grande dame dealing with a potentially recalcitrant servant. She certainly has the apartment to back up the attitude.

It's palatial: 5000 square feet on Sutton Place, in ten large turn-of-the-century high-ceilinged rooms overlooking the East River, each room trimmed with ornate molding, the doors and door handles enormous, ceilings high, and every parquet floor as beautiful as marquetry cabinets you'd see in a museum. The 20' x 20' foyer is marble-floored (black and white squares); the guest toilet, hung with hunting prints, is up three stairs behind a trompe l'oeil door; the living room seems as large as an Olympic-size swimming pool, with six embrasured windows framing the lights of the 59th Street Bridge, and decorated in expensive Empire reproductions: a wilderness of pale yellow silk and burnished sphinx heads and wings. The whole apartment is pristine and exquisite, the kind of home that makes you wish you were Greta Garbo, haunted and tragically beautiful in a trailing gown. Well, that's what I wish, anyway.

Obviously it's not her salary that makes all this possible.

I can understand that she's very nervous, trying to keep all the details for the party clear in her head (flowers, music, the constantly shifting menu, trouble with a caterer), but thinking I would sleep with one of her guests strikes me as funny, because I've never slept with anyone, male or female, guest or host. The Sexual Revolution may be blazing all around us in New York, but it hasn't taken me prisoner yet. At twenty, my homosexuality is like the miraculous handful of fire primitive men supposedly carried and guarded across desolate savannahs—something precious, fragile, strange.

Now my sister, she's talked about it endlessly, looking at different theories of homosexuality, different explanations, as if she were worrying at a Chinese puzzle box, hoping that somehow she'll turn it over and open the right drawers to find— Well, frankly, I think my sister wants the box to be empty. She wants to explain my homosexuality away, make it disappear, like a phase, a fad, an adolescent passion for collecting stamps or dissecting frogs.

It hasn't gone away, but I feel so caught up in her struggle to keep me from "making a big mistake" (our family taboo) that in hot and humpy mid-'70s New York, I'm like someone driving a station wagon through one of those theme park zoos—with the animals so fascinatingly close and thrilling—but always viewed through panes of glass. You see, when our parents retired early to Albuquerque, and I got accepted at Columbia, I decided to move in with Stephanie and her husband Martin, so she feels Responsible. My sister does not want me to make any mistakes, it's the taboo that her perfect life has never violated. First there was Radcliffe, then marriage to a Harvard Law man whose family owned a chain of New England inns, then her brief but incredibly lucrative modeling career (she was a perfect size eight with "lingerie legs") which helped them buy the apartment.

I can't blame holding back on her, entirely. I'm afraid, too.

See—I didn't even masturbate until I was fifteen, because I knew exactly what I would long for as my hand traveled up and down my cock, knew that once I had crossed the line and shot my wad with a man in my thoughts (forget about even in my room!), I would be doomed.

But my junior year honors English class forced me to come out, at least to myself, when I was assigned James Fenimore Cooper's *The Pathfinder*. Don't laugh! I had a crush on my teacher, Mr. Ness, who also taught gym. He was short, stocky, built like a wrestler, curly dark hair foaming at his open collar, his cuffs. A beautiful brute I might think if I met him now. Once I got a mesmerizing glimpse of him in the locker room as he padded naked from the showers. He was so beautiful I was as stunned as if by the news of a tragedy, sitting there at my locker, head down, dizzy. I heard what I thought was the slam of his locker, eventually, and that brought me back, a little. After that, I started fantasizing showering with him, soaping up his dark, broad back because he had a sore spot he wanted me to massage. . . .

Anyway, something about the image of Natty Bumpo and his Indian friend in *The Pathfinder*, alone out there in the forest, took me over, and reading that book in bed early one morning, I ripped my pants open and helplessly jerked myself off in a literary frenzy, my thoughts a blur of Mr. Ness and trees and moccasins and running water. I did it again three times that afternoon, twice that evening, and in a few days, my cock was swollen to twice its normal size, and still I did it, through the pain, my hand making only infinitesimal movements across the rim of my cock head—(which was all I could stand by then)—and even that was enough to make me come, though pitifully, a mere drop or two (you can imagine how I went wild when I found *The Song of the Loon*).

In a week I calmed down, I gave in, but I never risked touching another guy, resisted every opportunity—and there were lots. The guys who'd have you over to their house after school, talking about "pussy" non-stop, and read aloud from SCREW magazine, leering; or the ones who liked to try out wrestling holds on you; and the ones constantly talking about how horny they were, about their boners, even in the locker room, naked, laughing, flicking themselves and saying "Down boy!" Each one of those moments of possibility was like a sunken treasure chest waiting for me to dive deep and thrust open the coral-encrusted lid, plunging my hands into gold. But I stayed on the surface—I was no Jacques Cousteau.

Mr. Ness's class, we read Melville after Cooper and I was terrified by lines in *Moby Dick*: "in the soul of man there lies one insular Tahiti, full of peace and joy, but encompassed by all the horrors of the half known life. God keep thee! Push not off from that isle, thou canst never return!"

So it didn't help that when I came out to my sister, she freaked. We were on the phone; I had called her very late from our parents' house in Riverdale. I was sixteen.

"I want to tell you something, something personal."

"Are you having girl trouble?" She laughed indulgently, as if she were somebody's granny rocking on a back porch, face creased with mirth over the foibles of The Young.

"You could call it that, I guess."

"What's her name?"

"There isn't anybody. That's the problem."

"Now honey, you've got to be more confident about yourself, not tear yourself down, and you'll find someone, someone really nice who'll—"

"But I want to find a guy."

"Oh my God! I dreamed something like this just last week!"

That threw me. Like most people, I was warily curious to know what I had done or been in someone else's dream, as if it were a parallel universe on *Star Trek*. Temporarily diverted, I asked, "What happened?"

"It was disgusting. Believe me, Ben. Listen, we've got to get you into psychoanalysis. You can't be a— You're just confused."

I wanted to say, "I'm horny," but I didn't feel the moment could bear that much honesty.

"You were a model," I said. "Didn't you work with gay guys?"

"Sure, but they kept it to themselves!" She ranted and raved for awhile, leaving me feeling as unfairly picked on as the one kid pulled out of a crowd of troublemakers by the principal.

She kept pushing therapy, but I told her that talking to a counselor at school—who was helpful, and not shocked—was what had given me the courage to tell her. She then suggested reading, as if there were some magical book whose every turned page would strip all this "nonsense" and "trouble" away from me. I told her about having discovered *Giovanni's Room, Another Country, The City and The Pillar* (I didn't mention *The Pathfinder*).

She had me come down the next weekend, and she and Martin took me to see *A Little Night Music*; we had dinner at Lutèce. Somehow, I think she expected all this coddling might purge me of perversion: as if she wanted to show me that being gay would in some way bar me from the finer things life offered. Though why she imagined only straight people dined well and enjoyed the theater, I'm not sure. At the Sondheim show, I was hypnotized not just by the music and those swirling clever lyrics, but by the audience full of couples and groups of clearly gay men. Afterwards, whenever I listened to the cast album, I lost myself in the vague images of the wonderful lives all those men must have.

Strolling through the Guggenheim Museum that weekend, while my brother-in-law was working at home, Stephanie told me, "Martin thinks it's just a phase. He said he had very close friends when he was your age, and they . . . did things."

"But I haven't done anything!"

Now that was a mistake, because from the moment of my confession, she was determined to keep my body undefiled, and my secret safe from Mom and Dad, who as Sociology professors at Fordham University surely would have at least heard of homosexuality. Not the way my sister had it: "This will kill them, Ben, you can't tell them. Besides," she concluded, "There is nothing to tell." I suppose any other approach of hers would have been alien to how we were brought up: avoiding unpleasant information. A newsletter, produced by someone who didn't live with us, would really have been best in our family. We then could each read it privately, without embarrassment or surprise, and not have to deal with even the mildest of confrontations. We were living some archaic ideal of behavior, like those New Yorkers in the Edith Wharton novel I read in senior year of high school, the people "who considered nothing was more ill-bred than 'scenes,' except the behavior of those who gave rise to them." By that standard, though Stephanie had taken my coming out poorly, it was my fault for having forced her off balance.

The root of the problem, I suppose, was my mother's desperate attempt to fit in. She was the daughter of Russian Jews who had fled a pogrom for America. It was something I had only discovered during the Yom Kippur War in 1973, when my mother watched the news with a fever I found compelling and ugly. "That could be me, there," she said, and when she gave me her stingy explanation, I felt no inclination to ask anything more, just anger and contempt. I asked Stephanie how long she had known we were Jewish, and her "Always," made me once again feel insignificant. For years in our family, I would hear something discussed at dinner and say, "What? When did that happen?" only to be answered with, "We told you already. Don't you remember?" The question always quashed my resistance; though I was sure I hadn't been told—about a new car, a promotion, an upcoming publication—I couldn't insist, because that would make me feel even more unimportant. And now, this.

I knew nothing especially positive about Jews, though I understood that technically, because of my mother's birth, I was Jewish whether I liked it or not. Her blurted confession left me intolerably vulnerable; I cringed when I heard Jewish jokes, and Christmas began to seem menacing, the source of conflict and shame.

I began to see everything my mother did or said as dishonest. She wasn't Catholic, but had chosen to teach at a Catholic college. Her grace and attention to clothes was no longer impressive but a quietly hysterical attempt to be invisible, I decided, like those Jews hiding out during the War, desperately stifling their own or someone else's coughing to keep from being discovered by the Nazis. She lived in fear, I thought; the smooth low voice, the impeccable hair, the careful jewelry were all weapons in a battle against discovery. It was crazy to me, and my father and Stephanie had conspired in Mom's craziness, and in keeping me ignorant.

Soon after Mom's revelation, I was relieved when they decided to retire to the Southwest because of Dad's health, relieved that I would not have to continually pretend to be unconcerned about the past. But moving in with my sister was not much of a liberation since she and Martin were not very different from my parents: generally benign and uninvolved, and always, implicitly superior. And like my parents, they weren't at all physical, touching only to shake hands, or accidentally, when passing something at the table.

I don't really know anyone coming to Stephanie's big party, and I'm not excited at the possibility of meeting anyone famous. She's said it was "semi-formal," but I gag at the thought of a suit or even a shirt and tie, and settle for jeans tucked into black knee-high boots, my best *Saturday Night Fever* shirt and a matching long scarf tied with one of those brass double rings. And lots of 4711, of course. Having taken my hair out of its ponytail, I think that I do indeed look like Keith Richards, the way Stephanie has said. We've both seen The Stones in Madison Square Garden that year, my sister blushing when Mick played with that enormous balloon phallus—as if she were a nurse in charge of a shell-shocked World War One soldier whose convalescence was disturbed by a sudden thunderclap.

The night of her party, the party that becomes my party, I feel like a child too young to read the labels at a museum: baffled, overwhelmed. I stay in my room at the other end of the apartment until an hour after guests start arriving. Then I just wander the enormous noisy crowded apartment, my boots clacking on the shiny, intricate parquet floors. People seem to be enjoying themselves—talking loudly, with their mouths and their free hands. Some jerk in a green velvet tux sees me and says to no one in particular, "I thought this party was "semi-formal." "No," I say, smiling. "Semi-normal. Welcome to my nightmare." Stephanie, in rose silk and pearls, her hair up, looks as good as when she was a cover girl; she just shrugs when she sees how I'm dressed. Martin doesn't seem to notice—he's too busy telling a joke about President Ford.

In the kitchen I find a handsome man, who half-turns from the sink, smiling: "Hi! I'm Rick. Rick Fischer." He is washing out some pots. "You're Ben, Stephanie's brother, don't you remember me? I'm sort of your cousin, pretty far removed, but tonight I'm Mr. Chef. Have you tried the hors d'oeuvres? The caviar salad dressing? The salmon mousse? No? Are you on a diet or something?" Rick is tall, slender, pale and freckled, with a round open face and masses of curly, carrot-colored hair. "No," he continues, as if I've asked. "I'm not Irish. Jewish, but you already know that, don't you? There are Jewish redheads, my Dad, for one, though it's not very common, and there's lots of folk superstition from Europe among Jews about how redheads are in league with the Devil and can't be trusted. But you can trust me."

One of the anonymous-looking waiters comes in with a tray, murmurs something to Rick and then departs.

I sit at the messy, dish-laden table as if I've been struck. I don't remember having met Rick before, which seems remarkable, because he's so beautiful and so obviously, triumphantly gay. And close, just a few feet away from my hands, my mouth. I want him. I feel hot and shaken. Rick's simple sexy chattiness, and the thick outline in his jeans down the inside of his right thigh, have utterly exposed me, annihilated my years of reserve and fear, and Stephanie's warnings, like the wind tearing away newspapers from a sleeping bum.

"Hey," he asks, squinting, "Are you all right?"

"I'm almost twenty," I manage to say, as if those words mark a lifetime of failure. "And I've never—" I feel as stupid and gross as Henrik in the Sondheim musical, when he laments, "Doesn't anything begin?"

Rick frowns and steps a bit closer, wiping his hands on his jeans and then his eyes widen with understanding. His arms cross, he cocks his head at me as if I'm a challenging exhibit in a gallery. "You're a virgin?"

I nod, turning red.

Now Rick stands in front of me, framed by the gleaming red and gold kitchen like a dancer gracefully, powerfully poised before the curtain to take his bows. The hired pianist is playing "Night and Day" out in the cavernous living room. "Well, sweetie," Rick says, grinning, "We can fix that. I mean if Nixon could resign, anything is possible in this great land of ours. Martin suggested I sleep in the guest room tonight, rather than shlep all my stuff home when I'm tired. Are you down that hallway? Then wait for me later. I'll find you."

He moves to the refrigerator, and rooting around in there for something, he knocks out a half-carton of eggs, spilling yolks, whites and bits of shell at my feet. "I'm always doing that!" he laughs, completely relaxed (I would be cursing at myself for such clumsiness, hot under my sister's disapproving silence). "I'll take care of it," he says, getting paper towels and a sponge to quickly clean up the mess. "We'll make the omelette later, huh?"

I drink in the dimly-lit study, "waiting," for hours, perhaps. It's a cold sort of room. My own room is crammed with masses of worn and underlined paperbacks. Here, the books are all objects, beautiful and untouched, chosen for their value, shopped for, not savored and enjoyed. The room makes Stephanie's editing job seem too much like a caprice.

People look in now and then, and eventually, well after midnight, I wander out to where just a few guests are sitting in that lovely afterglow of a good party, snacking on their favorite party foods, steeping themselves in the view. I've missed Grace Paley, Stephanie whispers, but I don't care because I want Rick. Martin is sprawled on the floor by the fire, his broad handsome face flashed by light. Off behind him, Rick's lolling on a settee, massaging his bare long feet, while accepting compliments about the food. His feet are incredible—enormous, high arched, like something out of The Last Judgment. I can't believe how turned on I am by the power and nakedness of those feet.

I wave at everyone and say goodnight, hoping that's a clear enough signal to Rick.

My room shares a connecting black and gold bath with the guest room, and washing up, I keep expecting Rick to come find me, but I end up crawling into bed and falling asleep with a light on.

"I'm done," someone's saying. It's Rick. "Your sister's pleased—it went great." In a lower voice, he says, "They're asleep."

I can almost hear the hum of traffic filling the room.

He's sitting on the edge of the bed. He takes my hand, turns it over as if to read my palm. "You're so pretty," he says, and then, strangely, starts to tell me about his cooking career as if it's a bedtime story that's supposed to soothe and calm me.

"You're so young!" he says. "I'm thirty-two." He pulls my other hand out from under the cover. "Nice arms," he says.

I want to tell him about all the times I could have had sex, or at least the times I'd imagined it was possible, and how fear has kept me chained, so that he'll know how much this means to me.

But I say nothing. I watch him stand up and undress. Rick has all the ease of someone whose body is no source of shame or fear, and I long to be that comfortable in myself. He's utterly hairless except for the bright patch of pubic hair, and his fat wrinkled penis, with a dark blunt head, hangs half-swollen between his thighs. I stare. He's so much bigger than I am, but it seems appropriate, not embarrassing.

I feel very sober and intent now; I want to drown in his flesh. Rick moves back to the bed, kissing, stroking, his slim body very warm as he slips under the covers with me. Watching his expression as he touches and explores my body is incredibly exciting—he seems so pleased to be with me.

When he says, "Can I fuck you?" he's already crouched and licking my ass before I've even finished saying "I think so, yes." It's astonishing to feel his tongue enter me, and his hot forehead against my balls.

"Is there any oil or something in the bathroom?"

I know the cabinet has Oil of Olay, but I'm not sure what he would need. Rick jumps up and comes quickly back with Vaseline, which we apply to his cock with the intensity of two besieged fighters preparing a Molotov cocktail to hurl at a tank.

What does Petra say about her first time in *A Little Night Music?* Something about it being "better than a Rolly Coaster." Well, that's how I feel, rushed into the sky and then plunged downward too quickly to breathe, whirled upside down, all of it—though it's Rick who is riding me. I can't focus on what's happening. I'm too dazzled, and details keep escaping me.

It hurts, at times, but when he sweeps into me with a final small triumphant groan, I don't care. Rick kisses my eyes, my nose, my forehead, as if learning my face with his lips, and then starts to jerk me off. He stays inside me after I come, and I feel that this one orgasm is a manifesto, a declaration of independence from my family, my past. I'm free, or at least no longer the same frightened guy who walked out into the party.

But then, with my thighs back and legs in the air, resting on his shoulders, I suddenly feel as helpless as a crab on a beach flipped belly up by vicious kids armed with rocks. He withdraws just then, and hugs me.

"Beautiful legs, beautiful ass," he says, and I feel as joyous as a puppy leaping in a snowbank, digging its muzzle down and splattering the snow up into the air.

We lie there awhile, he strokes my chest.

"Let's shower," he says, just as I think I could fall asleep, and though I follow him into the bathroom, let him wash my hair and soap me all over, it's like a dream, even when he turns from me and leans over, bracing his arms on the tiled wall, with the hot water splattering around us, and says, "Your turn."

I'm ready.

Back in bed, I'm no longer sleepy, and I keep touching him, a little surprised that he hasn't disappeared. The heavy, strange weight of his cock in my hand seems to anchor the moment in reality.

I say, "You know, I'm Jewish, too, sort of." But then I realize it's no surprise for Rick if he's a cousin of ours.

Rick's branch of the family is actively Jewish, and he tells me about it.

"Doesn't it bother you?" he wonders. "Having a Christmas tree, pretending to be something you're not?"

"I don't know what I am, really, anymore. But it's not like we ever went to church or anything." I try to explain our vague upbringing, the way I see that our mother settled on no other religion in contrast with Judaism, just an absence.

"Did you always know you were Jewish? You found out when you were seventeen?! Weren't you pissed off?"

I hesitate.

"Well it pisses me off! I was at Stephanie's wedding, but you probably don't remember us. She almost didn't invite me and my folks because my Dad's a cantor. Your mother told us to try being a little less obvious, you know? And I swear she had people at the wedding keeping an eye on us, so we wouldn't get too close to Martin or his parents—because they're so anti-Semitic. At the wedding I heard Martin's father bet someone that the Jews would get wiped out in Israel. It was 1967—it was just before the War. I wanted to deck him."

This is all new to me. I don't know what to say.

"Boy, you need dynamite," Rick says. "Or serious drugs. You have to open up. Which reminds me." As we've talked, his cock has been swelling in my hand so that I can hardly hold it. Now he rolls me onto my stomach. "Beautiful," he says, as he slides right in.

The first thing I hear in the morning is a phone—Stephanie and Martin's phone (I have my own line).

And then there are quick footsteps down the hall and when the door swings open I leap out of bed, as if standing there naked, with Rick groggy but unmistakably in the bed behind me, will hide or disguise everything.

"It's Mom and Dad—" Stephanie says, even while taking us both in. She rushes out of the room, and grabbing my robe from the back of the door, I follow her, belting it.

"Stephanie!"

She is in the kitchen, trembling, having just hung up the phone with "He'll call you later, he's still asleep." To me, she says, with her teeth grinding, "I can't believe it." She slowly spins around the kitchen, hands thrust into her skirt pockets as if she's afraid they might punch or break something. "In my house."

"I live here, too."

"And he's your cousin! Our cousin."

Somehow, we are no longer brother and sister, individuals with a past, but actors in some tired generic family drama: one accuses, the other denies. I sit down, exhausted by the thought of arguing with her.

"It was just one time," I say. "I didn't even like it. Really."

"Did he force you?"

I shake my head, looking down but trying to keep her in focus, hoping she will not see that I'm lying as I never have before. Her anger, her resistance suddenly dissipate. She seems to feel sorry for me now, and comes forward a little.

"We'll talk about this later."

When I return to my room, Rick has taken a quick shower and is already dressed. I'm not sure what to say, or how to touch him, now that I've denied the importance of our night together to Stephanie. I feel like a liar and a creep.

"It was fun," Rick says. "But I should split, huh?"

I hear him off in the kitchen, gathering pots and pans, knives, chatting with Stephanie, both of them sounding very amiable and relaxed—perhaps because I'm not there, intruding my awkwardness. After he's gone, we have a lot to do this Saturday, cleaning up with Stephanie's maid whatever didn't get done right after the party, and the vacuuming, mopping, wiping, loading the dishwasher several times take us through the day. We are fueled by leftovers (which Stephanie does not talk about, since that would bring up Rick).

I keep wishing we'd had a romantic parting, something at least more personal than his simply saying "Bye" and patting my cheek.

It's only toward evening that I realize he hasn't given me his phone number or said anything specific about getting together.

That night, I wait. I watch TV with Martin and Stephanie, feeling a little like a juvenile delinquent they are guarding from rushing down to the park to rejoin his gang. We chat about the programs, and Martin asks me about my classes—questions he's asked before, and asks now as if to remind me that my life is waiting for me on Monday, the safe and undisturbing life I was living until that moment.

"I never called Mom and Dad!" I realize at a commercial.

"I called them back," Stephanie tells me, calm.

"What'd you say?"

"That you were out, with friends. That everything's fine."

Since our parents' move to the Southwest, they have become like what I imagine grandparents might be: more distant than ever, cheerful and full of vague noisy approval for the smallest things I do. No matter what I say to them, I seem to repeat myself, as if shouting to people who can't hear very well. It's depressing.

Stephanie and I do talk a little at night, but I continue lying, as if all the anguished conversations she and I have had the last few years didn't take place.

Several times she tells me, "I feel so awful that it happened in my house."

"At least it wasn't one of your guests, like you were worried about."

In bed, returned to where Rick and I slept together, I imagine going on vacations with him, sharing an apartment, seeing movies and plays. I think about what it would be like to wear a bracelet that he gave me, and wonder how long it'll be before he thinks of it.

Late Sunday morning, Martin and Stephanie have gone out for brunch and to shop a little, so I'm alone. I hurry to the desk in their marble-floored foyer, and take out the leather-bound address book to look for Rick's number. Now, more than any other time since he left, the sex returns: I feel opened, entered, lost, almost trembling as I sit at the desk and dial his number.

He's home, and he laughs when I say it's me: "But I was just going to call you! Are you in trouble with Stephanie and Martin? Are they mad at me? She was cool when I left, but—"

I tell him he has hardly been mentioned, and that I'm alone. "Why don't you come over?"

"Sure! Half an hour."

It's an hour. During which I shower, change my sheets, put on too much cologne, wash it off, put more on again, change the radio station several times, and rush to the door every time I think I hear the elevator stop at our floor.

I'm glad there are splendid flower arrangements left over from the party, all through the house: colorful and lush.

When he shows up, he grins and gives me a big arm-flapping hug that leaves me a little shaky, and right there at the door, he's suddenly down on his knees, pulling down my zipper and tugging at my pants—with his coat still on. His hands roam my ass, my thighs, my belly. It doesn't take much for me to come, pushing against his head, my hands deep in his curly red hair.

"Jesus," I breathe out, leaning back against the wall, my cock half-hard and cum smearing the head. Still on his knees, he licks, gently now.

"I wanted to call you," he says, "But I didn't want to talk to Stephanie. We're not really friends, you know, I think she just called me because she thought it'd be cheaper—or maybe some other caterer canceled, I'm not sure."

I manage to pull myself together, and offer him champagne I have on ice. He expertly uncorks the Bollinger and pours like a waiter. Sitting in the kitchen, I feel like a conspirator—like the times I smoked dope with friends my parents didn't approve of, back in Riverdale, the basement reeking from all the incense cones.

"Have you ever done drag?" Rick asks me, and though I know what he means, I'm surprised, and a little embarrassed, because I've often wondered what it would be like. "You'd be great! You have your sister's bones, and your eyes are much sexier."

While I'm blushing—from his compliments, from the champagne—he pulls out his wallet, and shows me a picture of an elegant woman in a sequined evening gown and tiara. "That's Glorene," Rick says. "Green's her color."

"You're beautiful," I say. "Both of you, I mean—" I imagine myself being dressed by Rick, and him fastening a necklace on me. . . .

He crosses his arms. "Ben-Ben, what'm I going to do with you? I keep thinking of taking you to bars, to the docks, everyplace, but I also want to take you to my synagogue. It's so weird."

"How about both? You'd get extra points." I hand back his picture.

"You're so cute!" He reaches over to ruffle my hair, and I try to look even cuter. I've downed several glasses of champagne by now, and I blurt out, "Will you give me a bracelet?"—as if I'm a little kid in a sandbox asking another to be his friend.

"Well, I had thought of handcuffs, honey, but let's go to bed and talk about it."

When Stephanie and Martin come back, Rick has gone, and we've made plans to have a late dinner that night. Putting her coat away in the foyer, my sister asks what I've been doing.

"I called Rick. I invited him over. We went to bed and I liked it, even more than the first time. He's got tickets to see Nureyev next weekend and I'm going." I do not add that Rick has seen Nureyev dancing shirtless in a disco, burning someone's nipple with a cigarette.

Stephanie glares at me, as fierce as the statue of some avenging angel.

I say, "I'm calling Mom and Dad."

Stephanie frowns, hesitant. "You want a vacation out there?"

I can't believe she doesn't understand where I'm headed. "No, I want to tell them what happened . . . and I want to talk to Mom about her parents."

Now Stephanie looks disgusted, as if I've revealed stealing money from her purse. But even with her face ruled by distaste for what I've said, she looks beautiful, untouched. I see her now as our mother's greatest success, a front, a shield against her own threatening past.

"You can't do that to Mom," Stephanie says, lips tight. She means, of course, that I can't do that to all of us, I can't question the rules, the silence, that have shaped our family's history. I feel reckless, free, as if I am the child of an alcoholic who finally has the courage to scrap a lifetime of avoidance, hesitation, untruth, who can say at last that something is deeply, darkly wrong.

Standing there, I want to snap out something cruel and defiant.

But then I feel as sorry for Stephanie as if she's Sondheim's "poor old Fredrik" discovering his young wife has left him, the delirious fantasy of his middle age stripped away, destroyed.

Martin has drifted off to make himself a drink.

"I have to call them," I say. "I want you to sit with me when I do."

"I can't."

I head for the study to make my call and she adds, "Not yet."

But despite that, she follows me to the phone.

The Story of a Plant

Dad had not wanted anything alive at home, except us. No pets, no plants. The long Riverside Drive apartment facing the park, the Hudson and the squat dark factories of New Jersey was not a farm, he said, or even a house: "So why pretend?"

Jerry and I didn't understand the notion that denied us the hamster, the rabbits, birds, puppy, cats, guinea pigs, African violets, spider pants and Boston ferns we had craved at one time or another. Dad didn't warn us of responsibilities we would neglect, he simply said we lived in a city and that was that.

In case you're wondering if we grew up to be veterinarians, you're close. Jerry majored in Agricultural economics at Cornell and spent two years with the Peace Corps in Gabon. His French is charming, I've been told, but he speaks most fluently about snakes and skin ailments.

My revolt was more modest. After graduating from Smith College I settled in Western Massachusetts on four acres of deer-crossed land in a stone house with a cockatoo named Max, and four Cairn terriers. My husband Jerry teaches in the Jewish Studies program at the University of Massachusetts in Amherst and he dreams of owning his own horse.

But this is not just my story, it's the story of a plant.

Remember how "Kremlinologists" used to analyze official pictures of Soviet leaders to see who was standing where at state occasions and spend hours guessing what it meant? Well I was like that growing up—for a while. A parentologist. Jerry was too busy playing with blocks, making up songs, talking to his teddy bears, and later, just reading, to study our parents. That was what I did, and even in first grade I felt that they had secrets and powers I could discover if I was careful enough. My teacher said I stared too much for a girl—I'm not exactly sure what that means. Dad, slim and prematurely grey, and whose engineering work I never understood, was pretty reserved. He seemed most comfortable reading a newspaper or napping on the living room couch, or just gazing out at the river and the Palisades as if there were something free and admirable in the view. Mom was one of those warm quiet women who baked and smiled, the kind who people with crazy mothers always say they wished for.

Well let me tell you, it's not what they think. For years while I'd sit in the kitchen babbling about school and Mom fueled me with strudel, chocolate cake, fruit tarts and simple questions, I guess I waited for her reserve to burst like a dam. But I was wrong imagining she had built up a flood of feeling. She was really more like a clear unhurried stream. She looked it, too: pale oval face, blonde hair pulled loosely back and up, wide pale eyes, like one of those tall and graceful women in a Botticelli you could never imagine shouting, or stepping on the gas.

Despite all the treats, I was hungry, reading her pauses for a clue to what I thought she had hidden away from the world. Sometimes she seemed as beautiful and exotic to me as the great aunts and cousins in her photo album, magical in clothes, hairstyles and hats of other years.

I suppose her silence, and Dad's, had something to do with Jerry playing by himself so much, imagining he was one of ten children called "The Jerries," and why he liked reading *Cheaper by the Dozen* over and over, and later on, Dickens or any book that seethed with life and noise. And I suppose the silence had some connection to my wanting to become a writer.

Well, picture us one Sunday, Mom baking, Dad asleep with a section of The New York Times dripping onto the floor, Jerry cheerful in his room, building block castles and knocking them down, me staring out my window at the wide still Hudson down which barges poured like honey from a jar. I was ten that Sunday when Mom got her plant, going through a plain squinty-eyed stage that left such brutal snapshots as evidence.

Mom had gone out into the hall with the garbage and found a one-inch cluster of leaves broken off at the black door of the incinerator chute.

"They threw out a plant," she said with the grim wonder of someone coming upon a desecrated gravestone. She held out the pale green and white survivor. "Your father doesn't like plants," she went on as I followed her to the kitchen. "He hates things dying."

They were simple but frightening words for me.

I sat at the kitchen table. Mom took out a small glass, poured in some water and gently set the plant bit in as if finishing the last icing rose for a cake. She put the glass on the wide soot-dusty sill, watched it so intently I thought she was praying. I sensed in her then the same tenderness that could make me cry when my dolls got chipped or bruised and she held them.

I rushed to hug her.

Dad was cool that afternoon when he saw her plant. "Why waste your time? It's so ugly."

But Mom only shrugged and the little plant stayed. The first week, when it began to root, Jerry tried to make it fly, and asked if it was a vegetable, but the plant survived, and Mom set it into a pot tiny as a toy when she judged it ready.

"Do you like plants?" I asked her.

Washing soil from her fingers, she said, "I don't know. Growing up in the Bronx we had flowers sometimes, from a shop. Birthdays, holidays." She smiled. "With ribbons."

"Dad doesn't buy you flowers."

"No."

Dad bought clothes, watches, things that could be repaired, always things. Our apartment was more the expression of his taste than Mom's: monochrome, somber, uncluttered, as if the glistening linoleum floors were those of a museum gallery and we were only visitors. He was like that when he cooked, spending serious hours slicing, tasting, stirring; he allowed no conversation or interference. The nights he cooked his complicated and spicy Czech meals, I was sick with fear that I wouldn't understand the care and subtlety of his work. Jerry always messed up his food, young or old; only Mom could dreamily close her eyes, murmur *prima*, kissing her fingertips like someone in a movie. I got the feeling that Dad was either dangerous or very sad those evenings, and Mom was taking care.

"Your grandparents owned a well-known restaurant in Prague," Dad told me once, as if claiming descent from Michelangelo, or at least a king.

This was how we always learned about the past—in headlines. The stories themselves never came, but over the years I pieced together a terrible sketch of his war years. First there was Munich in 1938, betrayal. Fervid supporters of the Czech nation, his parents ultimately committed suicide when it crumbled. He tried to flee eastward to the Russia of his ancestors, but couldn't get across the border, and was almost killed by a Soviet officer with a hand grenade. There were escapes, disguises, and finally he made it to the house of distant cousins in Budapest, on *Shabbos*. It was there he was captured and sent to Bergen-Belsen. Even what little I knew was wild, incomprehensible. This calm silent man had not only been close to death, but immersed in it like the three angels in the Book of Daniel who emerged from the "burning fiery furnace" unsinged.

Once I heard him say something about the War to a neighbor: "That was another man, not me."

It must have been, I thought.

The plant flourished tentatively, grew too big for the pot, but still seemed fragile to me, uncertain.

"Trauma," Mom explained. "Shock, when something bad happens." She added that *Traum* was German for dream, and I wondered what a plant could dream of.

That very summer, the Russians invaded Czechoslovakia, and while for me it was only strange news, Dad broke down. He read every report and stared at the television like someone going blind storing up his last minutes of sight. "First the Nazis," he kept saying. "Now the Russians." The War, the nightmare had come back.

I heard Dad late at night in their bedroom, talking, talking, an endless stream of words as if he could never say enough. And Mom's softer voice, calming him, perhaps, or maybe saying, "Go on, I'm here." That's what I would have said.

Dad went off at night for long drives because he couldn't sleep, gave up reading entirely, and seemed as crushed and diminished as the little plant had been when Mom found it. Jerry cried whenever Dad tried to hold him. Dad watched Mom tend her plant, now almost half a foot high, with new shiny leaves, watched her set it in the tub for its monthly light sprinkle of "Rain," watched her croon to it, as if he were someone in a wheelchair eyeing people walking by in the rich unconscious gift of free movement.

A year later, on a night treacherous with rain, Dad's car skidded on the West Side Highway into a lamp post. Death was instant, the police said, but I wondered how they knew, or even what the word meant. Tell me, what is an instant of death?

For a few years, while we lived on the insurance money and Mom tried to figure out what next, Jerry did poorly in school, had trouble sleeping, fought with me and cursed. Mom filled the house with music, the stereo or radio was always playing Frank Sinatra and Big Bands, and I became a viciously good student, as if forcing the world to acknowledge me.

The plant grew from pot to pot. We almost had a ceremony with each transplanting, Jerry setting out the newspaper on the kitchen table, me making lemonade, Mom slipping on the gardening gloves we had bought her. When it was a foot and a half high, Jerry and I got a bamboo stand one Mother's Day and we set it in the living room where it seemed to glow with the life of the park across the street.

Mom eventually recovered the couch and chair in a floral pattern as if encouraging her plant. It grew, oh it grew "like nobody's business," as Dad might have said, large enough, strong and broad enough for Jerry and me to take cuttings. Mom decided to go to Teacher's College and when she finished, we moved to Long Island where she taught first grade and I entered high school.

The day I went off to Smith, I took my cutting. Like Jerry, I had come to associate the plant with Dad, even though he didn't want it, even though Mom had been the one to rescue and nurture it. When I graduated summa cum laude in journalism, and found a job on a newspaper here in Northampton, Mom told me that Dad had lost his entire family by 1945, even his friends. "*Bakanter un farvanter*," I could hear him saying in Yiddish with his rare smile (because the phrase rhymed): friends and relations. While I had guessed at the depth of his losses, I had never felt brave enough to press for more, I had just waited, and now I regretted that his family history was closed to me.

"He didn't trust life," Mom said.

I was twenty-two, finally as pretty as her and full of my own wisdom and achievements, so I said, "Why should he?"

Now, five years later, with Jerry's wife Ruth expecting her second child, me my first, and both of us with plants that have become large imposing trees, six feet high in their terra cotta tubs, I realize he was probably right, for him. But loss has many lessons. It taught me that even though people die, you can still love them and have them close. I dream of Dad a lot. I don't remember what he says when I wake up, but I always feel that he's not gone.

Recently Jerry and I watched some new footage on *60 Minutes* of the camps being "cleaned up" after the Liberation, film we'd never seen before. Each stick-like corpse flung into a mass grave as if it had no connection to hope, to love, to dreams or anything human was like a thunderclap that shakes not only your windows but your very sense of yourself. I held on to Jerry, staring, crying, wondering how any cameraman could record such horror.

Stunned, I went to the kitchen for my watering can, and Jerry followed.

Whenever I water or tend the monstrously healthy plant that towers in our living room near the phone, I feel us all close, Jerry, Mom, Dad—and I am not afraid of life.

Roy's Jewish Problem

When I told my parents that I was moving into a Jewish students' co-op, they were as quietly, stupidly ecstatic as the parents of a daughter who's been unable to have a baby for years, who's tried every possible medical treatment (and even rubbed herself with herbs in strange places)—and the daughter tells them she's been diagnosed with twins, no less. My parents stifled their grins and hugs in a desperate attempt not to remind anyone of the years of anxiety and shame.

You see, I had been a problem child. More specifically, a problem Jewish child. Not wild, not into drugs or petty thefts or deliberate stupidity in school, but stubbornly resistant to being Jewish—despite the marking of my flesh, where the scar of my circumcision seemed like a ring marrying me to the generations of Jews who had suffered before me, starting with this painful and uncivilized ritual. And if anyone tells you infant boys are too young to feel pain—don't believe it! I'm not arguing from my own experience, but from more than one bris I've attended, where the boys wailed and gasped and coughed their anguish and outrage. It wasn't surprise, it wasn't stage fright, it was PAIN.

Now, my parents may not have said much about my sudden "conversion" when I decided to move into the co-op, but I knew they would want to. I could see them smugly letting their friends know that I was choosing to do something openly, proudly Jewish. As a boy I had fought them about Hebrew school and been kicked out twice for cursing at my teachers. I had resisted a bar mitzvah until I realized how much money was involved, and then only memorized the tapes of what I had to read, rather than learning what—if anything—it all meant. And I had even once made my mother walk through shit. See, she had driven me to Hebrew school and I had locked the car doors automatically as soon as she got out when we were parked. She stormed around the car, slapping windows with her palms, screaming at me to come out (or let her in), and then she stepped in some dog shit, whipped off her shoe and brandished it at me. I was so grossed out, I fled out the other side, away from her, into the school where I knew she would be too embarrassed to follow. Given moments like that, my deciding to move into a Jewish co-op at college was an event worthy of catering.

Like that time she tried to brain me with her show, I wasn't choosing the co-op for itself. Mostly, I was moving to escape the dorm, and more specifically, my roommate, Marvin. I've heard Italian-Americans call a stereotypic Italian with thick accent and gold chains a "Guido"—well Marvin was the Jewish equivalent, and I hated him. Even though Marvin Gross worked out every day, and had a stomach that a Hillbilly band could use as an instrument, he disgusted me, he was—there's no other word for it—gross. Like an anti-Semitic cartoon: hooked nose, slumped shoulders, pale face, no chin at all. And when he was just standing around, he rattled change in his pocket like an old man, an old Jewish man, I thought. I felt an almost physical repulsion around him, as if he was one of those stooping men on the East Side trying to pull me into a cave-like smelly store. He reminded me of all the times I crossed the street in New York as soon as I saw a Hasidic Jew whose black hat and beard were as frightening to me as the pirate skull and cross bones once were to a merchant ship.

I may not have worked out, but I was not gross. And I was very glad that I had dark blond hair, a small nose and grey-green eyes, could pass for a goy, and that my last name wasn't Steinberg, Greenberg or any kind of Berg. It was—are you ready?—Smith. An Ellis island substitution for Scziemanski.

There were other reasons besides my roommate to leave the dorm, but I don't want to get into that right now.

When I say I moved into a Jewish co-op, this is what I mean: we were all from New York or Lawn Guyland and enjoyed Woody Allen movies because they could make us feel superior both to the goyim, and to Allen himself, since lots of people couldn't get his jokes (we claimed) and none of us were such schlemiels.

Some people called us the Hillel annex, but we weren't connected more than going down the street to their brand-new building for deli lunches and films sometimes. We were Jewish and we were students and we co-operated—paid our bills on time, cooked and ate together, shoveled our snow, raked our leaves and always bagged our garbage.

The co-op was in a shabby old mock-Victorian house that shifted every night like an old dog trying to be comfortable. Downstairs there was a huge ratty kitchen, a toilet, living room and TV room full of refugee furniture donated by community members, parents and even our landlord. The better stuff went to Hillel.

163

Upstairs were six small bedrooms (subdivided from the original three) with doors marked by Shalom signs and some Israeli postcards and El Al posters. We all shared the one large bathroom and it always seemed crowded: someone showering, someone spitting toothpaste into the sink, someone else desperate for aspirin.

I was comfortable there, until I met Roy. It was Ilana who told me he was coming to interview for the Fall opening at the co-op: Roy Lichtenberger.

"Roy?" I couldn't help smirking. "Well at least it's not Kevin. Or Clifford."

We met Roy in the TV room. Ilana, blond and self-conscious, draped herself on the couch like an afghan to show off her legs. Ruth, small dark and suspicious, was primed with a tightly-held pad and two pens "in case." Jesse, in his red running shorts and sleeveless t-shirt was trying to stay awake. He kept strange hours and always seemed to be coming in from the track on campus. We used to joke that his major was Comparative Track. Redheaded Nicole, who looked like a very freckled Lauren Bacall, was listening as always to Bryan Ferry on her Walkman.

Roy looked nervous, maybe even excited. He was short, wide-eyed, with a dark mustache that made him seem older than a senior. But he was only twenty-one like the rest of us. He had a gymnast's build and I realized he was probably handsome when Ilana, wanting a better look, sat up in stages to avoid being obvious. Ilana used to say that men either had "potential" or "possibilities." I guess she thought that Roy had both. Even Ruth relaxed some, and Nicole lowered the volume on her tape.

We introduced ourselves.

"I want to be Jewish," Roy announced after thanking us for having him over.

"Aren't you?" Jesse wondered, stroking his thigh.

"Not enough. I want to feel it, I want to do Jewish things."

"We've got lots of Jewish dishes to wash," Ilana drawled, and Ruth frowned at her.

"I'm the secretary." Ruth took over, filling Roy in on every household detail imaginable. She would've made a great committee.

Anyway, Ruth was explaining the intricacies of garbage collection for the second time when Ilana cut in: "Let's order pizza."

"You don't keep kosher?" Roy asked.

I confessed we'd given up after making half the stuff in the kitchen *treyf.*

"They're kosher at Hillel," Jesse pointed out, but we all knew the Hillel co-op had no vacancies.

Pizza and soda opened things up. We talked about our programs—Roy was in Psychology—and what we liked doing in town and our favorite restaurants and clubs back in New York. Roy surprised us all by saying that he hated New York. I was tempted to ask what his problem was.

"You hate it?" Ilana paused in mid-slice to figure that one out.

"The City scares me." Roy's eyes were wide; it was obviously no joke.

"But you grew up there? You live there?" Ruth had to check her grasp of the facts.

Nicole eyed Roy over the rim of her Coke can and in an unexpected silence her swallowing was loud and embarrassing. She blushed.

It turned out that Roy was the only one of us who had ever been mugged and had a car stolen and been pickpocketed on Fifth Avenue in the Christmas rush.

"That's pretty heavy," I said. "So Roy, you ever been kidnaped?"

We took him in, of course. Ruth thought he was "serious"; Ilana thought he was "cute"; Jesse thought he was "nervous but okay"; Nicole was excited that he'd not only heard of Bryan Ferry but seen him in concert once; and I, well I thought he was in trouble. I wasn't sure why I felt sorry for Roy, but I did. The eyes looking out of that strong face were very sad. Jewish eyes, maybe. My grandmother said a Polish woman once told her that all Jews had the same quiet fear in their eyes, like they were waiting for things to go wrong.

Roy moved his stuff in from his dorm and took over Laura's room, the one with the smallest windows, facing north. None of us had liked Laura, who was always telling us what to do, so we were glad when she chose a year abroad to improve her French.

Roy moved in three weeks before classes started and since his room was next to mine I got to know him first, and maybe last, too. He wasn't very social; he listened a lot, watched us like he was hungry. We weren't really interesting, though, or very bright, but I guess we were Jewish and that was the point.

On his shelves were rows and rows of psychology paperbacks: Karen Horney, Freud of course, lots of Jung, Rogers, Adler, Sullivan, Fromm, Laing, Kaufman. Though he worked out every day at the campus gym, there were also a barbell and dumbbells in his room. He was in terrific shape, and looked a little like Mark Spitz, I decided.

There wasn't much to check out in his room, typical student posters and knickknacks, but over his desk hung a black and white photograph framed in lucite I knew I didn't want to get close to, but couldn't avoid. At the back of it was a wooden tower, barbed wire, and on a path parallel to that a double file of men in those camp uniforms, the striped ones, being led and followed by guards with machine guns. There were also guard dogs. It looked like a work detail and it could have been any camp—it was every camp, really.

Roy was sitting on his bed when I turned from the photograph. He said, "I keep that because my father could be in there. You never know."

I sat down, feeling that sick curiosity I'm ashamed of.

"Your dad was in a camp?"

Roy nodded. "Treblinka."

"That was one of the worst," I offered and when Roy smiled I felt really stupid. It was as dim as the time I saw Katie Couric scrunch up her face and ask a psychiatrist, "Now, schizophrenia, that's a serious problem, isn't it?"

"What about your mom, too?" I asked. I knew survivors tended to marry other survivors.

"She was in Auschwitz."

Picturing her numbered arm, I wanted to leave, but Roy's voice was so low I sat at his desk as if I'd been ordered to stay.

"I guess since you're a Psych major you've read that stuff about survivors' children?"

He had, but didn't find most of it applicable to him. We talked a little more but I had to make dinner and he said he needed to write some letters.

When I told the others, Ilana looked upset, Ruth fidgeted with the newspaper, Nicole looked away and Jesse seemed more awake than I'd ever seen him.

Roy fit right in to the co-op; he was a decent cook, never left dishes for other people or wet towels greasing the sink, seemed to enjoy shopping and watching TV with us. Roy took the sixth space in the co-op but he didn't claim it, shape it to fit him. He merged with the group in a few weeks without becoming a member of it.

"Do you think he likes us?" Ilana asked me one evening when Roy was at a class.

Clanking and scrubbing dishes in the sink, Jesse shrugged. "You mean does he like *you?*"

"I like him," Ruth said primly, fussing with leftovers and Tupperware. "He's very quiet."

Nicole turned down her music. "What?"

"Too quiet," Ilana decided. "Maybe he thinks we're—" She settled onto one of the bar stools at the counter.

Ruth shut the refrigerator. "What?"

"Maybe he thinks we're not Jewish enough," Ilana brought out carefully like a waitress setting down a very hot plate, and when no one commented, she rushed on: "I mean are we?"

"Oh, please," Nicole murmured.

I asked Ilana how Jewish was enough, but even I knew that wasn't an honest question.

We dried and stacked the dishes and moved to the TV room. Small, carpeted in red, curtained in brown, with a fat scruffy-looking blue couch, it was the center of our life in that house. There, with the comforting presence of the huge scarred color set, we drew in on ourselves, as if in contradiction to the TV screen that could connect us with millions, or maybe it made re-

166

flection easier somehow—it's hard to say. Often we just read there, relaxed, waited for things to happen.

Jesse pulled out a New Yorker from a pile of magazines on the floor and stretched out with his back to the wall to read the ads. For some reason, they all made him laugh.

"What are you worried about?" Ruth asked Ilana, looking for a dust rag.

Ilana shrugged and sat next to me.

I'd known her for two years now (we were both Communications majors) and she'd never done anything more Jewish than talk about Israel like everyone else did and make jokes about "us" and "them," but even those were so casual I'm sure she didn't believe there was a difference.

Us. My Dad, whenever he heard or read something about anti-Semitism, would shake his head and you could always tell he was thinking "The Goyim." His contemptuous silences used to rile my mother. She'd sit up sharp: "Jack, you can't say that!"

And then they would dispute about something he'd only thought. My Mom was a high school Social Studies teacher and big on Civics, so she argued Democracy and my Dad argued History. Both of them had relatives who remembered Russian pogroms and my Dad had seen the camps in 1945 with the Army. He didn't trust non-Jews and my mother wanted to; that was the difference. I don't know which of them was right.

We all read for a while and Ruth, small and intent behind her pump spray Pledge, cleaned around us.

That evening in the TV room, that silent evening in which we only spoke to read bits of articles aloud, we all seemed to be asking Ilana's question: how Jewish were we?

I'd never seen Jesse with a yarmulke before and the Saturday afternoon he appeared upstairs in a suit, too, I wanted to laugh—he looked so respectable. He plopped onto my bed:

"I went to shul at Hillel with Roy. You know he's never been? And no bar mitzvah, nothing. He's like one of those kids, you know the ones in forests that were lost and come out not speaking anything, like animals?"

"Feral children, you mean?"

"That kind, yeah." Jesse seemed as surprised by his own wordiness as Roy's past.

"Did he go to any kind of Hebrew school?"

"No. He's teaching himself Hebrew, but he couldn't figure out the siddur."

I said it was good that the prayer book they used at Hillel had so many footnotes.

"When they opened the Ark I thought he was going to cry or something."

"He's never been to shul?"

"No—and he liked it more than I do. I explained what was going on and he kind of ate it all up." Jesse grinned. "I know it and he feels it—put us together you got one good Jew."

Jesse seemed to like teaching Roy about the service and they went every Saturday after that. I felt kind of funny about that, as if I should have been going with Roy. Roy didn't talk about his "conversion" but I found him in the TV room a few times wearing a black yarmulke and reading the siddur he'd borrowed from Hillel.

"Listen," he said once, reading aloud first in fumbling Hebrew and then in English: "Thou hast changed my mourning into dancing; thou hast put off my sackcloth and girded me with joy; so that my soul may praise thee, and not be silent."

His voice was soft, reverential, as if the words were healing him. I felt a sharp ache for the sense of discovery and wonder Roy had.

"I've read books about Judaism," he said, "but now I'm doing it."

"Why now?" I asked.

Roy looked down at the siddur. "You'll think this is dumb, but I found a copy of *The Dybbuk* in a used book store and it was a whole different world I didn't know anything about. And when I started thinking, I saw I didn't have any Jewish friends, never dated Jewish girls. Maybe I didn't even like Jews." He glanced up, eyes pained and defiant, expecting criticism, I guess, but ready to counter it, or try. "I didn't really know any Jews. I probably didn't want to."

It was times like that Roy seemed most alien to me, most foreign to how I lived and thought, yet something in the core of me responded to him, as if he was the voice of a darkness I had no suspicion existed. Maybe my living in the co-op was a way of masking my lack of involvement. I didn't read Jewish books, didn't do anything particularly Jewish. It embarrassed me when Roy would ask questions I didn't have answers for. I lent him books, like Milton Steinberg's *Basic Judaism* and stuff I'd gotten for Chanukah, but that was so little compared to what he needed. I didn't have much information and I had less spirit, yet I wanted to help him, and felt frustrated that there wasn't anything more that I could do.

I went back down to Queens for the High Holy Days, which was the endless usual bore. Ruth and Jesse both lived in Lawrence and belonged to the same congregation; they invited Nicole. Ilana, who stayed up at school, didn't tell us what she did. Roy went to Hillel by himself and fasted for the first time in his life. He said it was "exciting" and that he almost cried during the "*Hineni*" ("Here I am—") prayer in which the leader of services declares his worthlessness before God.

"At least Roy's not crazy," Ilana confided to me unexpectedly one Wednesday night when we were cleaning the kitchen. Her face was red and blotchy from bending over the steaming soapy pail and shoving the heavy mop across the worn linoleum. I was attacking the stove, Nicole was scrubbing the counters in time to the music I could hear buzzing from her headphones: "Love is the Drug."

"I mean, he's not a potential Hasid or anything."

I scraped away with a knife at spilled coffee under a burner. "Do you think we should try keeping kosher again?" I asked.

Ilana shrugged.

"I've been reading about it."

Ilana looked up, curious.

I explained that I'd gone over to the Hillel library to read about the *kashrut* laws in the *Encyclopedia Judaica*. I'd never bothered with the reasons behind them and I liked the interpretation that explained them in terms of putting limits on oneself, learning spiritual discipline. I talked too long, I think, because Ilana smiled.

"I've been reading about how the Reform movement began," she said. "I got a book about Isaac Mayer Wise from the library. I wonder what Jesse and Ruth are up to?" We both looked at Nicole, unable to imagine that anything could tear her away from Bryan Ferry.

At dinner the next night Ruth sat down chattering about Eli Wiesel. Someone had lent her *Souls on Fire*.

Jesse cleared his throat, pushed his ice cream plate away. "Since I'm cooking Friday, let's have a *Shabbos* dinner. How about it?"

"With candles?" Ilana asked, pleased. "And *hamotzi?*"

"Would we have to *bentsh* after?" Roy looked a little nervous.

Jesse assured him we could do what we wanted. "But you can borrow a *bentsher* from Hillel if you want to learn."

Nicole asked what everyone was supposed to wear.

That night I heard Roy whistling a Shabbat melody in his room and it didn't seem ridiculous. Friday we were all excited. Ruth lit the candles, Jesse blessed the wine, we all washed our hands and Roy did *hamotzi*. His hands shook as he placed them on the challah Ilana had baked that morning, but his voice was clear and strong: *Boruch atah Adonoy Elohaynu melech ha-olom, ha-motzi lechem min ha-aretz*. Blessed art Thou, O Lord our God, King of the universe, who bringest forth bread from the earth."

The English had never sounded so beautiful to me before, like prayer and not just translation, and when Roy cut the five slices of challah, salted them, ate from one and passed the others to us, I wanted to clap his back and hug him.

We were all high, talking nonstop, except for Roy. He seemed dazed, as if he'd passed some kind of boundary he was afraid would hold him back.

We sat up late in Roy's room telling stories about high school, past loves, drunk on our confidences (though Roy mostly listened). Ruth relaxed and even Nicole seemed connected. When the others drifted off to bed, I stayed. I felt so proud of Roy, wished he were my brother. I may even have said that, I can't remember. I know I hugged him at one point.

With his eyes half-closed, Roy leaned back in his desk chair and explained what had really brought him to the co-op. It was a combination of anti-Semitic hassling in the dorm, and a growing fear of his own Jewish ignorance sparked by someone asking him to explain Shavuos. He had no idea what the holiday meant. Neither did I, and I flushed when I realized that Roy was like me in some ways: he had rejected really being connected to other Jews.

I asked, "Do your parents talk about the War much?"

"It's a blank." He shook his head. "I think they were too ashamed of what happened to them, ashamed of being powerless and trapped, and that they lived when people they loved, people they admired, didn't."

That night as I fell asleep I imagined us at my cousin Jeff's large and isolated cottage on Lake Michigan, a place I had been going to with my parents since I was four or five. I pictured Roy and me swimming in the lake.

I decided to go to shul the next morning with Ilana, Jesse and Roy, watched Roy kiss the tallis and put it on, shake hands and scatter "*Gut Shabbos*" as if he'd always come there.

I felt like the outsider, and the service bored me. I read the English translation when I wasn't singing in Hebrew, stared out the window, watched Roy's contentment and grace with envy. Did it take deprivation to make all this meaningful?

Roy got an *aliyah* and did the blessings at the *bima* as if he were a much older man; the Hebrew gave his voice richness and authority.

"He's good," I whispered to Jesse, who beamed like a shy parent.

Afterwards, at kiddush, I saw Roy talking to a tall, short-haired girl who was as dark as he was, and as good-looking in her own way.

"That's Shelley Stein," Ilana informed me. "She's a Jewish tornado: collects money for all these groups, teaches Sunday school, heads some coalition. If it's Jewish around here, she's connected to it. Her father's on the Hillel board."

I vaguely knew some of that.

Roy went back for *Shabbos* lunch to Shelley's and I felt cheated, somehow.

Because midterms were coming up, the house was very quiet and meals went quickly. Ruth holed up in the library and Jesse stayed in his department building most of the time. Ilana and Nicole were in and out, involved in study groups, so I pretty much had the co-op to myself, which was good because I sometimes had trouble reading if there's more than street noise. We were lucky to live on a block away from Main Street and Fraternity Row; the worst noise would be dogs at night sometimes, daring each other from behind locked doors or gates, their barks echoing off the silence. It's funny I needed it to be quiet, because I grew up in Queens under a flight path to Kennedy and our house had the shakes a couple times a day. Living in a small college town had got me used to less noise, less hassle all around. It was easier to study, easier to concentrate on things because there weren't as many distractions.

After midterms Roy started spending all his time with Shelley. All his time; they saw every campus movie, lunched together, studied together, went biking, out for walks. She did the talking when they were together, and Roy drank it in. Shelley had gone to Jewish summer camps, spent a year in Israel on a kibbutz, knew Hebrew and Yiddish, read the *Jerusalem Post* and half a dozen Jewish magazines, belonged to enough organizations to fill a small office building.

I didn't like her. None of us liked her. She knew too much. She talked too much. At dinner in the co-op, any Jewish topic brought out the lecturer in her. She'd wave a fork and jab words at us like we were hopelessly stupid.

Roy thought she was wonderful.

One night in a blaze of rhetoric about Jewish contributions to world something or other, Shelley spat a few times as she spoke. I glanced at Ilana; we winked.

After that dinner, we called Shelley "Spitfire" and even Ruth and Jesse managed a few mean remarks now and then, but we never let Roy know, not that it would've mattered. He had plunged into Shelley's life, her concerns, her activities and opinions as if he wanted to be her or know everything that she did. It was unpleasant, it was not love or even devotion. Roy's commitment to Shelley scared me, made me see that the void in him must've been enormous. I'd run into them holding hands or with arms locked in town, on campus, Shelley hot with explanation, Roy attentive, submissive. No, it was more than that—he seemed extinguished next to her. And I felt shut out.

We started *bentshing* after *shabbos* dinners and even Ruth and Nicole came to shul but our new-found observance did not really include Roy. We missed him.

A few weeks before Chanukah and finals, Shelley came over very late one night. Through the thin old walls I heard murmuring, heard the pop of a champagne cork and then after a silence, the radio, just loud enough to filter out other sounds. I read myself to sleep like I sometimes do; homework always works.

Not much later, I woke when the front door slammed and a car started up, drove off. A few minutes after that Roy knocked softly, opening the door and asking if he could come in.

I pulled on my robe, called "Yes" and turned on the desk lamp.

He was just wearing gym shorts and seemed so blank that I reached for the Dewar's under my desk, quickly poured him a shot. He sat in my desk chair, silent, eyes down, did three shots before he said, "I'm all right."

I didn't believe him. I sat near him on the edge of my bed. I couldn't tell what was wrong, but he looked sick to me, feverish. His mustache seemed very dark against his pale skin. It was cold in my room, but I didn't offer him a shirt.

"Have you ever had trouble in bed, with a girl?"

"Sometimes." I flushed, not sure what he might say next. "If I'm nervous." I was always nervous with girls, the few I'd gone out with.

"Not me—never. Until Shelley. We keep trying. But I can't."

I thought of all his psychology books next door.

"I've never been to bed with a Jewish girl," he said, as if I was supposed to understand what he meant. And then he added, "I'm not circumcised. My folks were afraid. Lots of Jews were caught in the War just because of that, it gave them away. . . ."

I remembered that I'd read about Virginia Woolf's husband seeing a photograph in 1937 of storm-troopers dragging along a Jew with his fly ripped open, and bystanders laughing. I told that to Roy; the words rushed out of me because I had to say something.

Roy said that he'd gone to a mostly-Jewish elementary school and always felt embarrassed at the urinals, that guys made jokes about him in the showers in junior high, one classmate leaving scissors on his desk and alerting everyone, that he'd always felt like an outsider among Jews, isolated from history, the past.

"I couldn't talk about it with anyone," he said. "I've never been able to talk about it."

Looking down, I managed to say, "Does it really matter?"

He reached over and grabbed me by the chin, forced me to meet his angry terrible eyes. I could feel his boozy breath steaming my face. "You don't understand, do you?" He let go of my chin, and I felt as if I'd been slapped.

"My parents wanted me to be safe, but instead of protecting me, they made me feel like I'm nobody, like I'm not part of the past. My father told me once that we were Levis, you know, descended from the guys that sang the psalms at the Temple? But I'm not the same as all of them. I've thought of getting circumcised, but it's too late, I'll always feel like this."

All I could do was shrug.

"I'm *treyf*," he said. "I'll always be *treyf*."

I was close enough to smell the drying sweat on his body. I asked, "What about Shelly? Do you really like her?"

"She's so Jewish," he said, shaking his head. "She's perfect."

I felt helpless, and my silence made him angry. I almost thought me might hit me, but he just left the room.

Brushing my teeth the next morning, I wondered what I should have said, but didn't come up with anything.

After classes, when I got back to the co-op to help Ruth with dinner, she told me that Roy had loaded most of his things and driven down to New York.

"I don't know what happened. He wouldn't talk to me," Ruth said. "I tried."

"He's not coming back?"

Ruth shrugged, checking the rice.

"But the semester's not over!"

"He can take incompletes." Ruth didn't turn around. Did she know? Had Roy told her?

I thought about Chanukah in a few weeks. We had all talked about having a party, baking, putting up decorations, chipping in on a really nice menorah. I had been imagining shopping for a gift for Roy.

Later, Ilana insisted we call Roy in New York, but Jesse kept shaking his head: "He'll blast you."

"How do you know?"

"Because I would." He sounded so sure that Ilana gave up. I knew I couldn't call. I was too stunned.

We were in the TV room with the news on low. I asked Ruth again what Roy had said to her.

Ilana grimaced as if she, master detective, would have never let the suspect escape. But what were we supposed to do? I felt like a traitor, somehow, like I should have told them everything. But I couldn't. There was too much to tell, and it was his secret, not mine.

When I finally went up to bed, I found Roy's concentration camp picture propped on my desk. There was no note, so I couldn't tell if he had left it for me, or simply gotten rid of it.

I saw Shelley in the Union cafeteria the next afternoon and she waved me over.

"Have you seen Roy?" she asked.

"No. He's gone." I piled my down parka over hers on the third chair and sat opposite her. Shelley was prettier than I remembered, with a fresh round face I could picture in an Ivory commercial.

"Then you know what happened?"

I nodded carefully.

She sat back from the small square table, shoulders loose in a gold cashmere sweater. Fiddling with her empty Styrofoam cup, twirling it in one hand. I dreaded what she might say, as if I were back in high school where people's feelings were never expressed directly, but relayed, filtered through friends. Shelley wasn't asking anything of me, though. She was just stumped. "I know his . . . his being different from other Jewish guys is a problem for him." She frowned. "But he could just go to a doctor and have it done."

Then he'd have two wounds that would never heal, I thought.

Shelley looked to me for a response.

I made myself shrug and say, "Yeah, why not?"

Secret Anniversaries
of the Heart

David could never seem to translate his mother's life into English. When she talked about *gymnasium*, he saw the ropes, mats and parallel bars of his gym instead of books and blackboards. When she described her blue pleated skirt uniform, David pictured the Catholic school girls with their matching satchels giggling on the No. 5 bus as it lurched down Riverside Drive. And when she talked about the authors she had loved reading—Jules Verne, Stefan and Arnold Zweig, Sinkiewicz—he drew a complete blank. Who were those people? What world did they come from? The names were as remote as cities Alexander the Great conquered in his war against Persia, strange names clotting the text of a picture book he'd read as a little boy.

And the rare and frightening times she spoke about her war years—the ghetto, the camps, the endless suffering—language failed him. He didn't know what to say. What could he say? He listened, always feeling as if he were trapped on one of those barrier islands on the Atlantic Coast and the roaring black hurricane was bearing down too fast for him to save himself. The words annihilated him.

He could not imagine his mother reduced to a number, an object, a starveling. In the heavy-covered photo albums, before the War, before the concentration camp, his mother had the tentative exotic beauty of a Dietrich. Distant American relatives had saved these pictures whose originals had gone up in Nazi smoke and she was dreamy there, foreign, her rich dark hair coiled and fragrant-looking even on dead paper.

"They shaved my hair," she sometimes said, to no one in particular. "It never grew back so full as it was." And her thin hands would twitch as if she wanted to reach up and reassure herself that she was no longer bald.

She might say this when David found her staring mournfully at her bed-room window, the only mirror she seemed able to stand, as if somewhere north, far north, up the tic-tack-toe of Manhattan streets lay the answer. Escape? She was thinking about the War, her hair, her stolen life.

But David saw color and life from his tenth-story bedroom in their Washington Heights apartment. He loved to watch Manhattan stretch and narrowly poke at the Bronx. Red, gold and brown apartment buildings rose and fell over hills that Indians and farmers claimed long before the stolid German Jews who strolled along Broadway and Ft. Washington Avenue on Saturday nights and filled the benches in Riverside Park to gaze across at the green, forbidding Palisades. His building, hulking across half a city block, with massive cornices and leering griffins, was not the highest spot in the city. His fourth grade teacher had told the class that The Cloisters in Fort Tryon Park, two miles north, bore that honor—but on his hill he could imagine he was higher, and feel curiosity for those who wanted to live Downtown or off in flat and dreary Queens which his mother said was built on garbage.

Their building was built on history, or its image. The great dim lobby below, three steps up from the outer hall, three again from the street, was walled and floored like a Hollywood castle. Its mirrors shone back heavy blistered tables to rest packages on while waiting for the scarred and pan-eled elevator that sank and sighed with its burden of more than fifty years. At night this heavy murmur came to David distantly, like the creak of some sleepless relative rocking, rocking to keep still.

Up high, it was quiet, and when his mother cooked and left him alone, he liked to wander from one high-ceilinged room to the next, his own parade, a conqueror of foreign lands, dramatically pausing in archways, sweeping open the glass-paneled doors. He wasn't David any more, but Alexander—a name of steel and stone.

"*A mawdneh mensh,*" his mother observed in Yiddish, frowning, when she found him playing this game, a sweater around his neck to make a cape, an umbrella his sword. Yes, he was strange. Stranger than she would know for a long time, and then stranger than she would want to know.

He understood her Yiddish, respected it in a way. She was always com-plaining about friends who spoke "*peylish*" Yiddish; and when he heard that variety, it made David wince with its vowels ugly as crooked teeth. His mother, a Vilner, proudly spoke the best and most beautiful Yiddish, a remarkable memento of a lost world, like the ostrich plume court fan a neighbor's grandmother saved from the *Bolsheviki*—as she called them—enfolded in red velvet and guarded from light. English for his mother was a language of directions and instructions, neutral, just a tool. Yiddish was the treasure she emerged with from the bowels of the War—but who wanted it? In this dying language, she taught classes at a Workman's Circle school like someone gravely feeding a fire when the logs have drifted into ash and only pine cones, twigs await the flames.

David refused to speak Yiddish, even though he understood it perfectly, the way he was persistently mediocre in school, spitting into perfection only for the standardized tests. "Not fulfilling his potential" was the red-ink complaint which he ignored because he thought talking about his potential was like picking the stuffing from a rag doll.

His mother complained about his grades as if each were a public disgrace.

"I don't listen to your mother," his father would say. "I tune her out."

There was a lot to ignore—if only David could do the same. His mother was given to sorrowful exclamations. "I'm so ugly," she could moan at dinner, unexpectedly, and David would stare at his pot roast and green beans. To him, she was always beautiful, so her complaint itself was ugly.

"How is it possible?" she went on.

His father, as if fumbling for the button to stop a clock's alarm, sometimes would try jokes, denial, full of pity, love. But David felt hysterical, as if a ghost had howled into their home and kept them prisoner.

"So ugly."

"She's not ugly," he thought. "She's crazy." And many years later, when his mother was unable to tell what day it was, or remember what she had read in the paper, or match her clothes, or find her keys because she had forgotten their name, and carried her favorite clutch purse around with her in the house, David thought that the seeds had always been there.

And she, the crazy one, with clear despair, sometimes she seemed to hate them: her smug husband with his good job as a custom tailor, her pale son, wide-eyed, scared.

"Staring, always staring!" She blasted David from his chair to the bathroom where locked inside, he sobbed into a towel. He was seven that time.

"Mommy's sorry," his father said, coaxing at the door, then left him there.

No, David was sorry, because he couldn't stand her mood swings, her inconsolable grief that coming to America, marriage, a son, had not touched. Like sailing an ocean in a thimble—impossible. He could never really please her. She would unexpectedly beat him down with criticism about the smallest things: picking at the way he walked, stood, combed his hair, ate his cereal, buckled his belt. She could have been a frustrated sculptor cursing at recalcitrant clay that always let him down.

And if it wasn't him, she could explode about anything, and none of it seemed real. She was trapped in nightmares as if an Iron Maiden pierced her peace and easy sleep.

Her murdered father was rich, important, a *gevir*, and always grander than her husband, despite the new cars, the color television before any of their neighbors had one, the trips to Florida. She called Washington Heights a slum.

David didn't understand. Slums were dirty and dangerous, but their streets were clean, safe, and full of trees.

"I have nothing to wear!" his mother's cry might break at night, familiar and estranged like a buoy marking passage, with its bells, as dangerous, unwise.

The raving about money or clothes was so common David even heard it in his sleep. His father would placate, explain, then storm into another room, derided and pursued: "Coward! Old Lady" Until his father, who had learned Yiddish from his parents, shouted "*Genug!*" and there was silence. Enough.

It didn't make sense to David—his mother's closet was jammed with clothes. He knew this too well. He had plundered his mother's closet all those years when he was six or eight or even eleven, and left alone, to feel the ice cream smoothness of her dresses, to stroke them like a genie's lamp, to slip inside whatever beckoned, to rope and pile her necklaces around his eager scrawny neck, squeeze her large earrings on, totter in her shoes, and stare into her bureau mirror, with no one home, no one in the world but him, turning, looking beautiful, like her, but like himself, a distant and imagined self. What was in his mother's clothes that bathed away his fears and pain, in the cotton, silk narcotics, alligator bags and gauzy slips, all smelling so much like her they were more than her, more than any woman, a world of vague and promised bliss?

And why didn't this world of wonders please her?

Well, he knew from his father that nothing, nothing could ever heal his mother's worst betrayal. A shattered young girl who had survived the War alone, she had been brought to New York by a rich relative, a cousin twice removed. He promised her a college education, but was only generous with words. She served as proof of his benevolence and had to live constant gratitude in the maid's room of the vulgar over-heated West End Avenue apartment, working as a maid. And her husband was no rescuing knight, no healing force, only a transition to the lesser realms of hate. The cousin left her nothing in his will and for David that dim figure and his kin were mixed of gnome and devil, witch and fox, gobbling up her freshness and her smiles, casting evil spells, pursuing her in the dark. When his mother finally lost her mind and threw plants and books at his father, screaming in German, she was screaming at this cousin, calling him everything she had kept back for all those years, a geyser of abuse. And then she fell silent, became a monument to loss and waste.

But silence had bristled between them for too many years before that. He had told her hat he was gay when he graduated Columbia's School of Journalism, and all she could say was, "Why spoil everything?"

So he never mentioned meeting Jake when he moved to a Detroit suburb and joined a group for children of Holocaust survivors, and how their first night together turned into a lifetime.

"She doesn't want to know," his father warned him.

"But I have a good life," David protested, proud of his job at the Detroit newspaper, his lover's position in the counseling center at the University of Michigan. When would it be all right? After they'd been together more than seven years, the length of an average marriage? Ten years? Fifteen? By then it turned out to be too late, because his mother had disappeared into Alzheimer's and would never return. Her death was almost an afterthought since she had been lost to him for well over a decade.

And when his father died soon afterwards, Jake insisted it was time for David to write about his mother.

"What, as therapy?"

"As writing."

They were sitting in matching wide burnt orange armchairs by the fire in their mid-century Ann Arbor ranch house. The style and colors of the room were warm even without a fire—everyone said so, relaxing as soon as they entered, admiring the cherry floor, the tan grasscloth on the walls, the soft, eerie landscapes by David Grath from northern Michigan. They had redone most of the house when they moved in twenty-five years ago, eventually adding a suite at the back with a separate entrance and its own path from the driveway so that Jake could see clients at home in preparation for retiring early from the university. He had made a lot of money consulting to various state organizations about the corrosive impact of shame in interpersonal relations and was planning to just do consulting and some private practice before he hit 55. It wasn't that far off, now.

Jake said, "You write book reviews, you do Arts coverage, why can't you do something of your own?"

"That stuff is my own. That's what I'm known for."

"It doesn't touch your heart," Jake said, the five words like unassuming rabbits slipped blinking from a magician's hat and sleeves, each a white and tame surprise.

"Don't do that," David said. "Don't be right."

Jake shrugged. He was short, slight, bearded, with the kindest eyes David had ever seen: round, deep, accepting. Jake had a ringing tenor voice that made you think he was a singer or radio personality, but there was nothing stagy in his presence, just a sense of powerful compassion in reserve. That had led David to remark to all their friends more than once in 2000 during the presidential campaign that George Bush didn't know the meaning of compassion—despite declaring he was a "compassionate conservative"—it just wasn't in his makeup. "Look at George Bush's eyes. They're always angry and detached. Cold. I know what compassion looks like, and it's not that yahoo."

Now, David took a sip of the Macallan they'd poured nightly fingers of (made possible, they liked to joke, by their daily workouts at the gym). He said, "I can't see myself in some class with freshmen. Or even graduate students. I'm forty-eight, I'm too old."

"Too old for what? You mean you'd be embarrassed, right?"

"Don't do shame therapy on me."

Jake shrugged that off. "So look for something else—a night class—or something untraditional. This is Ann Arbor—somebody's got to be able to offer you what you need."

David grinned. "I've already hit pay dirt there," he said, and Jake accepted the compliment.

But David did start looking, and found that a retired faculty member was teaching a writing workshop in the spring that would meet weekly in a reasonably private room of one of Ann Arbor's best independent book stores. The setting was ideal for David: serried ranks of books of all kinds, quiet, and no sense of going back to school, though he was uncomfortable that people there knew who he was. Everyone knew who he was in Ann Arbor, or seemed to.

But their instructor, Imre Meloth, did not seem to know or care about any of the ten amateur writers' professional lives. After the first introductory session, Meloth had looked progressively paler and more wrinkled. Hungarian-born Meloth was a bulging fat pyramid in shabby grey suits and wrinkled polo shirts, slant-eyed. David imagined him sleeping in his file-crazy little office on campus when he taught there, and drinking cheap wine not only at class breaks but whenever he was alone. Maybe he came to the group drunk, as some of the students suggested quietly, or perhaps had enough alcohol in him to not ever need another drink. As the semester went on, Meloth was more and more like the victim of a hit-and-run unable to shake the surprise or the collapse. But that was only when he wasn't tearing into their writing.

Meloth rarely liked anyone's work. He let people—all of them around David's age and all with jobs, families or both—comment on a story or a poem in their rambling casual way and then hacked at the fragile plant of their approval with blunt and vicious sheers: "Juvenile! Excessive! Meretricious! Limp!"

Attendance was consistently poor, and even though David went to every class on Thursday evenings, the same combination of students was seldom repeated. No one talked to anyone else much before Meloth arrived. They could have been strangers drawn to a huge drafty train station at night where the benches grew cold as stone and the longed-for whistle didn't come. Meloth was never helpful, never offered inspiration or joked or even smiled. He seemed to hate being in America, hate being in Michigan. And he raided their writing like the birds in *Suddenly Last Summer*, those terrible birds diving and tearing at the helpless baby turtles scrambling down the beach to the sea.

David was too shy to read aloud from his novel-in-progress (or was it a memoir?), but some students did, like Gabriel, the short intense Bolivian with a carved, unreadable face. The elegant way he sat and dressed and spoke seemed to invite admiration, but only from a distance.

Which was why David didn't expect Gabriel to read a prose poem about a guy making a pass at him in the steam room at a local gym. David had heard that a lot of gay men went at certain times, though he didn't know when that was, and he wasn't interested himself.

Everyone in the small group that evening looked astonished at the amazingly sexual images in Gabriel's piece filling the room with unexpected heat—like "cock hair dense as caviar." There were only seven people there as Gabriel read words completely out of keeping with his shy, restrained demeanor. Gabriel's unaccented steady soft voice was like the confident warm strumming of a guitar, incantatory, enveloping. David could feel himself turning red, and he looked down.

When Gabriel finished, one or two of them made some bumbling remarks, but Meloth lurched into action, a trembling avalanche of contempt that ended with: "You could write such garbage in your sleep. It takes no skill, no inspiration—only Vaseline." Meloth announced they were ending early, as if outraged by Gabriel's writing, and they all decamped from the book store.

Driving home David felt haunted by Gabriel's rich voice and Meloth's contempt, and David called Jake from his car to tell him what had happened.

At home, they sat together by the fire while David felt besieged by the image of Meloth in the workshop, the silence after he spoke, David's inability to comment, disagree, the glare and buzz of the neon lights in the store. It was as if a monstrous snake, jaws unhinged, were surrounding, engulfing its poisoned helpless prey, drawing it deeper, slowly into darkness in demonstration of a principle much older, more terrible than itself.

Jake had put on calming music, Lorraine Hunt Anderson singing haunting Bach cantatas, but the music didn't touch David.

"I should have said something!" he complained. "Not just slunk away like everybody else."

Jake stroked his hands, his hair. "You didn't feel safe."

"You would have told Meloth he was full of shit. I mean, I'm forty-eight years old, I'm totally out, and I still couldn't speak up."

"Coming out takes a lifetime. It's never over. And even though it's not a class with grades, Meloth's still the authority figure. He's got the power."

"He's got a lot of nerve. And why didn't anyone else say something? This is Ann Arbor, not Alabama."

"They were probably shocked, like you were. And embarrassed. It paralyzes you. And we may be in Ann Arbor, but we live in George Bush's America, remember? Listen, how about a video tonight to cheer you up? We can watch something funny. *Bullets Over Broadway*? *Jumping Jack Flash*?"

"No. I want to see people get killed. Violence."

Jake looked at him, nodded. "Sure." They picked *Aliens*. Later, when Jake was asleep, David lay awake thinking of all the things he could have said to defend Gabriel or at least put Meloth in his place. He wasn't sure how good the writing was, but it didn't deserve being slashed.

At the next workshop, Gabriel was not there. The tall, fortyish, burly redheaded guy named Chase sat next to David and nodded like a fellow passenger on a bus plunging uncertainly through snow and slush, as if to say "Some night, huh?" In the circle of chairs, the four other would-be writers were either reading, journaling, or just spaced out. A few minutes after class was supposed to start, a clerk from the bookstore they were meeting in came over to tell them that Meloth had phoned to say he was unable to make it that evening.

"Too bad," Chase said. "I was hoping he was in a car crash. You up for a drink?"

Chase had barely nodded to him these past weeks, so the invitation was unexpected. Out on the street, David studied him and thought he looked as large and heroic as one of those figures in a WPA mural—worker, farmer, American.

"Sure."

Catty corner from the book store street was a bar with a Sixties jukebox and tonight, a Thursday, the place was unexpectedly dead. They sat in an isolated booth and ordered Heineken drafts. Chase spoke with the stiffness of rehearsal: "I read your stuff in the *Free Press*. You're good." And before David could thank him, he went on, "You know, when Meloth said Gabriel's piece was shit, I wanted to deck him. I wanted to say, 'Fuck you, what do you know about being gay?' " And Chase nodded as proudly as if he actually had done those things.

"You're gay?"

"No. You don't have to be gay to think Meloth's a jerk." Then he lowered his voice. "But I mess around."

"Oh." The one piece Chase had brought in to the group was about his wife. Chase finished his beer, waved to the waiter for another. When it came and the waiter was back near the bar, he said, "Marriage is one thing, getting laid is something else. My wife's not into sex and I like to have a fuck buddy now and then." And his eyes drilled David's, the invitation obvious. "I know you're hooked up with that shrink guy—"

"—We're married, except for the ceremony and the ring."

Chase shrugged. That clearly wasn't a marriage to him. "We could have some fun together." Then he added, "You and me," as if it might be unclear.

Despite himself, David felt a surge in his crotch, imagining that magnificent body looming over him. Under the table, Chase nudged his foot.

Then David smiled when the Doors' "Break on Through" started thumping from the jukebox, ending the stream of Temps and Four Tops songs. He drew his foot back.

"Thanks, but I don't fuck around. I'm actually pretty straight for a gay man."

Chase nodded a few times, as if taking that in or making a show of taking that in. Then he switched gears: "You think Meloth imploded and the workshop is over?"

"Maybe."

"Well, I'm in the book, call me if you change your mind. My last name's Borenstein."

"You're Jewish?"

"What's the big deal?"

"Your name. . . ."

Chase smiled. "Coulda been worse. Claude or Dorian or something like that."

David laughed and they headed outside. Chase slapped his shoulder and said "Seeya."

Back home, David had to tell the story of Chase's pass several times. Jake grinned, like a parent proud of his shy kindergartener's first reports of playground companions. They had gotten stoned to watch *Lara Croft: Tomb Raider* for the fourth time but talked through most of it.

"You think it's hot," David said, "but I feel sorry for him. It's 2004 and he's on the down low."

"That's his choice."

"I don't think so, I think the choice isn't free when so many people hate us, when even Jews are homophobic. You've met guys, we both have, who are active in the Jewish community around Detroit, they win awards, but they're closeted. We're still not free."

"Well, I'm going to bed," Jake said, pulling off his sweater, stretching his rich heavy shoulders and arms, the dark nipples tightened by the brush of wool. Jake went off to the bathroom. He was a short man, but powerfully built, someone you could imagine saving others in a plane crash or other terrible accident. And hadn't Jake saved him?

When they met so many years ago, David had been like one of those storybook characters lost and bewildered in a terrible forest, who finds a shelter dazzling in its safety and warmth. So dazzling that its outlines never become quite clear. Jake had rescued him, released him. And moving in together had been like opening a long classic novel he'd always heard about—*Anna Karenina*, perhaps—to follow the beckoning first lines that promised a chance to live another, richer life.

He had that life. Or nearly had it.

David watched Jake walk back into the room wearing the blue silk robe that matched his eyes, and David glowed as if they were already in each other's arms after sex, nuzzling, sleepy, safe. He could still remember the years growing up and whenever he had looked at a man he thought attractive, he had cursed himself inside, jeering, "You faggot." The voice was his own, but the feeling of disgust, the sneer was his mother's.

"Oh my God," David said, and Jake sat down opposite, curious but not alarmed. "I just figured it out. Meloth reminded me of my mother! That kind of crazy hammering she used to do on me. That's why I froze."

"It makes sense."

"But doesn't it ever end—don't we ever get rid of them?"

"There's that amazing line from *Mourning Becomes Electra*, remember? 'Why don't the dead die?'"

"But your parents weren't like that, they accepted you. They accept us. My father didn't even use your name when he called, he just said, how's everything going? And I was supposed to figure out that meant you."

"Listen, my parents gave up trying to change me—that's a better way of saying it." Jake reminded David about the therapist he'd had as a teenager, a beautiful black woman who sounded like an actress. After only two sessions, she'd called in Jake's parents and said, 'Your son is gay, and that's not going to change. You can fight him, and fight it, but you'll only make yourselves miserable, and you won't help him at all.'

"Let's get ready for bed."

David followed Jake and started to wash up in the pink-tiled bathroom that was original to the house and they'd left as it was in what David sometimes thought was a surplus of irony.

"I feel besieged," he said. "It's not just Meloth and thinking about my Mom, it's the whole fucking country. How can *Will and Grace* be so popular but people still hate us the way they do?"

"Because that show is a fantasy, it's a gay *Amos and Andy*, you know that. It's unthreatening and goofy, it's not real."

In bed, David was still fuming, and Jake tried calming him down.

"Accepting yourself also means accepting that some people, that most people won't accept you—and you can't make them. They're irrational. Being queer scares lots of people. That's why they go nuts about gay marriage as a threat to marriage when it's adultery and booze and getting married too young and just plain being fucking stupid that makes marriages fall apart. Before that it was AIDS, but that was just an excuse because people hated gays before AIDS. Jews and queers, we just have history screwing us over. You think you can ever get people to stop being anti-Semitic? Look at Israel—how many Jews figured, 'Great, our own country, now we'll be left alone.' But being more visible, knowing who you are, means you take more risks."

David sat up in their cherry sleigh bed, arms crossed over his t-shirt from the Stratford Festival.

Jake kept talking, and suddenly he seemed both calmer and more excited, as if he hadn't realized before that he was lost. "Just because you're happy, *we're* happy, that doesn't mean it can change the world. Or change the U.S. You know, when I retire, we'll have enough money, I can give up private practice, and if you want, we can move to Canada. You know they'll have a national marriage law next year for sure. We can apply for citizenship, however long it takes, and get married there. It'll be better than this."

"Never. I'm not going to move away from my home. I don't want to leave my whole life behind to be free. That's why people have always come to America, from the beginning. Isn't it? That's why my mother came here, and your grandparents. And now you want me to be a refugee? This is my home."

"The Nazis took your mother away. You think this government couldn't take us away if it wanted to? There's plenty of hate to go around."

"It's not that bad yet. We're not living in a fascist state."

"Give it time." Jake shook his head and reached to turn out the light. "They've invaded Iraq, they're invading us. All of us, every day, with lies and fear and bullshit."

Despite his harangue, Jake fell asleep first as usual, and as I drifted off myself, I remembered something strange my father had told me after my mother died. For all the years of their marriage, she had kept a suitcase packed with toiletries and clothes under her bed. If she ever had to escape. She'd take it out and update the contents once or twice a year, always on the same date. Why those particular days? She never explained, but the bag was always ready, and so was she.

— III —

Dancing on Tisha B'Av

Brenda was already used to the men, sitting on the other side of the chest-high wooden *mehitzah* that separated them from the women, saying that they needed one more "person" to make the *minyan* while she and sometimes as many as six other women might be there. Like now, suspended in summer boredom, their conversation as heavy with heat as the sluggish flies whispering past in the small green-walled shul on the musty ground floor of the Jewish Center. Sometimes they all waited half an hour before continuing with services, for a man, any man, to be tenth. It amused her that even the dimmest specimens counted when she didn't—shabby un-showered men who shouted rather than sang and read Hebrew as if each line were the horizon blurred by heat; yawning men whose great round gasps for air seemed their profoundest prayers; men who sneeringly hissed game scores (and had to be hushed) to show how immune they were to the Ark, to anything Jewish and sacred.

Sometimes, on the other side, her brother Nat corrected them and said, "Man. You mean another man." And she smiled at his embarrassment for her.

Though raised Conservative, she had come to like the Orthodox service. Here the purpose was prayer, not socializing, showing off Judaic knowledge, filling the shul, or even getting away from the kids for a morning: People sometimes joked, but the service itself was serious. At the faculty-dominated shuls in their university town the persistent chitchat and laughter were like the desperate assertion of rationality and control in the face of what was mysterious—as if to let go, to be silent and feel, would be an admission of nakedness and shame.

"Too many Ph.D.s" was Nat's comment, and she, a graduate student in history, had felt accused. A junior, Nat had been attending the Orthodox services for two years, and his commitment was as fierce and sullen as the clutch of a baby's hand on a stolen toy.

Nat went out now to practice his Torah portion in another room. Thin, with the twitching walk of a jerky marionette, and that pale and narrow face, he seemed a genetic rebuke to their handsome family, a warning that all gifts were uncertain. As a boy, he'd been aloof, watchful, building castles out of blocks and bricks, pretending to be powerful, a knight. He never cried, never apologized. Spanking him was pointless, scolding absurd. The little mean eyes just shut inside, his face grew stupid and closed.

"*Red tsu a vant!*" their father would shout in Yiddish ("Talk to a wall!"), uneasily admiring the stubborn boy. The stocky pharmacist would peer down at Nat, hands clenched, as if wishing they were equals and could fight.

Nat was sullen and silent until he went into theater in high school, stunning Brenda with his intensity as Tom in *The Glass Menagerie*. He had felt, to her, more maimed by life than the girl playing Laura. Onstage, his walk, his thin face were larger, more compelling; his authority was beautiful. It had been the same here at State the few times he did a show.

What did their parents think?

Their mother said, "He takes makeup very well, it doesn't look like him."

His father, when he didn't fall asleep in the darkened auditorium, smirked, "Sure . . . here he can act—so what? Try Broadway!"

They were just as supportive of Nat's slow move to Orthodoxy, his father shaking his head. "What I gave him isn't enough—he has to go to *fremdeh menshen*, strangers, to be a Jew." And their mother wondered if Nat would be allowed to touch any woman he wasn't married to, and was he going to Israel to throw stones at cars that drove on Saturday?

How much this all affected Nat, Brenda didn't know. He had always refused to acknowledge successes as well as failure, living, she thought, in stubborn exile, unreachable, untouched.

Nat had learned to tie his shoes too early, was too neat and alphabetical in his approach to life. It was as if saying "First things first" and making points in conversation by clutching successive fingers could order and control the world. He read Torah in a dry triumphant chant as if the letters piled around him in tribute. He was a vegetarian and drank only mineral water and herb teas. He ran seven miles a day, even in the winter. He loved men.

Brenda had known this, known something, for too long. When she was sixteen and Nat eleven, she found a folder in his pile of *Life, Car & Driver*, and *Reader's Digest*, crammed with pages sliced from magazines, all ads. They were men whose exquisite eyes and hands and hair, whose tough hard bodies shot one hopeless accusation after another: You are not beautiful—you never will be. Nat had distilled this terrible poison from harmless magazines.

It was that year Brenda found an open notebook on his desk in which he'd written out pages of new names for himself, first and last, a parade of loathing.

Before these discoveries, Nat had been annoying to her, or unimportant, or sometimes, unexpectedly cute. Suddenly, he was dangerous, unknown. In the next years, she'd wait for Nat's oddities to burst from the neutral box of his silence like trick paper snakes, but he was only more sullen, blighting family dinners like the suspicion of a pitiless disease. Her father gave up cursing and her mother shrugged, as if Nat were a strange country she'd never been able to find on a globe. When her mother did talk about Nat, she had the brisk bored sound of a librarian stating facts that anyone could check.

"He doesn't have wet dreams," her mother announced, folding laundry in the basement. "I've checked his sheets, Bren."

Brenda, nineteen then, tried to think of something adequate to her surprise.

And when Nat was in high school: "Bren, why doesn't he date more? I think he's afraid of sex. Your father said he blushed when they talked about condoms."

"Wait till eleven," a man on the other side was saying now. "We always wait."

"Forget it." That was Nat. "I called this week and no one's in town." He listed all his calls.

She knew that Nat was right; the Orthodox *minyan* drew on a very small group of Jews, and strangers rarely joined them. The women behind her stirred the pages of their prayer books as if scanning merchandise in a dull catalog. They were mostly the bleak girlfriends of men who ran the *minyan*, wearing artless, dowdy plain clothes and talking after services about movies or food. She imagined they would welcome marriage and the children who would release them from regular attendance. She thought of them as The Widows, because though in their mid-twenties, they already seemed isolated, like survivors of historic loss.

Around her, the heat, spread by a weak ceiling fan, settled like a film of soot or car exhaust her light dress, sandals, and short hair didn't help her feel cool.

"Brenda, you look very nice today."

Clark, the law student who looked like Al Pacino and thought he was Bruce Springsteen, hung over the *mehitzah*. He was from Bloomfield Hills, and always talked to her with the smugness she remembered in adolescent cliques, as if his good looks and hers bound them in undeniable complicity.

Before she could say anything, Nat was, back at the door, bleating, "*Gut Shabbos!*"

At the chipped bookcase with the prayer books and Bibles stood a tall muscular tanned man who looked thirty to her, blue-eyed, with thick close-trimmed mustache and beard that seemed very black above the tan summer suit and white shirt. He slipped a prayer shawl from the wooden stand, covered his head with it as he said the blessing, and found a seat up near the front of the men's side, shaking hands, nodding, After finding out the man's Hebrew name (for when he'd be called up), Nat marched to the lectern.

It was a blessing to be the tenth man, she thought, as services continued with unexpected excitement. They sang and chanted like forty people, not fourteen. When there wasn't a *minyan* and the Torah had to stay in its plainly curtained ark, she felt a fierce longing to see it borne around the shul to be touched with prayer books, prayer shawl fringes, or kissed like a bride as some of the men did.

When the stranger, *Moshe Leib ben Shimon haLevi*, Mark, was called to the Torah for the second blessing, he loomed over the lectern like a dark memorial in a way that dried her throat; his back seemed broad and forbidding. But his voice was sweet, smooth, rising and falling with the self-indulgent sadness of a Russian folk song. He sight-read the first portion without a mistake. They were all impressed.

Nat, always well prepared, read badly today. He made mistakes even she could catch, and it was painful watching him struggle with easy words. The silver pointer in his hand usually paced serenely along each squarish path of Hebrew, but now it was as listless as an uninspired divining rod. She looked away from him, from her Bible. Nat would probably tell people after services that he was tired, and because he never read poorly, no one would doubt him. She hoped.

What did people say about him? Could they tell?

"He should date more"—that was his mother's verdict. Mrs. Klein often mentioned friends' daughters to Nat at holiday dinners as if genially passing a liqueur, but to Brenda she had recently said, "Is he gay?"

"No!"

"You're sure—?"

"Mom."

Her father had said nothing directly or indirectly to Brenda; if it concerned him that Nat had hardly dated, he probably classed that with Nat's habitual stubbornness. Besides, she imagined her father sneering, "With that *punim*, that face, who would want him?"

For Brenda, Nat was Coronado discovering the Seven Cities of El Dorado everywhere—in the pumping bare thighs of bikers on campus, the ripe curves of jeans-tight butts, the heavy twin swells of runners' chests under cool molding cotton—flash after flash of heaven-sent gold in hundreds of men around campus. But he was a Coronado without armor, without guides, troops, provisions, maps, or even a commission. He had only his hunger.

She never spoke about this with Nat, never asked about dates or parties, had no idea what his life was like. Nat lived in his dorm and she in her apartment in town, with the huge ecstatically landscaped campus between them. They had lunch sometimes, she phoned him, they met at services and occasionally drove home to Southfield together, but she seldom mentioned that her brother was "up at school."

She was ashamed.

In her freshman year, back at the University of Wisconsin in Madison, on her coed floor, there had been a lovely dark-haired boy named Tom who did up his single room with Japanese fans, silk scarves, and other gentle souvenirs of summers abroad. Cool, quiet, musical, literate, he was the eye of a storm: doors banged, voices hushed and growled, or cracked with laughter, and the jocks on their floor simmered like guard dogs on maddening chains. One morning, a camping ax was found buried in Tom's door, the handle chalked, for clarity, "Faggot Die." Tom moved off campus, and that was what she feared for Nat—violence in the night, a scandal.

Having drifted away during the Torah reading, she didn't reenter the service, but stood and sat with everyone and prayed aloud mechanically as if she were in an educational filmstrip, each action large and stiff. Mark, the stranger, had asked to do the last part of the service, and his Hebrew was fluent in the thick summer air.

On the way out after the last hymn, Mark wished her *Shabbat Shalom*.

"You read well," she said as they milled at the table set with kiddush wine and cakes in the little social hall.

And then Nat was there, grinning, his pale face spattered with excitement. After blessing the wine, Nat pulled Mark aside to talk about the next week's Torah portion.

Helen, Clark's cousin, bore down on Brenda. With her thin ugly legs and heavy shifting hips and rear, she resembled a pack mule struggling up a hill.

"*Gut Shabbos*," Helen murmured, round face doleful, as if she was passing on unpleasant gossip. "Isn't he terrific?"

"Mark?"

"Uh-huh. What a spa."

"Spa. . . ."

"Sure, he works out . . . look at his chest, those shoulders. Yum."

Brenda watched them; Mark with the cool, one-dimensional beauty of a brass rubbing, Nat grasping at him with a sickly smile. She ate a dry piece of pound cake.

There were at least a thousand Jewish students on campus, but hardly any came to the Orthodox *minyan*, which was a mix of graduate students, one or two shabby faculty members, and several university staffers. Mark's arrival was welcome, Brenda knew, because he could take some of the burden of leading services from Clark and Nat and the others who sometimes felt like, prisoners of their obligations. An assistant to the Registrar, Mark spoke little about himself, but seemed to have for Nat the impact of an analyst whose silence and concern at last permit an entrance to oneself. Nat told Brenda that he talked about his acting, his Russian and French classes, his desire to enter the foreign service, about everything. He was like a child dragging pretty treasures from pockets, under the bed, from drawers, to entertain, attract, possess a fascinating friend.

Brenda saw in Nat, for the first time, a resemblance to their mother. Generally, Mrs. Klein was like an antiques dealer displaying a find—herself—with chic reverence. She was slim, wide-eyed, fashionable even in a bathrobe, especially in a bathrobe whose rough folds set her off like a pretty girl's plain best friend. But sometimes their mother emerged from this haze of self-absorption to talk with merciless charm to strangers or her children's "little friends." She asked them endless unimportant questions until they found themselves like flood victims forced onto the roof of their self-possession, praying for the waters to subside.

Brenda saw Nat talking with that intensity to Mark one Sunday afternoon two weeks after that first Shabbat, at a restaurant in town, saw him through the wide front window, face twisted and alive, fingers plucking at a sugar packet. Mark sat deeply back from him, sky-blue tennis shirt open at a dense-haired throat, heavy fine arms crossed, a smile, some kind of smile nestled in the mustache and the beard. Mark was not just passively beautiful, she realized as she hurried on to buy her *Times* at the chain bookstore down the block, not a man to merely watch, admire, but warm, receptive, inviting. It was the lush curves of shoulders, chest, the gleaming hair and beard, the hard-lined nose and high cheekbones, the paintable mouth.

Not her type at all, too dramatic, too intense. The men she dated were at most "cute," and their ideas about Third World debt or German reunification gave them more color than the way they walked or dressed or were.

"They don't scare you," Nat had concluded, and it was too obvious for her to deny.

Mark and Nat started running together at the high school track near her apartment, like a boy and his puppy eager to show off how fast it moved. Mark's legs were hairy and dark, strong admonitions to the pale, weak.

They'd stop at her place afterward for water, to towel off, talking about the weather and their wind, old injuries. Mark spoke even then as if emerging from a past that wasn't his but something he had learned, borrowed details of a spy. He sat on the floor, back against her gray-green sofa bed, heavy legs out, relaxed, holding the tumbler to his face and neck. Nat looked wild and flustered, as if he couldn't decide whether to yell or leap or cry.

In late July, when the whole estate settled into a heat wave that seemed as inexorable as lava sweeping down a barren slope, Nat made an announcement to her one Friday afternoon.

"Mark has the use of a place on the lake, near Saugatuck, and he invited me to go next Saturday night after Shabbat and spend a day or two at the beach." Nat's face was so surly that she saw him as a boy again, daring their parents with his refusal to eat beans, or wash his hair, or turn from the television.

"Does he know you're in love with him?"

Nat gave her a liar's grin, stalling. "What?"

She looked down at her cool plate of deviled eggs, potato salad, tabouli, as if the food were an exhibit in a museum case, proof of customs stranger than one's own.

"What?"

She felt guilty now, tight-eyed. "If he's not gay, he's being very cruel."

Watching Nat lean away as if the sprigged tablecloth were dangerous somehow, she understood how strong soft people really were-they could retreat across vast plains of silence, disappear.

"I wrote him a poem," Nat brought out heavily, a pauper facing his last, most. precious coin. And when he turned away, she jerked from her chair to crouch by her brother, hold him and ease the ugliness of tears.

Mark called after Nat was gone, to invite himself over that evening. From Nat, she'd learned that he and Mark had spent many nights together since the first Shabbat in June, at Mark's apartment near the university and then the one he moved to in a nearby town.

Mark wore white jeans, Top-Siders, and a white Lacoste, as if to show her he was normal, American, no threat. But sitting in her small cramped living room, he looked like a model posed in an unlikely spot to throw his beauty into high relief.

They drank coffee.

"I was married," Mark offered. "Nat didn't say? In New York. We split up two years ago; I moved to Philadelphia, then here." He nodded like an old man in a rocker whose every motion confirms a memory.

"Children?"

"We couldn't."

She wished, in the quiet, for a clock that chimed, a noisy refrigerator, dogs outside, something to ease the tension in her neck and hands. She imagined her parents there: Dad scornful, incensed; Mom peering at Mark with distaste, curious, purring, "But he's handsome, don't you think?" Closing her eyes, Brenda saw the ax saying "Faggot Die" like the afterimage of a too-bright bulb.

Nat had pursued Mark, she knew, even if Nat didn't, so there was no blame for her to spatter on the canvas of Mark's silence.

"What about AIDS?" she asked.

"I've been tested. I'm okay. And Nat was a virgin."

"How about people seeing you at the Lake, or in town?"

"It's not a secret for me being gay."

"But Nat's only twenty-one." She rose to bring the coffeepot to them. "It could destroy him."

Mark shrugged.

She asked about the house on Lake Michigan two hours away, and Mark described the drive there, the beach. While he spoke, a thought crossed her mind with brazen clarity: even though she felt warmer to Nat after, his crying confession, she didn't love him, still, and feared what people would say about her more than what might happen to Nat. I'm like Mom, she thought. Cold.

The weekend was fabulous, Nat raved, returning with color, some new clothes, and a haircut that made him subtly more attractive.

"He wants to take me to Paris next year!" Nat crowed.

"On his salary?"

"He has friends there."

Friends, she thought.

At services, Nat sat next to Mark, the fringes of their prayer shawls touching, perhaps, beneath their chairs. Nat had coolly talked about Mark's divorce to most people there, had reported it with enough vagueness and somber gaps to make it seem a tragedy of some kind, a wound too open to discuss. "That's why he came to Michigan," Nat would conclude, delighted with his subterfuge. He could've been a child pretending there were dragons in the dark that only he could slay.

"Mark doesn't like me talking like that," Nat smirked.

Did she? Did she like any of it? When she wasn't plowing through the book list for her last comprehensive in September, she wondered what she felt. Mark was apparently kind to Nat, and luckily not one of those bitchy homosexuals whose standards were as vigilant and high as satellites, but he was real, and puzzling.

"What do you see in Nat?" she asked one noon in town, where she'd come across Mark waiting to cross a street to campus. He frowned and she felt exposed, her lack of understanding, her contempt as clear to him as diamonds on blue velvet.

"He's very shy," Mark said. "I like to make him smile."

She remembered Nat years ago, little, awash in bedclothes, small eyes tight with disapproval as their mother brought tea, sat on the edge of the bed holding the saucer in one hand, bringing the cup to his lips and back in a steady hypnotic beat, meanwhile telling him a complicated silly story to get him to smile.

Mark and Nat started spending less time with her after she asked Mark that question, as if she, a bumbling parent, had mortified a group of teens by trying to be sincere. Mark was busy helping Nat prepare for Tisha B'Av, the late summer Ninth of Av fast, teaching him Lamentations. She didn't like the fast memorializing the Temple's destruction by the Romans, which reading Josephus's *Jewish Wars* had made more awful to her. The slaughter, the terrible thirst, starvation, and ruin were all too real for her, too historic, harbingers of camps and numbered arms. At least. Mark and Nat, leading the services, would have something to do to keep them from falling into the past—or so she felt.

Her parents were even less sympathetic to Tisha B'Av; they liked the more decorative holidays, like Passover and Chanukah, and suffered through the High Holy Days as if paying stiffly for their pleasure later in the year.

Less than a week before Tisha B'Av, Helen's grocery cart pulled up next to hers at one of the mammoth vegetable counters in the town's largest market.

"Is your brother a fag?" Helen shot, and the two women feeling tomatoes nearby glared up at them. "Because I saw him coming out of Bangles downtown last Saturday, and honey, he was drunk. Mark, too—what a waste!"

Rigid, Brenda imagined a dump truck dropping tons of potatoes on Helen, sealing her away forever.

Helen grinned, looking like a grotesque carnival target. With more strength than she knew was in her legs and arms, Brenda moved her cart away and down the aisle, then left, as if the metal burned, and hurried out to her car. Getting in, she thought of flight, retreat no one would ever find her, hear from her again. But starting the Toyota seemed to drain the panic through her hand into the key and she drove out along the interstate to Mark's apartment complex ten minutes away.

"You moron! Why'd you go there!"

"I wanted to dance," he said, sitting down, untouched by her distress. "So did Nat. I love dancing with him. He's beautiful then, the way he moves, his eyes—"

Brenda flushed. She had only seen Nat dance at wedding receptions, and then he had seemed to her stiff, embarrassed, dancing only because he had to. She didn't know him at all, she thought dully.

"I hate it, I hate thinking about the two of you together. I don't understand what it means."

"Do you have to?" asked Mark.

"Don't be so cool."

"I'm thirty-five, he said. "What should I be?"

She felt inflamed by her father's angry pounding voice, but didn't know the words to destroy Mark.

"Well," Mark said, "how about a drink?"

"Yes," she said. "I will."

He joined her on the beige pillow-backed sofa that was as neutral and expensive-looking as everything there—prints, cushions, lamps.

"You know it doesn't bother me now," Mark began. "But for years I thought God would get me, like Aaron's sons when they offer up 'strange fire' and get zapped? My best friend all through school, from way back, was gay, too—in college he told his rabbi about us and got sent to Israel."

"Did it help?"

"Well, he got married."

"Was he like Nat?"

"Nobody's like Nat."

One point for you, she thought, and asked for another drink.

Nat showed up just then and she tried to tell him about Helen. Nat said he didn't care, and they went off to the best Szechuan restaurant in the county for a lavish dinner. Later, they drank at a bar like witnesses of an accident, desperate to blur the vision of that crash, the blood and smoke. Nat wouldn't discuss what had happened; each time she tried to bring it up, he looked away.

Two days later, Brenda came to Shabbat services late, right before the Torah reading, and everyone was up, jabbering, flushed. Clark stood at the lectern, his back to the Ark, as pale as Nat and Mark, who faced him from the narrow aisle between the men's chairs and the *mehitzah*.

"Get out," Clark was saying. "I won't let you touch that Torah. My grandfather donated it."

"You're crazy," Mark said.

"You're sick."

Brenda wavered at the door, disgusted by the ugly atmosphere of children squashing worms to make them writhe, exploding frogs with firecrackers.

"Come on," Mark said, slipping off his prayer shawl, jamming it into the gold-embroidered red velvet bag. Mark smiled relief when he saw her, squeezed her hand. White-faced, Nat followed, and Brenda was surprised that he didn't forget on the way out to touch the mezuzah on the doorpost and bring the fingers back to his' lips. No one speaking, they drove away in Mark's Volvo to his apartment, as if speeding on the road could strip away that scene.

Upstairs, Mark dumped his blazer on a chair, wrenched off his tie to sit with an arm around Nat, who was still pale and silent. Mark said, "I didn't think it would happen. They need us, it's our *minyan*, too."

"Technically," Brenda said, "it's not my *minyan*. " But no one smiled.

"We'll move," Nat finally said. "We'll go to New York!" Mark smoothed Nat's stringy hair with such gentleness that Brenda felt unexpectedly released. Their closeness warmed her like a Vermeer, rich with circumstantial life.

198

Tisha B'Av was the next night and they made plans to attend at one of the faculty shuls. Leaving, she surprised herself by kissing both of them.

Nat didn't call her that night and she hardly slept, awash with a sort of amazement that the children they had been had gown to see such ugliness. She longed in her restless bed for escape, for some wild romantic lover, a Czech perhaps, a refugee musician who'd fled, in '68, whose loss was larger than her own, a nation's freedom instead of a woman's pride. He would have an accent, she decided sleepily, imagining herself in a sleek black dress, and have a mustache a bit like Mark's. . . .

Mark was alone when he arrived Sunday evening. "Nat isn't coming. He went out."

"Out?"

"Bangles. To get drunk. To dance. He's furious." Mark smoothed down his gray silk tie, looking much too calm.

"He's dancing on Tisha B'Av?" She sat at the dinette table, more confused now than ever.

Mark pressed his hands to the back of his neck, massaging, stretching. "He had this dream last night, that he was swimming far from shore and there were sharks. He woke us both up. Shouting. He couldn't get away."

Brenda could feel her dress sticking to her back despite the air conditioning. "What if he sleeps with someone? He'll get herpes, he'll get AIDS!"

Mark eyed her steadily. "I think he'll just dance."

She followed Mark out to his car, and on the drive to the faculty shul, Brenda knew she was feeling the wrong things. She should be understanding, compassionate now, not think that. Nat was doing something ugly and vindictive, desecrating the fast day that he believed was solemn and holy. She should be happy for him, happy that he knew who he was, what he wanted, could feel his feelings, had found Mark—all of that.

She could hear her father snapping out the contemptuous Yiddish phrase for when two things had absolutely no connection: *Abi geret*. Says who?

As they pulled into the temple's parking lot, Mark asked, "You okay?"

She wasn't. What she wanted now was to slip out of the past months as if they were only a rented hot and gaudy costume she could finally return.

What she wanted more than anything on this burning night of Tisha B'Av was to forget.

Another Life

Nat had not started coming to Michigan State's small Orthodox congregation two years ago to look for a man. He expected to feel safe there, hidden, because it was not like his parents' huge suburban synagogue outside Detroit—all gleaming polished oak, a theater, a social hall, a stage. In the Jewish Students' Center at the edge of campus, they prayed in a bare, high-ceilinged, narrow room that was like an exercise in perspective, drawing your eyes inexorably to the plainly curtained ark in front. His first time, he'd sat in the last row, on the men's side, alone, after putting on his prayer shawl and slipping a prayer book from the crowded chest-high bookcase behind him.

At the small slanting-topped lectern, a man was praying aloud wrapped in an enormous black-barred wool prayer shawl as large as a flag. Nat's little polyester one, gold-embroidered like a sampler, seemed incongruous, almost ugly-though it was what he'd always used since his bar mitzvah. The man came back to shake Nat's hand at the point where waiting for enough men to continue with prayers began, and got Nat's Hebrew name for when he would call him to the lectern. Nat always regretted just being a Yisroel, one of the vast majority of Jewish men. Levis claimed descent from the Temple functionaries who sang the psalms and were entitled now to the second Torah blessing at services. Cohens were descended from the priests and had the first Torah blessing in synagogues. Nat liked this remnant of the Temple hierarchy even though he was at the bottom (his sister, Brenda, said, "Well then, that leaves me underground!").

Only six of the thin-seated black plastic and chrome chairs were filled that first morning, by guys who would have been unexceptional on campus or in town but here looked costumed and exotic in prayer shawls and skullcaps. They all chatted for a while. Most were graduate students, but for Nat they had the authority of much older men, because of their deep Jewish knowledge and the way they prayed.

The few women—wives, a girlfriend—were pale, plain, undemanding. Nat was glad they were on the other side of the five foot-high wooden barrier—the *mehitzah*—separate, even after services, even talking to the men, still as private and inaccessible as ducks brooding by the river on campus. They came to consider him shy, he knew, because he seldom initiated a conversation.

Nat had always watched other men pose, lean, grin, and entertain women, as if from a distance, thinking they looked like clownishly intense animals in mating desperation, all puffed up on display. Nat couldn't mimic the flattery and ogling, because women had never stirred a desire even to pretend in him. They were merely figures in a landscape.

The Orthodox service on Saturday mornings was very long, almost four hours, and some of the prayers and melodies were unfamiliar at first, but the direction and sequence were similar to the services he'd grown up with, and coming every week, he began to fit inside this new structure for belief. Nat's Hebrew, always better than Brenda and his parents knew, blossomed, until he felt confident enough to offer to do part of the service. It was such a small congregation, usually less than fifteen except on holidays, that praying here was intensely private for him, thankfully not a time to see relatives, friends from high school, or be shown off by his parents as a faithful son. Sometimes he was so moved, he covered his head with the large new prayer shawl he'd bought in Southfield, shutting the world and everyone out as the truly Orthodox did.

The singing, the absence of English, the spiritual concentration—kavannah-seemed—beautiful to him, as if they were all, at the most powerful moments, the fabulous gold cherubim on the Ark of the Covenant, over which hovered God's presence. Sometimes he felt that holy, that moved beyond himself—but who could he tell? The few Jewish acquaintances he had at State weren't interested in hearing about his discoveries. Most people would just class him as a fanatic, as his parents seemed to (Brenda listened, but not with enthusiasm), and even the congregation's regulars stayed away from talking about feelings or anything verging on mysticism. For them, the service was simply the right and only way to pray.

Yet he welcomed their self-absorption. He had really come here, at first, before he was seduced by the service itself, hoping that the Orthodox congregation, the *minyan*, might be a bath of acid in which he could burn away like verdigris from a bronze his obsessions about men. He'd heard about druggy friends saved by joining Orthodox communities in Brooklyn, lazy and almost criminal "trouble" students at his high school straightening out in Hasidic enclaves of Jerusalem, and had hoped for a similar miracle. Nothing else had worked.

Acting had not helped him lose himself, but brought him into a terrifying world of men who blared their availability and were always making reconnaissance raids on guys who didn't. Learning French and starting on Russian had only given him new words, not a new identity. Running did make him fit, supplied a hobby and completely new range of conversation—shoes, tracks, breathing, diet, shin splints, marathons, stars, books, and magazines—but he was still only Nat for all those miles. And he only admired other runners more, became a connoisseur of those wonderful high round asses, those long and heavy thighs. When he watched track and field events on TV, he waited for close-ups or slow-motion shots to see the heavy weight inside a favorite runner's thin and clinging shorts whip and swing from thigh to thigh.

Even at services, alone with the other men, trying to stay deep in prayer; his thoughts sometimes wandered: to a barefoot guy in cutoffs hosing down his car across the street, who'd glanced at him one morning as Nat entered the building; or two wide-backed, tanned bikers damp with sweat and exhaustion shouting to each other as they cut down the street; or even Italian-looking Clark, who helped run the *minyan*, Clark whose weight lifting had left him as bulging and tight as a tufted leather sofa. Nat's private gallery. He felt then lonelier than ever, tracing the path of his unquenched thirst for men, to be a man (was that different? the same?) back to childhood. When he had not felt this way? And what would it be like never to look at men but only see them: pure registration without excitement, interest, pain? He was always feeling helpless, like turning a corner in town and almost bumping into a guy in sweatpants with those seductive gray folds, whose belly seemed harder, flatter over the shifting, jock-rounded crotch, or watching someone's tight, jutting ass in the locker room at the gym as he bent over to pull up his shorts.

Still, he could lose himself in prayer often enough, long enough. And then his sister, Brenda, finishing her Ph.D. at State, began to join him at services after he'd learned the cantillation for reading the Torah. With her, he felt more anchored, sure this might be an answer if only he waited. Brenda wasn't pleased with sitting on the women's side at first, but she respected what he'd learned, or at least all the weeks of practicing at her apartment with a tape recording, chanting to himself there because it drove neighbors at the dorm crazy. And he was pleased that his pretty sister drew attention from the men, as if her presence made him less of a shadow or a blank, less suspiciously alone. With Brenda at services, he felt he could be normal—or seem that way—and sometimes it was easier to concentrate. Thoughts of men were not so intense; she was like a powerful signal jamming pirate broadcasts.

"I didn't think I would, but I like the service," she admitted after a few months. "I don't even mind the *mehitzah* anymore. I don't get distracted looking around, like back home."

At men, he thought, wondering what she had guessed about him. Perhaps she knew everything and didn't want to mention it, like the Jews in polls done by national Jewish magazines, who overwhelmingly supported civil rights for homosexuals but didn't want to have to see what that meant in their own lives. This unspoken demand for invisibility was more enlightened than Judaism's traditional distaste for homosexuality, but Nat could not find the difference very comforting.

Nat watched Mark's strong shoulders inside the black-striped prayer shawl on Mark's first *Shabbos* at the Orthodox congregation. Mark read Torah with a slow, persuasive rise and fall, beautiful large hands flat on the lectern, rocking softly, and Nat found himself staring at Mark's smooth thick lips when Mark brought the Torah around and he touched his prayer book to the velvet-sheathed scroll: Mark nodded.

Mark was a Levi, and Nat imagined him in the Temple, strong feet bare, curly hair and beard fragrantly oiled. With those deepset blue eyes, beard growing high on his cheeks; and the muscular frame, he looked distant, romantic, like someone's burly wild grandfather in an old photograph: a man who had disappeared on an adventure in Australia or Brazil. Nat drank Mark's every movement on that criminally hot and dusty June *Shabbos* Mark first came to services. When Mark kissed his prayer book on closing it, or bowed during certain prayers, the gestures were smooth and authentic expressions of a certainty Nat found seductive, and that made Mark unlike anyone else he knew.

In the little crowd after services, they discussed Mark doing part of the service next week. Mark talked briefly about having just taken an administrative job at State after a similar position at Penn, and Nat told him about being raised Reform. He described their invisible choir and organ, the three gowned rabbis who had seemed like Hollywood extras, watching them high on their stage from a sharply raked auditorium. It was theater to him back then, distant and boring.

Mark smiled. "So how'd you wind up here?"

Nat hesitated.

And Mark invited him back for *Shabbos* lunch after they chatted with Brenda, who assured Mark she had other plans.

They walked the mile or so from the Jewish Center in an almost incandescent heat—even Nat's skullcap seemed too warm and heavy to be wearing. Nat did most of the talking, and felt very young again, excited, as if he was on the verge of a birthday present, or a longed-for trip.

The air conditioning had left Mark's place blissfully cold. "This is just temporary," Mark said, explaining the boxes all over his featureless apartment. "I'm looking for somewhere nice."

They set the table and Nat tried not to falter when he handed Mark the silver laver at the sink after washing his hands and drying them while saying the blessing. Sitting opposite Mark, Nat watched him say *hamotzi*—the prayer over bread—long hands on the swelling, shiny challah. Mark sliced a piece, salted it, and gave Nat half.

"This is beautiful." Nat fingered the linen cloth, the. silver.

"Wedding presents." And then he shrugged "That was a long time ago, in another life. It's not important anymore."

After lunch of a traditional *Shabbos* cholent—the meat and beans stew that baked overnight—and singing the prayers, they played Scrabble and read the Detroit newspapers in a silence so comfortable, Nat felt as purified and free as after an hour in the campus steam room.

"Why don't you stay?" Mark said near six o'clock.

"For dinner?"

Mark smiled and slipped off his skullcap, then shook his head.

"Stay with me. Come on, aren't you gay?"

Eyes down, Nat said, "I've never done this."

"But don't you want to?" Mark came to hold him tightly, stroking his hair, his arms and face, taming the wild beast, fear, and then led him into the bedroom. Mark stripped. His body was statue-hard, blazingly dark and public—as if all the men Nat had ever gawked at padding from the showers to their lockers; or lifting weights, shoulders and face bulging as if to hurl themselves up through the roof; or lounging near the pool in bathing suits no larger than index cards—as if their essence had been focused like a saving beam of light into this room, for him.

He pulled off his clothes and moved to hug Mark, entering that light which seemed now to blaze up inside of him as he rubbed himself against Mark.

"Wait."

Mark led him close to the mirror on the closet door, slipped behind him. "Look. *Look.*" With one hand, he held Nat's head up so that Nat was forced to see his own wide eyes, and Mark's guiding him. He leaned back into Mark as if cushioned by water in a heated pool, floating, hot, abandoned, as Mark lightly ran fingers along his sides, down to his thighs, and back up, circling, teasing, calling up sensations from his skin like a wizard marshaling a magical army from dust and bones. Nat watched his body leap and respond as if it, too, were urging him to keep his eyes open and unashamed. Mark slipped one dark and hairy hand down from his waist to grasp him; the other stroked his chest. Mark kissed his neck, his ears, his hair.

"Don't look away."

The words came to Nat as if in a dream in which he was a solitary tourist lost in some vast but familiar monument whose history and meaning he strained to understand in a shower of pamphlets. He struggled, he gave in, staring into Mark's eyes watching him watch an incomprehensible act that ended—for now—with a savage rush as he came, and Mark grinned, laughed, right hand wet and white.

Later that night, they took a walk to campus, and it was a bit cooler where they sat by the river.

"Sometimes I feel transported, completely," Mark told him, explaining why he was often intoxicated by *davening*—prayer. "On Rosh Hashanah once, I saw my shadow on the wall in shul, yarmulke, beard, and it didn't look like me. It could've been anyone, any Jew, who knows where, how far back."

Ducks, white and startling in the dark, idled against the river's current. Nat breathed in the faint sweetness of Mark's skin and hair, wanting to brush a hand in his beard.

"You know," Mark began, "There's a legend that the Torah is written in letters of black fire on white fire. Sometimes I can almost see it."

Nat admired how for Mark, being Jewish was home, not a foreign land to be approached with guidebooks and a map.

He thought about black and white fire the next *Shabbos*, and found himself crying when they sang "*Av Harachamin*," Compassionate Father, before the Torah was taken out of the Ark, their voices blended and thoughtful, not loud as usual. As Mark's soulful voice rose above the others, Nat felt open and faint, wanting to rise, enter, disappear.

When Mark blessed the wine after services, he was beautiful in his brown slacks and beige shirt, brown and beige Italian silk tie, not at all like the other guys in the *minyan* whose shabbiness was almost boastful.

"Are you okay?" Brenda asked Nat. "Are you getting a cold or something?" She was their family's smart one and the beauty: slim-hipped, gray-eyed, magnetic, her body built for bikinis, with curly, almost red hair, face wide and kind and striking, with Dad's strength and Mom's charm, but Nat no longer felt like her plain and unimpressive tag-along little brother.

"I'm great," he said.

Nat helped Mark move to a larger apartment farther from town. It was splendidly cool, neutral-toned, all gleaming glass and brass, a construction, perfect and complete. And with its balcony view of a man-made lake, it was like a brand-new eraser wiping Nat's ugly dorm room from a board like a hopelessly misspelled sentence. He hated leaving Mark's place, which felt like his first real home.

At the dorm, he had to laugh at the jokes about getting laid, about faggots, had to be careful not to stare at anyone getting out of the shower or even stare into the mirror at the reflection of someone half-dressed, or nude under an open robe, shaving, spitting, scratching, praying for consciousness. Here he felt safe, could shower with Mark, stroke his back; go nude, bite Mark's shoulders in the kitchen, be completely free, or at least grow toward that freedom. Because even when they just went out for dinner, or to a movie, he was not relaxed. He felt stared at, wondering if they looked like more than friends.

Mark insisted that here in a college town it was different than in New York; most people wouldn't assume two men together were together: "Look at all those jocks, and the fraternities." But Nat disagreed, worried about the ten years between them, wishing that he, too, were big, broad, and dark, bearded, gray-eyed, hairy, so that they could look like brothers or cousins.

Nat's fear led to their first explosion. Mark had bought them expensive seats for an upcoming Chicago Symphony performance on campus—an all-Russian program of *Russian and Ludmila*, *Le Sacre du printemps* and Prokofiev's Fifth Piano Concerto. But Nat just set aside the card with the tickets and didn't smile at his surprise that came with dessert.

"That's a date," he said. "Everyone will see us."

Mark was silent after that, rinsing off the dinner dishes in their sink of soapy water, starting the dryer, wiping the counter. He hung up the dish towel, his movements heavy, admonishing.

Nat sat at the table, waiting out the silence, feeling like he'd entered a room of celebration with news of someone's death—important but guilty.

Leaning back against the sink, thick arms crossed, not even looking at him, Mark almost spat out, "What is wrong with you? Why is everything so fucking secret? You won't even tell your sister about us!"

"We're not in New York, this is Michigan, and we're Jewish, and it's wrong."

"Sure! And tell me you voted for Reagan! Is it wrong for you, does it make you a monster? Will you stop lighting candles now, stop being a Jew?"

"Sometimes at services, I feel like I shouldn't be there, shouldn't kiss the Torah or do anything."

"That's what your parents would say, your rabbi, not you! You don't believe that, you can't. When are you going to stop hating yourself?"

Mark went on, and Nat hardly listened, but he felt the passion in Mark's voice and felt near tears, wishing Mark's message of acceptance was not like the anguished cry of someone aboard a ship that was pulling out to sea who called back to the dock, "Jump in, hurry, swim!"

And then he was crying, and Mark handed him a napkin, and said, "Oh fuck the concert."

"No," Nat said. When Mark had wanted to enter him on their first night together a month before, Nat had pulled away as if slapped. It seemed impossible—too brutal and strange, and painful proof of how far he would have traveled from his incoherent fantasies of being with a man. He said no then, and had kept saying it, but now his fear of what it meant, what it would feel like, fell from him in a rush, like the fan-shaped leaves of his parents' ginkgo tree, which could drop in one cool fall day. He smiled. "No, fuck me."

With Mark's weight around and inside him, Nat felt like all those characters he'd never understood in *The Rainbow* and *Women in Love*—-annihilated by sex, transformed beyond words.

When Mark was finally asleep, Nat imagined his parents bursting in on them, Brenda horrified, old friends nodding, "Sure, I always knew." What could he tell them?

It was oddly like the first time he had prostrated himself on Yom Kippur at the Orthodox services during the Service of the High Priest, the only time Jews ever did that in prayer. The service described in lavish detail the High Priest's preparation for entering the Holy of Holies and everyone, many thousands of people at the Temple mount throwing themselves to the ground when the Priest pronounced the Name of God in a way lost to history and the multitude crying "Praised be His glorious sovereignty throughout all time! *Baruch shem kavod malkuto layolom v'ed.*"

With his forehead touching the floor, tired, hungry from fasting, intent, awed by the moment kept intact through two thousand years, Nat had known that his final, unexpected willingness to surrender to something beyond his understanding was a border, a crossing that would always mark him as different from what he had been.

Abominations

At eight in the morning, it was cool and misty on campus as Brenda headed across the wide concrete bridge to the low and spreading library fronted with broad, shallow beds of scarlet, mauve, and white tulips. This bridge across the tiny Red Cedar River was one of her favorite spots at Michigan State; the aged weeping willows here were so dense and hung so low (like flowering trees after a downpour) that looking off either side of the bridge, you couldn't see any buildings at all. Especially in the morning, you could easily think you were isolated, alone-not surrounded by thousands of students.

Halfway across, she was stopped by white scrawling letters chalked inside jagged circles: KILL ALL FAGS, DEATH TO HOMO QUEERS, STOP FAG DAY, FAGGOTS MUST DIE, GAY? GOT AIDS YET?

She stared. The crude white letters grew larger, pushing her slowly back against the round steel railing. She could feel herself unable to breathe.

She heard laughter.

Two handsome runners in fraternity T-shirts came loping across the bridge, the incarnation of power and ease. "Awright!" one shouted. "It's about time." The other laughed. "Man, I hate fags," he said, and their pounding effort drew them away.

I have to do something, she thought, trying to feel resolute and strong.

But someone had beaten her to it, perhaps. A skinny kid with masses of thick black hair streaked lime green was crouching at the other end of the bridge, taking pictures. He kept saying "Oh wow!" Behind him, a campus police car crept along one of the paths to the bridge, lumbering and out of place.

"Hey," the kid called to her, "I'm with campus paper. Can I interview you?" His voice was heavy with the nasal twang of western Michigan.

She wanted to run, but he was over in front of her, armed with a pad and a wide-eyed look of attentiveness he might have bought at the campus bookstore along with his journalism course materials.

"My name's Jim. Can I ask you some questions?" He was already writing in his pad, as if he knew her answers.

She wanted to shake up this kid so fashionably dressed in black T-shirt, jeans, and high-tops.

"It's like Selma," she started.

"Wait—" He squinted at her. "Who? What? I don't get it."

"Like Alabama, the bigots. The lynchings. It's sick. Whoever did it should be arrested and expelled."

He chuckled as if pleased by her intensity, made notes, and then asked for her name and major. He grinned when she said she was a former graduate student and now a temporary assistant professor in history. People on the way to morning classes were stopping on the bridge, pointing.

Off behind the little reporter, two campus policemen with barely concealed smiles were examining the scrawls. Brenda rushed over to them. "You have to find these morons."

She realized she was being loud—and at MSU, any raised voice except at a sports event, or if you were drunk, was the source of instant contempt, people turning, staring, appalled at your rudeness: where could you be from, for God's sake, New York?

"They're dangerous."

The two handsome policemen who looked like ex-jocks—thick-necked, wide-shouldered bodies straining at their blue uniforms—nodded, eyeing her a bit suspiciously, as if she had done it.

Desperate for some kind of response, she blurted, "My brother's gay."

They glanced at each other. "Too bad," one brought out.

Back at her apartment, she was shocked at how nothing around her reflected the uproar she felt—not even the mirror. She just looked tired, flushed.

She found herself remembering how years ago her mother had woken her up at three in the morning to say, "Come kiss Silky goodbye." And she stumbled downstairs after her mother, pulling on a robe, to find their miniature collie lying on his side in the basket near the front door eyes wide and blank, body slack. The vet had been very negative about Silky's chances of surviving a cancer operation, but the day, oh the day had started out beautifully even though Silky was too old and sick. That morning, looking out the kitchen windows to the backyard, washing her breakfast dishes, Brenda had been unable to turn from the sassafras trees, their large oval leaves blushing like peaches—creamy red and yellow, as if sprayed with fall. So rich, so captivating—surely the whole day would be as soothing.

But her father and Nat were getting dressed upstairs for the ride to the vet clinic, and Brenda and her mother crouched by the basket, weeping, trying to, hold Silky; the collie was beyond being comforted or even touched—lost in pain, too stunned by it to even whimper.

That's how she felt now. She sat in a stupor for an hour or more, with those vicious slogans from the bridge whirling around as if she were being attacked in *The Birds*.

Finally, though, it was time for her to get back to campus, to teach her afternoon sections of Women in America. And she recalled her mentor at the University of Michigan (where she had done her M. A.) revealing after Brenda graduated that she had taught a class the morning her mother died: "I had to. I had to hold myself together. It was like falling from a plane, with no parachute. But I never hit the ground. . . ."

Hurrying back on campus, Brenda felt unavoidably pulled from her sense of outrage and disgust, eyes drawn always outward: to trees and shrubs finally blooming after an ugly, dry winter, lush forsythia and lilacs, exquisite hawthorns; to former students she smiled at; to the bicyclists snaking through crowds of students in jeans and Florida suntans.

At her grim department office in one of State's oldest, dirtiest buildings, she heard other faculty members talking about the bridge.

"Well, it's ugly," one said. "But you have to admit that those homosexuals are getting too pushy."

She turned. It was Jack Callahan, the fat, greasy, red-nosed expert in Soviet history who looked like an English Toby mug. His office was near hers and she had once heard him telling someone that he thought enough had been written about the Holocaust.

His colleague, Sandra Sparrow, almost as plain as here last name, nodded, adding as if parlaying gossip, "And they want to be able to go to fundraising dances on campus and dance together!"

Brenda snatched up her mail and fled the office.

Five minutes away, in Berkey Hall, she found her class of thirty was embroiled in an argument she could hear in the hallway.

Brenda stopped at the door.

"Those fags make me sick," Lynne was saying. "They are all over."

"How can you say that!" Teresa shot back. Small, squinting, incredibly shy, she produced papers that surprised Brenda and everyone in class with the power of her writing. But in class, she was almost always silent. And people were smiling at this outburst, some nervously, others as if they were thinking, Finally. . . .

"How can you say that? You should drop this class. You think it's cool to complain about men treating you like you have no brain, like you're not even a person because you're so pretty but it's okay for you to dump on gays, right?"

"It's perverted," Lynne dropped, primly.

No one had turned to Brenda, who had quietly joined the circle of chairs; they already were used to her not riding herd on every discussion as they read each other's papers written in response to the assigned readings, in small and large groups.

Teresa went on: "You want everybody to be like you?"

Lynne tossed her head, blushing.

Two of the half dozen guys in the class were muttering to each other. One, a Tom Cruise look-alike had practically cried in Brenda's office last week about how hard it was doing his two-page response to an article on homosexuality and American politics, because of how he felt "so close" to his roommate, and he wasn't sure what that meant. But now he was sneering. The other guys looked bored and blank. They had not signed up for this course but had been bumped into it by a computer error, and Brenda felt relieved that they liked the class enough to declare a truce of sorts: they would not hassle her if she didn't force them to talk.

"You wouldn't say that if they'd written stuff about blacks, would you?" Andrena chimed in, pointing a pen at Lynne. "But it's acceptable for you to hate gays, you can say it and not be ashamed. Well, girl, you should be ashamed."

"Listen." That was Paul, the psychology major who Brenda suspected was either dyslexic or had learning disabilities. (How had no one noticed?) "Listen. The Bible says—"

Half of the class rolled their eyes, looked away, or started leafing through their essay books, shut off from what Brenda knew they thought would be another tirade like those delivered near the campus bridges in the spring by all sorts of Christians, inveighing against sin and degradation, which they saw everywhere around them. Their ferocity could make you think Michigan State University was a thundering pit of evil, like New York or Los Angeles.

"Enough," she said. "Let's leave the Bible out of this. Let's forget about the damned bridge and get to work."

In the silence, she could hear the humming of the banks of neon lighting.

"Are you okay?" Teresa asked after class, Andrena and a few others lingering by the door, close enough to hear. Brenda had explained her first day how important it was to her to have a feminist classroom, in which she was not the sole authority, "You never pull rank like that. . . ."

Brenda wanted to scream at her, at someone, anyone, but she could only shrug and head for her next class.

This incident made her feel as awful as last summer, when her brother Nat had been kicked out of the Orthodox congregation here in town because someone had seen him and his lover, Mark leaving a gay bar in Lansing. She had felt assaulted then, helpless, exposed. She kept waiting for a phone call from her mother or father in Southfield; surely they would've found out, but Nat insisted they wouldn't.

"No one in the *minyan* will say anything. That's gossip."

And she thought of the Hebrew term for gossip: *lashan harah*, evil talk. It was one of the things you confessed during the High Holy Days, several times, perhaps because it was one of the easiest sins to commit.

"Besides, it would be bad for them," Mark pointed out with a cynical smile, "because you're supposed to protect the honor of the community."

Still, though her parents didn't seem to have heard of the incident, and none of her Jewish friends in town brought it up anymore, she did not like the idea of the three of them driving down to Southfield that fall for *Kol Nidre* services on the eve of Yom Kippur.

As they drove down that Monday morning in September, Nat thrashing around in the front to talk to Mark, who was quieter than usual in the back, she felt party to a lie. Introducing Mark as a friend, or even Nat's friend, when she knew what he really was, made her feel like a child anxiously watching waves lick closer to the sand castle built with hours of fantasy and concentration.

It was sad driving up the curving street to their ranch house—all the crab apple trees in front had lost more than half of their leaves, and fall that day seemed melancholy and not beautiful. Her mother opened the door with such a Loretta Young sweep of her arms, Brenda expected one of those breathtakingly vapid greetings like "I've heard so much about you," but she only said, "I was tired of waiting." And smiled.

"Are we late?" Nat asked while his mother said hello to Mark, who introduced himself.

Her father was showering, and they had coffee and fresh marble cake in the long, gleaming kitchen, Mark sitting so impassively, saying so little even for him, that Brenda felt sure he was willing himself not to seem "obvious" in any way, though she doubted anyone in her family would guess someone so masculine and attractive could be gay. Mark made no request for a tour or even a look at photos, no interest in favorite *tchatchkehs*. He was being very cool.

When Nat led Mark off with their clothing bags to change, Brenda's mother said, "He's so attractive. Where did you meet him? At services?" She smiled as if picturing herself victorious on the phone: to meet a Jewish man at services—!

Brenda didn't correct the misapprehension, and they chatted about the job she had gotten right after finishing her Ph.D. at MSU. Even though it was only temporary, her parents kept telling her that they bragged about their "Professor."

Nat was smiling when he came back in a blue three-piece suit that made him look like an uncertain law student. Mark wore a charcoal gray blazer, black slacks, white shirt, soft-striped tie and seemed almost embarrassed at the silence in the room, which was obvious appraisal on her mother's part, stifled reverence in Nat, and something indefinable on hers. Mark looked more than ever like a tall, bearded Robert De Niro. She wanted to think of him as an intruder, a fraud, a pervert. But there he was, ready to go to services, to be part of their world in a profound, historical way.

Her mother had always set a magnificent table for holiday dinners, with French china and crystal, and silver so heavy that each movement of your hand seemed to mark the importance of the meal. In the gold and white dining room, Nat kept saying how wonderful everything was (Mark's praise was more judicious), but Brenda was lost in imagining the future. Would Mark be having more family dinners with them, coming to shul and bar mitzvahs, or would he be banned from their house, along with Nat? Would their relatives smirk and hold back, or be unpleasantly kind and attentive, as if talking to someone whose cancer left them only months to live?

Her mother told several of her long stories about the children of friends of theirs who were in debt, divorced, having trouble with finding a job. These always sounded like oblique warnings to Brenda.

Her father, red-eyed, crumpled in his blue suit, asked them how the traffic had been, and if Brenda was maintaining the Chevette, a birthday present now three years old. He did not seem to like Mark. It was, Brenda thought on the way to services in the family Delta 88, the average man's suspicion and envy of any man whose excessive good looks invited contemplation for themselves alone. Only women were supposed to be that striking.

There were so many temples in Southfield with Beth in their names (Hebrew for house), like Beth Shalom and Beth Israel, that Nat had always called their temple Beth Greenberg, after a girl he'd had a crush on in fourth grade. No one ever laughed at his joke, but Mark did as they pulled into the jammed temple lot, and her father turned around, frowning.

Inside the round, high, gleaming pine sanctuary, she sank into a seat by her mother, Mark at her right, Nat beyond. Leafing through the holiday prayer book, she read notes about the shofar, the ram's horn, "whose purpose it is to rouse the purely Divine in man. . . ." It had to be naturally hollow because attaining God was impossible by artificial means: "no sound which charms the senses, but does not appeal to man's better self, can raise you to God—indeed, you might surrender yourself again to your low, base way of living."

Low, base. The simple words were suddenly more awful to her than the translated doom of Torah: this was a modern voice, and she was condemned along with Nat and Mark.

She felt the peck and jab of glances and unheard remarks from neighbors and old friends, and when the service began, she was unable to respond with anything more than the memory of previous feelings in previous years. Nat kept grinning at her like a jewel thief positive of diamonds and pearls just an evening's work away.

Afterwards, in the showcase-ridden lobby (photos of the congregation's history, a shofar display, gifts), nodding, smiling, clasping hands and kissing friendly cheeks, she wished the admiring glances were honestly hers, that she were dating Mark and could truly hug the woman who took her aside for a kiss and "Such pleasure to see a beautiful boy and girl!"

Two white-haired cousins, the Feingolds, as lined and creased as a blanket cold with neglect, crept up to her, dim eyes somewhat more focused than usual. Slim Mrs. Feingold, from pre-War Poland, always seemed defeated by her efforts to understand the logic of her expensive, too-stylish clothes.

"So?" she asked. That meant Mark, of course, who was off across the chattering lobby, talking to a couple. Brenda didn't recognize. "How long you know him?"

"A few months."

"Get married."

Brenda laughed.

"You'll work, he'll work, it will be okay."

Expressionless, Mr. Feingold said, "Wait."

"What wait?" his wife snapped, not turning to him.

"When I get married," Brenda said warmly, "you'll know."

"Good." Mrs. Feingold stretched up to kiss at Brenda's cheek and moved away.

"Wait," her husband told Brenda as flatly as someone in a bakery ordering a loaf of bread.

In a few blurred hours, she was in Nat's room, already wishing she didn't have to fast through tomorrow night. Mark was down in the basement guest room, maybe already asleep.

"I loved it!" Nat whispered, pushing both hands through his hair.

"It's not a game. People take it seriously. They thought he was my date. Mom did, or she wants to."

"So did Dad, but he doesn't like Mark." Nat smiled at having reached their father once again by annoying him, even indirectly. It was, Brenda knew, his surest and sometimes only way of making an impact.

She wanted to say, "No more. I don't want to hear about it, I don't want to get involved." But she was involved.

Brenda couldn't sleep later and wished she was one of those people who had elaborate strategies for conquering insomnia—like meditation, or a bath, followed by a potent weird drink—or for submitting to it. She felt helpless, afraid in her room. The dolls and stuffed animals, the Nancy Drew books, the old Beatles posters, all struck her as emblems of a past she had betrayed.

She took down the leather-bound Holy Scriptures their" congregation had given her at her bat mitzvah and leafed through the thin gold-edged pages, found at last *Vayikra*, Leviticus, and looked at what she had read before with no comprehension but much embarrassment: "Thou shalt not lie with mankind as with womankind, it is an abomination." Coming after the terrible crescendo of forbidden sexual unions in those pages, and before a prohibition against bestiality, it seemed uglier, more perverse.

Her brother was an abomination. And Mark. And she did not protest or understand—it was impossible to picture them.

She felt unbearably hungry. Brenda went out softly to the living room and found her mother there, reading a mystery with only one lamp on.

"The New Year—and fasting!—makes me a little restless, and a mystery helps . . . you know everything works out very nicely."

Brenda joined her. Setting down the book, her mother asked, "Mark is how old?" "Thirty-five."

"Not bad, five years. I know, I know. I'm not talking about marriage, but even dating."

"He's just a friend."

"The age can make a difference," her mother went on, "he's getting older. It changes you sometimes. Life isn't so open anymore. You can get angry, or scared, maybe. But he doesn't look like that. He seems happy. That's good."

It was a rare moment of listening for Brenda; usually, she tuned her mother out or ended up snapping at insults she half-imagined.

"We won't date, Mom."

"Why not? He has somebody?"

"He's divorced."

"So? One mistake doesn't mean you retire."

"Do you like him?"

Her mother nodded. "Except for one thing. He should be in a movie, not in my house. He's too good-looking."

They drifted off to talking about the service, and soon Brenda was kissing her good night, and as always, her mother did not object but did not really respond.

The fatigue and hunger of the next day, and her exhaustion by the time services were over and they were breaking the fast at the temple the next night, kept her from thinking about Nat and Mark too much.

Her mother had stopped nagging about Brenda's romantic life ever since the time she had said she was dating a Dutch Reformed teacher from Grand Rapids. Her mother was clever enough not to push and create a crisis by lamenting Brenda's choice. And true to form, her mother was cautious in mentioning Mark's name after Yom Kippur, but every time it came up, Brenda hated herself for lying, and hated Nat.

The day after Brenda discovered the slogans on the bridge, the campus newspaper downplayed the graffiti incident, keeping it off the front page, and making sure it was "evenhanded," Brenda guessed, by quoting students who were against the upcoming Gay Pride Day, calling it sick, perverted, and un-American (the reaction this year was worse than ever before, perhaps because of Reagan's second victory). Since those vicious comments were put in a sidebar, the article was really an editorial in disguise, damning MSU's gays and gays everywhere.

She had been afraid to call Nat because she could hear him saying, See? That's what I have to live with, and she would feel implicated, part of the world that had spit out those ugly white scrawls.

Mark phoned. "Is Natty there?"

"Why?"

"He's not in his dorm, didn't leave any message, nothing, and we were supposed to go out for dinner. Now that you're in *The State News*, though—"

"What do you mean?"

"He must've freaked when he saw what you said in the article."

"About Nat? I didn't say anything about Nat." She grabbed up the paper, trying to keep the phone to her ear, and forced herself to read more slowly than she had before. And then she found it, the phrase: "My brother's gay!" That punk green-haired reporter had heard her, had written it down. . . .

"Oh my God. I was so upset, I—"

"Nat didn't want to come out, but you did it for him."

Mark sounded so measured and calm, she asked him to drive over, quickly, as if he could somehow save her from her own guilt and shock. She felt suddenly stiff with fear: what if something had happened to Nat, someone had beaten him up, pushed him off one of the bridges, run him down? It happened, she knew it happened all the time—just not here at MSU, not yet.

When Mark walked in fifteen minutes later, she hugged him, held on as if he were her brother, an older brother who could speak soothing platitudes that would tranquilize any pain.

"You should sit down." Mark sat by her, held her hand.

"There's nothing terrible you can say to me I haven't said since I hung up." She slapped both hands to her forehead, covering her eyes, starting to rock and cry, able to let go now that she was no longer alone. Waiting for him, she had felt like a traitor, branded by her own shame.

Mark slipped an arm around her.

"He won't hate you, you know. He might even be glad."

"But it wasn't mine to tell," she said.

"Some people might hassle him at the dorm, but he isn't over there that much, and he's got a single room." He shrugged. "You know, the janitor at my apartment complex figured us out real quick, and once when we were leaving the apartment, I heard him down the hall say something to another workman about hating faggots near him."

"Nat didn't tell me!"

Mark smiled. "He probably didn't think you would listen."

"What happened?"

Mark leaned back with the ease of someone in a mammoth dark library in an English country house, twirling brandy in a snifter, wreathed in cigar smoke. "I said, real loud, 'Don't worry, you'll be fine, most gays don't like effeminate men.'" Brenda laughed like a delighted child discovering a present under her pillow, clapping her hands. "Wasn't he furious?"

"Sure—but he was such a scrawny sonofabitch, so was his buddy. What could they do to me, or Nat?" He was right, she knew. Nat had taken to working out with Mark so seriously in the last six months that he already had a different body, more imposing, broad-shouldered, with a firm, tight chest. His whole outline and presence had shifted.

The doorbell shot Brenda from the couch and she sprang to open the door.

Nat was standing there, smiling. "Since when did you take on public relations?"

And he hugged her, ruffled her hair. They all sat on the couch like spies who'd escaped some dangerous and unexpected blockade of a civil war by pretending to be tourists: smug, delighted with themselves, but suitably rueful. Nat had to tell her three times where he was when he read the paper, and then, how many people knew his sister taught history, and how he'd just driven around for hours that evening, unable to cry, but thinking perhaps he should, now that the secret was out, "And with a bang. Jesus, Bren—"

Mark went to a nearby party store to get a bottle of champagne. "Let's turn it into a celebration," he said, and they drank toasts to each other. She watched him as Nat might, not just someone handsome—those blue eyes!—but the center of his life now. And Nat, grinning, a little drunk, was invested with a kind of grace. She had to admit that he was no longer so tense, so watchful, but sat with his body open and sprawling. His face was smoothed out, relaxed, as if before he had always been on the edge of a migraine, and she saw that he had never really been as plain and unattractive as she believed merely downcast, lonely, and even unformed. He was becoming a man, and would be quite interesting at Mark's age, she thought.

"What're you staring at?"

"You," she said. "Just you."

Mark sat on the floor, back against her couch, one arm tight around Nat, who lay back against him, reaching up now and then to stroke Mark's face.

217

As always, she couldn't help thinking how their parents would react seeing this simple closeness, it would disgust and shame them. Jews don't do that, they'd think. But just this past Chanukah, her mother had told her that she finally had figured out why a friend's daughter had moved to Argentina to teach English, deeply upsetting her family. "She's a lesbian, Brenda," and the word sounded almost quaint coming from her elegant mother, as old-fashioned and uncommon as "sodomite." "She must be, remember how she never dated much, and how her mother would always say Laura was 'different.'" Brenda had said nothing, waiting for a judgment, a comment, but all her mother added, while putting on her earrings, was a cool sigh: "The world is changing."

Brenda told Mark and Nat about her first class yesterday afternoon.

"But it's not just gays," Nat said. "That black girl you told us about, Andrena? She was wrong. I mean, maybe people wouldn't say it in class, but you should hear guys at the dorm talk about 'niggers' and 'kikes.' This black guy on my floor told me how he got beat up in an elevator once, it happens all the time." He looked up at Mark. "Glad you moved here from the East Coast?"

She made them each drink several glasses of water before she let them drive back to Mark's apartment. In the year she had known Mark, and known about him and Nat, finally watching Nat let himself be gay, she had relaxed a little, no longer feeling like their bond was some ugly and mysterious blight withering a lovely spring garden, or that she was the owner of a flawless lawn, driven wild by discovering a network of mole tunnels one morning. Yet she still wished that Nat and Mark hadn't been kicked out of the Orthodox *minyan* in town when people found there out they were gap, wished that everything could be smoother—on the surface, anyway.

Getting ready for bed, she heard a far-off fire engine's blare, so different from the usual late-night hooting trains, and thought it would be like that for her parents when they finally found out about Nat—a crisis, an emergency in which they would probably panic, but might, just might, she was beginning to hope, rally and find some strength. Maybe they would be glad it wasn't AIDS, and even relieved that Mark was Jewish. And such a Jew, she said aloud, shaking her head in the bathroom mirror with a satisfied grin. Orthodox, even!

She was pulled from sleep by her insistent doorbell and she glared at her alarm clock as if it should have protected her from this intrusion. She shoved it off the night table, found her robe on the floor, and hurried out to the door, rubbing at her eyes.

It was Nat, sickly pale, eyes down, hands cold when she grabbed them to pull him inside. He smelled strange to her.

"It's gone," he said, drifting to her kitchen, mechanically filling the fat black teakettle with water, setting it on a burner.

His car's been stolen, she thought—or vandalized. She saw white letters of hate and then wondered if it wouldn't happen to her car, too. . . .

"It's all gone. My dorm room."

She sank into a chair at the table as if his words were heavy hands weighing down her shoulders.

"I went back to get some stuff for my eight o'clock class. And from the parking lot across the street, I could see this big black hole on the first floor of the dorm. Fire, I thought, and then I saw all these puddles of sooty water and you could smell plastic, burned plastic. It was my room. Everything's gone, my clothes, the books, even the phone is melted. I found the RA, Dave, he said it happened at night. It looks like someone broke in and torched the place—and they were lucky it wasn't worse. Lucky? Someone called the fire department before the smoke alarm even went off. The marshal said it looked like arson to him, but he wasn't sure."

She realized then that Nat smelled of smoke, as if he'd been in a bar all night. "Everything's gone?" She was suddenly flooded by all the terrible film she'd seen of Germany in the Thirties, with JUDEN RAUS ("Out with the Jews") whitewashed across Jewish-owned storefronts, synagogues collapsing in flame, religious Jews beaten, bloody, dead.

He looked at her, eyes heavy, grim. "Except this." Nat reached into his jeans pocket and tossed a two-inch black button onto the table. It had one of those Gay Liberation pink triangles she had argued with Mark about. "But you're Jewish, too!" she had said. "Don't you hate that they use something from the camps? You never see Jews wearing yellow stars in a parade!" Mark had tried to convince her that the triangle's origin was precisely the point: shocking people, reminding everyone of the worst that could happen, that did happen.

Now, the pink and black button glared up at her like a baleful witch in a fairy tale, gloating over the princess's crucial mistake which was about to plunge her into darkness and slavery. Nat was telling her about the campus police, how aloof and matter-of-fact they were, even wanting to know where he had been all night, how much insurance he had, if any, and how everyone on his floor said they had no idea what had happened, hadn't heard or seen anything. Nobody would look at Nat—as if it was his fault, as if he had humiliated everyone in the dorm by not only being gay but also the victim of an attack.

"I called Mark . . . I asked him to meet me here. Okay? Is that okay?"

The teakettle—*tchynick* in Yiddish—started whistling and Brenda said in her father's Yiddish, "*Hock mir nisht kein tchynick*"—don't make such a fuss. It was stupid, not at all funny, but Nat smiled a little as he made some instant Folger's, stirred in three teaspoons of sugar, which she knew he'd given up years ago. It was as if he were retreating to the year he had begun drinking coffee, when he was fifteen, a year safe from all this.

"Nat, what can I do?"

"Just sit," he said, sipping his coffee. "Listen." And then he went through a terrible inventory of everything he'd checked and looked for in his room. She couldn't stop thinking of all the Jewish homes and apartments through-out Europe that had been looted, burned, destroyed, trainloads of plundered bloody goods snaking back to the Fatherland: not just gold and jewelry but mattresses, pianos, candelabras, coats.

Mark rang sharply, and pushed past her, flushed, rumpled, smelling of sleep and sweat. At first, Mark and Nat held each other's arms without hug-ging, peering at each other like relations meeting at an airport after forty years, not quite sure they had the right person. Then Mark embraced him, looking fierce and defiant, like a king sending off his armies to avenge his honor.

"I've been making lists of phone numbers. We're calling all the papers, the ACLU, the FBI, because it's arson. You need a lawyer."

Nat moved to the couch and sat. "I need a room."

"Couldn't we leave?" Brenda asked, arms out like an, opera singer implor-ing the tyrant for her lover's release. "Just today—go home and get out of this place? I'll cancel my office hours. I want to go home."

Mark shook his head. "I'm staying. We've got lots to do."

"No." Nat stood up. "Brenda's right. Not today. I want you to come down to Southfield with us, so we can all tell them what happened before they hear about it on the news, in the paper—"

"Or in the supermarket," Brenda put in. "From a neighbor."

Mark and Nat grimaced. They decided to go back to Mark's, shower and change, and Brenda would meet them there in an hour.

Washing her hair, she thought of Scarlett O'Hara, dirty, desperate, fleeing the flames of Atlanta for her beloved Tara. For the first time she understood the longing to be released from fear by simply being someplace you loved.

She fondly pictured their enormous backyard, a full acre, blooming now thanks to the unusually warm spring. Putting on the blue silk dress that her mother said made her look like an actress, Brenda saw them all sitting out in the lacy high-peaked gazebo Nat had always dreamed about and finally gotten this last year with money he earned as a waiter. They would sit in the deep cool shade, admiring the parrot tulips springing up at the back of the house, and breathe in the rich sweet smell, of the thirty white lilac bushes her parents had planted themselves on their thirtieth wedding anniversary. The stench of burnt clothes would be banished.

Her parents would have to be on Nat's side—the fire would be too famil-iar and threatening, like synagogue bombings, cemetery desecration.

She slipped Nat's triangle button into her purse before she left. She would have to ask Nat the date of Gay Pride Day, and where people would be marching and what time. In her car, before putting her key in the ignition, she remembered the myth about how the king of Denmark had worn a yellow star when the occupying Nazis started persecuting Danish Jews. It never happened, but it felt true, given Danish heroism.

She took out Nat's button and used the rearview mirror to help pin it to her dress.

The Children

"If you bring Mark to the bar mitzvah," Brenda warned her brother Nat, "He's your date, not mine. I'm not pretending."

The first time the three of them had been together with her family was back in September, for Yom Kippur services down in Southfield. Even though she and Mark never touched, they did end up sitting next to each other, so everyone had assumed that Mark was her date, and had beamed at seeing "such a lovely Jewish couple." It was inevitable, and one more appearance together—especially at services—would confirm everyone's speculations.

Her parents knew the truth now, and resented it so much that they had told no one, behaving publicly as if Brenda and Mark were at least a potential couple.

She couldn't stand being on display, couldn't stand the false position. That was why she had given up trying to go to the faculty synagogues in East Lansing, after Nat and Mark were expelled from the Orthodox *minyan* when people there found out they were gay.

Showing up at the other synagogues with Mark, she had felt as stared at and fussed over as celebrities getting out of a limousine for a movie premiere. The Jewish community in East Lansing was so small, even compared to the one in Ann Arbor, that any new couple, any new individual, was sometimes greeted a little hysterically—like a sail on the horizon discovered by survivors of a shipwreck. She fled the intense interest and excitement: the invitations to lunch, dinner, pool parties; weekends up north at Lake Charlevoix or near Traverse City; theatre parties headed for Chicago, Toronto, Detroit. Too many people wanted to know them, welcome them. "Just tell everybody you're gay," Mark had suggested, grinning.

It was easy for Mark to joke about it: he was out of the closet, and older than Nat and more secure. But Nat was only a senior at Michigan State, and Mark was his first lover. Her brother's circumspection as well as his delight in fooling their parents determined how the three of them behaved together. Nat had the subtle tyranny of the shy; it was unexpected, but so much stronger than loud and arbitrary demands: she had often ended up doing what her brother wanted, even though it made no sense, even though it was clearly wrong. Like going to Yom Kippur services with Mark down in Southfield last fall and never saying a word when relatives, when her mother, had assumed Mark was her boyfriend.

With his close-cropped thick black beard and mustache, his swarthy good looks, Mark often made her think of a buccaneer, but that picture always brought up images of plunder and violence. He had stolen something from her life—security, comfort.

"Don't worry about the bar mitzvah," Nat said now in her East Lansing apartment. "Mom and Dad won't notice who's with who, they'll be too busy griping."

Brenda knew that he was right. Their cousin David's bar mitzvah in a Detroit suburb was at a congregation Brenda's parents hated having to go to: Kehillat Olam, "KO" to its congregants, "Chaotic" to its detractors. First of all, there was no rabbi, and there was really no synagogue. The egalitarian congregation, which for years had met in church basements, had finally bought an old brick elementary school building, which no amount of El Al posters and Jewish-themed prints could alter. The few times Brenda had gone to services there, she expected to hear the grating shriek of those silver flutes she played in third and fourth grade, or see little kids with enormous scarred wooden bathroom passes in the halls. Hanging up her coat on one of the low metal hooks (high enough for children), she would feel swamped by memories of home room, recess, and art projects, and felt oppressed, as if she had forgotten her homework.

"Egalitarian?" Her father would sneer whenever someone mentioned KO. "I know what that means. Everyone's a *yentah*."

She agreed, a little: at least when she had been there, there was too much serene self-congratulation by the men and women leading services, and others piping up to explain what they thought the Torah portion meant. It was like being trapped at the worst kind of graduate seminar where showing off passed for insight.

Her father was always scathing about KO. He couldn't stand that members of the congregation leading services chatted to their "audience" about what they were doing, with the smarmy nonchalance of a dentist saying, "I'm going to turn on the drill, now."

But what most disturbed Brenda's parents was that the Ark, always on the Eastern wall of a synagogue, so that you prayed facing Jerusalem, was on

223

the south wall, because that wall already had built-in cabinets (for art sup-plies, maybe, or books), and it was "less trouble" to store the Torah scrolls there than to build something new. Her father yelled when he found out: "It doesn't make any sense!" Even her mother, whose cousin Fran (the bar mitzvah boy's mother) belonged to this congregation, would shrug and say, "Live and let live, okay, but some things have to be not okay."

"*Moyshe kapoyr!*" her father would snort—Yiddish for hopelessly screwed up.

It certainly was disconcerting to pray there. At all the moments when you were most conscious of facing the Ark, Brenda was uncomfortably aware that she wasn't facing Jerusalem, but Detroit, or perhaps Canada.

She didn't really mind the informality, though, especially since women could participate as fully as men, but even she had to admit that a service at KO was like spiritual junk food—it filled you up, but you weren't nour-ished.

Nat, despite his having been immersed in the Orthodox *minyan* at Mich-igan State University for two years, was surprisingly more understanding than any of them: "At least they're trying, they mean well."

"It's not enough," his father snapped. "They should also *do* well!"

Brenda had her own reasons for not being eager to go to David's bar mitzvah: his mother, Fran. Though ten years younger than Fran, Brenda had always been compared to her because they had both done graduate work in American Studies, and were both college professors. All the relatives who hadn't exactly understood what either one of them had been doing in graduate school took refuge in the fact that their family boasted not just one, but two "Doctors"—and wasn't that nice?

But while Brenda had published articles in academic journals, Fran had done something very different. After her mother and father died of cancer, she started writing limp and shallow novels about children whose parents had cancer, novels in which only the disease and its treatment had any life. Even Brenda had to admit that Fran could describe chemotherapy, side-ef-fects, hospital rooms convincingly. But that was all. Everything else in her books was lifeless, empty, dull.

These novels did not hit any best seller lists, yet they apparently sold well enough to make Fran a family celebrity, and the recipient of countless fan letters from around the country. Fran seemed to have a loyal following among Jewish women who read turgid family sagas, and Brenda was always having to smile and nod when someone mentioned Fran's latest literary excrescence. It was even worse when they jokingly linked Brenda to Fran's novels: "Darling, maybe some day you'll write an article about your cousin's books—they're so descriptive."

"That's right," Brenda thought, "I'd love to do an essay about the Cath-eter in American Fiction."

Fran had never been encouraging to Brenda, whose dissertation was on American-Jewish women writers. At parties and family gatherings Fran had often made her feel as if she were a whining little girl with a drippy nose desperate to play with her older sister's friends. She could not remember a single nice thing Fran had said to her, but she remembered all the put-downs. Once at a conference at the University of Michigan, Fran had come up after Brenda read her very first academic paper and said, "Listening to you, I'm so glad I write fiction!"

That was all. No hello, no good wishes, no falling back on the academic catchall of "I enjoyed what you had to say."

Brenda was crushed, especially since Fran's cheerful comment was loud enough for all the people crowding around the panelists to hear. Brenda seethed through the conference lunch right afterwards, accidentally seated at the same table with Fran, wanting to reach across and stab her hand with a fork. She went home in a rage, called Nat, her parents.

Her mother was not helpful that time. "It can't be easy," she had said. She meant, easy being Fran. The two cancer deaths, of course. And then Fran had been divorced twice, and was so deeply distressed that her pale doughy face often had the frozen frightening look of a Mask of Tragedy. Brenda's mother was sympathetic by reflex; after all, it was *a shandeh far di goyim*, a shame that non-Jews should see such things as divorce among Jews. But Brenda's father despised Fran, and when he heard about her third divorce, from David's father, he snapped "Of course! What I can't figure out is how she ever got married in the first place. Such a *meeskeit*, so ugly, and so sour, all the time so sour, never anything nice to say to anybody. Just like her books—cancer, cancer, cancer. Can't she write something happy for a change? Or at least pick another disease for God's sake!"

Fran had taught at several colleges before landing a tenure-track position at the University of Indiana, but returned to Michigan, so the story went, to be near what was left of her family, who, as Brenda's father pointed out, "A) Don't really like her, and B) thought Indiana was close enough."

True to form, Brenda's mother had said, "Well still, it's nice when family is together. And she's so famous now with all those books, she could teach anywhere, so it's lovely she's back in Michigan."

Brenda exploded. "She didn't come back to be with her family, Mom! She just didn't get tenure. She was fired, basically, because she hasn't published anything worth a damn, just those crappy novels. And I bet she's a lousy teacher, too. Nobody leaves a Big Ten school to teach at Central unless they have no choice!"

Her mother took that in, and then nodded. Even she knew that teaching at Central Michigan University, a bleak and conservative wasteland a few hours north and west of Detroit, was no prize position.

It pleased Brenda that Fran's teaching career had not been successful, but the continued success of her novels irked Brenda, and she wished for a more public and obvious downfall, perhaps proof of Fran having plagiarized someone's else's book. Or something more humiliating, like a series of blistering reviews burying some novel of Fran's under cold drifts of scorn. But that was impossible, since Fran's mediocre fiction consistently got reviews good enough to supply zippy blurbs for the jacket of her next book.

No one else in the family seemed to recognize how vacuous Fran's fiction was, so Brenda had to suffer her novels appearing on everyone's shelves or coffee tables, and Fran spreading the story of her terrible marriages and her worries about her "little boy" at family get-togethers, to relatives who were too polite to be unsympathetic, too gullible not to feel sorry for her, or too impressed by her publishing.

"But why do you dislike Fran so much?" Nat wondered.

"Because she's a phony, because she's a bitch, because she doesn't care enough about people to bother constructing a single real or interesting character—"

Nat whistled his surprise. "God, you are really jealous of her. But I don't get it. It's not like you want to write novels, do you?"

Embarrassed, Brenda muttered, "I've thought about it. . . ."

Reasonably, Mark said, "You'd never write the kind of tripe she does, so—"

Nat cut him off. "Brenda, this is all like something from another life, something that never got resolved."

"Don't tell me it's karma to have a cousin like that!" But Brenda did find herself wondering if it wasn't just that. Why else did she sometimes feel obsessed by Fran's success, even imagine getting to write a review of one of her books, a review that would start off gently, as if she were walking up to Fran with a smile and an outstretched hand, and then blast her with both barrels of a shotgun.

Brenda, Nat and Mark drove down together from East Lansing, but got to KO early, and so they stood chatting in the hallway. Mark leaned back against a blue tiled wall, while Nat shifted and turned, as restless as a puppy in a car.

"Relax," Mark smiled.

Down the hall, voices and the clatter of pans came from the kitchen where people were preparing for the kiddush afterwards. A small table draped with a gorgeous lace tablecloth was set up near the sanctuary door and there were already some presents and envelopes on it.

Nat liked being early, Brenda knew, but it never made him comfortable, just antsy. She knew her parents would be late, because it was KO, because Mark's presence unnerved them, and because Fran's third divorce was so recent, having occurred halfway through planning for the bar mitzvah. Her mother had intimated that it had been a vicious break-up.

"I can tell you, Brenda," her mother said, "I just don't want to go. The thought of them together after what happened—"

"What did happen?"

"Don't ask."

The front doors of KO opened now, and with a blur of voices, David, the bar mitzvah boy, his mother and her family surged into the building. The expensive blue pin-striped suit made little David look about ten years old to Brenda, not thirteen; he was pale, wide-eyed, like a kid caught cheating on a test. Brenda felt almost like her mother as she came forward chirping bright false compliments: "You look terrific. New haircut? What a great suit." And she was shaking hands with Fran, who grabbed and hugged her, teary-eyed.

Brenda was painfully aware of Nat and Mark hanging back, and of the heavy embrace of Fran's arms and perfume.

Fran's eyelids drooped knowingly. "So you brought Mark," she murmured.

Brenda wanted to say, "He's Nat's lover," but it seemed so bizarre in that hallway, with those people, a profanation of the day itself.

She waved Mark and Nat over, already beginning to feel her opposition, her sense of self battered by the storm of family, which could sweep away all the tiny landmarks of individuality she was forever trying to establish and cling to. She hated lying, but the words of greeting and accommodation slipped out of her despite that, maybe even because of that—to cover over any possible embarrassment.

Nat followed Mark over, leaned down to talk to David. "How's your Hebrew?" he asked with a grin.

The hallway was filling up with congregants and their kids, many of whom were trying to pose nonchalantly in their new and uncomfortable clothes—the boys burdened by either ignoring the girls or by trying to impress them.

"I heard you got hired full-time at Michigan State," Fran was saying, her arm in Brenda's as if they were about to stroll through a park. Something good, like knishes, was being heated up down the hall, and Brenda felt very hungry, and a bit nervous that she had lost sight of Nat and Mark in the swelling crowd.

"We always expected the best of you," Fran said sententiously, as if she were eighty, and really pleased. "Your parents must be very proud."

It meant nothing to Brenda, it was annoying, the same empty words of praise anyone could say, the same words she was used to hearing from her parents, words that were laden with expectation and claim. You are proving me right—your success is really mine. And how could it come from Fran? What was going on? What did she want from Brenda?

Then she realized it was a setup, because Fran said, "My new agent just got me a two-book deal with Ballantine. In the high six figures! It's amazing! I can finally build a house on that land I bought up in Leland."

Suddenly Nat was tapping her shoulder, muttering "Mom and Dad." Brenda pulled away from Fran.

Her father walked in as if he were an angry factory owner confronting a hostile union meeting—defiant, almost sneering.

"He looks good," Nat said. They all turned, and Fran and her mother embraced while her father nodded hellos in several directions, without specifically acknowledging Nat or Mark. He did look good—distinguished in his double breasted black suit, glistening grey-streaked hair brushed straight back, like a Twenties crooner, his face and hands refined, his eyes watchful and cool.

She glanced from him to Nat, and from Nat to Mark.

"How nice to see you, Mark," Brenda's mother was saying with just the right amount of warmth, elegant in her taupe silk suit.

Fran nodded encouragingly again at Brenda, who wanted to hiss at her, like John Malkovich playing Valmont in *Dangerous Liaisons*.

The hallway was full now, people chatting so loudly they could have been in a subway car trying to make themselves heard.

Her mother said to Brenda, "*Gevalt*, there's poor Ralphy."

Ralph Benveniste, Fran's ex-husband, despite the romantic Sephardic name, was a chubby, balding little man who had the stooping, inconsequent air of a generic nebbish—despite his successful career as a chiropractor, his Jaguar, his trips around the world. Brenda's mother always called him "Poor Ralphy." Brenda watched Fran turn her back to her ex-husband—her face stiff, lifeless—and move away.

"What happened with Fran and Ralph?" Brenda asked softly, but her mother had slipped away.

It was near ten o'clock, and people were drifting into the Sanctuary, where the chairs were arranged in two groups facing each other, with the podium in the middle, near the windows, opposite the cabinet holding the Torah scrolls.

Seated, Nat and Mark had become preternaturally quiet and attentive, like dogs at point. She knew at once that they were staring at some man, and it disturbed her to feel so excluded and unimportant.

"What?" she whispered to Nat as they sat two rows behind David, his mother and her parents.

Nat raised his chin a little, and she followed the direction of its arc. The ranks of seats opposite them were filling up, and standing in the last row was a young man she had not noticed before. He was dark and lanky, long-haired, about 30, she thought, with the thick-lipped sexy look of a rock star, and the clothes to match: black leather pants and tie, wide-shouldered black jacket, grey silk shirt. He looked cocky and amused, delighted to fill the space around him. It was the kind of self-satisfied expression she had seen in paintings of grinning Flemish burghers who radiated a childish glee in just being themselves, in being alive.

Who was he? Was he Jewish?

Nat was whispering to Mark, who grinned like a cardsharp about to fleece a rich victim.

And then she realized that Ralphy and this guy were gay. That was what had been bothering Brenda's mother. There could be no doubt about it. Ralphy was trying so hard to look normal, to look as if he belonged. Hadn't Brenda seen Nat look like that sometimes, expending who knew how much energy on neutralizing whatever he suspected about himself that could bring down criticism?

But the other man, the rock star, looked cocky and unconcerned, the way Mark often did. She had a sudden wicked vision of herself asking Fran after services, "Was Ralph gay when you married him, or did you turn him off to women yourself?"

"We're ready to begin now."

That was Mark Voss, a Teacher Education professor at Wayne State: short, curly-haired, squinting, prim, with the perpetually disappointed expression of a father who has caught his children in an obvious lie about when they got home the night before.

"I'm so glad that David asked me to open services for him. It reminds me of something I saw on the Joan Rivers show—" He went on to tell a pointless dim anecdote, and then, perhaps because there was some murmuring from the older people in the room, he said, "Some of you new to KO will be surprised by not seeing a rabbi up here." He tried to grin. "But at KO we believe men and women should be equal, and anyone should be able to lead services if they can. But even more important, we believe in sharing our experience of prayer with you while we pray."

"*Genug shoyn*," Brenda heard her father mutter in Yiddish: "Enough already."

"Now, these opening psalms are meant to establish a meditative but exalted framework for us as we establish a deeper sense of Shabbat peace, the peace of removing ourselves from everyday concerns, of finding rest and spiritual tranquility. . . ."

Brenda stopped listening, because Voss seemed to have no sense of where he was—his delivery was so large and stiff (despite the casual words) that he could have been lecturing to 300 ignorant freshmen. Besides, she had never been able to experience Shabbat the way she sensed that Nat and Mark sometimes could, as a complete release, an entrance into a different kind of time. And she was unlikely to enter any relaxing frame of mind sitting next to Nat and Mark now as they seemed to drink in every detail of the sexy guy across the room.

Mark Voss was still talking about the glories of the sabbath.

Around her, Brenda could feel those unused to KO's digressions and announcements stirring with suspicion. Wasn't the service ever going to start? She wondered if the out-of-towners assumed that this was how Jews worshiped in Michigan.

She glanced at her father. He was sitting with his head down, one hand massaging the bridge of his nose while her mother sat as gracefully attentive and relaxed as a beautiful girl waiting to be asked to dance at her high school prom: she knew the moment was coming.

There, Voss was singing at last.

Brenda flipped through the prayer book which she had closed while looking around, but she suddenly felt a wave of incredulity. What was she doing here? The whole day was meaningless and gross. David was probably like most bar mitzvah boys, eager for attention and primed for the wave of checks and presents that would wash over him for days. He would buy a new bike, a boom box, a gold chain, brag about his swollen savings account, and this moment that was supposed to mark him as an adult and a full member of the Jewish community would be an empty ceremony, a chance for his parents to outdo their neighbors at the kiddush, and then at the lavish reception. It was vulgar and stupid and had nothing to do with religion. Even sitting there she felt part of a cultural fraud. When it was all over, the congregation's president would give David an insipid speech about how well he had read the Torah, and how proud everyone was, and how this was a great day in his future as a Jew. *Bubkes*, she almost muttered aloud, feeling as cynical as her father: Beans!

Brenda's mother had told her that Fran forced David to go to Hebrew school when he wanted to stop, and would probably force him to continue going to services. Was this going to make him feel glad to be a Jew? For the rest of the service, she fought a desire to just walk out, imagining everyone staring, talking about her afterwards—half-pleased at the stir she would make, half-shocked that she had come to this point of disillusionment.

She realized now that Nat's own return to Judaism, or his search for a more meaningful form of expressing it, had almost hypnotized her. He was so serious, and she was so captivated by watching him enter Orthodox belief with all the intrepid industry of one of those little hermit crabs disguising its shell. First it was kissing the mezuzah on the way into services, which she had never seen him do before, then it was wearing his skullcap on the way home from services, then going to Detroit to buy a prayer shawl, a real one, not the polyester stoles that were little more than Jewish scarves, but a black-barred wool one that covered and enfolded him, cut him off from the world. He would drape it over his head sometimes, and the effect was not charming and sweet, like in those colorful engravings of Orthodox men that you found in catalogues of Jewish ritual objects, books and knick-knacks—pictures that were as much a connection to your faith as signing a petition was a connection to real protest. No, the effect was different, and he seemed driven, remote, intense, as when he started swaying back and forth in prayer.

She came to enjoy the liveliness of Nat's small Orthodox congregation, all the fierce singing that was so unlike the sometimes dirge-like, mournful chanting at her parents' synagogue. She had liked that Nat's *minyan* at Michigan State met in just a small room instead of a cavernous showy hall, and that whoever lead services faced the Torah, not the congregation. In her parent's synagogue, almost every one she'd ever been in, the rabbis and cantors were on a stage, elevated, remote. Prayer by proxy. And yet they were often complaining about "unaffiliated Jews," but why would anyone want to be affiliated with something that was so pretentious, so off-putting and stiff?

She stood, she sang, she bowed through all the rest of the service, feeling herself to be a fraud for participating. She tried to smile and look proud through David's whiny reading and his appalling speech which was mostly a detailed list of thank you's to various relatives for helping with the bar mitzvah. At the end, she rushed from the Sanctuary outside to gasp in some air, eyes closed.

Her father was tapping her on the shoulder. "*Sheyninkeh*, sweetheart, is everything okay? Your mother said you weren't looking good. Are you getting enough sleep?" Brenda turned and hugged him fiercely. She felt blissfully transported to a younger time when pleasures were simple, direct, easy to comprehend: a new game, cookies, a kitten, getting read to and kissed at night, making a new friend.

"It's nothing," she said. "Let's go inside."

She had missed the blessings over the wine and bread, but Nat and Mark, who spotted her in the buzzing hallway, had saved her a piece of the enormous challah.

"Do you know who he is?" Nat asked her. She knew he meant Mr. Leather. "David's Hebrew teacher! He's Israeli. His name is Shimon. What a hunk."

"They all are," Mark said. "I went nuts in Israel. The men are incredible—"

She didn't laugh appreciatively, as they probably expected her to, just followed them to the social hall, where the tables arrayed with treats were as dense and rich as a model battlefield in an exclusive toy store window.

"Can't you ever turn it off?" she asked sharply, her voice low, reaching for some baklava. "Can't you ever just be yourself, instead of acting like a faggot?"

Nat stared at her, but Mark nodded, as if he had expected this moment.

"I hate lying," she whispered, trying to move away from the crowd. They were standing off to the side, beyond the tables. "Why should I have to lie about you to everyone? Forget Mom and Dad and their *mishegoss*, what about me?"

"Who cares what your parents think. Tell everyone the truth," Mark said, and Brenda felt like a clown who'd been clutching at the air around a tightrope for balance, suddenly falling into the net below, free of struggle.

"Maybe I will," she said.

Nat was pale.

Family and guests whirled off behind them, loading thick paper plates with food. Cameras flashed. She fled from the crowd, down the hallway to the Girls' Room, but before she could reach the door she was stopped outside one of the empty classrooms. Through the glass pane in the closed door, she could see Ralph Benveniste pushed up against the back wall covered with crayoned elementary Hebrew exercises, enveloped by sexy Shimon, who was kissing him with an almost savage hunger.

Brenda felt as helpless and appalled as she had years ago in her parents' sun room, when an enormous bluejay had slammed right into one of the glass doors and dropped onto the deck, quivering and jerking, while she could only stare.

In the cool dark Girls' Room, her mother was touching up her makeup at the mirror.

"Mom—did you know about Ralphy, about him and the Hebrew teacher?"

Her mother nodded grimly, closing her purse. "I just don't understand it," her mother said wearily. And as if she were a plaintiff seeking justice, she turned to Brenda and said sharply, "First your brother, now this. Tell me, if everyone's going to turn gay, who's going to make the children?"

You're Breaking
My Heart!

Brenda had never pictured her brother Nat and his lover Mark settling down in East Lansing, or even Michigan. She had imagined that after Nat had graduated from Michigan State, he and Mark would move to one of the coasts, and that she, on her loving and significant visits, would end up as a crucial link between them and her parents in Southfield. It was a situation she was aware she had vaguely concocted out of Victorian novels full of wrangling over wills, clandestine excursions, tears, oaths and threatened violence.

The fantasy did not include Nat living just an hour and a half away from their parents, living in the town she was beginning to think of as her home, and living not just in an apartment, but in a beautiful Tudor-style house in one of East Lansing's prettiest faculty neighborhoods. It was on a curving slightly uphill street lined with large old homes—mostly Colonials—and towering thick maples, oaks and elms. And though the landscaping and gardens were meticulous, there was a quirkiness and delicacy to the choice of flowers and shrubs that you didn't find in other, newer neighborhoods, where the plantings were unimaginative, or in the older subdivisions where the landscaping was overgrown.

Her father read the move as a provocation. "They're living right there in East Lansing!"

Her mother said, "I'm sure they'll have a lovely home"—as if it all came down to a question of drapes.

And in a way, wasn't it just that, even for Brenda? She had been off at a conference when Nat and Mark found the house, and again when they moved in, so she was unprepared for how beautiful it was. The previous owner had been an interior designer, and each large room was like a stage setting, with skillfully matched curtains, wallpapers, window shades, and rugs all washed in rose, cream and sky blue.

"It's kind of floral?" was Nat's slightly embarrassed comment.

Yes, it was a bit like living in a potpourri pot, with wreaths and vines and blossoms and stems curling, twisting, arcing on wall after lovely wall, underfoot, even on the trim of shades that matched curtains. Touching a chair, you expected your hand to come away fragrant. But Brenda was impressed.

Her mother would love it, and love that Mark and Nat had not filled the house with black oppressive pieces of "clever" furniture by way of protest or irony, but had bowed to the inevitable and settled for a comfortable English country look in what they bought. Jacobson's Store for the Home, she thought approvingly: East Lansing's very best. Mark had unexpectedly come into some money after a cousin died, and enjoyed spending it with Nat.

Her father would hate the house, Brenda knew, hate the oppressive sheen of elegance and perfection. This was not what a man's house should look like, he would think. And the Jewish items on display—the menorahs, the small shofar, the silver-bound Passover Haggadah, even the mezuzah on the front doorpost would seem defaced to him, because they were owned by homosexuals.

"Your father needs time," Brenda's mother said, with no trace of emotion or strain.

"How much time? A decade?" Brenda snapped.

Her mother shrugged, graceful, elegant, remote. Though she talked to Nat on the phone, she refused to visit his house by herself: "That would be dishonest."

Brenda had originally hoped for much more than stasis. She had expected to see Nat embraced by her parents and the world defied. After all, Nat's dorm room at Michigan State had been torched last year when other students found out he was gay—didn't that make him a victim, a refugee, someone to protect?

Instead, her father was outraged. Nat had humiliated the family, had humiliated all Jews by bringing so much attention to himself, to their family. There were stories in the *Lansing State Journal*, the *Detroit Free Press*—and worst, in Detroit's *Jewish News*, which was their paper—a record of engagements, marriages, sales and predictably undisturbing news of the Detroit Jewish suburbs.

"Jews don't do that!" her father had yelled, unwilling to look at Nat, Mark or Brenda who had come down to Southfield the day after Nat's dorm room was destroyed, to explain and inform.

Brenda shook her head. "Do what, Dad, get attacked?"

They were—incongruously for Brenda—in her parents' plaid on plaid family room, with no fire going, but surrounded by emblems of warmth: family photos, award certificates, bronzed baby shoes.

"Don't be smart with me! The Torah says it's filth."

Brenda wouldn't back down. "The Torah also says men and women shouldn't wear each other's clothing."

Her mother, in green silk slacks, crossed and uncrossed her legs.

"It's not the same." Her father shut his eyes as if hit by a migraine.

They got nowhere. When Mark tried to talk about a lawsuit, her parents quivered with dread and disgust—at the idea of publicity, and just as much, she thought, at Mark's intrusion into their lives, into their plans for Nat's future. He was as terrible as a revolution disturbing a tour group's Caribbean calm.

"I didn't raise my son to be a homosexual," her father said.

Nat exploded. "You didn't raise me at all!"

And even though the shouting ceased, and they all had dinner together, sitting at the table clearly marked the end of many things—of deception, and at least surface harmony among them, and worst, of Brenda's privileged spot in the family as straight-A student, scholarship winner, valedictorian, grant winner, assistant professor at Michigan State. Brenda was re-reading books for the Edith Wharton seminar she would be teaching in the English department, and she found herself feeling a little like Ellen Olenska in *The Age of Innocence*, being banished from comfortable, clubby Old New York in the guise of a cordial farewell dinner. It wasn't fair or kind, but Brenda had too clearly taken Nat and Mark's side, and so had to share in their disgrace.

She imagined Thanksgiving could change that, a little.

Nat and Mark were dubious.

"They won't come," Nat kept saying.

Mark wanted to know who would invite her parents. "Us? You? You and Nat? Nat?"

Brenda insisted she would try it herself.

Her father was incredulous. "—and I have to sit there while he carves?"

Brenda assumed that meant Mark. "You can carve, Dad."

"I don't want to!"

She could make no progress. Her father was as convinced of his position as a Sunday morning televangelist, and his face was just as full of anger and contempt. Any minute she expected him to be bellowing about how "the land would vomit them forth." What was the hold of Leviticus on Jews like her father who were not really observant, and for whom the Torah otherwise had little immediacy? Even she was spooked by the Biblical prohibition, when so much else in the Torah struck her as archaic and silly, mere time-worn regulations that were completely overshadowed by the truly lasting parts of Hebrew scripture—like the prophetic calls for social justice, the urging to love your neighbor, or the deep concern for widows, orphans, strangers.

"Homosexuals want to destroy society, destroy everything," her father insisted.

"But Dad—that's exactly what crazy anti-Semites always say about the Jews!"

Brenda's mother tried to take the historical approach to her father's anger and shame. "We've always been watched, honey, so we have to be better than the goyim."

"But gay isn't worse, Mom, Nat's just like you and me, there's no difference. He has a house, he has a job—okay, okay, not a great one but let's not get into that right now. He has someone he loves, who loves him."

Her mother stiffened a little at this.

"I don't think it's the same," she brought out. "Not exactly." Her mother now seemed ready to announce that there was no comparison between her marriage of thirty years and whatever path Nat and Mark were taking.

They were having coffee in the recently re-done kitchen, which was inexplicably modern—something out of *Star Wars*—white and chrome and bright, bright bulbs. Brenda missed the old colonial kitchen with its frilly cafe curtains and cheerful American eagle/butter churn/spinning wheel tile. Even her mother admitted the remodeling was an expensive mistake, and would have to be changed somehow: "I'm not sure what I was thinking of, Brenda." They were sitting at a cold and efficient-looking white marble counter, and facing each other was slightly uncomfortable.

"I don't understand you, Mom. You vote Democrat, you support practically every liberal cause that exists, but this is too much—"

"Because it's my son," her mother said a little primly, and Brenda realized she had gone too far. She sliced another piece of mohn cake, the poppy seed pastry unavailable up in East Lansing.

"I told you," Nat said when Brenda called him with her news, or lack of it.

"You're not upset."

"I'm relieved." And he wouldn't say anything more to her about it. That stubborn and immutable silence was what Nat shared with their father, though Nat would of course claim that he had a reason for not talking, while their father's silence was always arbitrary. She didn't know how to break through to Nat. Brenda's relationship with her brother had not changed enough since he met Mark over a year ago; Nat was still suspicious, tense, watchful—as if she would turn on him as brutally as their father had.

Mark was not encouraging when Brenda visited a week before Thanksgiving. "Why don't you just relax? If they come around, they come around."

"And if not—?"

Mark shrugged. While Nat seemed a little too unfinished to be quite at ease in their flowery new home, Mark throned there as if he were some lustrous businessman in a *New York Times Magazine* home section layout. Looking a bit like an Italian Renaissance prince, he was handsome and relaxed, at ease around expensive things, and she could hardly believe his parents were immigrants and had worked their way up from nothing.

"It's a loss, Brenda. Your parents have to grieve."

"Oh, please! I've read Kubler-Ross—and not everything in the world is about death and dying."

Mark smiled. "No? Nat's dead for them—the little boy they had dreams about? He'll never marry some neighbor's daughter, never give them grand-children—well, probably not. So isn't he gone?"

She flushed, because the loss he described was close to what she had felt, was still feeling from time to time. "Are your parents over it yet?"

Mark shook his head, and looked away from her. "But I've never been real for them anyway, nothing is, not here, no matter what they do, their real life was back in Poland, and the Nazis took it away."

"Why won't you tell my father your parents are Holocaust survivors? How could he push you away when he lost everybody in the War?"

"I don't like talking about it. And don't look at me like that. I don't have any incredible stories to tell. They don't mention the War, ever. Total silence. I mean, I know they were in Poland when the War broke out, and they were in Germany when it ended. That's it. That, and there isn't anyone in their families who survived. No one."

The books Brenda had read on the Holocaust, the films she had seen, even the pictures of the camps were always unreal to her in the face of some-one who was connected to all the horror so directly.

"How can you pray?" she brought out, having wanted to ask before. "How can you go to services at all?"

Mark shrugged. "I have to believe in something."

"We've got to tell my parents." Brenda was ready to head for a phone.

Mark waved his hand as if to confine her to her chair. "Because that'll be Nat's passport? Forget it, Brenda. You can't use something like that as a bargaining chip—it won't work. They'll just feel sorry for my parents—'To survive the Nazis and end up with a queer son. It's a *shandeh!*'"

On Thanksgiving Day, when Nat opened his door, Brenda smiled be-cause they were both wearing black. Nat looked almost glamorous in pegged pants, turtleneck and cardigan. "Wow," she said.

Nat flushed a little. "Mark picked everything out."

From the beautiful living room came the brassy confident sound of swing music.

Nat put her coat away, and she followed him to the kitchen, from which she heard a drawling *Masterpiece Theater* sort of voice: "Well, I think the perfect dinner party should be equal parts cotillion and train wreck—you want formality and terror."

"That's Adrien," Nat explained.

Brenda winced, expecting Nat and Mark's visiting friend from New York to be her worst cliche of a homosexual: someone fat, fiftyish, drowned in cologne and gold jewelry, and planted in a tasseled caftan. Nat had warned her that Adrien was "dramatic": "Just because we pay taxes, too, and vote and rake leaves or whatever, doesn't mean we're all just like you," Nat had said. And she'd had flashes of Gay Pride reports on national TV that always showed the most effeminate, the most extreme marchers.

She almost laughed when she saw Nat and Mark's guest sprawling at the kitchen table. Adrien was slim and tanned, only in his late twenties, with the intense angular face of Kevin Costner. His black jeans and white tuxedo shirt with sleeves rolled up showed off a runner's body.

"So you're the mostly sympathetic sister," Adrien said, rising with all the sweet shy grace of Audrey Hepburn making her ballroom entrance in *My Fair Lady*.

"I can't remember what Nat told me you do. Are you a writer?" Brenda asked, shaking his hand.

Adrien smiled. "No—I work for a gay magazine in New York. We don't write, we execute."

Mark was washing his hands at the sink, and he laughed. Nat was grinning at Adrien as if he were a parent watching his infant perform an amazing feat like bringing his foot to his face and chewing a toe. Brenda quickly understood that Adrien had their absolute approval to entertain by being himself, that whatever he said would strike them as funny. She felt a little tired at the thought, as if she were cornered at a bar mitzvah by one of her chatty pinching kibitzing male relatives who were always cracking bad jokes and talking about themselves.

"It smells great in here," Brenda said, accepting a glass of pop from Nat, and sitting opposite Adrien.

"That's the cup and a half of Grand Marnier in the stuffing," Nat said, and he handed her a worn and stained copy of a Silver Palate cookbook. She read the other ingredients aloud: celery, yellow onion, slivered almonds, herb stuffing, chicken broth, thyme, dried apricots, sausage.

"Wow."

"Sausage?" Adrien asked. "You mean you boys don't keep kosher?"

Brenda stiffened. Non-Jews seemed to only know one thing about Judaism, and that not very clearly. The word "kosher" itself often made them sneer or laugh, the way University of Michigan football fans did when they heard someone mention the MSU Spartans.

Adrien seemed to catch her reaction, because he reached over to pat her hand. "Don't worry, sweets, we're all in the same boat."

Nat explained: "His real name is Harold."

"Girlfriend, my real name is Adrien, it just took me a while to discover it. Harold's what my family calls me." He grimaced. "Harold Rosenberg. *Feh*! So, Brenda, do I pass, now?"

Embarrassed at her own relief that Adrien was Jewish, Brenda smiled and asked if he had changed his first name legally.

"Of course. I had a ceremony with flower girls and paper boys—or maybe it was the reverse. After the triumphal fanfare it's all a blank." He went on like that.

More relaxed, Brenda watched him wave his hands and pose with the stylized motions of a kabuki dancer. He sounded as if he were a much older, much more cynical and experienced man. Though what did she know about his experience—just because he was only in his twenties didn't mean— She drank some pop to drown the thought.

"Seriously, Brenda," Adrien said, "I wasn't making fun. I know how you feel. I like being with Jews, too. But Jewish queers—that's even better. I feel safe. That's why I joined the gay synagogue in New York. It's incredible—the services will make you cry. They have hundreds of members. Next time you're in New York you've got to come."

Brenda looked at Nat and they smiled. "Could you imagine Mom and Dad—?"

"It could happen," Adrien said, telling them about his parents at P-FLAG. "Shy? Maybe at first, but then they took over. It gives them a place to feel comfortable."

Eyes down, Nat said, "I don't think Dad will ever change."

And before Brenda could utter some comforting platitude, Adrien roared, "Aw quit it, you're breaking my heart!"

Nat and Mark laughed and had to explain to Brenda it was a line from *Mildred Pierce*.

"The movie about family values," Adrien said. "No where's that champagne you boys promised me?"

Nat brought out a bottle of Veuve Clicquot and they toasted one another's tolerance, good looks and the group's general sexual diversity.

Mark was quieter than usual, and she asked him why. "I'm tired," he said. "I'm happy. I'm drunk." He hugged her.

Dinner was laid out in the formal dining room with its built-in buffet along one wall topped with mirrors. She felt like she was in a holiday window display—the settings and the centerpiece of lilies were that ornate, and dinner superb. Like her parents, Nat and Mark had ordered a fresh turkey, which was so much juicier and more tasty than the frozen—and with that stuffing! The food was delightfully different: glazed lady apples and pearl onions; sweet potato and banana puree; Brussels sprouts in a maple syrup and sherry vinaigrette. But the feel was so much like her parents'

239

Thanksgivings that Brenda wished for their presence at this table, or at least their voices from the kitchen.

"It's all so colorful," she said, sitting opposite Adrien. A little guiltily, she thought she sounded as inane as her mother sometimes did, but no one seemed to mind.

Adrien was looking around suspiciously. "This does not feel like the Midwest," he said. "Where is the ambrosia salad? I was really looking forward to tiny marshmallows!"

Nat chuckled "Stop."

Brenda smiled, feeling suddenly proud of Nat, proud for him, and lucky that she was so much at ease with his lover and his very gay friend. It didn't disturb her anymore to see Mark and Nat hold hands or kiss, and even when they hugged Adrien or touched and stroked him while they talked, she smiled. She was a little drunk; they had moved to a second bottle of Cadillac.

The Eurythmics' "Sweet Dreams" was playing in the living room, and Brenda just sank into the pleasant haze of being with them all.

She was so glad not to be worrying about grading papers, not to be planning her Wharton course, to be completely free of all her projects and commitments. "This is fun. Does that make me a fag hag?" she asked at one point, spooning more mashed potatoes onto her plate, and they all stared at her.

"Honey," Adrien said, "You have to work to be a fag hag, you've got the manual to read, the night classes, the tape cassettes to listen to—it's not that easy!"

Mark raised his glass to her. "It's not like being a JAP—"

"Wait!" Brenda said. "How the hell can you use that word? It's sexist, it's racist, it's anti-Semitic."

Nat murmured, "It's just a joke."

"No," Brenda said. "It's ugly, it's a stereotype, and you of all people should be sensitive to that. If you use it, then non-Jews think it's okay."

"She's right," Adrien said quietly. "I was just reading a new novel by this gay Jew and he throws 'Jewish American Princess' around like it's funny. I guess he thinks it's funny, but I don't. His publisher even put it on the book jacket. They'd never put 'nigger' on there—you just know that."

"Thank you," Brenda said to him, impressed.

Adrien shrugged, and Mark apologized. They were all silent for a moment, until Adrien started to rave about property values in Michigan and how lucky they were to have such a great house. "Three quarters of a million at the very least where my parents live in the Five Towns, that's what this place would cost."

Brenda was silenced by the figure, and then Mark and Nat bawled at Adrien, "Aw quit it, you're breaking my heart!" and she laughed so hard she started to choke. Nat rushed around the table to slap her back. Mark was up, holding out a glass of water. She felt flushed and headachy, and stood up, trying to breath deeply. "I'm fine," she said.

Nat asked about her Wharton course, but interrupted her by saying he'd read Martin Scorcese was filming *The Age of Innocence*, with Michelle Pfeiffer playing, he hesitated, "that foreign woman."

"Ellen Olenska?" Brenda moaned. "Impossible! They might as well get LaToya Jackson."

Adrien almost spit out his wine. "Brenda! You—have—possibilities!"

"No, listen." She tried to explain her favorite Wharton novel to them, but Adrien interrupted.

"Was she a dyke?" he asked. "Edith Wharton, I mean?"

Mark threw his balled-up napkin at Adrien, who caught it gracefully, and shrugged. "I was just curious."

After coffee and a cranberry apricot Amaretto lattice-crust pie, they moved to the living room, which was hung with Japanese-inspired Whistler and Sargent prints. She crawled into an enormous claw-footed blue leather armchair, cradling a glass of Pineau des Charentes, which Nat had insisted she try. Was it good? She'd had so much to drink she couldn't tell.

"Are you staying over?" Adrien asked. "You could use the other guest room." Adrien grinned. "Sorry! I'm not the host, but I guess I'd love to have breakfast with you." He laughed. "I know you've heard that from men before, but this must be the first time it's coming from a *shvester*!"

Brenda smiled to hear him use the Yiddish for sister, the way Nat and Mark sometimes did when referring to gay Jewish men. She did feel comfortable, did think that staying overnight would relax her even more, bring her even further into Nat's life.

"Stay," Nat was saying. "We do have the room. And like Mom, plenty of towels."

Mark encouraged her, too: "It'll be fun."

"How could I refuse?" she asked.

"I'll get us more champagne," Mark said, winking, and headed for the kitchen. Adrien followed, swivelling his hips.

"Stop it!" Nat sputtered, but Adrien was gone.

"I don't mind," Brenda said. "It's good for me. I'm too used to tight-ass academics."

"Tight-ass, he's not," Nat murmured, and then started to turn red. "Sorry. . . ."

"Don't apologize. Don't censor things. I'm not Dad, I won't have a stroke."

"How come you're so different now, more relaxed?"

She looked away. "Maybe it's just the comparison. Dad's so extreme, even Mom in her way. . . ." She thought longingly of her parents. She wanted them to come around too; she wanted them to eat dinner with their son and their son's lover; she wanted them all to be family again. Was that impossible? Couldn't her parents realize that Nat had found what he needed, couldn't they see things the way that she did?

Adrien came in with fresh champagne glasses, humming something she recognized from *Die Fledermaus*, and Mark followed with a glittering loaded ice bucket.

"Why don't you all come to New York for Passover?" Adrien said, setting the glasses down and sitting on Brenda's chair arm.

"We always go to our parents' seder," Brenda said awkwardly. It sounded as embarrassing as an obvious lie.

Nat was shaking his head. "Brenda, let's try something else," he said. "We can't change them, you can't change them."

"But I'm so disappointed! I thought they were better people, deeper. . . ." Head down, she said, "Somehow I thought the bell might ring today—"

"—and Mom and Dad would be there," Nat finished for her. "Just dropping in? Oh, Brenda. . . ."

Mark popped the cork and poured them all champagne. Nat was looking into her eyes, and when he raised his glass to hers it was like a challenge. She clinked her glass against his, and as she drank, she imagined some glorious Cinemascope adventure filled with shouting crowds, banners, high intentions, defiance—and fear.

"Well," Adrien said, patting Brenda's hand. "It sounds like you three are coming. I'll start cooking as soon as I get back. You won't be disappointed in me, honey. I do a mean Four Questions," he threw off. "Very Post-Modern. And some years," he went on, "I stage this fabulous Passover pageant—before dessert—of the Hebrews crossing the Red Sea. You," he said, pointing his empty glass at Brenda, "You would make a wonderful Miriam. You'd be fierce with a tambourine."

The Author

Lev Raphael is the author of seventeen books published in a dozen languages. Winner of the Lambda Literary Award, among many prizes, he is the author of a popular mystery series and the host of BookTalk on Lansing Public Radio. He lives in Michigan with his partner and they recently married in Canada on their 21st anniversary.

ABOUT THE TYPE

This book was set in Garamond, a typeface based on the types of the six-teenth-century printer, publisher, and type designer Claude Garamond, whose sixteenth-century types were modeled on those of Venetian printers from the end of the previous century. The italics are based on types by Robert Granjon, a contemporary of Garamond's. The Garamond typeface and its variations have been a standard among book designers and printers for four centuries.

Composed by JTC Imagineering, Santa Maria,CA
Designed by John Taylor-Convery